HVNTED

MOLLY KERR

HUNTED

For information contact:
http://www.mollykerrauthor.com

Cover design by James, GoOnWrite.com

ISBN: 979-8-9903402-0-6

First Edition: April 2024

All that is gold does not glitter,
Not all those who wander are lost;
The old that is strong does not wither,
Deep roots are not reached by the frost.

J.R.R. Tolkien

For those who decide to take the long way round, this is for you.
We all get there in the end.

Prologue

S he was running for her life, and only had herself to blame.

It was the first truly clear night in a long while, and she'd found herself drawn to the stairs of the auction house where she worked as soon as the chaos of the latest auction had died down enough for her to slip away. The weather was fine, if a little cool. The breeze tugging at the sleeves of her sweatshirt had a crispness to it that meant autumn was on its way.

She'd at least had the presence of mind to change her clothes, swapping pantsuit and heels for leggings and a sweatshirt with a hood drawn up to cover her dark red hair, but she had little else with her, and that included a weapon. Any weapon.

And there were others who wandered the rooftops at night.

The street-side cafes below were full of people catching a meal or a few drinks after the auction or a show at one of several theaters that dotted this and the surrounding blocks. Even the tables on the patios lining the street were full, their occupants warmed by glowing heaters and propane-fueled torches. The air buzzed with conversation, laughter, and the clatter of plates and silverware. Music wove through the din, bass thumping from the club on the corner, jazz from the bar next door.

From the patio of the French restaurant across the street, a man put a violin to his chin and started to play. As the first notes of *La Vie en Rose* reached her, she found herself humming along, hearing in her mind the French lyrics, which she had always preferred.

So engrossed in the music, she almost missed the soft thump of feet landing on the gravel roof nearby. She turned slowly, keeping her chin low so her face was hidden in the shadows of her hood. Across the roof, a black silhouette stood, hands at their side.

"Sorry, Joseph," she said to the figure. "I know I probably shouldn't be up here."

The shadow took a step forward. The build was clearly masculine, and also clearly not that of the head of security. She sighed. It was going to be one of those nights.

He slowly raised his arm. The red dot of a laser sight slowly tracked up her thigh and continued up until it stopped on the center of her chest. The first shot sprayed chips of masonry from the wall an inch from where she'd been standing, but she'd already leapt behind the ventilation system, straight into the body of someone coming around the other side. It was like hitting a brick wall of muscle.

The behemoth grunted in surprise and made a grab for her, but she spun away and headed back the way she had come, sprinting for the edge of the rooftop, and leaping the short distance to the building next door. For several blocks they kept pace. Her heart hammered in her ears, as much from adrenaline as from exertion. The occasional bullet rang out, but she kept moving, ducking, twisting, and turning to keep available obstacles between them, jumping from one roof to the next.

The next roof was lower than expected. With a small cry, she pitched forward, but her balance was off, and she landed on her shoulder with an awkward crunch, arm caught awkwardly beneath her. The bone pulled free of the joint and she slid across the roof, scattering gravel in all directions.

With a grunt, she levered herself up on the good arm and shook her head to try to clear the ringing. Her pursuers had fallen back and were bringing their guns to bear. The muted pops sounded fake at this distance, but the bullets that whizzed close by and hit the gravel at her feet were plenty real.

The shouted orders grew unnervingly close as she stumbled to her feet, cradling her limp and throbbing arm to her chest. They had reached the edge of the next building, and were bringing their guns to bear, when she pivoted to the right and dashed across the next rooftop and down the fire escape on the other side.

She gripped the ladder in her good hand and rode it down. It lurched to a stop part way down and she fell, landing on the dumpster underneath with a crash that echoed down the alley and drove the air from her lungs. As she rolled off, the white-hot pain lancing through her shoulder nearly drove her down to her knees. Black spots danced in her vision, and she fought to keep from vomiting. There was no time for that.

Boots clattered on the stairs above her, but no more shots rang out. They were far too close to populated streets for even Hunters to keep firing and her path was taking her out onto a wide and well-lit street full of shops. She dove into the foot traffic and wove through the crowds, wincing as her shoulder was jostled.

After a few blocks, she ducked into the alleyway between two buildings and picked up the pace, running down deserted alleyways and ever quieter residential streets. Here there was little light. The few streetlights that hadn't been broken by kids with rocks or drug dealers looking to keep their business in the shadows cast feeble pools of light dozens of feet apart.

She pressed her back against a brick wall. Moisture from a nearby drainpipe seeped into her shirt and helped cool the heated skin of her back. Her fingers prodded around the shoulder joint, manipulating the arm bone back into position. It was difficult work with the muscles clenched tightly around the dislocation. She choked back the bile burning up her throat as she inched her hand up the drainpipe and grunted when the bone slid back in with a meaty pop.

She sagged against the wall as the pain was replaced with an almost pleasant tingling as if her body understood that now it could truly heal the injury. She glanced back the way she had come, at both street level and above, but in the darkness, there was nothing to see nor did any sounds of pursuit reach her ears.

She risked a few more idle moments until her breathing evened out and her pounding heart began to slow then pushed off the wall and continued on. Her pace was deliberate but no longer frantic, one that she could sustain for miles if she needed to. A block down, she rounded the corner into the wide alleyway between row houses, narrowly missing a homeless woman pushing a shopping cart piled high with trash bags bursting at the seams. The woman cursed at her as she rushed by.

For a few more blocks, she slogged through puddles and half-rotted garbage before stopping at the mouth of an alley that opened onto what she quickly identified as Market Street. By now, it had to be after midnight, but this part of town was full of shops, restaurants, and people.

Lots of people.

She ran her hands over her hair, tucking back curls that had loosened during her flight and slid into the streak of foot traffic. Her eyes never stopped moving, scanning the shadows, focusing on places where they were darkest, where it was easiest to hide. Among the hundreds of people that filled the street, she was about as safe as she was going to get. Even her enemies were smart enough not to expose their conflict to so many witnesses.

Despite the dangers, this city was a place that always drew her back. Where once a collection of crude wood-framed houses had huddled along the shore of a raging river, now stood a sprawling metropolis of more than three million people. This brick pedestrian way that wove between gently aging buildings had once been only a dirt road lined with carts and stands selling everything from vegetables and meat to silk, leather, and glass. Only decades ago, this neighborhood had been full of abandoned tenements, breeding grounds for vices worse than those that searched for her, but now it was crammed with boutiques and exotic restaurants.

At times, the growth and development in the city was disorienting, at times it was infuriating. So much change while she remained always the same. Despite all that, Kingston was the closest place she'd had to home in more than two hundred years.

But change was inevitable, time continued to move forward, and soon enough she was once again on the move to protect the few secrets she still managed to keep. Five years ago, she had returned, and if tonight was any indication, the Hunters were creeping closer, but this time she wanted it to be different.

Shaking free from her thoughts, she joined the crowd at a crosswalk and looked around, waiting for the light to change. The rooftops were empty, and the crowd concerned only with their own business. A smile curved her lips as relief coursed through her. Once again, she had escaped.

Once again, her enemies had failed to understand that no matter how hard they tried to kill her, in this city, *her* city...

She would always get away.

One

The doorman looked up from behind his desk, as the automatic door slid open. His face sprang into it's usual grin, teeth flashing a brilliant white against his coffee-colored skin. The smile slid away as she came fully into view, eyes going wide and round.

"Good evening, Fred!" she said cheerfully as she walked over to the desk and rested her elbows on the cool marble top and resisted the urge to press her flushed cheek to the stone.

"Good evening, Miss Dericault," he answered. "Had an eventful night, haven't you?"

She looked down. Her clothes were dirty, the shoulder of her sweat-shirt torn to reveal unblemished but equally dirty skin beneath. Her legs spattered with mud and worse. "Never better," she assured him, grinning. "Nothing like a run across the rooftops to get the blood flowing, eh Fred?"

"Oh yes, Miss Dericault." That absurd little red bellhop's hat bobbed a nod while his tone suggested he was none too sure that he would find the same enjoyment. In all the years she had known Fred, he had never lingered on the roof for more than a scant few minutes at a time. "Nothin' like it."

She smiled at him and laughed. He beamed at her in response but then his attention returned to the state of her clothes. "What happened to your arm?"

She waved dismissively. "Don't worry, it's already healed."

He merely blinked and nodded in a way that said he didn't understand but accepted it anyway.

There were very few people that she had ever trusted with her secret, but he was a kind soul, and a loyal friend who had been working the doors for twenty years. Those alert eyes never would have missed that the penthouse owner hadn't aged a day in all that time.

She tapped her hand on the counter and took a step back. "Well, I think I've had enough excitement for one night. Good night, Fred."

"Good night, Miss Dericault."

Her smile twisted slightly, and she touched his hand. "That's three times tonight, Fred. How many times have I asked you to call me Morgana?"

He grinned. "Too many to count, Miss Dericault."

Morgana shook her head and gave his hand a squeeze before walking into the waiting elevator. The ride to the tenth floor was short, but as the car rose, the adrenaline that had kept her on her feet finally ran out, leaving her to stagger across the lobby and into her apartment.

Her bed beckoned from the end of the hall, but she turned into the bathroom first, leaving a trail of dirty clothes in her wake. She headed straight for the shower and turned the taps. The grime of the rooftops and city streets blackened the water at her feet. But even after her skin was clean, she lingered under the spray, absorbing the heat deep into her bones.

She woke shivering and found herself leaning on the wall of the shower. The taps creaked as she turned them, cutting off the frigid water, and reached blindly for a towel. Wrapped in its warm softness, Morgana staggered down the Persian runner to her bedroom, paying no heed to the wet footprints she left in her wake.

She glanced out the window as she turned back the thick white duvet on the bed. The night wasn't as dark as it had been, but sunrise was still a few hours away, and as much as she would like to sleep long into the afternoon, she had an early meeting with a new client insisting he had something of interest for her.

It had better be something with lots of caffeine in it. She thought as she returned to the living room to complete her nightly routine to ensure that nothing in the apartment had been disturbed. The office door was still securely locked. The first edition of *The Count of Monte Cristo*, given to her by young Alexandre himself, still stuck out over the edge of its shelf slightly, the thread she'd left taped between the window and the sill was in one piece.

While modern technology ensured that the house was secure, old habits died hard. More than once a book out of place or a wet spot on the carpet under a window had alerted her to danger, so she kept up the practice. The wealth of antique books and artifacts arranged throughout the apartment made it a thief's paradise. Yet despite their value, she'd discard nearly every one of them without a thought if she had to leave town in a hurry.

The contents of her office were another story. Half her life had been spent researching the origins and histories of those like her and she had carefully recorded it all. Stories of love and happiness turned to panic and flight and ruin as her enemy gained in strength and numbers while her own people were driven farther and farther into the shadows to spend their days looking over their shoulders waiting for the final strike to come.

Their numbers were far too few, but neither she nor the Hunters could know exactly how many were left. Her heart clenched tight; a wave of despair rose up as it always did when she mused over the fate of her people. It was certainly possible that she was the last in Southwestern Canada.

If they knew, they'd line up to take their shot at her just for the bragging rights for freeing British Columbia from the clutches of those like her. Their motto was "kill what was feared before learning that it was no real threat at all."

Morgana snorted a laugh through her nose. All she'd ever wanted was to be able to live her life in peace. She was a historian, not a warrior or conqueror, and had only learned to fight because they'd forced her to.

But the other choice was death.

Sighing, Morgana climbed between cornflower blue silk sheets and pushed away the bitterness and misery that came at her when she thought of her people's fate and allowed the exhaustion to finally overcome her.

Two

Her dreamless slumber was broken by the buzzing alarm clock. Feeling as if she had just closed her eyes, Morgana swept it from her nightstand with a growl, and cursed the man who had invented the damned things in the first place. She crawled out of bed, got dressed, and made her way across town to the auction house.

As she pushed open the heavy mahogany door of the employee entrance at Albrecht House Auctioneers, the warm, familiar scents of aged paper and furniture polish drifted over her and lightened her heart a little after the events of the night before.

Her assistant sprung to his feet and emerged from behind the desk outside her office. His greeting as he bent to retrieve her phone messages, hit her like a shot of espresso. The thickness of the stack in his hand made her want to turn right back around. A corner of his mouth twitched and then he was launching into a recounting of his night, spent at a local bar, sharing drinks with a friend until the early morning. Yet here he was, seemingly unaffected. But that was just how the young mortal was.

On even her worst mornings, if she stood close to Alan long enough, some of his perkiness rubbed off. Some days, it was the only thing that got her through. Days like today.

"Good morning, Alan."

"Your nine o'clock is already here, and I took the liberty of showing him into your office." He smoothed a lock of dark hair behind one ear and fanned his face dramatically with the phone messages. "He is utterly divine. Send him my way when you're done, won't you?"

She chuckled and plucked the messages from his hand. "Sure."

Her heels clicked softly on the marble flooring as Morgana strolled into her office. It was just as well apportioned as her home, being the assistant director of the largest and most successful auction house in British Columbia definitely had its perks. The heavy emerald drapes had been pulled back from the two large windows, flooding the room with light. A large walnut desk took up most of the space, with a Tiffany lamp on one corner, the remainder of the space covered in layers of books and papers. A waist-high Ming floor vase stood between the two windows, while a tapestry from fifteenth century Flanders adorned one wall. A pair of Louis XVI chairs stood before the desk, one of which was occupied.

"Good morning!"

Her prospective client rose to his feet at the sound of her voice. His chestnut hair, lit with cherry-colored highlights from the sunny window, was long enough to brush his collar, but neatly styled. His blue eyes, framed by dark lashes long enough to be feminine on anyone else, followed her every move as she crossed the room. His charcoal suit hugged the muscles of his broad shoulders. A gold cufflink flashed at his wrist as he extended his hand.

Alan did indeed have good taste.

Morgana clasped his hand, the shake warm and firm. She gestured to the chair that he had just vacated, moved behind the desk, and examined her date book.

"Let's see... Patrick Davies." She looked up at her visitor with a raised eyebrow. "Of Davies & McNamara? That would make your father Stephen, would it not?"

"Yes, ma'am."

"Please don't call me ma'am, Mr. Davies." Morgana said with a smile. "It makes me feel old. You can call me Morgana."

"Then you must call me Patrick." His voice carried a cultured accent that couldn't quite hide his east-coast American roots. "Mr. Davies is my father."

Morgana raised an eyebrow as she turned to the small console table behind her desk. The son of her greatest business rival had something to offer her?

This should be interesting.

She considered the array of beverages on the table. It was far too early for her to offer him a cocktail, so she poured each of them a cup of coffee from the carafe. She handed one to Patrick and took a sip of her own, gesturing to the tray in front of him that held sugar and cream.

He ignored the tray and took a sip, then quickly added a healthy pour of cream, and stirred in a heaping spoonful of sugar.

Morgana smiled, "Alan likes his coffee to be strong enough to raise the dead, and sometimes there are days when it feels like it has."

Days like today. She mused, praying the caffeine would kick in quickly and do something to quell the headache suddenly pounding at her temples, only compounding her misery. It must be the bright light spearing through the window.

After a few sips, the coffee wasn't quite raising the dead, but at least keeping her eyes open didn't take quite as much effort as it had considering she was running on three hours of sleep. To make sure, she took another sip.

"Now, what can I do for you, Patrick?"

He leaned forward and set his coffee down with one hand while reaching into the briefcase at his feet with the other.

With the previous night still fresh in her mind, Morgana tucked her feet under her and gripped the desk with her free hand, prepared to push back and reach for the dagger in the console table drawer. When all he withdrew from the briefcase was a stack of papers and a pair of rectangular-shaped reading glasses, she took another sip of her coffee to conceal her relief.

Until he settled the glasses onto his nose with a slight twist of his head, and her breath caught mid-sip as a lazy tendril of heat started curling through her out of nowhere. She coughed once and set her coffee aside.

Concentrating on the stack of papers he'd propped on his knee, Patrick didn't notice. He leafed through, as if checking that the pages were in the right order. Satisfied, he tapped them into a neat pile on the edge of her desk and handed them over.

"These are scans from a rather remarkable book, which has only recently come into my possession." He sat back and crossed one foot over his knee. "I have heard through the grapevine that you are the resident expert on medieval books, and I hoped you could maybe tell me what it is."

Morgana took the pages and her breath caught again, her thoughts scattering as if from hurricane-force winds. The color scans were of a very old book, pages yellowed but largely intact, just a slight tattering of the edges to show their age. Her own handwriting stared up at her, the ink had browned but still leapt off the page. The shock turned to dismay when she tried to read the words. There was some resemblance to Modern French, but it was otherwise incomprehensible. The writing *had* come from her own hand, but a very long time ago.

"Where is this book now?"

At least her voice sounded relaxed even as she struggled to breathe. That she had responded in English was also good. She had a bad habit of reverting to her native tongue in times of stress. Not that it helped her here in the least. Her eyes continued to scan the pages, as snippets of dozens of languages and dialects ran through her head, but none helped her make sense of the words. She huffed out a breath, ruffling the strand of hair that kept trying to fall in her eyes.

"Safely locked away." Patrick's tone was neutral, but there was a hint of curiosity in his voice.

She risked a glance out of the corner of her eye. He was settled back in the chair, one elbow propped on an armrest, his thumb nail slowly moving back and forth over his lower lip. The sunlight reflected off his glasses a little, but it didn't obscure the fact that those blue eyes were trained on her.

She schooled her expression and returned her attention to the pages in her hand as the right language finally clicked in place in her head. Her lips mouthed the words as she completed the first page, stumbling as much from the poor penmanship as from the words themselves. As memory served, this had been one of her first literate languages.

Patrick shifted in his chair to reach his coffee cup. "It's written in a very archaic Old French dialect."

Clearly, he was mistaking her silence for confusion. Morgana tilted her head and cocked an eyebrow at him.

He chuckled. "It took me a couple months of research and study to even identify the language, let alone any of the words."

Morgana studied him a little closer. With his reading glasses on, he looked like someone who wouldn't look out of place in a library despite having a build that suggested he spent more time with a hockey stick in his hand than a pen or a book. But there was an intelligence in his gaze, as he studied her in return.

"*Parlez vous Français?*"

He barely hesitated, "*mais oui.*" He replied and continued in smooth, rapid French. "I spent more than one summer in France with my father on buying trips."

Morgana nodded appreciatively at his clear accent, albeit somewhat heavily Parisian-influenced, and the fluidity of his words. She returned her attention to the pages in her hand and continued in French, just to see if he could keep up though the sound of his voice in her native tongue sent another pulse down her spine.

She cleared her throat. "And you learned obscure French dialects on these trips?"

A corner of his mouth turned up at the sharpness of her tone and a hint of a dimple showed in his cheek. "Not at all." He replied, still in effortless French. "The book came in with a small collection of Oïl Language manuscripts and I was intrigued when what I originally believed to be Middle French turned out to be something entirely different. I spent nearly a week discerning as much as I could with the resources at my disposal here and only managed to identify a few place names."

Morgana's eyes found one of them right then as if the letters had turned red. *Aubrac.* She swallowed against the sudden lump in her throat.

Patrick continued on as if he hadn't noticed. "I then sent a few pages to a contact I'd made at the University in Amiens. Using their library, and several graduate students, I was able to get a reasonably complete translation in about two months."

Morgana was amazed at his persistence, and his linguistic ability. She switched to English, not bothering to keep the surprise from her voice. "You spent a long time on a book that could have turned out to be a daily accounting of the weather patterns at a fifteenth century vineyard."

"The trivialities of rain patterns in fifteenth century France may seem to be of little importance to twenty-first century Canada, true, but in order for the book to be—salable at D&M, we had to know what it contained."

The hesitation didn't go unnoticed, but Morgana let it go for now. "Davies & McNamara must employ as many research assistants as we do," Morgana countered. "Why would you take this on personally?"

Patrick did not respond for a long moment, giving Morgana a chance to read through another page. "It was a challenge."

She glanced up at the tone in his voice.

"Surprised?" The dimple was on full display now as he grinned.

Morgana considered for a moment and in the end shook her head. "Surprisingly, no," she answered and smiled back. Her gaze remained fixed on his, the light from the window throwing back gold flecks around his pupils, which were slightly larger than they should have been given the brightness of the room. "If I had been going through the same stack of manuscripts, this one would have leapt out at me, too."

Patrick nodded appreciatively. "What can you tell me?"

Caught up in the unfamiliar sensations coursing through her as their eyes continued to hold each other, his mouth had moved, but the words didn't register. She blinked hard to break the stare. "I beg your pardon?"

He repeated the question, the slightly distant tone in his voice suggesting that he wasn't completely unaffected either, but she turned her attention back to the words on the pages in her hand rather than risk losing control again.

"I believe it's a dialect once used only by a small monastery in northern France and the surrounding villages."

"How do you know that?" he asked.

Because I learned it there.

In her peripheral vision, he took his glasses down so that he could look directly at her. Even out of the corner of her eye, his were almost an impossible shade of blue.

For a moment, her thoughts scattered. What was her current cover story again? Had she studied at the Sorbonne this time or the University of Toronto? Was she born in Rouen or Marseille? Did she have siblings? Was she an orphan or just out of touch with her family?

Stopping the spiral was a physical thing, which she hid behind her coffee cup. Once her thoughts settled, she set the cup down. "I wrote my master's thesis about the monastery ruins at Aubrac." Morgana pointed to the name on the page. "It was a highly isolated church complex popular with travelers on the road to Santiago de Compostela."

It had also been a haven for her people until the Hunters had found it sometime in the sixteenth century.

"The hospice and monastery buildings tumbled to ruins centuries ago and only the walls of the church remain. I assisted on several archaeological digs on the grounds and spent countless months pouring over the journals of an abbot named Brother Ambois."

Patrick studied her for a moment as if he was measuring her knowledge against her apparent age and was having trouble making something add up. Morgana's pulse quickened again. At any moment, he could pull a weapon from the bag at his feet and declare that it had all been a ruse. A few frantic heartbeats later, he moved, but only to shift forward in his chair so he could retrieve the scans from her desktop.

"If I may?"

He took them back at her stiff nod. He replaced his glasses and scanned the pages until he found the right passage, then neatened the stack before handing them back to her. Their fingers brushed as she took them.

"Maybe you could help me with this passage." He pointed to a spot halfway down the top page. "See here the use of a word for 'ancients'? Now, at first glance, I thought that it meant a group of people devoted to old ways or an old religion, but if my translation is correct, and I think it is, the phrase is more likely a title, and from the context, it's the title of a group of people who *live forever*."

He removed his glasses and sat back, his eyes still on her, burning with a blue intensity that had her almost twitching with unease. "Now, you and I both know that people living forever is a figment of someone's overactive imagination."

"Yes, of course." She gave him points for being able to deduce as much as he had, but admitting it was likely bad for her health. "Though, given the fact that the church ruled everyday life, it could be a reference to the afterlife, which in Christian mythology is never-ending. *La vie sans fin*, if you will. A moment, please." She rose from her desk and paced to the window for the better light to read.

The distance from him didn't hurt either as the thrum between them eased a little. She leaned against the heavy brocade curtain, one ankle crossed over the other, a mask of calm hiding the chaos of emotion inside. Elation that one of her books was close at hand warred with confusion over how it had gotten into the hands of another auction house.

The prickling in her scalp warned her to be cautious of the man sitting in her visitor's chair.

All strangers were Hunters until proven otherwise. And the fact that he had one of her chronicles couldn't be a coincidence. Maybe the Hunters had their suspicions about her too, and this was all a test.

That all battled with the stirrings of something inside that had begun when he first put on his reading glasses. They did something to his face, allowed the intelligence in his eyes to project out, and did strange things to her normally unwavering composure.

When she was finished reading and had stuffed the bedlam in her mind into a box to mull over later, she turned back to Patrick. "I'll need to see the rest of it."

The dimple flashed in his cheek. "Come by my office and I'll have it ready."

"Can I keep these?"

Patrick nodded and rose to his feet. Over the desk, their eyes met and held, bright blue to dark green. Her skin started to prickle as the air between them hummed with something she couldn't identify. Morgana looked away first and carefully, almost reverently, set the papers on her desk. "Is there anything more I can do for you?"

"Not at this time, no." Patrick said, reaching into the inside pocket of his jacket. "Here's my card. I'll be expecting you at six."

"We close at four and I am pretty certain that Davies & McNamara keeps similar hours."

"Do we?" A light and almost teasing tone came into his voice. "Well, you'll just have to meet me for dinner then, won't you? We can discuss fifteenth century weather patterns some more." He smiled crookedly at his own joke as he finished packing up his briefcase. "Then I'll let you see it."

Morgana hesitated. For all she knew, he could be leading her into a Hunter trap. But a small part of her countered that he could just be a normal mortal man who had taken an interest in her, which wasn't in itself a rare thing. She had a slender, willowy build that made her appear much taller than her modest five foot three. Her dark red hair was long and wavy; eyes large and long-lashed in a heart-shaped face that wouldn't immediately be called beautiful.

But it *was* rare for her to have even a flicker of interest in return. Emotional entanglements were far too difficult for far too many reasons.

"On second thought..." he paused at the door and turned back. "I'll send a car for you."

As he disappeared through the door, Morgana sighed deeply and sat hard in her chair. She flexed her fingers, releasing her grip on the Mont Blanc pen she had instinctively grabbed at his sudden movement. It took several deep breaths for her heartbeat to slow, as she gazed unfocused at the door, the encounter replaying in her head. It usually took effort to shake her confidence, more to scramble her thoughts, still more to play with her emotions.

In only a few minutes, he had managed all three.

Her eyes drifted down to her desk to the scanned manuscript pages. Her Chronicle. Its contents so ancient and unfamiliar it could have come from someone else's pen, even as the handwriting screamed otherwise.

Taking up the scans again, she *could* almost feel the goose feather quill in her hand, smell the woodsmoke in the brazier in the corner, the iron-gall ink that spotted her fingers. The pages were vellum, skins tanned and scraped paper thin, later to be sewn into the book that Patrick Davies had discovered only God knew where.

The more she studied the pages, the more she became convinced that this was one of a half dozen she'd last seen in London in 1922. While the collection in her office was nearly complete, a few had been lost over the years when a Hunter attack forced her to flee. Some she'd eventually recovered, but others, like this one, had remained lost. Could it be possible that he had the others as well?

As for the one he had for sure, Morgana was prepared to do anything to get it back.

Three

The day passed in a blur as those following an auction always did with finalizing transactions, and readying pieces for delivery. Morgana moved from department to department for much of the morning before returning to her office to try to review resumes for an open appraiser position. As usual, she never quite finished an application before being called back out to unlock the vault to retrieve a piece so valuable it stayed secure until the moment the buyer arrived to sign for it.

By the time she got home just after five o'clock, she had only enough energy to pour a glass of wine and collapse on the depths of the living room sofa. Her body craved a soak in the whirlpool tub she'd installed the year before and her bed.

Not until I see that Chronicle.

With a sigh, Morgana pushed herself up off the couch. Wine glass in hand, she opened the door to her walk-in closet, fragrant cedar wafting out. After a few minutes of pushing through racks of dresses in every hue, she selected an emerald dress that matched the color of her eyes exactly and turned to the wall of shoes to select a pair of black heels. Her hair went up into a twist with the quick ease born of long practice on the way to the bathroom to touch up her makeup.

By the time she was transferring the essentials into a smaller clutch purse, her equilibrium was back, and excitement fluttered under her breastbone. Morgana glanced at the clock in the kitchen as she reached for her black wrap from the peg by the front door. She had to hurry to get back to the auction house by six.

Halfway out the door, the hall phone, which served only as an intercom to the front desk rang. Morgana retraced her steps and reached for the handset. "Hello?"

"There is a car here for you, Miss Dericault." Fred's voice was uncharacteristically excited.

The receiver nearly fell out of Morgana's hand. "T-Thank you, Fred." Her voice trembled slightly as excitement turned to something colder. "I-I'll be right down."

Morgana hung up the phone and went to the closet by the door to retrieve her smallest stiletto switchblade from the pocket of a leather jacket and slipped it into her clutch. Her mind was still reeling as she rode the elevator to the lobby, almost screaming at her that the car was headed in the wrong direction.

But curiosity won out. At least she would face what was coming next armed.

As the doors opened, she took a steadying breath and strode across the lobby and out to the waiting black limousine. A driver in a pressed suit held the door for her. With only the slightest hesitation, she slipped inside the dimly lit space and set her opened clutch on the seat beside her. As the car gently eased away from the curb and into the heavy traffic, she put her head back and closed her eyes.

"Good evening, Miss Dericault."

Morgana yelped, hand diving into her purse to clutch the knife. Before she could withdraw it, her eyes came to rest on Patrick emerging from the shadows of a side seat with two glasses of champagne in his hands.

He slid smoothly to the seat beside her and held out a glass. "I'm sorry if I startled you."

She released the weapon and reached for the dainty stem with fingers that trembled only slightly. "Are we celebrating something?"

He shrugged and took a sip from his glass, motioning for her to do the same. She balanced it on her knee instead, eyeing him warily. "I didn't know that the car you were sending for me would have you in it."

"Why not?" he asked with an amused grin. That dimple flashed again.

"Besides, I thought that maybe we could discuss the book on the way to dinner. I am intrigued to hear if you have any other thoughts about the pages I gave you this morning."

"I need you to answer a question for me first." She lifted the glass to her lips, but only pretended to drink. "How did you get my address?"

He raised an eyebrow at the question and shrugged. "Your assistant gave it to me when I was at Albrecht this morning."

"Well, he's fired." The levity in her voice was underlaid by seriousness. Privacy was rule one, and Alan should have known better.

Patrick barked a laugh and drank the last of the champagne in his glass. "Don't blame him," he answered as he set the glass aside. "I was charming."

That surprised a chuckle out of her. "It would have taken quite a lot to get something like my address out of Alan."

"I was *very* charming."

Morgana fought the urge to roll her eyes and smiled. "I'm sure."

His eyebrow went up again at the sarcasm in her voice.

She cleared her throat and reached across him to set her full glass beside his empty one. The car lurched, knocking her off balance halfway out of her seat.

Patrick caught her elbow before she fell into his lap and guided her back. His grip was gentle, his fingers warm on her bare skin.

They sat for a moment, side by side, his hand still on her arm, before Morgana shifted in her seat and his hand slid away. She deliberately resisted meeting his gaze, which was trained on her with something like curiosity.

She brushed a stray hair behind her ear and cleared her throat. "Now, about that book."

"Ah yes, the book."

Morgana reluctantly turned her head back. Even with the dim light inside the limousine, his eyes were very blue.

He studied her through those long lashes. "Well, like I told you this morning, the book only came into my possession a few months ago, through someone my best friend knows, but it took me until now to make headway because of the dialect it was written in."

A small knowing smile creased the corner of her mouth. "It definitely was difficult to read."

"I'm impressed that what took me months, only took you only a few minutes," Patrick answered. "Your reputation precedes you, and I'm happy to say, it's well earned."

It was impossible not to blush. "Well thank you, Mr. Davies. As I said—"

"Patrick, remember?" he corrected quickly.

"Right, Patrick."

The leather creaked as he shifted in his seat, turning sideways to face her with an elbow propped on the top of the seat. "Tell me your first impressions."

"Well, it was only a small taste of a much larger volume I assume." Morgana paused to consider her words carefully. To buy time, she settled back against the seat and crossed her legs at the knee, her hand drifting back to her purse.

The dress rode up her thigh, but to his credit, he didn't appear to notice.

"The pages read like an excerpt of a diary entry or a journal, though it was written long before either really became common practice. Few of those who were literate at the time could afford paper or vellum just to record their own personal thoughts, not to this extent. Fiction writing was typically confined to plays since printing was equally expensive."

"And this book strikes you as fiction?"

"How could it not be?" she answered. "The author talks about an encounter with a young man new to the monastery who arrived in the middle of the night with injuries that should have left him dead by dawn. The sun rose and it was like the wounds had never been."

"I will admit," Patrick said with a nod, though there was amusement twinkling in his eyes even in the dim light. "It does sound a little unbelievable."

Morgana chuckled. "Well, she was convincing at least."

His eyes narrowed. "One moment, how do you know the author is a woman?"

She schooled her thoughts and her expression to hide her pounding heart and resolved to be more careful with her words. He had probably selected those specific pages on purpose.

There was something about him that made her want to speak without an ounce of caution.

Time to use that reputation that he put so much stock in. "The handwriting, of course."

Patrick nodded and smiled slightly. "Monastic scholars in the Middle Ages spent years honing a style of writing that today would appear feminine."

"True," she conceded.

Damn, he's good.

"Contextually speaking, though, there is little in those pages that would imply a woman's perspective. Not by sixteenth century standards anyway," Patrick added. "What makes you believe that we have a female author?"

Morgana looked out the window for a moment, the bright lights of a theater marquee flashing dimly through the smoked glass as the car waited at a light, her features carefully blank.

After a few moments, her eyes met his and she shrugged. "I do understand your skepticism. As a general rule, unless they were of the high nobility, women were rarely taught more than their letters. Few had the education to write with such eloquence as this woman, whoever she was."

"I get the impression that she had many names, but while she lived in the monastery, she called herself by the rather melodic name of Jacqueline d'Arnault. My apologies." His phone had begun buzzing in his pocket. He pulled it out and responded to the message in a flurry of clicks and returned the device to his pocket. The buzzing continued, but he ignored it. "Where were we? Ah yes, well, she was a scholar, who must have spent her days in pious reflection."

Morgana snorted before she could stop herself, but he only raised an eyebrow. She made a wave with one hand that was half apologetic, half beckoning him to continue.

"It's the work she did by candlelight that has me intrigued. Like you said, this book is some kind of diary or journal. But I think that she wrote about her life, and about the men and women she encountered. She was one of these Ancients and she knew a lot about them, and hungered to know more."

"It's an amazing story," Morgana said, trying to keep the smile that threatened to break free at the thought of the writer's "piety." As memory served, the only reason she'd gone to services was because Brother Ambois required it as a condition of living at the monastery. *He* was the most pious man she had ever met, and it did not matter to him that most of his residents were devout pagans, still loyal to the beliefs prevalent in the years of their birth. Some were like Morgana, who had abandoned belief in any kind of deity when she'd woken up from her deathbed.

All went to services the required three times a day, at least, or they were asked to leave, putting them back within the sights of the Hunters.

And by then, she'd had her fill of running. The monastery was, for all intents and purposes, a godsend.

A little outward piety had been a small price to pay for some semblance of security and, with it, an opportunity to continue her research and to spend time with others like her. They shared meals and stories, how they found out they could no longer be killed, how long they had been alive, and what they had done with that life.

At night, as he'd suspected, she wrote it all down, carefully sketching out their likeness in ink to remember what each of her people looked like. It was those histories, those portraits, that made her chronicles such an appealing commodity. Her people never changed, so the Hunters could use her drawings to identify her kind. They had done it before.

"It still sounds like fiction to me," she mused, withdrawing from memories which were turning suddenly to regret, and also alarm. What exactly was in this particular volume?

Patrick chuckled. "If you read the entire book, you would think otherwise."

"That's why I'm here," Morgana said, unable to conceal her eagerness. They had been driving for a while, and she was just about to ask where they were going when the car slid to a smooth halt and the driver got out.

"But first, I'm starving." Patrick said as the car door opened and he slid out, and held his hand down to help her out, then tucked her hand into the crook of his arm and led the way to the door.

Morgana's eyes widened as they passed through a pair of glass doors, the name *Sophie's* gracefully etched across them. It was the most expensive and lavish restaurant in town. The interior was all cream walls and candlelight, red tablecloths, and soft music. The kind of place where elite businessmen rubbed shoulders with local politicians and visiting celebrities on a nightly basis.

She cut a glance at him to find him openly waiting for her reaction. A corner of his mouth turned up, and a blush began to rise on her cheeks. The air inside was pleasantly warm, the clink of silverware on porcelain mingled with the buzz of conversation and the quiet notes of a grand piano tucked into a small loft above the dining room.

Patrick guided her through the small crowd waiting for tables at the door with a gentle hand on her back and called the maître d' by first name.

The man behind the stand smiled and waved them over. He collected menus, and led them into the restaurant, ignoring the well-dressed and clearly impatient couple hovering by the stand who started to object. He placed the menus down on a table in the back corner, wished them a pleasant evening, and left.

Morgana had to admit that she was impressed. It was a beautiful space where the addition of a few candles, some flowers, and the right wine could completely change the tone of the evening.

But this wasn't a romantic dinner. It was just a formality Patrick was forcing her through to be allowed to touch her manuscript again. They were seated and served their drinks before either spoke again.

"Is your family from France?" Patrick asked. "Your name, Dericault, it's one I haven't heard before."

"I was born in France," she said, "in a little village north of Toulouse."

"Amazing, you have no accent whatsoever."

Morgana smiled and affected the accent her voice had carried for centuries before she had taught herself how to speak without it. "But of course, it is so easy to find it again."

Patrick chuckled. "*Touché*," he said, and sipped his wine.

The air between them was growing entirely too comfortable, too relaxed. She had been in his presence for no more than an hour and knew almost nothing about this man. She needed to steer the subject away from her. "And you, born in Brooklyn if my ears don't deceive me?"

He froze mid-sip, his eyes widening over the rim of his glass, and then he smiled. It brightened his whole face. Damn that dimple. "My father would be very angry if he knew how easily you figured that out," he said ruefully. "He tried to give me the best schooling in Manhattan, but then my parents separated when I was fourteen. He moved out here to establish the West Coast branch of D&M, and I moved with my mom back to Brooklyn. My education became somewhat... less orthodox, and the accent my father had tried so hard to banish came back. You see, cultured accents are what get you beat up in Brooklyn."

"Life on the streets can be tough," Morgana agreed. "And quite educational."

"Indeed," he said thoughtfully, but anything else he was going to say was interrupted by the arrival of their waiter. Patrick glanced at her briefly with a questioning cocked eyebrow, to which she replied with a wave of her hand. He flashed a grin and turned to the waiter, ordering their meals in perfect French.

"You didn't stay a street-kid," she observed, unable to suppress a smile.

"No," he said. "I moved back to Manhattan after high school, but on my own merit with what money I had, loans and hockey scholarships to pay for what I didn't. I have bachelor's degrees from NYU in Art History and Finance, my Graduate work was at Cambridge with summers spent in Paris. I worked as an intern at Sotheby's for a while as well."

"Impressive." While she herself had no such credentials, she had very clever and necessary forgeries, supported by knowledge and expertise cultivated over the centuries.

"What about you?"

Eager to change the subject again, but not wanting to be rude, she told him her current backstory. Born in France, she had moved to England at twelve and Canada at fourteen. At eighteen, a friend had gotten her a job at a small auction house in Toronto. By twenty-five, she had moved across the country to her current position which she had held for the last two years. If anyone cared to look, they would find birth records, school records, employment records, everything carefully fabricated to ensure no suspicion. In some ways, the electronic age made changing one's identity much easier, but in other ways much more difficult, but it could still be done.

None of it was true, of course, she had been back in her apartment after a decade away for five years, living in the same building she'd had built two hundred years earlier. It was a necessary ruse.

Patrick refilled her glass from the bottle chilling in a bucket beside the table. The glass froze halfway to her lips when a shadow crossed the table.

"I thought that was you!"

The voice froze Morgana in her seat, unable to even reach for the clutch inches away.

They both looked up at the man who stepped up to the table. He was dressed in dark pants and a white shirt, but no tie. The collar was unbuttoned, and the sleeves rolled up to his elbows in a haphazard way that suggested he'd done it quickly to perform a task rather than for fashion. He had a long face with a sharp, clean-shaven jaw even at this hour of the night and his straight, dark hair was pulled back in a neat ponytail at the nape of his neck.

She would know that face anywhere, but his cunning brown eyes weren't looking at her.

Patrick's face broke into a broad grin as he got to his feet and extended a hand. They embraced warmly, slapping each other on the back.

By the time he returned to his seat and looked at Morgana, her mask was in place, her clutch in her lap and open, but her skin had gone bone white.

"Now Pat, who is this delightful creature?" He swept up Morgana's hand from the table and kissed the knuckles.

"Morgana Dericault, this is Jacob Martel."

"*Enchanté*," Jacob said releasing her hand.

Morgana took her napkin from the place setting in front of her and placed it in her lap, using the movement to try to rub away the feeling the contact had left on her skin.

"*Enchantée de faire votre connaissance.*" Morgana replied automatically.

Jacob smiled and he settled into an open chair at Patrick's invitation. She fought the urge to shift away from him but Morgana, the young auction manager, had nothing to fear from this man.

Morgana, the immortal, on the other hand was suddenly very much on guard. While she always went to great lengths to keep her identity a secret, she knew his face well. Martel was the leader of the local group of Hunters.

"Jake has been a really good friend for a long time," Patrick said. "Until he married my sister that is."

It took every ounce of strength to keep Morgana in the chair, and her jaw from hitting the floor. Her hand went reflexively to her throat, and quickly camouflaged the movement with a slight shiver.

"Are you cold?"

Morgana drew her wrap up around her shoulders and smiled as she reached for her wine glass. "I'm fine."

Except that I spent last night dodging the bullets your friend sent my way. The wine slid down to form a ball of ice into the pit of her stomach.

"Pat, I wanted to let you know that Soph's having a barbecue on Saturday. Why don't you bring Morgana here along?"

Soph? as in Sophie? Suddenly, the choice of restaurant became more suspicious.

"Oh, I wouldn't want to intrude," Morgana answered quickly.

"Nonsense," Jacob said with a wink. He rose to his feet and shook Patrick's hand. "See you Saturday." He clapped his friend on the shoulder and walked away, greeting people at other tables before disappearing into the kitchens.

"Does he work here?" Morgana asked, eyes fixed on the still-swinging door.

"He owns the place," Patrick said, eyes following hers. "Are you alright? You look like you've seen a ghost."

"No more than usual," Morgana murmured, her heart still hammering in her ears, drowning out the piano playing above them. "So... he owns this place, and Sophie..."

"Is my sister," he finished. "Hence the name. Are you really sure that you're okay?"

She nodded. Being here, with him, was a mistake. If Patrick was friends with a Hunter, he almost certainly one himself. Morgana sized him up again. He didn't look quite as big as the Hunter she had collided with on the rooftop, but the encounter had been so quick. It could have been him.

Patrick continued to study her for a long moment. Her hands were starting to tremble slightly, and she put them in her lap, clenching the folds of her napkin to calm them. She was just reaching for her clutch to run when the food arrived.

"How well do you know your friend?" Morgana asked as she reached for her silverware. The plate was decoratively arranged, thin slices of perfectly roasted duck perched on a bed of root vegetables and bathed in a sauce of cherry and red wine. Her mouth watered as the delicious scents reached her nose, but she found she didn't have much of an appetite.

"I've known him for twenty years. Why?"

"No reason."

He eyed her speculatively but didn't press the matter and observed that she was doing little more than pushing her food around on her plate and persuaded her to eat. She managed to force a few bites down, where they formed balls of ice in her stomach. Soon enough, he signaled for the check and paid the bill from a money clip. He helped her to her feet and straightened the wrap around her shoulders.

Once again, his hand slipped to the small of her back as he guided her from the restaurant. The night was cool, and she gathered her shawl tighter, but they only waited a moment before the limo rolled to a stop and the driver emerged to open their door. He took her hand to help her inside, but Morgana paused, looking back at Sophie's and up at the surrounding buildings as if she was simply taking in the beauty of the evening, when she was really scanning for Hunters perched in the shadows.

"Morgana?"

She brought her gaze down to him, heart still hammering in her ears. "Please take me home."

Four

J acob had just settled into the creaky office chair when his phone began to ring. He patted his pocket out of habit, but the sound was coming from somewhere under the layers of receipts and bills on the desktop. He lifted one pile after another, finally locating the phone just before it went to voicemail. He'd been playing phone tag with Patrick over the last few days since he had come in with the striking redhead in the emerald dress, but the voice that spoke wasn't his best friend.

"Check your email."

Jacob scowled at the gruff voice, but tucked the phone to his shoulder and reached for the mouse. "I'm fine, Winter, thanks for asking. How are you?" he drawled as he logged into the private network that separated his restaurant files from his Hunter ones and opened his email.

Brian Winter chuckled. "Sorry, boss."

Jacob ground his teeth as he opened the email to find only Winter's automatic signature and a date stamp. "What am I looking for?"

"Open the video file."

Jacob clicked on the attachment and sat back while it loaded. Camera footage appeared on the screen from one of the customs agent's booths in the immigration hall at Kingston International. The camera appeared almost perched on the agent's shoulder as a well-dressed young businessman, maybe in his early to mid-twenties with light brown hair and oversize black glasses, handed over his passport. The agent's computer screen was in full view of the camera but the resolution on the video wasn't good enough to make out the traveler's information when it appeared onscreen.

"I'm going to assume that the video has loaded by now."

"Watch the tone, Winter," Jacob snarled. Just because the man was their eyes and ears at the airport and spent his day running a facial recognition program in the background while performing normal inspection duties didn't mean that he could be an asshole about it. "Who am I looking at?"

"Open the other file."

The document that appeared on screen was a summary report of the immigration interview. There was a scan from the man's American passport and a photo taken at the booth along with a fingerprint. "Alexander Richman, age 24, came in from San Francisco. Don't tell me that your fancy program finally got a hit."

"He lit it up like a Christmas tree." Winter's voice was smug.

It was his pet project. Winter had built the software, and had deployed it, at no little personal risk, onto the government equipment at the airport. After almost two years with no results, the expense hadn't seemed worth it.

Until now.

Jacob sat up straighter in his chair. He opened the third file before Winter could prompt him and found a report containing biographical data attached to a handful of photographs. Some were of questionable quality as if taken from a distance on a low-res cell phone camera, but there was one photo that stood out, a professional headshot. "Alasdair Bromley," Jacob murmured as he read. "Says here that he's CEO of an investment company in San Francisco with a $50 billion portfolio. That's no small amount of money."

He put the headshot and the immigration photo side by side. Other than the glasses and slightly different hair styles, they looked like the same man. "Interesting. So why is Alasdair Bromley carrying a passport for Alexander Richman?"

"Keep going in the file."

Jacob continued scrolling down past the headshot and stopped, eyes widening on a photo from a scanned newspaper clipping. There was a small group of people dressed to the nines, and there to one side was the same face, partially obscured by his arm holding up a celebratory drink. "Anthony Bailey, London Art Gallery, New Years Eve... 1957?"

"Yep," Winter confirmed. "Either this guy is the spitting image of his grandfather, or he hasn't aged a day in seventy years."

Jacob's heart started to race. He flipped back to the immigration paperwork again. "Says he's visiting for business and staying somewhere," he squinted at the address, "over on the east side of town. I'll have someone check it out. Nice work."

"I'll be expecting that nice bottle of Scotch you promised."

Jacob scowled at the phone as the line went dead and dropped it back down among the mess of papers on his desk. For a few moments, he poured over the photographs and reports from one of the databases the European Hunters used. There wasn't much but, from the looks of it, this guy had managed to stay hidden for much of the last fifty or so years, at least until recently.

Jacob sat back for a moment, fingering his chin as he stared at the headshot of Alasdair Bromley. After a moment, he picked up the desk phone and called the bar. Brennan picked up after a few rings, the music dimly heard through his office door on the far side of the kitchen blasted through the earpiece, the clamor of people at the bar almost as loud.

"What's up, boss?"

"Can you come back here for a minute?"

"Pretty sure you can hear all these thirsty people through the phone."

"Why is everyone giving me attitude tonight?" he growled. "Now."

Brennan sighed and agreed and then hung up. A knock sounded on the door a few moments later and Jacob yelled for him to enter.

"What's so urgent?"

Jacob motioned him over where he could see the computer screen and explained what Winter had sent him. Brennan's eyes widened and he brushed Jacob's hand away from the mouse, taking control to look through the other records. "Well, I'll be damned."

Jacob took back control of the mouse and pulled up the immigration record. He dug through his desk for a pen and a slip of paper and jotted down the address. "I need you to check this out. See whether this guy actually gave a real address or not."

Brennan took the paper and tucked it into his shirt pocket. "I'll do it first thing after I drop Kaitlyn off at school in the morning."

Jacob nodded, though impatience tore at him. He could go himself except Sophie was expecting him home early tonight and they had an appointment in the morning. He took a deep breath and calmed his voice. "That's fine," he replied, "thanks, Bren."

"No problem, boss," he replied. "Looks like we're in for some excitement. And if this paperwork is any indication, we might be in for quite the payday too."

Jacob clapped his friend on the shoulder and Brennan returned to the bar. An excited smile spread across his lips as he looked back at the computer screen. It had been a while since Jacob's last kill, since before he had moved to Kingston, but he had continued to train his body and his mind to stay ready for the next one.

As he closed the files and logged out of the private network, something still nagged at him. No immortal would risk crossing an international border without a good reason, and it likely wasn't for business. If that were true, there had to be someone already here waiting for him.

Five

A lan barged into Morgana's office without knocking for the fifth time in as many hours. He slapped down the phone message slip on top of the pile of others and waited for her to look up. "If you don't call him, I will," he told her, a mixture of annoyance and amusement on his face, and sauntered out of the room.

Morgana stared after him, brain too fuzzy to think of any kind of retort. He deserved a good telling off after giving away her address, but she found the words died on her lips. Despite the lapse, he was the best assistant she had ever had. So, she'd held her tongue and he'd kept his job, though she'd warned him not to expect a raise anytime soon.

Glancing at the clock, Morgana let out a relieved sigh. The day, like much of the week, had passed in a blur. After a few fitful nights' sleep expecting a Hunter attack that never came, today had started out with a crashed computer system and two staff members resigning to move back east together. Not to mention Patrick Davies had called four—she looked down at the messages—no, five times. And that was just today.

Morgana tossed down her pen and reached beside the desk for her briefcase. She stuffed her laptop and the scanned pages of her chronicle inside, adding the phone messages on top, and headed for the elevator.

Once home, the shoes were the first thing to go, the cork from a bottle of wine soon followed. After a long sip, she turned back to the island where her briefcase had fallen on its side, the contents spilling out onto the white marble.

She gathered up the yellow phone messages and smiled as she read through them for the first time. They'd become scrambled escaping from the bag, but Morgana was able to put them in order going by what Alan had written, each bolder and more annoyed than the one before it. The last one said in overlarge lettering, "For the love of GOD, call him back" with as many exclamation points as would fit.

Morgana chuckled and set the pile of messages down on the island and took her wine with her to change out of her work clothes. As she emerged from her bedroom, she stopped at the closed door of her office.

It had been weeks since she had opened the door, let alone sat down to write. And if she was honest with herself, she had avoided recounting the rooftop chase and her encounters with Patrick Davies the following day, because it meant she would finally have to analyze how those events had affected her.

"Coward," she muttered aloud and swallowed the remaining wine in her glass.

It took two keys, retrieved from hiding places on opposite sides of the apartment, and just as many codes to open the door to her office. There was a slight hiss of a released seal as she opened the door and flicked the lights on as she stepped inside. There were no windows, a concession to security given that the walls, floor, and ceiling were fire-proof. If the building burned down, this room would survive intact, protecting her life's work.

For all its security, the room was a cozy space. The floors were inlaid with maple hardwood like the rest of the apartment, with a thick carpet in shades of cream covering all but a foot of wood before the heavy bookcases that lined three walls from floor to ceiling.

Most of the widely spaced shelves were packed with leather-bound books, distinguishable only by their age, some well-worn, some very new, waiting to be filled. The fourth wall was painted a warm, inviting honey color. A framed print of DaVinci's *La Scapigliata* hung on the wall, gazing serenely down at a sturdy mahogany desk with a leather chair the color of warm caramel before it.

She paced the room, trailing her fingers lovingly along the spines of her chronicles. The current volume lay open on the desk, resting on a wooden writing stand, which was sloped slightly with a space in the middle to accommodate the binding. A half-completed sketch on one page called for her to finish it.

Morgana set to mixing the ink, carefully measuring out the powders into water in a bowl and stirring. The familiar work helped to calm her mind. She tapped the glass stir stick on the side of the bowl and wiped it clean with a rag, stained from long use, and went to the kitchen to refill her wine glass while the ink mixture developed.

She returned to the desk and placed the open wine bottle off to one side where it wouldn't get knocked over and stood, glass in hand, while she flipped back through the last few pages to refresh her memory. When the ink had turned a dark bluish-black, Morgana filled the glass inkwell on the desk, settled into her chair, turned the pages back to the sketch, and got to work.

Sometime later, she put the pen down and picked up the wine glass, watching a small fly bounce in and around the lamp shade as she worked out a rough outline in her head. After a few moments, it disappeared back through the open door, and she traded the glass for the pen. She turned to a fresh page, and with precise strokes and a flowing script, Morgana recounted her flight across city rooftops after surprising two Hunters on the rooftop of the auction house, and her suspicions that Jacob Martel and possibly Patrick Davies had been the men who had given chase.

Satisfied with the entry, she refilled the inkwell and her glass of wine, and slowly began to record the encounter in her office and the chronicle that he had brought back into her life.

> *Throughout the meeting, which took not quite an hour, there were moments that I was certain that he knew absolutely nothing about the world described in the text, but then there was something about him, and the careful but rapt attention that he paid to our conversation that made me suspect that he was testing me. As if one wrong word and he would reach into the open briefcase and pull out a weapon instead of a sheaf of papers and a pair of reading glasses.*

At the thought, an echo of unfamiliar heat that had gone through her the first time he'd put that pair of dark blue lenses on shot down her spine, and she tried to shake it off.

I am still of two minds over whether or not he is involved, and that scares me.

Morgana paused and stared at the words.

She *was* scared.

Her pen hovered over the last statement, her fingers itching to cross it out as if that would somehow make it less true. Writing her chronicles always brought a clarity that simply thinking or talking about an event never could. And she had never once censored her own writing, so the thought stayed.

The idea that he might be a Hunter is unnerving, particularly since he somehow managed to convince my assistant to disclose my address. In the days since our meeting, I have expected an attack through door or window, or for someone to be waiting when I emerge onto the street.

But truthfully, what scares me is how I feel when I'm around him after only having spent a few hours in his company. His eyes are a crystal sapphire that could pull an unsuspecting person inside its matrix and never release them again.

His hair is auburn, thick, and rich like the coat of a chestnut stallion, and when the sunlight from my office window shone on him, there were so many shades of red, I couldn't name them all, at least not from across the room.

He's tall with a fair and clear complexion, surprising for someone with hair like his to have. There is not a freckle or mark on his skin. He exuded confidence that bordered on cockiness, but there were moments where that demeanor could have been affected.

He speaks French beautifully, and I sense an intelligence that he has let few people truly see. He had the wherewithal and the connections in France to translate the chronicle from a very obscure dialect into English. I teased him about this, joking that the book could have contained weather records and he replied that his father's auction house (Davies & McNamara, a prestigious auction house in Kingston, New York, and London) needed to know the contents before it could be sold.

As our meeting progressed, I felt as though his interest was very different than obtaining an executive summary in order to value and sell a book. It also struck me as odd that he did the work personally. At the conclusion of the meeting, we agreed to meet for dinner, though in hindsight, I very much wish I had declined. He said that he would send a car, but I was unprepared for where that would be.

Morgana recounted the events from that night, from the car arriving at her home, to the surprise encounter with Martel and the revelation of the relationship between the two men. By the time she finished, her hand was cramped, and the inkwell was running low. She reached for the reserve ink and found the bowl empty.

Sighing, she rose to mix more and swayed slightly, catching herself on the desk, as the blood left her head from too much wine on an empty stomach. Leaving the ink to develop, she went to the kitchen to make some food. After setting a pot of water on the stove to boil, Morgana loaded her arms with chicken and vegetables from the refrigerator and turned back to the island, where she had to bend and sweep the chronicle scans aside with one forearm to clear room.

As she prepared the ingredients, her attention drifted to the pages, her own handwriting calling out to her as it had in her office. She cleared the chicken from the cutting board into a pan of melted butter and oil with the scrape of a knife and turned to the sink to wash them.

A familiar sensation suddenly ran through her, the buzzing of a hive of bees, the rush of the sea during a storm, and the clamor of ringing bells all at once filled her head, but the sounds didn't come through her ears. Morgana dropped everything with a clatter, but the knife missed the edge of the sink, and she danced awkwardly back to avoid spearing her foot.

She swayed against the counter as a current went through her, as if she had touched a live wire. As quickly as the sensation had come on, it faded away, leaving behind a rush of adrenaline, a pounding heart, and a headache just above her eyes that had nothing to do with the wine. It had been four long years since she had last sensed one of her kind. For some, it was a pleasant sensation, but for Morgana it was a tidal wave.

Morgana retrieved the knife from the floor and dumped it in the sink, then waited with her hand on the phone in the front hallway and snatched it up when it rang. "A visitor, Fred?"

"Yes, Miss Dericault," Fred replied, surprise in his voice. "Well dressed one too. Says his name is Alasdair Bromley. Shall I send him aw—"

A grin spread across her face. "Send him right up," she said and hung up the phone, dashing to the sink to wash her hands and to give the pan a toss. Moments later the doorbell rang, and Morgana dashed back, drying her hands on a towel.

On the doorstep was a young man in a three-piece suit, dark brown hair carefully styled, with trendy, slightly oversized, black eyeglasses. He had an overnight bag over one shoulder and a bottle of red wine in one hand. He cried out her name and held out his arms.

Morgana held him close, breathing deep the scents of sandalwood and sage with just a hint of pepper from the cologne he had been wearing for the past seventy years.

He released her and set her back at arm's length, taking in her capri leggings, baggy sweater and hair twisted up with an enameled chopstick. "You look beautiful."

"Flattery will get you everywhere with me, Alasdair." Morgana kissed each cheek and released him. "Make yourself useful, you know where the corkscrew is."

She went back to the stove to turn the chicken and add pasta to the water.

"Looks like I'm just in time," he said popping the cork out of the bottle. "What are you making?"

"Nothing fancy," she replied, adding the vegetables to the chicken pan. "Can you get the lemons and tell me how you've been! The last time I heard anything of you, you were in over your head somewhere in—Vienna, was it?"

"Prague." Alasdair corrected her, dropping the bag of lemons onto the island with a thump. "And don't remind me. It wasn't one of my finer moments."

Morgana chuckled as she stirred the pasta and then washed the knife and cutting board in the sink. She carried them back to the island and started slicing lemons. Alasdair placed a glass of red wine within her reach and took a seat on the other side of the island.

"Life has been fairly uneventful of late," he said and raised his glass.

Morgana clinked her glass to his and took a sip. The burst of fruit and spice exploded on her tongue, her eyes momentarily rolled back. Alasdair had an exquisite taste in wine, and an expensive one.

"Unlike you, from what I hear."

Her eyes snapped open. "Excuse me?"

Alasdair shrugged. "I heard the police have been receiving calls about strange people running around on rooftops. Gunshots in the night in some of the posher areas of town."

Her sip of wine turned into a gulp and a cough. She set the glass down with a clatter and turned back to the stove without a word to squeeze lemon juice over the pan.

When she didn't speak immediately, he continued, "just because I live in San Francisco doesn't mean I can't keep tabs on an old friend."

She looked back over one shoulder and raised an eyebrow.

"I have a detective friend in the KPD that keeps me in the loop," he admitted with a shrug. "Obviously, I put two and two together."

Morgana drained the pasta and filled two wide, flat bowls with food. She walked past the island, motioning with an elbow for Alasdair to retrieve her glass and carried the bowls to the coffee table in the living room. She heard the rattle of the silverware drawer and the glug of wine refilling glasses before he joined her.

"How casual," he remarked with a chuckle as he removed his suit coat and vest before sitting down. His cufflinks made gentle clinking sounds on the glass table. He rolled up his sleeves to the elbow and reached for a bowl.

He took a bite as she settled beside him and smiled. "Delicious, as always."

"Thank you."

They ate in companionable silence for several moments before Morgana finally put her fork down and turned to him. It was his turn to lift an eyebrow. "Okay yes, I did have a little run-in with a couple of men with guns on the roof of the auction house last week and led them on a bit of a chase."

He sighed. "Indeed."

She patted his arm and went back to her food. "It's been too much too long, Ally."

He grimaced at the nickname, one that he had always referred to as "horrid," and that was why she still used it. Their friendship was one that spanned centuries and a little light-hearted teasing wouldn't have any adverse effect on it now.

Morgana laughed and traded bowl for wine glass. She scooted back on the sofa, tucking her feet up under her and recounted the story as he finished his dinner. "I love that you're here, Ally, but there *is* this newfangled thing called a telephone." Her face and voice were gentle but serious, though the faintest of smiles played at the corner of her mouth.

He stared right back for several moments, but as always, he blinked first. "Thought it was a good enough reason to visit an old friend."

When she didn't speak, he held up his hands with a chuckle, defeated. "All right, all right," he cried. "I was worried, and I just wanted to come and be sure that you were all right. Are you satisfied?"

Morgana rose to her feet and retrieved the wine bottle from the kitchen. "This is the first time in the better part of a year that anything has happened."

"You *should* move, you know, get away from Kingston and stay away for good!" Alasdair called after her. When she returned to the sofa, he had taken off his glasses, and was dangling them by one earpiece over the side of the sofa. His hair was disheveled from at least one hand run through it.

"You've been here far too long, and you keep coming back. It's only a matter of time."

"I know," she answered with a sigh. She took a sip of her wine and studied him over the rim of her glass. Without the black frames, and careful styling of his light brown hair, he very much resembled the rakish and brash nineteen-year-old who'd had his first death on the losing end of a duel. After nearly four hundred years, he still regretted his reckless youth.

"What's on your mind, love?" he asked as she continued to look in his direction, but wasn't really seeing him.

Morgana shook her head and her eyes focused. 'Sorry."

Alasdair caught her hand as she set her glass aside again and pulled her gently against his side, tucked under one arm.

She smiled, and there was the hint of a laugh in her voice when she spoke again. "And I *have* been thinking about it. Moving, I mean."

"What is so funny about moving?"

She smiled. "There is nothing funny about it, and I really don't want to ever do it again."

She swatted the air in front of her wine glass where it sat just out of reach with his arm around her.

Alasdair rolled his eyes and plucked the glass from the table and handed it to her.

She smiled gratefully and took a sip before continuing. "If you must know, I was just thinking about that night in Weimar, the dinner after Berlioz conducted at the Staatskapelle."

Alasdair's chest vibrated under her cheek. "Ah, *that* night. We'd had two too many bottles of red wine and nearly ruined a one-hundred-year-old friendship."

Morgana smiled and reached up to twine her fingers in the hand draped over her shoulder. "And after nearly two hundred more, where do you think we would be if we had?"

She'd meant it as a joke, but the heaviness of the silence that followed spoke volumes and she squeezed her eyes shut. *Stupid*, she thought.

When he still didn't speak after several moments went by, she brushed a lock of hair away from her face and turned the conversation back to the original topic. "At my age, all I want is to find a single place to live and stop running for good."

Alasdair nodded. "Would that we could, love."

"I honestly thought that I had found that here." Morgana took another sip of wine. "But much as I am loathe to admit, I might have already been discovered. But it happened days ago, and I have yet to be attacked. So, maybe not."

He craned his neck around to get a look at her face, locked his gaze with hers to stop the rambling. "What are you on about?"

She sat up and bracing one hand on the back of the couch, the other on his thigh, lifted herself up and twisted so she faced him, landing cross legged on the cushion. Her heart started racing with some of the earlier excitement returning to her voice.

"Never mind," she said with a wave of her hand. "One of my chronicles has been found!"

His eyes widened and he smiled, the tension in the air easing. "What? That is spectacular!" He crowed. "How? When?"

Her answering smile nearly stretched ear to ear as she leapt to her feet. The movement dislodged the chopstick from her hair, so it tumbled down her back as she raced back to the island to retrieve the scans and deposit them into his hands. "A man named Patrick Davies brought these scans to the office a few days ago. It's the one from the monastery, the oldest one I'm missing. And it looks to be in very good condition for its age. Only issue is that he said that he had acquired them from a friend of his brother-in-law."

"I fail to see the connection." He picked up his glass and took a casual sip.

"His brother-in-law is Jacob Martel."

He choked, and then coughed. "Ah."

"Yes, 'ah'." Morgana said wryly.

"And this Martel knows where you live?"

"No, but Patrick does. The same night that he came to my office, he sent a car to take me to dinner." She ignored the eyebrow that popped up at that. "Obviously, I assumed that the car would come to my office, but it showed up here."

His eyebrows nearly disappeared in his hairline. "How did he get your address?"

"From my assistant."

"Well, off with *his* head," Alasdair quipped sardonically. "Does this Patrick know what you are?"

"I don't know," Morgana said, settling back against him. Alasdair picked up a curl within reach and started winding and unwinding it around his fingers. It was an unconscious habit of his and it soothed her nerves, so she let him.

It would have been so simple if only she reciprocated his feelings. Alasdair wouldn't age as a mortal did. Perhaps, after a century or two, they would get sick of each other and go their separate ways, but Morgana didn't see him as any more than a dear friend, a brother.

"That's the problem. I am not entirely convinced that he doesn't. He could be a Hunter and I wouldn't know it."

"And that thought troubles you?"

She sprang up to her feet again and started to pace. "*Bien sûr, ça me trouble!*"

Like any well-educated English aristocrat of his time, Alasdair understood French, but she still took a deep breath and forced herself to find the English words. "You of all people know that even when I was mortal, I never stayed in one place very long." She said, remaining just out of reach of his attempts to take her arm. "I've created a nice life here; I don't want to move on yet."

Alasdair lunged for her again and finally managed to grab her wrist. After several gentle pulls, she allowed him to guide her down to perch on the edge of the coffee table. "Want to or not darling, sooner or later we all must move on."

She swallowed against the cold knot of fear in her throat and nodded, her face mostly hidden in a curtain of auburn curls. They sat there in silence, his thumb rubbing the back of her hand, as he gave her the space to steady herself.

"Were you writing?" he asked suddenly.

She raised her head and glanced over her shoulder at the open office door and nodded again. "I was getting the entries up to date and was just working on my meeting with Patrick when I took a break to eat and then you arrived."

His eyes returned to hers and he studied her for a moment. "What?"

"What aren't you telling me?"

Morgana sighed, "I told you that he had sent the car for me, and that it came here?" She reached for the wine bottle and waited for him to hold out his glass. "Well, let me tell you the rest."

Alasdair listened as she spoke, occasionally taking a sip of wine, but mostly he just held her hand. The pulse at her wrist skittered and jumped with an echo of the panic from that night, and it took several moments for her to meet his eyes as her words ran out. When she did, he was surprised to see what looked like shame.

He squeezed her hand. "You should call him."

Her eyes widened and she cleared her throat. "That was honestly the last thing that I thought you would say."

Alasdair rose to his feet and drew her up with him. Still holding her hand, he led her across the living room and down the hall to the open office door. He pointed inside. "*That* is why you will call him. *These* books, that you have spent your life writing. Patrick says he has one of them, and it is up to you to confirm that and bring it home."

He gave her a gentle push into the room with a hand on her lower back, and led her to the desk chair, pivoting it so she faced the bookcases. Alasdair waited for some of the tension to ease from her shoulders before he spoke again. "I completely understand your concern about him. Morgana, you have survived for over seven hundred years on your wits and your instincts, neither of which has let you down to this point. Take a deep breath and tell me what they're saying."

When she didn't say anything for many minutes, he spun the chair around to face him. He retrieved the pen resting beside the open chronicle and pushed it into her hands. He crouched down so he didn't loom over her.

Morgana looked down at the pen and then back at him.

"If you can't tell me, then write it." he said patting the open pages. "Tell the book what you think you should do."

A corner of her mouth twitched up. For a few moments, she turned the pen slowly in her hands. After a moment, she pushed back and brushed past him to refill the inkwell.

"It's a good thing that this is where I left off in the book anyway."

Alasdair took up position behind her and read over her shoulder. The words came slowly at first, but soon her hand almost flew over the page.

The chronicle, according to Patrick, belonged to a friend of Jacob Martel who brought it into the auction house, and presumably asked for help in getting it translated so it could be sold. There is also the possibility that the friend knew exactly what the book was and gave it as a gift from one Hunter to another...

Of this, I am still skeptical. There were times when I was certain that I was in the middle of a Hunter trap and, at other times, I was certain that he knew absolutely nothing about his brother-in-law's life.

Yes, Patrick is connected to the Hunters, but I am of two minds over whether or not he is involved.

This could all be an elaborate ruse, to wait for my guard to come down, but Patrick has known for the better part of a week where I live, and all he has done is call. And who can blame him after I abruptly cut the evening off?

As good as I normally am at controlling my emotions, the tension and, yes, fear that went through me sitting at the same table with Martel could only be contained for so long.

But was it fear for myself, or was it something else?

She paused for a moment as if considering the answer. Alasdair's hand twitched from its perch on the seat back, and he suppressed the urge to touch her shoulder to reassure her for fear of breaking her concentration. Then her chin came up and she reached to dip the nib in ink again before continuing.

The truth is that the fear wasn't entirely from the possibility of being attacked. There was plenty of that, to be sure, but there was also fear that Patrick could be innocently unaware of how his brother-in-law spent his nights. And if that is true, I do not want to be the one responsible for revealing that, and so many more secrets despite their long history.

Yet, if I want to bring the chronicle home, I must go through him, and risk revealing so many more truths, and my connection to the events described in the book itself.

Morgana stopped again and placed the pen in the inkwell with a clink of glass meeting ebony. "And there it is."

Alasdair spun the chair around to faced him. She looked very small in the oversized chair with her knees tucked up to her chin. "Do you feel better?"

She nodded. "Thank you, Ally." This time, she smiled when she said his name. "I've also decided that I'm not going to be scared anymore. I never should have let myself get that way in the first place." She pushed back the chair and stood. Their bodies nearly collided. Alasdair reached out to steady her just as Morgana swayed and caught her balance on the edge of the desk. Her face was flushed.

"I think I'll call him in the morning though," she said, her voice only slightly slurred.

He gently adjusted the neck of her sweater, that constantly threatened to slip off one shoulder.

"You'll stay, won't you?"

"Of course," he agreed. "Might I suggest some water though? You may be immortal, and won't die of alcohol poisoning, but you're not completely immune to a hangover."

"The address is a no-go, boss."

Brennan's voice was barely audible over the din of food prep in the kitchen as Jacob hurried through to the quiet front of house. As the door swung behind him, silencing the clang of pans and cutting boards, the shouted orders, he asked his second-in-command to repeat himself, the words clearer the second time. The dining room was quiet and empty, almost eerily so. The calm before the storm when they opened for service.

He scowled. "Figures."

"Yeah, building looks like it was a hotel at one point in its life, but it's not one now." There was a slam of a car door and a growl as Brennan started the Jeep's engine.

Jacob swore, and yanked the phone away from his ear before the blaring music deafened him.

"Sorry, boss." Brennan's voice in his ear was contrite but distant, as if he was on speakerphone. "The building looks to have been converted into an artist's commune. One of those places where a whole bunch of people have their studios. It's not residential."

"Damn," Jacob replied as he started weaving through the empty tables checking centerpiece candles and place settings. "Thanks for checking. I'll start putting together a patrol plan, put some feelers out, see if we can track this guy down."

"Think he's involved with the female?"

Jacob scowled. "Maybe." He adjusted the cutlery on one table, and turned to find another that was half set, the candles barely stubs, the centerpiece askew. "I have to go tell Aubrey off and get her out here to finish her damned job."

Brennan chuckled. "Go easy on her, boss. Her mom's been sick."

He deflated a little. "Sure, take the fun out of it."

Now he was laughing. "Well, we'll just have to hunt this Bromley down. Then you can have all the fun that you want."

Jake's answering smile was more of a curl of his lip, a thrill of antici-pation went through him. "I'll see you tonight." He hung up and stalked back to the kitchen to find his lead hostess and tell her—nicely—to finish setting up.

Six

A s he always did on a Monday morning, Patrick settled behind his desk and nursed a large mug of coffee while his computer booted up. To kill time, he checked his voicemail messages and took down notes, with each one hoping that he would hear a certain smoky voice. When the red light turned off, he put the handset back with a little more force than was strictly necessary.

With a sigh, Patrick took a sip of coffee from his mug and turned to his computer, the desktop finally loading with a fanfare of recorded horns. His inbox followed, displaying an unnecessary number of unread emails that had accumulated over the weekend. Mentally, Patrick calculated the amount of time it would take to get through it all, and groaned, then toggled over to his calendar. Hopefully, his department wasn't slammed with meetings, or he'd never get any work done.

Only a few colored areas blocked out time for meetings, but he immediately zeroed in on the first one of the morning. He expanded to the full view to be sure, but there it was at nine o'clock.

Morgana Dericault, Albrecht.

Patrick glanced at the clock; it was only seven-thirty. He swore under his breath and raised the coffee mug to his lips, only to find that it was empty, and it was far too early for that. He emerged into the small maze of cubicles normally occupied by D&M's cadre of researchers, assistants, and finance staff. As Vice President of Finance, one step below the company CFO, the latter group was his. At this hour, most of the desks were empty, only the staff who worked directly with the London or Milan offices were on site this early.

He could have had a coffee maker in his office, or have an assistant fetch it for him, but Patrick preferred to spend time "in the trenches" whenever he could. So, he wove his way to the small kitchenette on the other side. It gave him the opportunity to stop at the desk of one of his team leaders to say hello and catch up on the weekend's events.

The kitchenette was empty except for one slightly bedraggled member of his Milan finance team eating breakfast. His collar was open, tie loosened, and his brown hair also looked like it had already had a hand or ten run through it. It was lunchtime in Italy and his shift was half over.

"Rough morning, eh Glenn?" Patrick reached for the full coffee pot and poured the steaming black liquid almost to the brim. He hadn't slept very well the last few nights, and the first cup hadn't been of any help. Hopefully, the second one did the trick.

Glenn ran his hand through his hair again, a sheepish expression on his face. "How could you tell, sir?" He laughed. "Had some systems issues this morning, which got this week started with a bang, a whistle, and a very loud explosion. All fixed now though, I think."

"Good." Patrick took a sip of his coffee to bring it down to a safe level for travel and wove back to his office, closed the door, and settled back behind the computer. Might as well get through some of these emails to pass the time.

Sometime later, a knock on the door startled him out of the quarterly report he was proofing. Patrick straightened in his chair and adjusted his tie. "Come in!"

The door opened and June, one of the front desk secretaries poked her head in. "I have a Miss Dericault for you, sir, from Albrecht's House."

"Is it that time already?"

She nodded and stepped back to allow Morgana to step inside. She was dressed in an emerald jacket and black pencil skirt that went just past her knees with a pair of black heels that were high but still business appropriate. The jewel tone made it clear that her eye color was true green, not hazel, and made her auburn hair, which was twisted up and pinned at the back of her head, shine a bit more crimson. "Hello, Patrick."

There was that voice. He came around the desk and held out his hand. Morgana shook it firmly with a business-like smile. She stood with her back straight and her eyes met his directly, with no discernable emotion. The last time they had met, those eyes had been filled with uncertainty, and if he wasn't mistaken, fear.

"Please sit." He gestured to the chair beside him. "Can I get you anything?"

"Water?" she replied as she settled into one chair and placed her black leather tote bag on the other.

"Be right back." Patrick jogged back across the floor. Glenn was gone, and the coffee pot was down to an almost-burnt inch of black liquid. He turned it off to prevent stinking the floor up with burnt coffee and dashed back to his office. Curious eyes followed him, but he ignored them. Just outside the door, he stopped and reentered the room at a more normal pace.

Morgana glanced over her shoulder at the sound of the door and accepted the water bottle as he passed.

"I half-expected you to not be here when I got back."

She twisted the top off and winced. "After our last meeting, I don't honestly blame you." She took a sip and looked for a place to set the bottle down on the desk, and not finding one, held the bottle in her lap instead. "I did want to apologize for how the night ended."

He studied her for a moment.

She sat upright in the chair, one foot tucked behind the other, hands in her lap. This was the Morgana he had met in her office at Albrecht, not the Morgana who had gotten into the car later that evening.

He must have waited a half-second too long to speak, because they both started speaking at the same time. They stopped and overlapped again.

Morgana chuckled and waved a hand for him to speak.

"Why did it end the way it did?"

She studied him for a moment before replying. "My home address isn't something I normally disclose or allow others to disclose," she answered. "So, when the limo arrived at my front door, I was a little surprised to say the least."

"And at the restaurant? You seemed a little on edge there too, almost as if you were spooked, for lack of a better word."

Her eyes dropped to the water bottle, and passed it back and forth between her hands for a moment before unscrewing the cap. A corner of her mouth turned up. "Your friend reminded me of someone from my past. That's all. But I wasn't fair to you to cut the night short." She took a sip and replaced the cap. "Did you have a good time at your sister's party?"

He blinked at the quick change of subject. "Uh, yeah, it was very nice. It's not so much a party as an-every-couple-of-weeks kind of thing. Sophie loves to cook and have people over to eat it. You should come sometime. Jake *did* invite you."

Morgana nodded. "Perhaps."

"I have to tell you Morgana," he said, steering the conversation back. "I was very surprised when you asked me to take you home after dinner, especially given how interested you seemed to be in the pages that I brought to your office."

She grimaced. "That's partly why I came here today. I would still like to see it, and I brought you something that I think might help." She reached into her tote bag, withdrawing a folder, a rather thick folder, and placed it on the desk.

"What is this?"

"A bit of fair play."

He eyed her quizzically for a moment before the idiom came to him. "Ah, I get it. I came into your office with a surprise folder so you're doing the same?"

She nodded, and if he wasn't mistaken, a slight blush colored her cheeks. His eyes lingered on her as he slid the folder closer and opened it then looked down. The first few pages were handwritten, and underneath was a neatly bound document.

"This is some of my research from Aubrac and a copy of the thesis that I wrote. It contains everything that I have about the history of the location and everything I could find about the local dialect of French that was spoken in that area. The same language in which the pages you brought to me were written. I know you already had it translated but I thought maybe it would be helpful."

Patrick skimmed eagerly through the handwritten notes full of neatly printed columns of words, comparing English, modern French, and the Aubrac dialect, but there were other research notes as well.

"Now I wish that I had come to you first," he said. "Next time I'll go to the expert rather than spending the time and effort to do it myself. I'm a finance guy, not a linguist."

"You did very well," Morgana replied. "Surprisingly well, considering the material."

Her praise was unexpected and started a little flutter in his chest.

"Speaking of," she continued, "I was hoping that the offer to show me the manuscript was still good? I do very much want to see it, to see if there is anything that I can help you with that I couldn't manage from just a few pages."

He cleared his throat and took a sip of coffee to keep himself from making a run for the car right then. "Of course, I'm available most of this week."

"Sooner would be better, considering I've already wasted enough of your time as it is."

By avoiding my phone calls, you mean?

"Is tonight too soon?"

"Not at all."

"Well then, since we're talking about turnabout, and I already have your address..." He reached for a cube of sticky notes and scribbled down his address and instructions for the elevator and handed it to her. "Is seven o'clock, okay?"

She nodded with a smile that was softer and warmer than the one she had given him when she'd arrived and rose to her feet. She took a moment to straighten her jacket and brush down her skirt before holding out a hand. "I'll see you then."

This time when he took her hand, the shake was a little less rigid. Her fingers looked dainty, almost fragile in his grip, and he found himself holding on, or at least not consciously letting go. She wasn't pulling away either, not at first, but just as the moment started to stretch out, she did remove her hand from his and turn to gather her belongings.

"Is there any type of food that you are in the mood for?"

"You cook?"

"I have learned a thing or two in my travels."

"Surprise me then."

Seven

P atrick was washing prep dishes when the elevator dinged, signaling
that his guest had arrived. He shut off the water and dried his hands
on a towel as he crossed to the metal doors and pressed a button. They
slid apart and Morgana stepped inside. The smile she initially turned on
him went a little slack as she took in the large, open space.

He chuckled. "Can I take your coat?"

Morgana set her purse at her feet and shrugged out of the hip-length
waxed canvas jacket, still damp from the rain outside, revealing a violet
top with long, loose sleeves and a draped neckline that showed a panel
of cream lace underneath. Gray tailored trousers with damp hems had
replaced the pencil skirt, but she was still wearing heels despite the rain.
A simple, but elegant, emerald necklace circled her neck. Her hair was
still twisted up, but low on her neck now, a few shorter curls had slipped
loose to frame her heart-shaped face.

He took the umbrella from her hand and went to the closet to hang her coat. The scent of lilies rose from her coat and filled his nose.

Morgana's heels clicked on the wooden floor as she crossed the room to place her bag down on a living room chair.

He closed the closet door and turned to see her looking around with interest. "The building was built in 1878 as a textile factory, this top floor was the offices. It was renovated and converted into lofts about twenty years ago, but I've been here about five. Bought it on the spot after seeing this wide-open space. The bedrooms and bathrooms are down that hall." He pointed beyond the kitchen and dining areas. "Ten-foot ceilings, original hand-hewn white oak floors. The windows are all original except for the balcony doors along the west side."

"Your place is very nice," she said over her shoulder as she crossed to the window.

In this part of town, his building was one of the tallest, and when the sky was clear, the North Shore Mountains were visible to the south, though the view was better from the bedroom windows. The rippling, island-dotted Pacific coastline was directly ahead, not quite visible with the low clouds and fading dusk.

"The sunsets must be spectacular."

"You just missed a good one, peeking through the storm clouds. Maybe another night." He gestured to the large dining table along the far wall and headed for the kitchen. "Please, have a seat. I just need to plate up the food. Do you want something to drink?"

"On that thought..." Morgana retrieved a bottle of wine from her bag and walked over to hand it to him. "I wasn't sure what you were cooking so I took a guess on what might work."

He looked down at the label and nodded appreciatively. "This will do nicely. Take it to the table, please. I'll be right there."

Morgana placed the bottle of wine down and sat at the place he'd set that put her back to the bedroom wall, leaving the seat at the head for him.

Patrick poured the vinaigrette he had mixed earlier onto the salad and gave it a toss then plated the lasagna. He tucked a bottle opener in his pocket and carried the food to the table, plates balanced along one arm as Jake had taught him.

Morgana sniffed appreciatively at the food and placed her napkin in her lap as he pulled the cork and filled their glasses. They served salad onto side plates and ate in silence for a while. But it was comfortable silence, unlike the dinner the week before at *Sophie's*.

Although she had given him an explanation for her behavior that night, it certainly wasn't the whole story. But he didn't know her well enough yet to press too hard for more details or she might just bolt again. And there was a part of him that really didn't want that to happen.

When they were finished eating, he rose and reached for her plate.

"I can clear," he told her when she also got to her feet.

"You cooked," she protested. "Least I can do is help clean up."

He didn't argue, and she followed him into the kitchen with the salad bowl and a small stack of condiment containers. She set them on the counter next to the sink and went back for the wine bottle and glasses while he loaded the dishwasher and put the leftovers in the fridge.

"I suppose we should get to the reason you're here?" he asked, motioning for her to go back to the table, and smiled when her heels clicked rapidly across the space. Yet, despite that burst of eagerness, her face was perfectly calm while he changed the tablecloth and set out a pair of gloves.

As he turned up the hall, Patrick's stomach was a ball of nerves, his hands almost shaking as he tugged on a pair himself. He removed the book, wrapped in a protective suede cloth, from a wall safe beside the only fireplace the builders had left in the unit. As he emerged from the hall, she turned and the change in her expression was immediate and startling.

She scrambled for the gloves, and tugged them on, white teeth flashing in a brilliant and infectious smile. Patrick couldn't help grinning in response as he removed the wrapping before setting the book with its battered but beautiful leather binding in front of her.

Intrigued by her reaction, he found himself unable to look away even as he drifted back to the kitchen to refill the wine glasses. Not taking any chances with the book, he set hers an arm's length away on the table and took up a position leaning on the counter.

The fascination on her face as she ran a hand down the remains of gold leaf embossed into the cover, sent a shiver down his spine, as if she was touching him and not the book. He shook the feeling off as she tucked a finger under a corner and turned to the title page.

Les Chroniques Des Anciens.

Morgana smoothed the page with her gloved hand, fingers slowly tracing the intricate twists and turns of the elaborate illuminated border. Her lips parted slightly, eyes sparkling from the light over the table.

He raised his glass to his lips.

"Tell me again how you got this." Her voice was breathless, reverent.

The sip turned into a gulp. He coughed and set the glass aside. "From a friend of Jake's."

Her eyebrows drew together for a moment as she studied the silhouette of a stag in one corner, but the look was gone before he could identify what it meant.

"He brought it into my office along with a few other unrelated books, pretty much the same way I brought it into yours." Patrick said.

She nodded, as she turned the page and began to read. Before long, her face became dreamy, as if greeting an old friend after a long time apart. A butterfly took up residence in his stomach and he picked up his glass. She didn't react as he resumed his seat at the table and continued to read almost as if she had forgotten about him all together.

An hour passed, then two. A myriad of emotions flickered across her face, eventually taking on an absorbed passion that started his heart pounding. At one point, about halfway through, her shoulders drooped, and a lone tear slipped down her cheek unheeded. She sat back slightly, head bowed, her mouth moving silently as if in prayer.

He resisted the urge to touch her or get up for tissues for fear of breaking her concentration as she took a deep, shuddering breath and kept reading. It had to be the entry that described the destruction of the monastery in 1562, by men the author called Hunters, and the death of the monk who had sheltered Jacqueline and her compatriots. The last sentence trailed off half completed with a streak of ink. A large gap in the dates between entries followed and when they resumed four months later, she didn't recount those days, or complete the last thought, as she valiantly wrote around the scatter of small burn marks.

Throughout the earlier pages, she hadn't shied away from writing about the bad experiences, which by far outweighed the positive ones. Yet those months following the fall of Aubrac were never recounted, and there was no evidence that any pages were missing.

Endless years of running. Countless attacks.

So much loss.

Another hour passed before Morgana turned to the last entry. By then, Jacqueline had found safety in Geneva and changed her name to Aline Caro.

Patrick marveled at the author's adaptability across entries that spanned the better part of a decade, and the life that forced this chameleon-like quality on her. In that obscure French dialect, the quality of the lettering and ink varied, sometimes a hasty scribble of cramped letters, other times full of drips and blobs and inconsistent lettering as if the materials had been of a poorer quality. By the last entry, the lines were smooth and sure, and written in a more recognizable, more modern French. A third of the book was empty, the book abandoned before the author could finish filling its pages.

"What is your price?"

Morgana's voice jolted him out of his reverie. There was color in her cheeks and a burning intensity in her slightly reddened eyes, fixed directly on him.

"Pardon?"

"You mentioned before that you were looking for information so you could price it for sale." She stripped off the gloves and set them beside the book. "I will take the book off your hands immediately. Name your price."

"I did say that, didn't I?" he murmured half to himself. "It's not for sale, not quite yet anyway."

One russet eyebrow lifted, as she reached to rub a tight muscle in her neck. He was already on his feet before he was conscious of the decision. "I want to *understand* the book. Who was Jacqueline, or Aline, or whatever her name was?" He took a step around the corner of the table.

Her eyes followed him, but she didn't otherwise react.

"What was it that made her, and the people she wrote about, unable to die?" He stopped behind her, one hand hovering just over hers where it had stilled on her shoulder, close enough that he could feel the heat of her skin.

"May I?"

At first, it looked like she would refuse, but then her hand slid slowly down to her lap, and she lowered her chin. He clenched his hands into tight fists briefly and then stretched his fingers wide before settling finally on her shoulders and got to work.

His hands slid over the silk covering her skin as he pulled and kneaded the tight muscles he found there. The muscles released one by one; her body slowly pressing into his hands until her head almost rested against his chest. The sweet scent of lilies rose from her skin, both as soft as the flower's petals, and filled his head. The room tilted around him.

The world shrank to just the two of them. Only the tick of his watch and the pulse of her heartbeat under his fingers told him that time still existed. When she finally spoke again, her voice was deeper, almost languid. The sound sent a current through him.

"Patrick, I'm serious. Name any price."

His hands came to rest on the curve of her slender shoulders. He needed to put some distance between them but found that he was unable to step away. "I feel like you know more about these people than you're letting on."

She leaned forward slightly, so she could turn to face him. His hands slid away, leaving his forearms balanced on the top of the seat-back. His hands clenched into fists in an attempt to keep the warmth of her skin from fading away.

Her green eyes were hard and determined, in contrast to the sound of her voice a moment ago. "Maybe I do." Her hands rose to circle his wrists, the movement drew her slightly closer. "Maybe I don't. But I'm a collector of books from this era. It would increase the collective value immeasurably. The only copy of an original work of fiction from the mid-1600s intact, despite its condition would be invaluable."

"I don't believe it *is* fiction."

She tipped her head to one side and a smile twitched at the corners of her mouth. Clearly, she thought that he was crazy, had watched too much television as a child, or both. "People healing in one night from fatal wounds? Dying only by decapitation? Travelers who roamed the world for hundreds of years? It's not true." Morgana's voice was dismissive. Then her gaze locked with his.

As if a circuit had closed, a bolt of electricity shot down his spine.

Her next words were only a whisper. "It can't be."

Patrick's lips twitched slightly. She was so close; her perfume filled the space between them. Her pupils were wide, the irises a brilliant ring of emerald surrounding them. A faint trail of freckles peeked out from under her light makeup, running down one side of her nose and across the cheekbone.

He leaned slowly forward as if the current running through him came from a wire that was pulling them closer together. They were a breath apart when she released his wrists and slid out of the chair.

She stopped a few steps away from the table and turned back to him. Her eyes were still wide, but now there was a fine tremor in her hands, her chest rising and falling rapidly.

She wasn't the only one.

"Take some time to think it over, Patrick." Her voice was barely a whisper, eyes fixed no longer on him, but on the book. She cleared her throat and her voice became stronger. "I could make you ve—"

He took a single step toward her though the table remained between them.

Though she didn't move away, she stiffened, and the fingers of one hand clenched tight then released slowly as if it was an effort for her to straighten them again.

"Sophie is having another get-together this weekend. Come with me."

She blinked. "What?"

"I'll take the time to think." He took a step back and assumed a casual position against the wall, hands in his pockets. Something inside him was still churned up, and he was sore from standing. And she needed space. "But I might as well spend that time getting to know you."

"I don't think—"

"Jake invited you out to the house, and you missed the last one." His tone was gentle, but invited no argument. "I know that Sophie would love to meet you. She loves antique books, just like you. She practically has a whole bookcase of first editions, including some of Charles Dickens' lesser-known works."

Her head tilted as if that got her attention. But then her gaze turned inward for the span of a few heartbeats. Ultimately, she sighed and murmured an agreement.

"Excellent! I'll pick you up at your place around three."

Morgana walked back to the table, but kept it between them. She bent over and delicately stroked the cover with her fingertips, as if saying goodbye, then looked up to meet his gaze, hands braced on the back of the chair. "I still don't know why I haven't fired Alan for that yet."

"Oh, if I were you, I would give him a raise."

She smiled, but only one corner of her mouth moved. The wall had come back up in her eyes. He half-expected her to bundle the book under her arm and make a break for it. But she didn't.

Instead, she held out a hand. The movement was stiff, mechanical. The shake was formal and quick. "Thank you, Patrick, for dinner, and for giving me the opportunity to read such a fascinating work. But it's late, and I think it is time for me to go."

"Of course." His head was spinning. How had they come back to business-like formality? How had it become something else to start with?

Morgana collected her belongings from the chair in the living area and headed to the entrance and pressed the call button.

He pushed off the wall and scrambled over to retrieve her coat and umbrella from the closet. When he held the coat out for her, she slid her arms into the sleeves. But this time, when his hands lingered on her shoulders, she stepped away.

"Do you want me to call a car?"

"No thank you, I drove." She dug in her tote bag for her keys and placed them in her jacket pocket.

The elevator doors opened and Morgana stepped inside. She turned back to look at him. "Good night, Patrick."

"Good night, Morgana." He stepped back to release the doors.

As they started to close, she leaned back against the wall and her closed eyes with something like relief.

His heart squeezed, and he swung his arm out, hitting the safety bar inside the door just in time. It retracted with a clatter. "Wait, Morgana!"

She sprang upright again. "Yes?"

"I'm sorry."

Her eyebrows drew down low over those emerald eyes. "For what?"

"For whatever I did or said to make you afraid of me. I just need to find Jacqueline's other books. If more exist. There are answers in them that I need."

She smiled, but again it didn't reach her eyes, and nodded.

He stepped back again and allowed the doors to finally close with a dull thud that reverberated through him and, for a moment, he was unable to move. When he did, it was to pinch the bridge of his nose with one hand and shake his head in frustration, mostly at himself. Her scent lingered in the room; he could still feel the softness of her skin in his hands.

Leave it to him to turn a business meeting into something else entirely.

He walked back toward the dining area, to put that much more distance between them and his eyes came to rest on the book. Her interest went deeper than mere historian's curiosity. She'd nearly begged for him to sell it to her.

Had he been a greedy man, he could have taken her for thousands, and she would have paid it. But Morgana was the key. She had to be.

As he approached the table, the sight of her empty chair brought back the brief moment when she had relaxed completely under his hands. He pushed that thought away with some effort and gently wrapped the book and returned it to the safe. It filled most of the space inside, the rest taken up by a few other books, none quite as exotic as this one, and some heirloom jewelry from his great-grandparents.

He sealed the safe and closed the cabinet door, then turned to the window. With the room lights off, the city sparkled in the clear night, as it only did after a good rain. The clouds had parted, the buildings reaching for the starry night above. Beyond the downtown, a long string of lights illuminated a cargo ship as it moved out of port, heading for open water. He watched it for a while then turned away. A throbbing pain in the middle of his thigh brought him to a halt with a hiss of pain escaping his lips. Cursing himself for being on his feet too long, he rubbed at the spot until the pain eased.

He slowly made his way back into the main room to turn off the lights, then trudged back to his room to get ready for bed. But once under the covers, he found himself staring at the ceiling, his thoughts too wired to sleep. When he finally could close his eyes and drift off, it was only an hour before dawn.

Once the elevator car was safely moving down, the wall was the only thing that kept Morgana on her feet. Her chest was too tight to get a good breath. Her head throbbed from a potent mix of alcohol and memories.

"*Mon dieu.*"

As soon as she'd turned the cover, the rest of the world didn't matter. She was back in the seventeenth century again as if the time in between had never passed. Incense and wood smoke, the chiming of bells calling the faithful to worship, the low drone of the monks chanting their prayers had all filled the air of Patrick's apartment as if it was the hewn stone of Aubrac.

There was something about being in Patrick's presence that put her at ease without much effort. The fact that she had let him touch her spoke volumes about that.

And those hands...

They had moved across her skin, deftly releasing muscles she hadn't realized were tense until they weren't anymore. With each tug and pinch, her awareness of him had grown, his warmth sinking into her skin. Cedar and something spicy had filled her head. Under his touch, something in her that had been dormant for centuries had begun to awaken. And that was terrifying.

The elevator arrived on the ground floor before she could think any further on the subject. The lobby, which took up most of the first floor, was dimly lit at this hour, and empty.

A bright path of lights suspended from the open rafters lit a carpeted walkway that stretched from the elevators to the front doors, past cozy meeting areas with sofas and bar tables interspersed with gaming tables.

Once outside, Morgana closed her eyes and focused on her breathing, filling her lungs with cool, fresh air, faintly tinged with the sea. She exhaled through her mouth, in through her nose, and out again, forcing a rhythm that released some of the tension in her neck and shoulders. Tension that Patrick had so deftly smoothed out but had immediately returned at the mere mention of Martel's name.

The rain had washed the humidity from the air, and the street sparkled in the light of passing cars. If only she could give in to the sudden urge to walk home to enjoy the night, stretch her legs, and clear her head. But it was nearly twenty blocks as the crow flew, in high heels no less, and she wasn't suicidal.

After all that, maybe I am a little. Going to Patrick's apartment alone knowing the company he kept was, at minimum, reckless. And then, agreeing to go to a party with Patrick, whom she barely knew, at Martel's invitation and at his house...

With a sigh, Morgana adjusted the strap on her shoulder, and pulled her keys out of her pocket, gripping them tightly in one hand, a key jutting from between two knuckles. The sidewalks were almost empty, but she squared her shoulders and walked to her car.

As Morgana entered the lobby of her building, the woman sitting at the desk looked up. Jessie, the thirty-year old ex-Marine who traded desk duties with Fred, greeted her with a cheerfulness that only someone an hour or two into their shift could. It was far more than Morgana was capable of at this time of night.

Once inside the apartment, her keys landing in the bowl on the hall table seemed to echo in the large, open space. The kitchen lights seemed abnormally bright as her bag and coat thumped onto the kitchen island, her shoes clattered onto the tile. Her arches ached as her feet adjusted to being freed from their confinement as she walked to the fridge for a bottle of water.

The apartment had an odd, empty feeling to it. Alasdair had stayed the night in the guest room, and was still eating breakfast when she'd left for her meeting at Davies & McNamara. But he was gone now, to check into a local hotel with a promise to remain close by for the next week or so before going back to San Francisco. She owed him dinner after cancelling to go to Patrick's place instead.

Though weariness dragged at her limbs, Morgana made her rounds through the house, to be sure nothing had been disturbed. The bedrooms were as she'd left them, the office door securely locked. When she flicked the switch to brighten the living room, she stopped in her tracks. The candles that had been arranged on the wide sill of the window leading to the fire escape were scattered onto the floor.

Eight

———✦———

Morgana dashed to the window, heart hammering in her throat to find it still tightly locked. She narrowed her eyes as she crouched to retrieve the candles and found a small slip of paper tucked under one of the red cylinders. She hastily unfolded it and collapsed against the sofa in relief.

Just kidding.

Morgana crumpled the note in her hand and found herself laughing as she replaced the candles on the sill. She dug her cell phone out of her bag and found Alasdair's number in her recent calls. He picked up on the first ring.

"Why hello, Morgana." His grin carried through the phone.

She called him an unkind name in French and continued in English, "I would strangle you, if I thought that it would do any good."

He laughed. "How was your night?"

She tucked the phone between chin and shoulder as she moved about the room, recounting the evening while she rearranged the other signals starting with the bookcase. She pushed Dumas back into place and pulled out a Robert Frost on the shelf below as she told him about dinner.

"And the book?"

"It is in remarkable condition." She adjusted the wide fan of dried flowers on the table between the windows, which he had also messed with. "I can't describe what it was like to touch it again, even for a little while. The subject matter wasn't exactly cheerful, but I'm just going to count the days until I get it back."

"Wait, love," he said, "you mean, you didn't bring it home with you?"

"He wouldn't part with it, not yet at least. And I didn't want to raise suspicion so soon by being too eager," she said. "But I will get it back no matter what I have to do. I certainly have time."

He chuckled. "Done rearranging your living room?"

Morgana settled onto the sofa and curled her feet under her. "You think I'm paranoid, don't you?"

"We all have our quirks," he answered. There was a creak and a rustle, as he shifted on the hotel's bed. "If rearranging books or setting obstacles at windows makes you feel better, then by all means."

"I can't get careless, Ally," she told him, "especially now that they might know where I live."

"You could always come back with me to San Francisco."

HUNTED

In her current state, she couldn't tell if the offer was for her benefit or another proposition. When he prompted her, she sighed. "I'll keep it in mind," she told him halfheartedly, getting to her feet. "It's late, Ally. I'll talk to you tomorrow."

Morgana hung up and went to run a bath and turned on the jets. Despite what she had told Alasdair, she was still wired to the point where sleep wasn't even remotely an option. She submerged to the neck in water that was just shy of being too hot with a soft moan of relief, the jets gently pummeling her back and legs. The oils she'd added to the water scented the air with eucalyptus.

The bath did the trick, and Morgana climbed out before sleep could pull her under. She wrapped herself in a robe and wiped the steam from the mirror with a towel. The reflection that stared back at her had dark smudges under the eyes. For a moment, the weight of seven hundred years of life pressed down on her, despite the fact that the face staring back at her was no different from the one she'd seen in the wavery silver looking glass at Aubrac. The same face that would stare back at her four hundred years from now. If she was lucky enough to live that long.

Sighing, she reached into the basket next to the sink for make-up remover and gave serious thought to calling in sick in the morning. Sleeping in on a weekday, and being anything but productive, was tempting. But she dismissed the thought as she swept her hair over one shoulder and braided it into a long rope. There was far too much work waiting for her. Morgana made a face at her reflection and shut off the light with a slap of her hand and went to bed.

Nine

The following evening, Morgana again found herself restless. She kept going over and over what had happened in Patrick's apartment in her mind. She needed to sit and write it all out to process it properly, but this kind of energy wasn't conducive to writing. In the past, the results had been an incoherent mess that even she couldn't read the next day.

She needed to move, to burn off some energy, to quiet her racing thoughts and there was one thing that might work. So, she dressed for the gym in leggings, a crop top-style sports bra, and a baggy hooded sweatshirt, then dug in the spare bedroom closet for her boxing hand wraps and headed for the twenty-four hour gym a few blocks away.

Standing in front of the door, Morgana dug the access card out of the depths of her wallet and held it up to the scanner. The clock above the vending machines said it was just before ten o'clock and there were only a handful of people scattered around the different areas of the gym. It was divided into several sections, one for cardio equipment, another area dedicated to weightlifting had both machines and stations with barbells and plates, and an area for stretching or yoga. At the back, in one corner near the almost floor-to-ceiling windows, was an area with a few weight bags hanging from the ceiling.

After getting her heart rate up, Morgana headed for the boxing area in the back. In the daytime, the only view was of the former mill building across a narrow canal that had once transported boats and powered the textile machinery.

The buildings were low, only a couple of stories, but sprawling, and the windows let in a lot of daylight. But now, there was only the glow from a scatter of lit windows across the way and the faintest hint of stars in the clear sky.

Morgana pulled off the sweatshirt, wrapped her hands and got to work. At first, every contact with the punching bag reverberated up her arms, but after a few moments, she found a rhythm. Jab, weave, a quick jab then cross, an occasional kick when the bag swung just right. Soon enough, her thighs were burning, sweat gleaned on her skin, and her mind had gone completely blank.

Gravel crunched under his boots as Jacob Martel hopped down from the top of the fire escape and onto the wide, flat roof of an old factory building a dozen blocks away from *Sophie's*. As usual, he had helped the restaurant through the worst of the dinner rush and then swapped polished dress shoes for worn work boots.

Some nights he walked the streets, others like tonight, he went up. And each night he ranged out in a different direction, sometimes heading toward the docks, other times staying in the more affluent areas, but tonight, he'd headed toward an area that, like Patrick's neighborhood, had been reborn over the last twenty years or so as vacant nineteenth-century industrial buildings were converted into offices, businesses, and residential spaces. This area was a little rougher, the businesses tending toward auto service shops, pawn brokers, or souvenir hawkers catering to naïve tourists.

Jacob moved to one edge of the building that ran along the street and stopped next to a stairwell door where he wouldn't be seen when he looked down. The narrow road was tightly packed with cars, their red lights flashing as traffic moved at a crawl. The sounds of squeaking brakes and the occasional honk of an impatient driver rose up. The game at the ballpark a half-mile away must have recently let out. From the lack of excited chatter and celebratory honking, the home team had lost. Again.

Fans dressed in home team green trudged by, some with drooping pennants or foam fingers tucked under their arms, heading for the garages that offered cheaper parking if someone was willing to walk a little.

Not exactly the best area to be in just to save a buck, he thought. But it was the kind of neighborhood to find people who didn't want to be seen or found.

It had been a week since Alasdair Bromley had appeared on their radar. Jacob and a few of his men had been pulling together leads as to where he might be staying or who he was in Kingston to visit, but so far, they had little to go on. What they did know was that the man was involved in something to do with money. So, despite the fact that

Bromley had been well dressed at the airport, Jacob decided that he would keep an eye on some of the seedier parts of town for a while. Large sums of money changed hands in places like the chop shop across the street that advertised as auto repair. The bar a block further up, whose neon sign he could just make out over the corner door, was a known mafia haunt.

The baseball spectators began to thin out as he lounged against the corrugated metal, soon replaced by women tottering around on the highest heels, the men who looked after them, and the men who were looking for their services. Finally, after about twenty minutes, a pair of men, one of which had Bromley's build, turned the corner, and started going in and out of the first-floor businesses, emerging from each rearranging the contents of their pockets as if they had picked up their latest round of protection money. Jacob pushed off the wall and kept pace with them, moving along the shadows of the rooftop where he wouldn't be seen by those down below.

When in doubt, follow the money.

He paused and adjusted his jacket against a sudden buffeting wind, watching as the pair disappeared into one of the auto shops, reemerging a few minutes later. When he ran out of roof, Jacob was forced to stand and watch them walk the last half-block and disappear into a basement nightclub.

When they didn't emerge after a few minutes, Jacob checked his watch. He had a good hour before he needed to be back at the restaurant for closing time cleanup, so he turned and headed along the alley towards the fire escape. After only a few steps, he froze. There was a figure standing off to his left on the other side of the roof looking down at something, much as Jacob had just been doing moments before.

But this wasn't one of his guys, he could tell that even from this distance. This man was dressed all in black, from boots to knit hat. Jacob silently slid his gun from its holster and flicked the safety off with his thumb.

The click the gun made as he pulled the hammer back echoed through the silence on the rooftop. "Anything I can help you with?"

The man whipped around.

Jacob still couldn't make out his face, but his slender, yet tall build fit Bromley's description as much as the enforcer down on the street had. He needed to get closer, so he raised the gun and started advancing slowly, step by step.

"Who are you?"

At first the man just held his ground watching him advance, then he was moving faster than Jacob could have expected. He shouted in surprise and fired off two quick rounds. Both missed, sending chips of masonry flying. Jacob cursed and dashed after him.

The stranger bounded for the ladder ten feet from where he had been standing and quickly disappeared from sight, the athletic movements almost inhuman.

By the time Jacob reached the top, the man had already reached street level.

The stranger looked back up and saluted before disappearing up the narrow walkway between the building and the canal.

Jacob cursed and holstered his weapon. He walked over to the spot where the man had been standing and looked down. Immediately below, the murky green water moved swiftly in the light flooding from the numerous windows. The walkway along the canal was deserted but something had held the man's attention.

After a moment, his eyes fixed on the first floor of the building across the way. A wide array of fitness equipment filled the space, most of which was unoccupied at this time of night save for a young couple trading reps at a weight bench, and a treadmill or two in use.

Through one window, a lone figure bobbed and weaved around a boxing bag, delivering punches and kicks with practiced skill as if facing a challenging opponent. She was small, but fit, dressed in black leggings and a crop top that revealed a toned mid-section, her hands wrapped in blue. A long, thick braid danced with her movements.

Like the stranger, Jacob found himself lingering to watch. After only a few moments, she turned away from the bag, and retrieved a water bottle from which she took a healthy drink. She set the bottle aside and looked out the window as she unwrapped her hands.

The face was familiar, and it took a moment for him to recognize Morgana, the woman that Patrick had brought into *Sophie's* the week before. He didn't know much about her, just that she worked at a rival auction house to D&M.

Morgana started on her other hand, still gazing out the window more or less in his direction, but he was standing just far enough back that he should be lost in the shadows. Suddenly, a milky light reflecting in the glass blocked all sight of her.

Confused, since he was already on the roof, Jacob turned his head. A fat crescent moon had emerged from behind a wisp of cloud. The glare passed almost as quickly as it came, revealing a smile on Morgana's face. A moment later, she turned away to gather her belongings and moved out of sight toward the other side of the building, and presumably the exit.

He made to follow her, but cursed when a quick glance at the canal revealed that the closest footbridge was at least two blocks away, and the gap was far too wide to jump.

Albrecht was across town, so for her to be in a gym this late at night, she had to live nearby. He thought back to the night at the restaurant where she had seemed so quiet. Timid. Yet the woman he had just seen in the gym had stood tall and confident, moving with the skill that came from long practice.

Something didn't add up.

Jacob resolved to keep an eye on his best friend's new girl as he finally headed back the way he'd come. Halfway across, his cell phone started vibrating in his pocket. He pulled it out and answered it.

"Sorry boss," Brendan called over the din at the bar. "We need you back at the restaurant. There's a situation."

"What kind of situation?"

"Mayor Blackman showed up without a reservation a half hour ago," Brendan said, and continued before Jacob could open his mouth, "don't worry, we took care of it and seated him right away."

"Then what's the problem?"

"Well, Mrs. Blackman just showed up, and the mayor wasn't exactly alone at his table."

Jacob chuckled and shook his head in disbelief. "Oh boy," he remarked, picking up the pace. "I'm on my way."

Morgana let the gym door fall closed behind her and swiped her sleeve across her sweaty brow, then pulled the hood down low. Her legs shook as she descended the handful of steps to the street. A satisfied smile tugged at her lips. Falling asleep wouldn't be so hard tonight.

She crossed the street behind a passing taxi and headed down the alley between buildings. The side streets were dingy and dimly lit, but it was the shortest way back home. After a couple of blocks, in the long stretch between two factory buildings, the clatter of a glass bottle being kicked across the alley made her glance back. A lone figure moving in the same direction as she, but was a good distance away.

The alarm bells stayed silent, for now, but still, Morgana slid her hand into an outside pocket of her bag and palmed a small throwing dagger. No harm, no foul, if it was just another pedestrian, but at least she had something in her hand if it wasn't.

The click of a gun a moment later put an end to the pedestrian thought. Morgana stopped and did a quick scan of the options available to her. There was a dumpster ten feet along to her right and the street, which was really only a single paved lane with sidewalks, was too narrow to make a dash to the next intersection. A Hunter would shoot her down and take her head before she could come back if she tried.

"Turn around."

Morgana obeyed the thickly accented order, which had come from much closer than she'd expected. He was young, no more than twenty, with a slender build born of too little food. His skin was dark, with greasy black hair in desperate need of a trim hanging into eyes that were wild in the flickering light, fixed on her with a kind of hunger.

This kid didn't look like Martel's handiwork. A street kid she could handle.

"What do you want?" She asked, one eye still scanning the shadows and rooftops in case he was merely a decoy.

He continued to advance, moving now with an exaggerated slowness, keeping the small black handgun pointed at her but tipped sideways, a ridiculous habit favored by those who really hadn't been trained to use them.

"Gimme your wallet."

It was always the wallet.

"I don't have one."

"Hand over the money then, cell phone." He gestured menacingly with the gun at the bag slung across her chest.

Her heart clenched even as a rush of adrenaline sharpened her mind and her vision. There were far too many desperate people like this, the ones who lived only for the next fix. She turned out the pocket in the side of the bag to show that it was empty.

Unsatisfied, he took another step forward, now only about ten feet away.

As discretely as she could, Morgana shifted her weight and adjusted her grip on the dagger, lying flat along her wrist out of sight. It wasn't a weapon that was meant to kill but to distract her attacker long enough to get away.

"Let's just take it easy."

There was a dangerous combination of agitation and desperation in the dark depths of his eyes as they darted to her hands, her feet, the street behind her. At this range, he would have to be blind to miss her, and she was not in the mood to have to buy new clothes if he did decide to shoot.

"Let me just reach in here," she motioned to her bag. "I think I have something for you."

He licked his lips in anticipation and his eyes followed as she lifted the bag up over her head with her free hand. The dagger flew from her other hand with a flick of the wrist. It stuck in his shoulder, and knocked him back a step, but it was little more than a bee sting for someone in his condition.

"Puta!" he cursed, glaring, and pulled the trigger.

Morgana was already diving for the cover of the dumpster, but not before pain lanced through her thigh. His frantic shot had gone wild but hadn't missed her entirely. The impact knocked her off balance and sent her crashing into the dumpster instead of tucking safely behind it. She bore down on the pain as she pushed to her feet, even as her leg threatened to give out under her.

There was a satisfied glimmer in his eyes as he advanced. A woman with nowhere to go and blood dripping down a leg she could barely put any weight on. Or so he thought.

The moment he was in range, she swung out with her bag, catching him in the shoulder and neck, the weight of phone and keys sent him staggering away.

The gun clattered to the pavement.

With the panicked look of the predator suddenly becoming the prey, he turned and scurried away. Morgana sighed in relief and looked down at her leg. The material was torn, but the blood little more than a darker wetness on her black pants. She ran her hand around her thigh over the sticky wetness and found a second hole where the bullet had passed clean through.

If there was one thing she hated more than getting shot, it was retrieving bullets. Her body healed at a remarkable rate, but it didn't heal fully around foreign objects like bullets or arrows; the obstruction had to be removed first. She was lucky this time, and the pain was already beginning to fade.

Morgana limped over to the discarded gun and stripped it into as many pieces as possible. She tossed them into the dumpster and pocketed the magazine, not that removing a dozen or so bullets from the street would make much of a difference in the grand scheme of things. But if someone was able to retrieve and reassemble all the pieces, at least they couldn't use it right away.

When she approached the main street a block south of her building, she stopped and looked back, scanning the shadows and rooftops for any more assailants, but all was quiet. When her leg would hold her up if she needed to run, she wove through the crowd and disappeared into the shadows of the alleyway on the other side of the street.

From her vantage point, Morgana missed the figure who stood in the shadows of the fire escape directly above her who had seen everything.

Ten

T he rest of the week passed in a blur of cataloging shipments, conducting interviews, and putting out fires. So, when a knock sounded at her door for the millionth time on Friday afternoon, Morgana expected it to be Jane or one of her other assistants. She barked out a command to enter around the pen clenched in her teeth as she had every other time, idly wrapping and unwrapping a curl around her finger as she studied the file of scans and x-rays of a new painting spread out across the desk.

"Ahem."

Papers scattered everywhere. She darted out a hand to save a few from the floor and a broad, long-fingered hand closed over hers at the end of the desk. Morgana looked up to find Patrick's smiling face only a foot away. He had his glasses on again, which muted the sapphire of his eyes slightly, but they still seemed to stare right into her.

MOLLY KERR

"A little jumpy?" His cheerful tone only made her more irritated.

"No, just busy," Morgana protested, gathering papers while rooting with one foot for her shoes under the desk. By the time she had them back on and rounded the desk, he had already gathered everything from the floor and was holding the stack out to her. "Thanks. Now, what can I do for you?"

"I just wanted to make sure that we were still all set for Sunday?"

"As far as I know." A trickle of ice went down her spine at the reminder that she would be spending all day with Martel. "But I half-expected a call before now."

He sighed, his eyes tightened briefly, almost quick enough for Morgana to think she'd imagined it. "My apologies," he said. "This week got away from me. But I told Sophie that you were coming, and about your expertise. She said to tell you that she's looking forward to it. 'A meeting of the minds,' she says."

From his expression, Patrick and his sister were very close. "I'd like to meet her too," she found herself saying, unsure if it was from polite habit or true curiosity.

Patrick smile lit up his blue eyes, all traces of his earlier fatigue suddenly gone. The sunlight streaming in through the window caught the cherry highlights in his auburn hair. "Good," he said.

The smile ensnared her. Their eyes met and held for a long, breathless moment, her traitorous heart pounding out of control. The connection between them thrummed again like a plucked string, but she forced herself to look away first. "Have you, um, changed your mind about the chronicle? My offer stands. Name your price."

Patrick shook his head and settled himself into one of the chairs. "It's still not for sale." His voice had an edge to it. "I don't need your money, Morgana; I have plenty of my own. What I need is information."

"What more can I possibly tell you about that book?" Morgana asked, putting the desk between them. "I don't know any more than you do."

A corner of his mouth twitched and he held her gaze as he propped one foot on the opposite knee, draped his arms over the armrests, and generally made himself comfortable.

Morgana really wished that he would go.

She clenched her teeth and started reassembling the folder on the Velasquez portrait and filed it away. She had too much to do, and the last thing she wanted was to slip up and give Patrick any idea how much that book meant to her. Or worse.

A half hour passed while she updated her date book and started reviewing the mock-up for the next catalog.

"I'm not going anywhere," he said. "I won't melt and disappear into the chair or have Scotty beam me up."

Morgana almost smiled at the last one.

"I'll tell you what, Morgana..."

The creak of the chair brought her head up. He was leaning forward, forearms resting casually on his knees. It was a position that looked natural for him, but not in that expensive suit. It strained across those broad shoulders. His collar stretched open to reveal the muscled column of his throat. His glasses dangled from one earpiece between his knees. Her heart pounded slow and hard, the impact reverberating through her body as those eyes drew her in.

"Help me get the information that I need, and you can *have* the book."

"What information?" she asked, turning to the computer screen but the lines of unread emails all blurred together.

"I want to find *l'Ancienes*." Patrick said. "I want to know who they are, where they come from. What kind of magic did Jacqueline d'Arnault and her people possess that allowed them to live forever?"

It was a question that Morgana had been asking since the frigid morning she'd woken to discover her husband crying into her hair only to be told that she'd died in the night.

There was another creak of the chair and Patrick's hand covered hers. Her breath shuddered out as she forced her eyes up. Terrified brown eyes and drawn, malnourished features were replaced by wide blue eyes and stubble-roughened jaw. She fought the urge to grip Patrick's hand for dear life, just to wipe away the memories of the days following her death that threatened to bubble up.

"Are you okay?"

He rounded the desk, never taking his hand from hers and stood over her. It wasn't meant to be threatening, or intimidating, just to reassure her that he was there. The circles he traced over her hand with his thumb sent jolts of electricity up her arm. At the same time, it was strangely comforting, and she managed to banish the ghost for now.

"I'm fine," she murmured, and stepped away to pour herself a glass of ice water. "I'm just tired and extremely busy. I'll see you Sunday." She took a sip, wishing that she'd poured something stronger. One tear slipped through her defenses, but her back was thankfully still turned.

Patrick remained by her desk and didn't press her, but frustration was radiating off him like heat.

Yet from her position by the window, a chill seeped into her that nothing could banish. She gripped the curtain with one hand, so she didn't turn back to him, clutching the crystal glass to keep her fingers from trembling. Dimly, she heard him turn and leave the room.

"Alan!"

Eleven

M organa sighed as she slid a hair pin into place and studied her reflection in the mirror. Her fingers shook as she reached for another. Sure, she was just walking into the lion's den with full knowledge that the king, and possibly many of his soldiers, were lying in wait.

Why be nervous?

She tried to remind herself that the Hunters didn't know her face, and she was always careful to cover her hair when in danger of running into one of them. And chasing someone down in the dark of night wasn't the same as picking someone out of a police lineup. Or a family barbecue.

It didn't help.

Impishly, she made a face at her reflection and flicked off the light. She cast a longing look at the locked door across the hall. There hadn't been any time recently, and her chronicle was calling to her. Maybe it was the calm that came only with the process of mixing the ink by hand, putting pen to paper. Putting her thoughts into words. Whatever it was, she was more at peace there than anywhere else. But she had agreed to do this, and she wouldn't back down now.

She paused at the end of the hallway and straightened up to her full height, which the spotless white sneakers did nothing to add to. It wasn't her first choice of footwear, but heels were out of the question. The street punk's frantic shot was shaping up to be one of those random wounds where the discomfort lingered, as if her body was still repairing damage deep in the muscle or bone. She wasn't limping, but something was still off, not completely back to normal.

With her purse and coat on the table beside the door, she set about putting her nervous energy to work by straightening the apartment, making sure that her signals were set. By the time her phone rang, Morgana was able to stride to the elevator with a high head and a better mindset.

She emerged into the lobby to find Patrick leaning on the high desk, talking with Fred as if they were old friends. He was dressed more casually than she had ever seen him in a white polo shirt and khaki pants. He'd also traded dress shoes for running sneakers, and instead of his reading glasses he had tinted aviator sunglasses that were much, much more dangerous.

The conversation stopped as she approached.

He straightened up and took off his sunglasses. He didn't speak at first, but he there was no denying the appraising look in his eyes at the deep violet halter top that left her back and arms bare and set her hair aflame, at the pale blue jeans that clung to her curves, or the fact that he clearly liked what he saw.

"Hello, Patrick," she said, and greeted her doorman as well.

"Morgana." His breath left him in a rush.

She forced away a smile.

He cleared his throat, and the sound was gone. "You look great."

"Thank you," she responded, fighting the urge to blush. They were not going on a date, she reminded herself. It had been a hundred years since she had been on a date. "Shall we go?"

He nodded and led the way to the glass doors with a hand on her lower back. He was close enough that the deep, rich cedar of his aftershave filled her head and made it spin.

That wouldn't do at all.

He led her to the silver BMW parked at the curb and she took his hand and allowed him to help her into the buttery soft leather seat. He got in and pulled smoothly out into traffic.

"I never thought to ask where your sister lives,"

"Jake and Sophie live in Dane," he answered mentioning a small town twenty miles up the coast.

"Oh, I figured they would live in town with them having the restaurant and all." Not to mention certain other nighttime activities.

Patrick shook his head with a chuckle as he merged onto the coastal highway. "Blame Sophie for that one."

The drive passed quickly as they talked mostly about their mutual love of antiques. Patrick told her more about his research into rare manuscripts that had brought the chronicle into his possession. His eyes grew distant when she pointed out that many of them focused on the arcane.

Morgana let the subject drop even when his reaction made her want to dig deeper. But she needed to stop. The conversation had been almost too easy, and she found herself wanting to say much more than she should about the chronicles, the Ancients, and herself.

After that, Patrick drifted into his own thoughts and Morgana was content to watch the farmland pass by until they made the last turn up the driveway of a large white farmhouse. Once a much smaller building, wings and additions had been added haphazardly, almost at random. The end result was sprawling yet charming. A three-car garage was set off to the side and behind the house, a tent stretched between the two buildings.

Morgana climbed out and took in the wide range of vehicles that filled the driveway and spilled over onto the lawn, everything from beat up farm pickups to sports cars like Patrick's.

How many of them belonged to Hunters?

She tamped down on the thought as she met Patrick at the trunk of the car and accepted the cooler bag he pressed into her hands. The gravel drive crunched softly under their feet as he led the way between cars to the back yard. The air was redolent with horses and dry grass. The bass beat of a stereo mingled with the splashes and shrieks of children as they played in a pool somewhere beyond the tent.

The sound took her nerves down a notch.

Surely the Hunters wouldn't launch an ambush with children around.

They rounded the corner of the house and found the party in full swing. Small groups were clustered around the food tables, energetic kids darted around the legs of the adults. Against the house, three young men argued over a laptop set between two large speakers. Across the tent, a group of young women, barely college age, sat flipping through photos on a tablet.

Out of nowhere, a little blonde bundle of energy sped past her and collided with Patrick's legs. He shoved the case of beer into Morgana's hands and bent to scoop her up, paying no heed to the water that dripped off of her. She giggled with delight and placed a sloppy kiss on his cheek.

"Well hello, Miss Kaitlyn," he said, shifting the little girl, who couldn't be more than four, onto his hip and brushed back the thick lock of hair that had fallen into his face.

"Hi, Uncle Pat," she said, her voice high and innocent. "I went swimming."

"I see that," he agreed and bounced her up and down eliciting squeals of delight.

His easy smile at the child's directness made Morgana grin. Her wet suit must be seeping through his clothes by now, but he continued to hold her, oblivious.

"Mommy let me have soda *and* chocolate."

Patrick laughed. "She did. Did she?"

"Uh-huh," she said, brushing damp curls out of her face with her whole hand in that imprecise way young children had that only made things worse. She looked over at Morgana through the wet ropes of her hair and her eyes narrowed. "Who are you?"

Morgana shifted her grip on the case and smiled at her directness. The child wasn't scared of seeing a stranger, just curious. "I'm Morgana."

"You're pretty."

"Yes, she is."

Morgana brushed a strand of hair behind her ear and looked anywhere but at Patrick.

He cleared his throat and placed Kaitlyn back on her feet, then took the beer back without meeting her eye.

Kaitlyn gestured for Morgana to bend closer. She crouched down with a smile. Kaitlyn gave her a kiss on the cheek and ran off.

Morgana put her fingers to the spot as she straightened up. "Uncle Pat?"

His grin turned sheepish. "Kaitlyn's mom, Courtney, is Sophie's best friend. Soph thinks it's cute that she calls me 'uncle.' Come on."

He led the way across a small, paved patio, adding the beer to the pile by the back door and stepping into the house. A small group of women gathered around a large island assembling trays. The music was quieter indoors, nearly drowned out by the din of conversation and laughter in the kitchen.

Morgana slid the screen closed behind her and turned at the sound of a cry of delight to see Patrick gathering a smaller, female version of himself into his arms. She looked to be a few years younger than him, and though they shared similar coloring, she had none of his height. Her head barely reached his shoulder, maybe only an inch or two taller than Morgana herself.

"Soph, let me introduce Morgana Dericault." He motioned her forward. "Morgana, my sister Sophie."

"Pleased to meet you," Sophie said shaking her hand warmly.

"Same here."

"Pat has told me a lot about you." Sophie said, then a mischievous glint came into her eye as her gaze drifted up over Morgana's shoulder. "Assistant Manager at Albrecht, huh? I'm impressed, you don't look nearly old enough. Most managers are decrepit, old, and ornery. Take Patrick's boss for example."

The comment didn't make sense until she saw the balding man in his early sixties who had just come through the door. Though his auburn hair was going gray at the temples, he was nearly as tall as Patrick, and just as fit.

"I take offense to that," he informed her, with a twinkle in his blue eyes as he wagged a finger at his daughter. "I am *not* decrepit."

"But you are ornery." Patrick walked across the room to embrace him.

Morgana knew Steven Davies by reputation, but hadn't met the man in person. She took the offered hand, and he surprised her by bowing low over it.

The surprises continued when his next words were in fluent French. "I finally get to meet the woman who has stolen so much business from us." It was a compliment, not a condemnation.

"Davies & McNamara does well enough for itself," she replied in the same language. "I haven't made that big of a mark."

"Modest woman," Steven said, switching to English. "I like that."

Patrick chuckled. "We could stand here and talk shop Dad, but we're here to have fun."

"Did you bring your suit?" Mr. Davies asked her with a raised eyebrow. It was an expression that his son had given her several times.

"No," Morgana answered. "But I think the kids are having much more fun than I would."

The elder Davies smiled. "Please, make yourself at home."

Morgana thanked him and allowed Patrick to lead her back outside. They got drinks, then Patrick led her to one of the few free tables. Morgana settled into a white plastic chair in time to see Kaitlyn go down the slide into the arms of a man who must have been her father.

There was something peaceful about having nothing to do except relax and have fun. This was surely no Hunter gathering, or if it was, they were hiding it well. She found herself putting her feet up on the chair next to her and settled in.

Patrick glanced over at her and smiled.

She caught it out of the corner of her eye as she continued to watch the pool. As hard as she tried not to react, one corner of her mouth twitched up and a flutter started under her ribs. She took a healthy swallow of her drink to wash it away.

"Thank you for coming with me."

Morgana set her cup down on the table. "Of course," she replied. "Your sister's house is beautiful."

"Yeah, Sophie loves living out here." Patrick replied, then chuckled, half to himself. "Growing up, she was a city girl through and through and hated being more than four blocks from anything she needed."

"You're pretty close, aren't you?"

"Let me put it this way," he said with a chuckle, eyes turning toward the house. "If anyone other than Jake had asked to marry her, I would have dumped him in the pool. In December."

"Glad to hear I'm held in such high esteem."

Ice slid down her back. Morgana took a careful, deep breath and met the smiling face with her calm mask in place, her posture relaxed, arms draped along the plastic arms.

Martel was dressed casually in swim shorts and a denim shirt left unbuttoned to reveal lots of smooth, muscled skin. His black hair was tied back neatly and was damp from swimming. His deeply set brown eyes held a look of brotherly affection.

Patrick gathered him into a backslapping hug. "You're just lucky that you're like a brother to me. Half the time I'm tempted to throw you in anyway."

Morgana's stomach clenched.

"Good thing, then," Martel said smiling warmly.

For his next trick, laughter.

Martel turned to Patrick. "Hey buddy, Matt needs help with the grill. He heard that you were here and asked me to come find you." He gestured toward the knot of men now assembled around a grill the size of a picnic table. "Besides, I want to get another look at the woman you brought into my restaurant last week. Trust me, I'll take good care of her."

"Paws off, man, you're married."

The thought of Martel touching her made Morgana's skin crawl, but she forced herself to maintain a pleasant mask as Patrick wove his way through the tables and confiscated the lighter fluid and matches.

Martel settled into the chair that Patrick had just vacated and took a sip of his beer.

Morgana smiled at him as warmly as she could and turned her attention back to the activity in the pool. She could feel his intense gaze on her, but he didn't immediately speak. Gone was the normal sneer she'd seen from rooftops as he ordered his men.

"I wanted to thank you for the invite," she said, silently marveling at the irony of her thanking a Hunter for anything. "You have a lovely home."

"You're welcome," he answered. "You and Patrick looked like you were having a good time at the restaurant. Have you known him long?"

Morgana shook her head. "Just a few weeks really."

Martel made a non-committal noise and took another sip of his beer. "I have to admit Morgana, that I was surprised to see Patrick come in with a woman. I can't remember the last time that happened."

Morgana laughed at his tone and shook her head. "Oh, no, that was a business dinner. We're not seeing each other. He brought me an excerpt from a book to look at, and we had dinner to discuss it, that's all."

"My apologies," Martel replied. "And what did you think of it? The book, I mean."

Morgana shrugged. "It's an interesting work of fiction."

"I'm surprised you could even read it," Martel remarked, and she couldn't quite tell from his tone of voice if that was a complement or not. "Thanks to four years with Madame Bazinet in high school, I could barely make out that it was some form of French. I had Pat take a look, because he can speak a hell of a lot more French than I can."

"I was born in France, and I'm good with languages," Morgana said, by way of explanation, keeping her voice calm. It was taking almost all of her will to keep from looking around in case he was serving as a distraction.

"Well, then I guess he went to the right person." Martel glanced up and locked eyes with someone.

Morgana clenched the armrest to keep from reaching for the bread knife in the middle of the table.

Martel slid the cutting board in his direction and cut a small piece off and popped it in his mouth. "Oh, here comes Pat," he said, mouth full. He got to his feet and took the cutting board with him. "Maybe you could tell me about it sometime soon."

Patrick clapped Martel on the back and plucked up the remaining chunk of dark bread as he passed. He handed half to Morgana as he took his seat again. She ate it with satisfaction as Martel disappeared back into the house.

"So, are we all going to starve?" Morgana asked, brushing crumbs from her shirt.

Patrick laughed, running a hand through his russet waves. Long enough to brush the collar of his dress shirts, he'd had his hair carefully styled the few times she'd seen him, but Morgana thought it suited him better like this, when the breeze could blow it into his face.

"Matt is a total moron when it comes to lighting grills."

The flutter in her stomach was back. She reached for her cup again only to find it empty and set it aside with a sigh. She wasn't out of the woods yet.

Especially given who his best friend was.

Damn, could things get any more complicated?

One glance at Patrick gave her that answer. He was watching the pool again, as if he had forgotten that she was there. The children were still splashing away, and there was a softness around his eyes, almost longing. That look again, the one that sent her heart pounding and a tendril of heat curling through her.

Morgana got up and went to refill her drink. She took several steadying breaths as she wove between the tables and waited for space to clear at the drinks table. She filled her cup with ice and studied the selection in front of her, deciding on the ruby red pitcher of sangria packed full of sliced fruit.

She took a sip as she turned back for the table, a burst of dark fruit and tart citrus on her tongue, and bumped shoulders with a blond-haired man coming the other way. She held her glass away, and narrowly avoided spilling red wine on them both.

"Sorry about that," the man said and took her cup and refilled it.

Morgana took the cup back. "No harm done."

He gripped the ends of the towel around his neck and smiled, then headed for the beer coolers.

She found herself smiling as she settled back into her seat. Her arrival finally broke Patrick's reverie. He blinked and the look in his eyes vanished. He turned to her and that dimple flashed in his cheek. "So, what did you and Jake talk about?"

"Nothing much," she answered, her throat dry for a reason other than thirst. "I just thanked him for inviting me. I am having a lot of fun."

It wasn't completely a lie.

"I'm glad. You seemed so tense on the way here," he answered. "Any particular reason?"

"You never know who you're going to meet," she said with a dismissive wave of her hand. "But your sister's lovely and your father's great."

Patrick chuckled. "Well, there's nothing you have to worry about with my family. We're all pretty laid back. Though Jake has his moments."

"You're telling me."

He frowned at her choice of words.

Morgana bit back a curse. Her tone had not been for someone she'd only known for a few minutes. Over by the pool, Kaitlyn's father was wrapping her in a towel that had a little hood with cat ears on it. An unfamiliar longing plucked at her heart at the sight.

As sudden as the flash of a camera, the small round face of her infant son, wrapped in a blanket filled her vision. Lost before he was even six months old, and dead for centuries, the image was still crystal clear. The phantom weight of him on her chest, made it difficult to breathe.

She couldn't quite smother a gasp of pain, and struggled with her calm mask, eventually forcing it into place.

Patrick was giving her an odd look. "Are you alright?"

She nodded. "I'm fine."

With impeccable timing, Martel came back out of the house, a huge plate piled high with steaks and burgers in his hands. Sophie followed with a smaller plate, laughing at something going on in the kitchen. Patrick jumped to his feet to help, giving Morgana the chance to put the memories back in their proper place. As the men started loading up the grill, Sophie came over to her and settled into Patrick's seat with a sigh. She closed her eyes and rested her head on the back of the chair.

"Let's let the men slave over the grill for a while."

Morgana nodded. A breeze blew through the tent to ruffle their hair. Sophie tucked a strand of hair behind her ear. It was similar to her brother's, with roan and cinnamon, auburn and gold all blended together, but hers stretched halfway down her back without a trace of a wave.

Morgana was surprised at how comfortable the silence was. She usually shied away from social situations, because close relationships with mortals always ended one way, with her alone, and in pain. They could die too easily, and far too quickly. At least when compared to immortality. For the better part of two centuries, she had been successful, but the Davies family was proving problematic.

"Patrick tells me you have quite the book collection," Morgana said, voice somehow steady and relaxed, when inside the opposite was true.

"It's nothing like the one he says you've amassed at Albrecht," Sophie countered, eyes still closed. "But I'm daddy's little girl as they say. I have an eye for books and manuscripts."

"I'd love to see them," Morgana said eagerly. "But you look so comfortable, I'd hate to make you get up. Maybe later?"

Sophie turned her head and opened her eyes. A smile spread across her face. "Nonsense," she answered and got to her feet. With a conspiratorial wink, she beckoned Morgana to follow her. "There are chairs in the library as much as there are out here."

Twelve

The room Sophie led her to was upstairs and down a long corridor, past and office and several fully furnished bedrooms set aside for guests. The stairs and upstairs floorboards creaked gently under their weight and the whole house had an air of well lived in antiquity. Maybe it was the lemon oil and beeswax scent that permeated the air, but the personality was comfortable, welcoming, and charming. Morgana quickly appraised that some of the artwork and the large grandfather clock in one corner of the entryway were worth far more than she made in a year. The benefits of being an auctioneer's daughter indeed.

Morgana stopped just inside and tried not to gasp. The room was quite large, with long floor-to-ceiling windows that flooded the room with late-afternoon light. Every remaining inch that wasn't taken up by the looming marble fireplace on the opposite wall, was covered with books and tasteful antiques. It was an eclectic collection, from paperback romances to eighteenth century first editions, some of which were remarkably rare. Patrick hadn't just been boasting about his little sister.

Sophie settled into a chair under the window, a little smile playing on her lips as Morgana wandered from bookcase to bookcase. Her hands settled across her stomach in a way that Morgana had seen countless times, and with her sitting back, her loose shirt revealed a slight rounding to her stomach.

"You're pregnant?" Morgana asked casually, her eyes trained on the books in front of her, but she caught the reaction from the corner of her eye.

The blue eyes, so like Patrick's, widened and she sat up straighter in her chair. "How could you know that?" she asked. "We haven't told anyone."

Morgana shrugged. "I'm just observant," she responded. "You can't be very far along though. Three months?"

"Four," Sophie confirmed. "Jake and I were planning on telling everyone after dinner. And I'm starving! My appetite is finally starting to come back, thank God."

"Congratulations."

"Thank you," Sophie said with a smile.

Morgana returned to examining the books in front of her, her mind turning over the news. Finally locating the Dickens book Patrick mentioned, Morgana passed it by since the one and only time she had met him, Charles Dickens had been an off-putting, pretentious ass. On another shelf, Nora Roberts and Isabel Allende were sandwiched between Mark Twain, Robert Frost and Alexandre Dumas. Sophie's copy of *The Three Musketeers*, in the original French, was older than her own. Not an easy feat.

MOLLY KERR

"Patrick hasn't told us very much about you. Do *you* have any children?" Sophie asked after a few minutes. It was Morgana's turn to be surprised. "Judging from your figure, I'd say not."

"Your body goes back soon enough," Morgana said, before she could stop herself, with a knowing tone she couldn't quite hide.

"Ah." Sophie's blue eyes were gentle. "Do you have a boy or a girl?"

"He was a boy."

"Was?"

"He died," Morgana's throat tightened. Her emotions were still swirling from earlier, stunning her with their ferocity. What was it about this family that burst through the tight control she usually had on her memories?

"Oh Morgana, I'm so sorry," Sophie said gently. "What was his name?"

"Henri," she answered. "It was a *long* time ago, but I really don't like talking about it."

"You must think horribly of me!" True remorse shone in her eyes. "I just met you and already I'm dredging up old memories."

"N-no, don't worry about it. You couldn't have known." She rubbed at her temple where a headache was starting. Panic suddenly seized her, and Morgana quickly crossed the room and crouched down next to the chair, taking Sophie's hand in hers. "Please, keep that between us." Morgana said, "Patrick doesn't know."

"Of course."

Morgana studied Sophie's expression for a moment and there was nothing but kindness and understanding in her blue eyes. Feeling a little foolish, she gave the hand in hers a squeeze and went back to the wall of books. The next bookcase was full of more classics, but the titles were not in English. A copy of *War and Peace* sat on a shelf with several other Russian classics all written in Dutch. Morgana's eyebrow went up and she asked Sophie about it. The next shelf was primarily in German.

"Oh, there was an action house in Berlin that closed down round about the time the wall came down. Times were tough then and Daddy got a lot of my older books there. Most are in German though."

"Do you speak German?"

Sophie chuckled. "Not really. I can muddle my way through some of it. Kind of a fun conversation starter though, aren't they?"

"Indeed," Morgana replied and bent to view the books on a middle shelf. She almost passed right by it at first, but something about the battered blue cloth binding looked so eerily familiar. Morgana leaned in close to read the title and held her breath. *Gullivers Reisen*, a German translation of the famous Jonathan Swift satire.

The stamping was faded now with only a trace of the gold leaf that had once announced the title. There was an odd scorch mark across the top of the binding, the product of the book getting too close to a candle. Inside, had she dared to look would be pages and pages where her own handwriting was crammed into every available space.

She had been Emilie Jardin then, in the late 1800's and this copy of *Gulliver's Travels*, the only paper she had available to her while on the run from a particularly tenacious Hunter. He'd chased her out of Madrid and pursued her across half of Europe. Forced to sleep in the woods or at the hearth of a friendly farmer before moving on, she'd only had a change of clothes and a few necessities that she had kept stuffed in a sack. Her chronicles remained in storage, and she'd written in the book's inside covers and flyleaves when she could find the ink to keep a record of her movements. Events tended to blend together before too long otherwise.

The book had stayed with her until she'd been forced to leave Munich in the middle of the night at the outbreak of the First World War, and thought the book was lost. Until now.

Morgana glanced over her shoulder at Sophie, to find that she had closed her eyes, hands still folded over her stomach. She smiled and had just pulled the corner of the book back when footsteps sounded in the hall and Patrick pushed the door open.

The book made a soft thump as it settled back on the shelf.

"There you are!" he exclaimed from the doorway. "Food's ready."

Sophie opened her eyes and pushed laboriously to her feet. "Great, I'm starving."

"Come on then." Patrick ushered both women out ahead of him.

Heart racing, Morgana quickly assessed options to retrieve the book. When they reached the bottom of the stairs, Morgana stopped.

"Where is the washroom?"

Patrick pointed down the hallway to her left. "It's the second door on the right. Want me to wait for you?"

Sophie swatted him on the arm. "It's not like she can get lost." She told her brother as she slid her hand inside his elbow and led him outside.

Morgana watched them go and caught at least one of the women cleaning up in the kitchen looking her way. She didn't need to go, but she went into the washroom anyway, and stared at herself in the mirror, wrestling with the choice between going back upstairs and retrieving—no, stealing—or asking Sophie if she could borrow it.

Maybe Patrick's sister had books in her collection that she had never opened and had therefore never seen her scribblings in Swift. Maybe she had seen the writing but hadn't made any connection to the more mysterious tome that her brother had. It had to be one of the two or Sophie would have already given the book to him.

The thought of stealing from Sophie made Morgana's stomach twist into knots. The scents of grilled steaks and chicken turned sour in her nose. And what would Patrick think once he found out?

But it was her own book. And Patrick was already keeping one from her, so it wasn't really stealing. Morgana also reminded herself that this outing was a social visit to convince Patrick to give the book back to her. Not a date. She'd probably never see Sophie again anyway.

After enough time had passed, Morgana flushed the toilet and ran the sink in case someone was being nosy enough to track her movements. She opened the door to find the house whisper quiet, all the sounds of plating food and washing dishes had stopped.

Morgana returned to find the kitchen empty. Before she could change her mind, she darted up the stairs, stepping carefully to minimize the creaking they had made earlier. Inside the library, Morgana plucked the book from its shelf and turned back the cover.

Her heart swelled at the sight of all those cramped letters filling the first few blank pages. For a moment, she'd almost hoped that she had been wrong about the book, that blank pages would have greeted her behind the cover. It certainly would have been easier that way.

She started back for the door and froze for footsteps had reached the landing at the top of the stairs and were headed up the hall.

Thirteen

The steps were heavy, purposeful and the book in her hand was like a grenade, a beacon of dishonesty should someone walk through the door.

The steps drew nearer, and Morgana held her breath. As quietly as possible, she tucked the book under her shirt and clamped down with her upper arm. The shirt was sleeveless, but the loose cut should hide any tell-tale bulges. She turned to the shelf, pretending to still be browsing, but the footsteps pivoted into the office.

Morgana lowered her forehead to the shelf. There was a rustle of papers on the desk followed by a satisfied sound as whatever the person had been looking for was found, then the steps moved back to the hall and away. She inched over to the doorway in time to see Martel turn the corner and head down the stairs, a small stack of plastic CD cases in one hand.

Her knees threatened to give out with relief, but Morgana forced herself to remain upright. She counted off several minutes in her head and then peeked back out into the hall, ears straining to pick up any sound from within the house. Hearing none, she checked her shirt in the mirror over the fireplace and stepped out into the hallway.

Martel had pulled the office door mostly closed but Morgana couldn't resist poking her head inside. The space was dominated by a desk so large that it looked as if the house had been built around it. A laptop computer off to one side was half-buried in papers and files. The walls inside were lined with bookcases almost bursting with books, but Morgana couldn't make out the titles from the hall.

Her hand hovered over the doorknob. Did she dare push it open? Were it her home, Martel wouldn't hesitate, she told herself and grasped the knob.

The door creaked softly, and she only opened it far enough to slip in. Morgana creeped across the wide floorboards to the desk. She forced away the tendrils of remorse that coiled in her belly as she turned to the laptop. She tried a couple of password combinations at random but stopped before the computer could lock her out, and hopefully before any kind of alert went out to Martel that someone was tampering with it.

Instead, she opened a compartment in the back of her phone case and withdrew a device the size of several credit cards stacked together. She tugged on one corner and withdrew a connector which she slid into a slot on the side of the computer.

With the press of a button, a light started blinking. A status bar appeared on top of the password prompt indicating the drive was copying the laptop's hard drive. It quickly jumped to twenty percent. Thirty.

Morgana drummed her fingers on the desk as the bar creeped along, continuing to listen for any sound from below. As the drive worked, she pulled open the desk drawers and gently rifled through. In one drawer, there were more stacks of papers and files, in the bottom of another, a small lock box for money or a weapon. She checked the center drawer for keys or a tool to pick the lock with but came up empty.

The drive was at seventy percent when voices floated up from downstairs, and a footstep sounded on the bottom stair. Morgana scrambled to close the drawers and sprang to her feet. She pulled the drive free at eighty-seven percent and sent the computer back to sleep.

She raced into the hallway, heart in her throat and pulled the door back to where Martel had left it. The drive was safely stowed when Martel turned the corner.

His eyes widened when he saw her, then narrowed. "Can I help you with something?"

Morgana smiled sheepishly. "I forgot my phone when Patrick came to get us." She waved the device at him and continued on as if nothing was amiss and her heart wasn't still hammering in her throat.

His eyes burrowed into her back as he followed her all the way outside. Music gently flowed over the sounds of silverware on plates and quiet conversation. Almost all of the tables were occupied, though a line of people were still making their way through the serving table. She found Patrick sitting at the same table, but now most of the other seats were full.

Martel took a seat next to Sophie.

"Everything okay?" Patrick asked as she took her seat.

Morgana nodded. She reached up to scratch a phantom itch on her shoulder, at the same time, releasing the book and guiding it down into her lap, still under the cover of her shirt.

"Can I get you something to eat?"

Morgana looked around the table, everyone else was eating. "You didn't have to wait for me." She protested. "But yes, I'm starving."

Patrick smiled and went to get plates. Morgana reached to the center of the table and retrieved her purse. She made a show of checking her cell phone for messages while using the other hand to stow it and the book inside. When she replaced the bag, she caught Martel watching her out of the corner of his eye and smiled politely. He quickly looked away.

Patrick returned with plates heaped with food, the necks of two beer bottles pinched between his fingers.

Morgana surveyed the plate, which had small amounts of everything, steak, several kinds of salad, a deviled egg, and some kind of bean mixture. She picked up her fork and tried to eat around the tightness in her chest.

What was there to feel guilty about? She had only taken back her own property.

The justification rang hollow. For a moment she ate her food in silence until a gentle elbow nudging her elbow brought her head up. All eyes were on her, and she blushed.

Patrick chuckled. "As I was saying... Morgana, this is Courtney, Sophie's best friend and her husband Brennan," he said, gesturing to the couple sitting on either side of Kaitlyn, who was still wrapped in the kitten towel, happily shoveling bits of hot dog and pasta salad into her mouth.

Morgana smiled and nodded her head. The conversation resumed and Martel joined in as the men started telling stories of their mischievous youths together spent breaking windows in abandoned buildings, stealing candy, sneaking cigarettes and alcohol once they reached their teens. Patrick made it clear that his hooligan days ended in his third year of high school as schoolwork and sports became the priorities, but they'd remained close. Courtney was a shy, but pleasant woman in her mid-twenties who provided a good contrast to Sophie's easily talkative nature.

"How did you all end up out here, then?" Morgana asked as she took a sip of beer. It coated her tongue with a bitter sourness that wasn't entirely rooted in her dislike of Pilsners. She set it aside with a grimace.

The three men looked at each other, but it was Sophie who spoke. "By the time I graduated college, Patrick had already moved out here to work for D&M, so I decided to go to grad school out here. I'm a software engineer, so I could find work just about anywhere."

She looked over at her husband and smiled. "Jake followed me, of course, and we loved it so much we bought this place. Then Jake decided to open the restaurant, and Brennan was looking for work, so Jake brought him on to manage the front of house."

"The rest is history." Martel lifted his wife's hand so he could kiss it.

"And your mother?" Morgana asked. "Is she still in New York?"

Sophie and Patrick exchanged a look. "She is," Patrick replied, his voice oddly hollow. "She's remarried, and happy on the east coast. We talk every once in a while, but we haven't seen her in three--"

"Four," Sophie corrected.

"Four years."

Tension thrummed between the siblings like a plucked string, as if both were suppressing the urge to squirm at the mention of their mother. Perhaps it was just the normal discomfort that came when parents divorced and remarried. But it wasn't something either wanted to talk about in mixed company. Brennan broke the silence a few moments later as he launched into a story about a mattress, a steep hill, and a bottle of cooking oil, and bursts of laughter erupted around the table.

After another twenty minutes or so, and everyone at the table had finished eating, Sophie nudged her husband, who nodded and rose to his feet. He called out and brought everyone's attention to him as Sophie got to her feet next to him and took his hand. When he announced their news, cheers and clapping exploded under the tent.

A slow, wide smile spread across Patrick's face. He leapt to his feet and swept Sophie off of hers, spinning her in a circle. He set her down and punched his friend playfully on the arm. Martel gave him a smug smile and returned the back-slapping hug. The pure joy on his face as he celebrated with his family brought a smile to her face and punched her in the gut at the same time.

"Congratulations, 'Uncle Pat'," Morgana called over her shoulder as he passed behind her to return to his seat.

He looked down at her, still beaming. "Thank you," he replied as he retook his seat. In almost the same motion, his hand came over to cover hers where it lay on the armrest of her chair and squeezed gently.

Morgana glanced down, but didn't move away, both because of Patrick's happiness, and because strangely, she didn't want to. Sophie caught her eye, looked at their hands and smiled gently before returning her attention to her husband who was thanking everyone for coming and announcing that there would be a bonfire lit soon. Morgana's cheeks grew warm, and she took a deep, steadying breath.

The party started to break up as families rose to clear plates and tidy up. The sun was starting to set. It was still warm, but there was a breeze coming through the tent now that made her glad for the light sweater she'd tucked in her purse. She helped carry platters of food back into the house and fell into companiable conversation with Courtney and a few of the other wives as they packed food into storage containers and stuffed the fridge so full the doors took a little extra push to stay closed.

Patrick came in as they were finishing, wood smoke and lighter fluid scenting the air. He wove his way through the crowd in the kitchen and stuck his hands under the running faucet and reached for the soap.

Morgana handed him a towel to dry his hands.

"All done?"

She nodded and reached for the strings of the apron she'd been given to cover her satin top. Patrick balled it up on the kitchen island and unhooked her purse from a chair back and passed it over. There were titters of laughter as he swept his hand dramatically toward the sliding door and ushered her through.

It was almost fully dark now and a bonfire roared a dozen feet in the air from the pasture behind the swimming pool, beckoning to them. Morgana paused to retrieve the black cardigan from her bag and shrugged into it. The material was thin, but it helped with the immediate chill.

The heat coming off the fire reached them from a surprising distance away. Those who hadn't left with sleepy kids gathered around it like so many moths, the ones left standing chased each other around with sparklers. The roar of the fire and the hum of conversation and laughter filled the air. Patrick spread a blanket in front of a hay bale they could use as a backrest and sat.

Morgana stretched out beside him, feet crossed at the ankle. She adjusted her sweater and turned her face toward the fire and let the heat seep into her. More immediately, the warmth radiating from the man beside her was like a physical caress, tempting and terrifying at the same time, though they weren't touching.

Slowly, more parents ushered sleepy children toward the driveway. Then Sophie bid her goodbyes and Martel followed with a wave.

Patrick returned the gesture, and the men shared a look, Martel's eyes shifted between his friend and Morgana. A mix of curiosity and something else filled his eyes. Patrick waved him away with quick flicks of his wrist and Martel went shaking his head in amusement.

With the Martels' departure, much of the conversation died as couples and families gathered together to enjoy the fire and watch the stars. Morgana and Patrick were almost alone on their side of the fire. Neither spoke, neither really acknowledged the other's presence, but both were all too aware of it.

The fire let out a pop like gunfire as a log cracked and released a pocket of sap. Morgana jumped, back stiffening. Patrick put an arm around her shoulders, his hand gently moving up and down her arm in a comforting way. Once her brain had sorted out the source of the noise, she relaxed.

She should have shaken his arm off but found herself softening into him, just a bit. When he gently pressed a kiss to her temple, a thrill zinged through her. She lifted her chin and looked at him, immediately mesmerized by the firelight flickering in the dark eyes fixed on her.

I shouldn't be doing this; I can't *do this*, part of her brain insisted. The other part of her brain, the less than rational yet suddenly dominant part of her brain, told the other part to shut up.

Neither moved at first, then the space between them started to shrink until she was pressed against him almost from shoulder to hip and her head drifted onto his shoulder. His hand slid down her arm and over her hip and drew her in even closer, while the other came around to lift her chin. Her breathing, only just returned to normal, began to quicken again.

Morgana wrapped her fingers around his forearm unsure whether it was to restrain him or to pull him closer. Their gazes locked, neither willing nor able to look away. Patrick blinked slowly as he searched her face. She did the same, and the intensity she found should have frightened her.

Then his lips were brushing hers. The contact was brief, but it shook her to the core. He pulled back to gauge her reaction, and she couldn't mask the tightening of her shoulders, the widening of her eyes quick enough. Some of the light went out of his eyes and he turned his head away. His arms began to slide away.

Morgana raised her free hand to his cheek and turned his face back to hers. Her fingers brushed back the hair at his temple, the strands as soft and silky as she had imagined in the few moments she'd let herself dream. She traced the curve of his jaw, feeling the roughness of a day's growth of beard under her fingertips. When he opened his eyes and met hers again, she took a handful of his shirt, and dragged his mouth back to hers.

This kiss was warm and sweet. He explored her mouth, tasting first one corner, and then the other, before consuming her mouth all at once.

Their tongues met, danced, tasting faintly of the beer he'd drunk and something much more potent that was all Patrick. He drew her hand from his face and linked their fingers while the hand at her hip swept up her back and cupped the nape of her neck. His fingers deftly kneaded the muscles there, sending little jolts down her spine to pierce her heart.

There was nothing hurried to the kiss. Morgana turned, one leg draping over his, so she could press even closer, her arms wrapped tight around his chest. The few remaining people around the fire could have disappeared for all Morgana knew or cared. A girl could get used to being kissed like this, like a part of her was being drawn into him.

When they finally came apart, he tucked her head back against his shoulder, drew part of the blanket around them, and linked his hands around her waist. There was such a tenderness in the way he held her, as if she was something extremely fragile and immensely precious. Her heart fluttered when he released a gentle, but satisfied sigh.

Morgana watched the flames dance, sparks swirling high in the air. Neither moved, except for an occasional glance or caress until the fire began to shrink and the blanket, even with their combined warmth underneath, was no longer enough to keep the chill away. They rose to their feet, and Morgana stretched the kinks out of her back while Patrick folded the blankets. Morgana rolled her shoulders, wincing as muscles tightened as the cool air reached them.

Then Patrick's fingers were there working their magic. Her head fell forward of its own accord, giving him better access. The knots soon loosened, and when he left her with a gentle kiss on the back of her neck, she shivered, but not from the cold.

Patrick added their blanket to the pile and led her to the car, gently guiding her with a hand once again on her lower back. He could have guided her to the edge of a cliff and over in her present state of mind. Strangely, she wasn't as alarmed by that thought as she should have been.

Maybe tomorrow she would feel differently, but not tonight.

They said little in the car, but Morgana's hand covered his on the shifter. The silence was easy and comfortable, as if they had been doing this for years. The kiss goodnight on the sidewalk outside her building was unhurried, and gently sent her head spinning, his arms strong as they surrounded her.

Her lips continued to tingle long after he got back into his car and drove away, refusing to fade even as she drifted off into sleep. That night, he was in her dreams, still in her head when she woke, and she had a premonition that it wouldn't be long before he was inescapably part of her heart.

Fourteen

L ate the next morning, Morgana rose, called Alan, and told him
to reschedule all of her appointments for the next few days.
Yes, she wanted him to call if anything came up that she needed to
know about. No, she wouldn't be coming in.

Her second call was to Alasdair, who luckily was still in town,
and told him that she had an emergency. A half hour later, she
opened the door, squinting and rubbing her temple from the
pounding headache, and immediately bent over laughing.

"Now, love, what could possibly be so funny?" It wasn't clear if
he was truly offended or just pretending.

She took the pizza box from his hands and ushered him inside.
He dropped the bags on the island, and unpacked pints of ice cream,
a bottle of wine, and a few bags of potato chips.

"I don't think I will ever get that sight out of my head. Pizza, junk food, and what's this?" She lifted both sides of his jacket, revealing a long dagger tucked in on one side of his belt and a handgun in the other and laughed again. "Were you planning on avenging my honor, or having me gain two hundred pounds?"

Alasdair shrugged and added the weapons to the mix, still smiling. "I didn't know what you meant by 'emergency'."

Morgana was still laughing as she put the ice cream in the freezer. It was well-established between them that Alasdair Bromley couldn't shoot a tin can from ten feet away or fight his way out of a paper bag. He'd lived to the ripe old age of four hundred sixteen by keeping his head down. The Hunters had no idea that the owner of a large San Francisco investment firm was so rich because he had made some smart financial moves more than two hundred years ago. He kept his name out of the papers and his face out of the spotlight so they couldn't catch on. And he was lucky that, so far, he had succeeded. "Best to be prepared."

Morgana chuckled and reached up to pull her fiery curls into some semblance of a ponytail, securing it with the elastic band from around her wrist, then went to get plates and silverware out of the dishwasher. "I need your help with something," she said as she lifted the lid on the pizza and inhaled deeply. "Starting with helping me to eat all of this."

Alasdair wrinkled his nose in distaste, but took a dutiful bite of the slice she put on his plate. "Would this something have a name?"

Morgana shrugged. This conversation usually worked in reverse. "Perhaps," she said, carrying her plate to the coffee table, then coming back for their drinks. When she went to pass him again, Alasdair caught the sleeve of her sweater and pulled her to a stop.

"What is it, love?"

She reached into her pocket and pulled out the flash drive.

Alasdair narrowed his eyes as he plucked the credit card-sized device from her fingers and examined it.

"What's this?"

"Most of the contents of Martel's home computer."

Alasdair jolted as if the device had shocked him. He dropped his plate on the island, the half-eaten slice of pizza forgotten and made a beeline for her laptop on the coffee table.

She chuckled and followed, chewing on a bite of pizza. "I got a start on decrypting it last night, but your tech wizardry is much better than mine."

Alasdair dropped onto the sofa and studied the data flashing by. The status bar showed only a little more than twenty percent of the files she'd dumped off the drive had been decrypted. "What are you running here?"

She perched on the arm of the sofa and told him. He laughed and shook his head. "Amateur," he chided playfully as he extracted a small thumb drive from an inside pocket of his jacket and plugged it into the laptop. New windows opened and closed as he typed for a few minutes. He hit the enter button one more time with a dramatic flourish and sat back.

Morgana glanced down at the new status bar that had already passed hers in just a few seconds. She scowled, thought excitement was tingling down her arms.

Alasdair looked over at her with a grin like the cat who had gotten the cream. He patted the seat beside him. "Come, tell me why you really called while we wait."

She sighed and went back to the kitchen for a drink and another slice of pizza. She added one to his plate and pressed it into his hands as she took a seat beside him, her own food balanced on her knee.

He frowned at the plate in his hands, then catching her eye, picked up the half-eaten slice and dutifully finished it.

Satisfied, Morgana looked away and concentrated on chewing. When she'd picked up the phone earlier, she'd wanted nothing more than to have him come to talk everything out. Now, with him only a few feet away, the words weren't there.

There was a rustling noise and then the plate was gone. A finger slid under her chin, and exerted enough pressure to raise her eyes to his. "What is it, love?"

His fingers were cool on her skin as he waited. Had she wanted to pull away, she could have, but she didn't. She could tell that he was worried, and deep inside, so was she.

"Yesterday was... interesting."

"Define 'interesting'."

Morgana dragged the brocaded throw pillow from behind her and hugged it to her chest.

Alasdair's hand fell away but he remained sitting close, leaning forward with interest and concern, one arm draped on the sofa behind her.

It was a few moments before she could speak. When she did, her voice was small, her words hesitant and disjointed. She told him about the trip out to Martel's home in Dane, of meeting Patrick's family, the easy rapport with his sister, and the news that their enemy was going to be a father. He choked on his wine at that, but thankfully did not spit it out all over the cream chenille sofa.

She told him about the library, and the book, and searching through Martel's home office, copying what she could to the flash drive before almost getting caught.

"Thankfully, he bought your story." Alasdair remarked when she told him her excuse about the forgotten cell phone. His face was neutral as she spoke, though the workings of that brilliant mind showed in his eyes, processing her words, slotting information away like the tumblers in a lock.

Finally, she told him about the bonfire, and even keeping out most of the details, her face heated. She looked away and took a deep gulp of her drink and looked back nervously to see another tumbler in the lock click into place. Morgana had always been jealous of his stone face. Hers had never been as strong, and lately, it hadn't been very effective at all.

Right now, she wasn't sure if he was shocked, or if he was just fighting some other emotion. *Say something,* she ordered silently as she took a large sip and looked back nervously.

Say anything.

Then the lock finally seemed to spring free as he took a deep breath and smiled. "It's about time."

Whatever she had expected him to say, that wasn't it. But before she could question him, the laptop on the coffee table beeped a warning.

Alasdair turned his head and read the new message. "That's odd."

"What is it?"

"The program's nearly done but it hit a whole cache of files that are stored behind several layers of additional security." He turned and gave his full attention to pressing keys and studying lines of code. Windows opened and closed faster than she could follow. A bead of sweat gleamed on his temple as he frowned at the screen.

"Extra security is good though, right?"

"Possibly," he said distractedly as his fingers flew over the keys.

The status bar, which had been frozen at ninety percent began to creep up incrementally as Alasdair waged war with firewall after firewall. The lean muscles under his shirt tensed and rippled as if he was yielding a sledgehammer to knock them down rather than a keyboard.

Finally, he flopped back on the sofa, breathing heavily. The computer let out a triumphant fanfare as the last files decrypted. Despite the guilt and worry still lingering from last night's memories, Morgana laughed in triumph. She tossed the pillow to the floor and sprung across the sofa to hug him.

His eyes flew open and his arms automatically wrapped around her. He set her back almost immediately to return his attention to the window now on screen, full of neat rows of icons representing each file and folder.

"Please tell me there is something good on there somewhere."

Alasdair's eyes flicked quickly over the screen and chose a folder at random. The screen filled with thumbnails of dozens of family photographs from ski trips, cruise ships, and monuments. Martel, and Sophie. And Patrick.

Morgana noted with some satisfaction that there were few photos of Patrick with other women, though one beach vacation included a stunning brunette in a small bikini with her arms wrapped around Patrick's neck. Both were tanned, smiling, and seemingly very happy.

Morgana swallowed as her stomach twisted, a hot wave of something almost choking her. She reached over and closed the folder. This wasn't about Patrick.

Alasdair eyed her quizzically as she took control of the laptop and started examining file names and folders. They were in no particular order, many coded. Eventually, she would need to go through them all individually.

Her eyes rested on a folder marked simply with the current year and opened it. Inside were a half dozen files marked with the initials JLM and a month. She selected the most recent one and waited for it to load but when it did her eyes popped wide.

The file contained monthly bank statements, investment accounts, stock balances, a dozen or more. Morgana recognized many of the banks and investment firms as old, prominent American institutions that usually catered to the very rich, the kind that kept clients for many generations. She had accounts with a couple of them herself.

Alasdair let out a low whistle as she scrolled through. "Quite the holdings for a restaurant owner."

Morgana nodded, some of the accounts had balances in the hundreds of thousands, some quite a bit more. She scrolled on to another statement and stopped. Where most had shown Martel's name with only the middle initial, this one had his full name. Her hand flew to her mouth.

Alasdair leaned in. "What is it?"

Morgana's other hand inched the mouse pointer across the screen until it rested on his middle name. She sat back, one hand on her chest, and concentrated on breathing.

"Jacob Lembaye Martel?" Alasdair stumbled over the name and scoffed. "What an odd name."

"You're saying it wrong." She spoke the name with proper French pronunciation.

Alasdair repeated it back to her and she nodded in confirmation. He made a face as if the name left a bad taste in his mouth. "Does it mean anything to you, love? You've gone white as a sheet."

Morgana rubbed at her temple. "I knew that Martel came from an old Hunter family back in the States. But I didn't realize just how old."

Alasdair looked at the computer again and then back at her.

Morgana felt the pizza trying to come back up. "Lembaye is a small village in the south of France. One of its nearest neighbors is Arricau. And as you know, many French surnames come from place names."

"So, he's from an old Hunter family that comes from the same part of France that you do?"

She nodded and swallowed hard. "Not only that, one of the oldest." A ball of ice lodged in her throat. "After I changed, I had no idea what had happened to me, just that I had died in the night, but for some reason I hadn't stayed dead. I thought for sure my husband was mistaken."

Her breath hitched, her throat tightening further. "I was alive, breathing, talking. I couldn't have died. But Jean wouldn't come near me. When I approached, he pushed me away and reached for a weapon. So, I ran."

Alasdair reached over and took one of her hands, and she clung to it like an anchor to ground her.

"And I kept running, my husband the tip of the spear following in my wake." She reached down and retrieved the pillow from the floor and curled herself around it. "He wasn't a Hunter with a capital letter, they weren't organized that way yet, but he was the first to truly *hunt* me. He gathered men to him, men who he got to believe that I was a demon who had stolen his son from him and then somehow cheated Death when he had come to claim me as punishment."

She took another shuddering breath. "One of those men was Roul de Lembaye."

Alasdair reached for his drink and drained it, his throat bobbing with each swallow. "You're kidding."

She clutched the pillow tighter. "I wish I was," she replied. "For twenty years, Jean and Roul and the other men chased me across France, Spain, and Portugal. Each time I saw them, they looked older, yet my reflection remained the same. Then I boarded a ship for Scotland in the dead of night and left Jean behind for the last time. It was another five years before I met someone like us."

She tossed the pillow away and gathered up the plates as a sudden urge to move overwhelmed her. "More pizza?"

From the sofa, Alasdair made a face.

She laughed as she refilled her glass and came back. As she passed, Alasdair caught her hand and drew her down to sit close beside him.

He studied her face, then reached up and tucked a strand of hair behind her ear. His hand cupped her cheek briefly then fell away. "He's not Jean."

Morgana pulled back. "What?"

"Patrick is not Jean."

She sighed and was silent for a long moment as those four words reverberated through a chest that was suddenly hollow. "If I were mortal, it would be different."

Alasdair squeezed her hand but didn't reply. The sympathy in his eyes spoke volumes, and also pinned her in place.

The questions she'd been hiding from all day finally crashed over her. Could she go on with her life as she had been living it? Could she keep holding herself separate from everyone she knew so that she wouldn't be hurt when they died? Could she continue to keep to herself to the shadows so that she could live in Kingston just a little bit longer?

Perhaps. But did she really want to?

Morgana put a hand to her forehead as her temples started to pound. She forced a deep breath through the tightness in her chest and waved a hand at the laptop. "Can we pick this up another time?"

"Of course."

Alasdair climbed to his feet and headed for the exit with Morgana following in his wake. He stopped at the door and held out his arms.

She stepped into his embrace, the roaring in her head easing slightly as she breathed in the cologne from his shirt.

"I will leave you with one question," he murmured into her ear. "Can you deny your heart and live another seven hundred years alone, when you could have had at least the span of a mortal lifetime with someone you care about?"

She went rigid in his arms, and he eased back, meeting her wide eyes with a sad smile. One hand rubbed her upper arm reassuringly for a moment and then he released her. The door closed softly behind him.

Morgana stood frozen until long after the elevator had deposited him on the ground floor. And when she could finally force her legs to move, she turned to the living room and stared down at the laptop, at the name that practically leapt off the screen.

The laptop closed with a snap and Morgana shoved both hands through her hair. She looked around the open space, at the clutter in the kitchen, the computer on the coffee table, the pillows and blankets scattered all over and walked away.

Cleanup, and the answer to Alasdair's question, could wait until tomorrow.

Fifteen

P atrick settled into the chair behind his desk with a weary sigh and fought the urge to lay his head down on the cool marble top right then and there. As far as long days went, this one took the cake and then some. He looked at his phone and its blinking voicemail light and grimaced. Beside the phone was a stack of messages from people who hadn't bothered to leave voicemails and had called one of his assistants instead. Too tired to talk to financial investors and auditors, he decided that he'd deal with them later.

Instead, he opened the top file on his blotter and got back to proofing the contract his Italian staff had sent for his review. It was a mindless, routine task, and something his brain could handle. Maybe. But after about fifteen minutes, the words just seemed to swim on the page. Sighing, Patrick pulled open his top drawer and dug though it for a bottle of ibuprofen. He came up with it a moment later and struggled with the cap while reading about costs relating to the new system being built to help share information between the Italian staff and the home office.

An hour later, he scribbled his signature and set the folder aside. The next folder held a report from the most recent auction, including photos of the items sold, and their reserve and winning bid amounts arranged in neat columns. Flipping through, he came across a page with a photograph of a porcelain doll with red ringlets, wearing a Victorian era dress and black shoes.

The face was elegantly painted with rosy cheeks and green eyes that were wide and intelligent and reminded him of another pair which were equally as striking. His chest tightened, not painfully, but he found it difficult to breathe, nevertheless. The photos slid from his fingers to the desk as he heaved another sigh.

When he'd first moved back to Kingston, Patrick had attended many auctions, both at Davies & McNamara and at other houses around the city to get some ideas on making improvements. One day at Albrecht about six months ago, he had seen her, standing off to one side with her hands clasped together watching the auctioneer and the crowd. She was dressed in one of the jewel-tone suits she favored, with her hair all but glowing in the light focused on the painting behind her.

He'd seen her a few other times, but had never approached, not until the translation had come in. Then her credentials gave him the opportunity to finally introduce himself.

But did he really know her?

It had only been a few weeks since he'd scheduled that first meeting at Albrecht. Since he first felt the softness of her skin under his hands. Since he'd tasted her by the bonfire. The lily fragrance of her, tinged with woodsmoke and hay, was burned into his memory.

No, he didn't know her, but he wanted to. He wanted to know everything about her.

But life had gotten in the way, meetings and appointments stacked on top of each other, so that once he did get a moment's peace and quiet to himself, he'd been too tired to reach out.

Then again, neither had she, he mused. Maybe she had been serious about their relationship being only business... He sat back in his chair and stared blindly ahead. In his mind, the memories flickered by like an old film. Dinner at *Sophie's*, the sight of her absorbed in Jacqueline d'Arnault's sad and miraculous life. Her sitting at a table with the people closest to him, laughing with them, as if she belonged there.

He threw his pen down and shoved the red-headed doll and the rest of the photos back into their file. He slapped the call button on his phone without looking. June tottered in on heels thin enough to snap and smiled at him.

"Yes sir?" she asked, her weepy brown eyes going soft with affection. At least he hoped it was affection. She knew that wrinkle between his brows, the one that said he was in pain. "Cancel my appointments for the rest of the day. I'm going home," he said, and took a deep breath before levering to his feet, fighting back the urge to groan as his knees and hips protested, still unaffected by the medicine he had taken.

"Will do, sir." she said and hurried off with her usual brisk efficiency.

Patrick crossed to the door and took his suitcoat down from the hook, checked that his cell phone and keys were in the pockets and walked out.

June let him pass without another word, telephone headset already settled over her ears.

Silently, he blessed the woman and made his way to the elevator. Once behind the wheel of his car with the air conditioning blowing directly on his face, he took a moment to relax, to decide what he wanted to do with the rest of his day.

Home was the last place he wanted to be.

He drummed his fingers on the steering wheel, and stared at the wall of the parking garage, thinking. A few moments later, it came to him, and he started the car. There was only one place to go.

The line of cars outside the auction house backed up the street for more than a block. He'd forgotten that it was an auction day, and knew that parking, while difficult on normal days, would be impossible to find at a rate that didn't cost a month's salary. Impatiently, he joined the queue and waited for the valet to take his keys.

The inside of the impressive four-story marble and red brick building was teeming with people. The controlled chaos was invisible to the casual observer, but he had practically grown up in an auction house and knew the signs. While the crowd wove through a small gallery to preview some of the items for sale, or settled into seats in the auditorium, the staff was flitting this way and that making final arrangements at a brisk but not quite frantic pace.

When he turned for the hallway that led to the staff offices, a young man in a navy suit, name tag, and yellow two-way radio detached himself from the shadows by the main doors and moved to intercept him. "Are you here for the auction today, sir?" he asked, gesturing to the large double doors to Patrick's right.

Patrick shook his head. "Not this time." It was a habit at Davies & McNamara to watch the competition at work, examining bidding strategy and pricing, but he hadn't been sent by his father as much in recent months. "I'm here to see Morgana Dericault. Do you know where she might be?"

The suit nodded. "She may still be in her office," he said and raised the radio. "Shall I let her know who's calling?"

"No, that's all right, I'd like to surprise her," Patrick told him. "I'll just go and see if she's still there. Thanks anyway." He left the usher where he was and pushed through the door.

It was one of those days Morgana dreaded.

One of the largest auctions of the year was supposed to be getting underway in less than ten minutes and even after she'd studied dimensions and values until her head was ready to burst, she was totally unprepared. And no wonder, given that every spare moment for the last week had been spent buried in Martel's personal files.

Her fingers tingled with adrenaline as she reached for the auction inventory that had been on the corner of the desk and found it gone. It had been there before lunch. She spun in her chair, her head whipping from one flat surface to another. Her phone rang as she circled the desk to see if it had fallen on the floor and she almost jumped out of her skin.

"Yes?" she barked, a little sharper than usual. *Who would be calling now?*

"There's a young man on the way to you, Morgana," Andrew, one of the ushers, said.

Her nerves kicked up a notch at the din in the background. She pinned the phone between ear and shoulder and kept searching. "I'm busy, Andrew."

"I know," he answered sheepishly. "He said he wanted to surprise you."

"Did he at least give a name?"

"No, ma'am."

She ground her teeth at being called "ma'am."

"Thank you," Morgana said curtly and hung up. She'd apologize later.

Alarm bells were ringing. Forget apologizing, Andrew should have known better. Her very strict security instructions were meant for days like this. Letting an unnamed man upstairs to "surprise her" would earn him a good tongue-lashing and then firing if she was around later to do it. Taking no chances, Morgana got to her feet and retrieved the small antique dagger from the drawer of the console table under the window. She quickly strapped the sheath to her arm under the sleeve of her jacket.

Moving silently across the carpeted floor, Morgana positioned herself beside the door and waited as the footsteps on the marble floor outside drew closer and closer. There was a gentle knock on the door and the knob turned. Morgana took a step back, fingers gripping the dagger as it opened. When her visitor appeared around the door, she jerked in surprise so hard that the dagger pulled out of its sheath and clattered to the floor.

Patrick turned at the sound.

Strain crinkled his eyes and tightened his mouth to almost a thin line, but much of that eased when his eyes fell on her. The change was immediate and startling, leaving Morgana both flattered and annoyed.

She bent and retrieved the dagger with a bit more force than she needed to, rising quickly to her feet only to collide with his chest.

He reached out and steadied her by the elbows while she stood frozen, heart pounding.

"Patrick, what are you doing here?"

There was a cautious smile on his lips, but his eyes were teasing as they had been the first time they'd met in this office. "Should I have made an appointment?"

"Of course not," she answered stepping out of his grasp and walking back to her desk. "But you could probably tell from the crowd you had to push through to get up here that we are very busy today."

"I'm not here for the auction."

"Then what?" She asked. "Did you change your mind about the book?"

He shook his head. "I wanted to see you, Morgana." His voice, normally deep and silky, was suddenly more so, though there was also the slightest hint of weariness that he couldn't quite banish.

Morgana looked up from her desk and was caught up in the intensity of his gem blue eyes.

"And to apologize for not reaching out sooner. It's been a crazy couple of weeks."

She didn't respond beyond looking away. There was no reason to doubt the sincerity of his words, but the time since the party had given her a chance to settle her thoughts and make some hard decisions. Mainly, that she couldn't risk her life, no matter what her heart, which was pounding almost out of her chest, thought otherwise.

She tried to ignore him as she resumed her search for the inventory, the last item she needed to head for the auction hall. She leafed through the scattered papers on her desk, through the stacks on the side, before coming back to the spread of photos and fact sheets in the middle of her desk, her movements grew more frantic as he moved closer to the desk.

One of his hands came down on top of hers and forced her to stop.

She didn't want to look up, but it was the only thing she found that she could do. His blue eyes were confused, his hair a little mussed as if he had run his fingers through it. He stared at her for a moment, then slowly circled the desk, his hand keeping in contact with hers.

Please don't.

Her thoughts started to scramble just because he was touching her. "What's wrong, Morgana?"

She tried to take a step back. He followed. Then, before she knew it, she was in his arms with his mouth hard on hers.

Her body responded before her brain could object. Her traitorous arms wrapped around his neck. She met his assault on her mouth with an offensive of her own.

His arms were strong and sure around her back, holding her so tightly against him that her toes only grazed the floor.

The pounding of her heart began to hurt as if it was trying to burst through her ribcage. She forced herself to put some distance between them before it shattered, by scooping up the dagger, and depositing it in the drawer where it belonged. The sheath she left around her arm for it would only invite questions. She remained there with hands braced on the wooden top, her back turned, and stared sightlessly out the window.

Patrick came up behind her and put a gentle hand on her shoulder. He didn't speak, but gave a gentle tug. Question enough.

She resisted the pressure intended to turn her around. She didn't dare meet those eyes. "I'm fine." she said, and returned to her desk, making a show of rummaging through the photos in front of her as if she was putting them into some kind of order. "I told you, I'm busy."

She heard him sigh. "I'm sorry, Morgana, for disappearing on you." His voice was pained, almost pleading. "Let me make it up to you."

"Please, Patrick, just go. I have to take care of this auction." The ice in her voice stung her as much as it did him, though the ache in her chest was worse. She wanted him to leave.

She wanted him to take her into his arms again and kiss away this pain.

He didn't speak but he did exhale strongly through his nose. He stood still behind her, close enough that her head filled with his cologne, her shoulder warmed from the hand that hovered just above it. After a few moments, each one long enough for a lifetime, he walked past her and left the room without looking back. The quiet click of the closing door reverberated through her more than a slam ever would.

Morgana braced herself on the desk, and took a deep, shuddering breath, and then another. Finally locating the inventory she'd been searching for on a side table, she took the back stairs to the auction floor to ensure that she didn't run into Patrick.

She scanned the room from the doorway to be sure he was gone before stepping onto the small stage and taking a moment to speak with her auctioneer. Satisfied that he was ready to go, she stepped down and mingled with some of her most loyal customers before standing to one side to watch. Afterwards, attendees stopped to shake her hand and tell her that it was one of the best auctions that Albrecht had ever had. While she accepted the words graciously and with a smile, little did they know that right now its manager couldn't have cared less.

Sixteen

From his pocket, his cell phone started to ring. Jacob cursed as the sound echoed across the rooftop and he scrambled to pull it free. On the screen was the restaurant's number. "Yes?" He growled, diverting the anger at his own carelessness onto the caller.

Brennan's voice was almost drowned out by the din of a busy dinner rush. His voice was harried and anxious. "I need you to come back in, man."

His first reaction, oddly enough, had nothing to do with a busy restaurant, or the Ancient he'd been making progress tracking. "Sophie?" he asked, surprised at the fear in his own voice. His wife was almost six months pregnant now, but after a few recent appointments, doctors had told her to cut back on physical activity for fear that she'd deliver early. It wasn't bed rest, not yet anyway.

"She's fine," Brennan said, and those two words were the best news he'd heard in a long time. "But she's also here."

A different kind of fear went through him. He rose to his feet, keeping to shadows just in case someone was watching the roof, and moved toward the fire escape. The building, a four-story complex of self-storage units, was just down the street from the heart of the theater district. His car was blocks away and *Sophie's* at least a ten-minute drive from there.

"Has she asked for me yet?"

Brennan sighed dramatically. "Would I bother calling you if she hadn't?" His tone had Jacob scowling at the phone as he descended the stairs. Despite his earlier fears, he was in too much of a hurry to try to conceal the noise he was making on the old wrought iron steps.

"I had her sit in one of the booths in the back where it's nice and quiet and brought her some chocolate cheesecake. I know it's her favorite."

Right about now he was too anxious to feel the gratitude he should have. "Where did you tell her I am?" It was his night to manage the restaurant and he had told his wife as much.

"Just that you were dealing with some problems in the kitchen and that you would be out as soon as possible. You'd better get your butt back here man."

"What the hell do you think I'm doing?" He hung up as he broke into a run. Jacob kept to the back streets, his jacket flying out behind him, no doubt revealing the handgun at the middle of his back, and didn't care.

His future rested on his wife remaining as blissfully unaware of his night-time hunts as she had been for the last five years. He truly had no idea what she would do, but he knew that it wouldn't be good. Once in the car, he broke countless traffic laws on streets he knew weren't patrolled by police.

He parked at the delivery entrance and jumped out. The scramble to his office to lock up his weapon and change back into dress pants, shirt, and tie was the fastest he had ever done in his life. With the sleeves rolled up, tie loosened, and sweaty from his mad dash across town, he looked like a man who had rushed around a hot kitchen all evening.

Even at this late hour—it was nearly eleven—the dining room was full, and loud with conversation, the clinking of silverware on china. He turned to his left to see the bar was just as crowded, nearly three deep all around, with Brennan and the three bartenders racing to keep up. The kitchen door opening caught his friend's attention. Their eyes met and he beckoned furiously. Jacob glanced again through the dining room and, noting that his wife was out of sight, went to the bar.

"There you are!" Relief bled through his voice. "What took you so long?"

Jacob narrowed his eyes and flashed Brennan a not so nice grin. "I was over in Dovetown. Where's Soph?"

"I told you, in the back." Brennan pressed a glass of water into his hand. "Here, she asked for this five minutes ago."

"Thanks, Bren," he said. "I owe you."

"Yeah, you do." Brennan turned back to his customers at the bar and Jacob started threading his way through the tables, smiling at regulars, occasionally stopping to exchange a few words with friends. In the back corner booth, Sophie's eyes were closed, a half-eaten piece of cheesecake on the table in front of her. Her hair was a loose cloud over her shoulders, only auburn in this dim light, unlike its normal fiery brilliance, and her hands were draped loosely over her belly, which in the last week or so had truly started to show. Her feet had been freed of their shoes and rested on the seat. Gently, he rubbed a knuckle over one arch until she opened her eyes.

"Hi," he said with a warm smile.

"Hi," she answered, voice sleepy. "How long was I out?"

"A few minutes," he guessed. "Sorry about the wait, Soph. We lost a line cook this afternoon and I had to do a little scrambling around."

"That's all right," she answered. "Everything okay?"

"It's fine." He took one foot in his lap and began to rub.

Sophie closed her eyes in bliss and Jacob finally began to relax, secret still safe.

"Are you alright? The baby?"

"The baby is doing the backstroke and the butterfly at the same time, but other than that, perfectly fine," Sophie told him, rubbing gentle circles with one hand. Her eyes took on that inward-looking expression that she had a lot lately.

"Soph," he called softly, repeating until she focused on him. "I don't want to sound like I'm not glad to see you, but... why are you here?"

She sighed and sat up a little straighter, taking her foot out of his hands and putting both on the floor. "I was visiting Patrick."

Inwardly, Jacob winced. But he wouldn't allow Sophie to see the expression. "How is he tonight?"

"Well enough," she said, eyes troubled. "He overdid it a bit yesterday running and is paying for it today."

"Makes two of us," Jacob said reflexively straightening and bending his sore leg. "Did he go to work today?"

Sophie nodded. "But Daddy wanted him to go to Albrecht for the auction and you can guess how well that went over."

"You think he's up for another visit?" he asked. "Maybe I can cheer him up."

"It's been three weeks, Jake," Sophie protested. "A whole truck load of clowns couldn't cheer him up."

"No, that would just scare him to death."

His attempt at humor was lost on her after the last few weeks, and her hands wrapped more protectively around her belly. He was immediately on his feet and sat beside her. "Soph, honey, I'm sorry."

She took a deep steadying breath and gave him a poor attempt at a smile. "I'm okay," she said, though she didn't look it. "And yes, I think he could use some cheering up."

"I'll go over later then," he said and slid off the seat bringing her to her feet with him. "But first let's get you to your car so you can go home and get some rest."

Sophie nestled her hand in his and allowed him to lead her outside to her little Volvo. She settled into the driver's seat, her belly taking up most of the space behind the wheel. It still amazed him how her petite frame had adapted to carry their child, and how much more it would need to grow before she reached full term. She leaned over when he bent for a kiss and then put the keys in the ignition as he closed the door. He smiled at her and took a few steps back, ignoring the light drizzle that had begun to fall, as she backed out of the parking spot and drove away.

Once her taillights faded, Jacob went back inside. He ran a relieved hand through his hair and pulled the band out. He fixed his ponytail on the way to the bar where he poured himself a stiff drink and, ignoring Brennan's curious glance, carried it to his office. He settled into his chair with a shuddering sigh and closed his eyes.

"That was too close."

It was nearly two in the morning before the last customers left, the kitchen and all the tables cleaned, and Jake could finally lock the doors and think about going home. Brennan was unloading the last load from the bar dishwasher as Jacob slid into one of the low-backed stools and put his head in one hand. Brennan reached for a bottle without looking and refilled the glass he'd taken earlier.

"Long night, huh, boss?"

Jacob tipped his head up only enough to glare at his second in command.

Brennan chuckled and pulled the two remaining glasses from the rack, wiped them dry and put them away before closing the dishwasher door with a flourish. He wiped his hands with the towel, slung it over one shoulder, and leaned forward on the bar. "It's been such a crazy night that I haven't had the chance to ask you how your patrol went."

Jacob raised his head and let his arm drop to the bar with a thump. "I feel like I'm starting to get closer to that male immortal. He left town for a while, but Nathan told me he's back again." He took a sip of his drink. "I think he's staying at The Mason, so I've been staking it out whenever I can. Saw someone going in tonight that fit the description, but you called me back here before I could get a closer look."

"Hey, I'm sorry about that, man." Brennan picked up a glass, spun it on his palm like some Eighties movie bartender and served himself a beer.

Jacob wanted to roll his eyes at the performance, but it was the non-Hunter reason he'd hired his friend as house manager in the first place. "It had to be done."

Brennan nodded his head. "I take it we're all good with Sophie?"

"Yeah, for now."

Brennan moved the cash register drawer to the bar and started counting. "What did she want?"

"She was over at Patrick's place." Jacob sighed. "I need to go over there and have a talk with him."

Brennan took a stack of bills and tapped them into a neat pile on the edge of the counter. "He could probably use the cheering up." He wrapped a slip of paper around the stack and wrote the amount with a pen.

"Yeah, maybe," Jacob replied. "I honestly still don't get it. I mean, he's acting like his heart's been broken, but I'm not sure they were ever truly dating. From what he tells me, she kept a lot to herself."

"Maybe she is just the kind of woman who gets off on stringing guys along, then breaking up with them." Brennan wrapped another stack of bills. "I'd hate to think that Pat would fall for someone like that."

Jacob considered that for a moment. Patrick had always been the type of guy to look for the good in people and that sometimes meant that he would completely miss the bad. Sometimes it worked in his favor, but often it didn't, especially with Patrick's dating history.

His mind drifted back to the first time they had met. He was twelve, and Jacob had just stepped in to rescue the scrawny new kid at school from a bunch of street kids who saw an easy target wandering around the Brooklyn slums. Little did he know that they would become such fast friends.

But the fact that Jacob came from an old Hunter family and Patrick didn't meant that there were always some things that couldn't be shared. In Brooklyn, their Hunter group operated like a street gang, well-connected and well-armed, defending their neighborhood and dealing with mortals from rival gangs as much as they hunted those that were a little harder to kill.

He'd had his first immortal kill at eighteen, and the first person he'd wanted to tell was Patrick. But that had been out of the question. Patrick had been naïve at that age, he wouldn't have understood, and even now, almost two decades later, he still wouldn't. His friend had never seen the real horrors of this world, not those you could experience on the street anyway.

Jacob left Brennan to his counting and went to his office to retrieve coat and keys. He left the restaurant and took the long route to the highway so that he could drive past Patrick's apartment. He didn't actually expect his friend to still be up at this hour, but as he passed the building, there were lights still on in the penthouse. Deciding that now was just as good a time as any, Jacob parked his car on the side street and let himself in the residents-only back door. He took the stairs and knocked on Patrick's door only a little out of breath from the six-floor climb.

It took a while, but finally the door opened.

Seventeen

He could sense her, but he couldn't see her yet.

Alasdair idly swirled his glass of whisky and waited. The day was beautiful. A slight breeze, bright sunshine, perfect for a crisp October day. In weather like this, he could stay outside all day and all night and not care.

Finally, Morgana rounded the corner to his right from the parking lot. Her eyes scanned the patio as she tucked her keys into her purse, finally coming to rest on him.

He smiled and she returned it, more brightly that he would have suspected given the circumstances.

She was dressed casually, but elegantly, in jeans and a form-fitting emerald sweater. Her ankle boots were high-heeled and painful looking, but they suited her lean figure nicely. Yet the circles under her eyes, visible through her light makeup, told him that she hadn't been sleeping well, and her hair was in a single, simple braid instead of its normal elaborate pinning.

He rose to pull back her chair.

She settled in and he motioned to the waiter to order her a drink. A silence stretched between them until she turned and aimed an irritated look in his direction. "What?"

He shrugged and sipped his drink idly while they waited for her wine, which appeared a moment later. It was a deep garnet red, an expensive French Bordeaux that he knew she liked. Morgana raised the glass and Alasdair tapped his into it with a clink.

Looking at her, he second-guessed going back to San Francisco again so soon. Work was starting to pile up, but she wasn't quite back to her old self. Plus, she would never admit that she needed help from anyone. She'd lived the definition of a solitary life, depending only on herself. But now the thought that she might not need to go it alone quite frankly terrified her.

She would admit to being scared only after she asked him for help. Which was why he had been forced to take matters into his own hands.

"I read about the Martin sale in the papers," he said hoping to get a reaction out of the Morgana-shaped statue sitting beside him. "Six point five million in just over an hour is no chump change."

Morgana just shrugged and reached for one of the menus propped up in the center of the table. Her face was passive, but he hoped that by bringing up the auction, her mind would dwell on the events immediately before it.

"The estate of a tycoon like Charles Martin, newspaper mogul who built half of this city? That's no yard sale, darling," he continued. Morgana simply made a noncommittal noise and continued to look for something to order.

Alasdair reached over and took the menu from her hands which remained frozen in place. It took a moment, but her hands pressed flat to the glass tabletop and her gaze turned in his direction. Her green eyes were simply curious.

"Are you going to order for us both then?"

"I'll order you something greasy and American that will clot your innards like a plug." Morgana made a face and Alasdair had to laugh. Her lips twitched once, twice, as she fought and lost the urge to smile. *Was that a chuckle too?*

"There, that wasn't all that hard," he said, flicking a playful finger down her nose. She nipped at his hand, and he pulled back sharply, but she was grinning. He motioned to the waiter who had just brought fresh drinks to a nearby table.

"Yes sir?" He pulled a pad from his apron.

"You order me a hamburger and you're a dead man," Morgana warned him in French under her breath. The ice in her voice enough to freeze a lesser man.

"I'm quite pleased to have my head attached, thank you." He said cheerfully in English. "*I'll* have the burger; she'll have the Cajun chicken Caesar salad."

The waiter looked nervously at Morgana for confirmation, at her crossed arms and eyes shooting daggers while he took their orders. But she nodded in approval. He offered to bring them new drinks and tried not to look like he was running away.

"Adding scaring off waiters to your list of talents?" He asked wryly.

"Ha-ha," she muttered, voice dripping with sarcasm. Then she shook her head a little and the look disappeared. "I guess the auction went pretty well," she finally admitted, brushing a stray wisp of hair behind one ear. "Some of the artwork went for more than one and a half times over reserve. There was one lacquered jewelry box that I wanted for myself. It went for fifteen hundred dollars! Real rubies and sapphires in the lid."

He could almost see her salivating. This was the Morgana he knew, the woman who had passion for the job she did that could talk antiques until she was blue, then purple, in the face. As she was doing now. But the mercurial mood shifts only heightened his concern for her.

Alasdair could hold his own only so far and soon he was forced to sit back, munch at the fries on his just-delivered plate, and listen to her excited babble about furniture, paintings, and books.

She ate as she talked, taking bites of salad between descriptions of items, their asking and selling prices. He fought back a smile for a long time, but in the end, he was grinning like an idiot.

"Now what?"

"I could count on one hand the number of breaths you've taken in the last five minutes."

She actually blushed.

He could count on one hand the number of times *that* had happened in all the years he'd known her.

She covered it nicely with a nonchalant sip of her wine. "Thanks for this, Ally," she said and the pure happiness in her voice was enough to excuse the use of that horrid name. "I haven't been up to doing much of anything for the last month or so."

The "so" being the last time she had spoken to Patrick at Albrecht right before the Martin Estate Auction. A brush-off that he had taken for a breakup, ending a relationship that had never truly begun. But given the fact that he hadn't reached out since, it had saved her the trouble of saying it in so many words. Not that it saved her the heartache or agony. Discretely, Alasdair checked his pocket watch under the table.

One raised auburn brow said he hadn't been all that subtle. "You have somewhere to be?"

"Nowhere, love," he said with a chuckle that was more than a little forced. His appointment was due here at any moment.

Movement across the patio caught his eye as a tall figure wound through the restaurant toward them. Morgana would thank him later, Alasdair repeated in his head almost like a mantra. But he couldn't help the little niggling sliver of guilt from ambushing her like this.

Morgana continued to sip her wine, unaware of Alasdair's plans for her. When Patrick stepped out of the restaurant, her head went up like a rabbit catching the scent of a fox on the breeze.

Her wide eyes went to Alasdair's face and then slowly she turned.

Their eyes met and held, and Alasdair wondered again why she was fighting so hard.

Or maybe now, seeing them together, he understood.

The mortal's face, so drawn and closed as he approached, brightened as if a lantern had been lit. He was a handsome man, tall with broad, muscular shoulders, though a little on the thin side, with hair that was every shade between ginger and crimson. His blue eyes were bright as jewels and trained on Morgana.

Alasdair wished that he could see more of her face, but what he could see told him that she was dangerously close to falling over that slippery edge, even after making up her mind that she wouldn't, and she was fighting it with all her will.

Good thing she had him to give her a little push.

Morgana couldn't think, couldn't breathe. For a moment there, her heart could have stopped too. But then it started again and pounded in her throat. Her eyes met Patrick's across the patio; met and held and she couldn't look away for a single moment.

He didn't smile, but he moved across the space between them with a determined step, still holding her eyes. When he bumped into a waiter and was forced to look away, Morgana found that she had the ability to move again and turned back to her meal, only to find that her appetite had deserted her.

Alasdair got to his feet and motioned to the waiter and handed him more money than was necessary for their meals, telling him to keep the change. It was probably a bigger tip than he had ever seen, and his eyes grew large and round. He thanked Alasdair profusely and hurried off.

All this Morgana noted with a kind of detachment as if she was off to the side observing the whole scene.

Then he bent to kiss her cheek and his whispered words broke through. "Remember what I asked of you? Whatever you feel, embrace it as real. Don't back away."

She was too shocked to answer and simply nodded woodenly.

"I'll call you when I land."

Before she could protest, Patrick reached the table and Morgana was aware of nothing but him.

"Alasdair Bromley?" He dug in his pocket and pulled out a slip of paper. "I got your note."

Morgana's head whipped around to look at her friend with an accusing look.

He ignored her. "Ah yes, you must be Patrick."

They shook hands and little else was said. There was a moment of unspoken communication as if they were sizing each other up and found the other worthy. Of what, Morgana didn't know, something male that she wasn't supposed to know about no doubt. Then Alasdair gave a slight nod, kissed Morgana's cheek again, and left.

Patrick stood for a moment as if debating what to do next. Morgana sat and waited; her salad forgotten on the table in front of her. Finally, he made up his mind and he took the chair Alasdair had vacated.

"You're looking well, Morgana." His voice, that silky, deep timbre, flowed over her skin. She pushed back at the little voice in her ear that was telling her that she was acting like an idiot.

"And you," she responded. "How have you been?"

He raised his eyebrow for a split second. "I've been busy," he said. "My father has kept me running around. I was in the Toronto branch last week overseeing a few things and I only got back yesterday."

"Toronto," she said, a slight wistfulness to her voice. "I lived there for a few years." Several times, once when it was still a collection of trappers huts and a French outpost.

"You mentioned that, I think." He raised his arm and gestured to the waiter who brought him some iced tea. He took a sip and then another longer one, downing the whole glass in long, deep swallows as if he hadn't had a drop all day. He caught her look and smiled. "No time to stop for anything."

She nodded. The air between them thrummed like a plucked guitar string and one end was attached to her chest. Her mind drifted back to that day at Albrecht. All morning, she'd agonized over what to say to him, whether the decision she'd made was the right one. Whether or not she would be able to face him and keep to that decision. And then, as her thoughts had summoned him, he had shown up at her office.

And now, he was just across the table. She stiffened her spine and took another sip of wine. She was not some hormone-driven teenager incapable of having an intelligent conversation with a man. No, she was an immortal, capable of holding her own with bullets flying in her direction. Matters of the heart should be easier than that.

And yet they weren't.

"I think we need to talk about this," Patrick said finally. His thoughts had obviously gone in the same direction.

"Look, Patrick, that day at Albrecht..." Morgana started to say, then her voice failed her, and she had to take a deep breath before continuing. "I was having a really bad day; the auction was stressing me out and then you came in."

"And you brushed me off like lint on your coat."

"Yes." She winced. "No. Don't get me wrong. When I told you I was busy, I meant that I had things to do. That auction was one of our biggest, but I was ill prepared and couldn't afford the distraction."

Patrick cracked a wry smile. "Kissing me was a distraction?"

"One I didn't need at the time." *And still don't*, she finished to herself. "But I did mismanage the way I asked you to leave." The words rang truer than she would have liked, and she rubbed the dull ache that was forming in the middle of her forehead. It wasn't exactly what she had intended to say.

It was hard to see that cautious look of hope in his blue eyes and not smile reassuringly. Her hand itched to reach out and touch the one he rested on the table beside his glass, palm turned up as if in invitation.

"But our time apart has given me some time to think."

"Me too. Morgana--"

She held up a hand. "Please let me say this while its fresh in my mind."

He snapped his mouth closed and settled back in his chair.

Morgana brushed at a wisp of hair on her cheek and took another deep, steadying breath. "I have a very solitary life, Patrick. It's always been my choice and I wouldn't have it any other way. The short time we spent together showed me what I could have, but also what I can't afford."

Patrick opened his mouth to protest, but she stilled him with two fingers on his lips.

"I lead a busy, complicated life and I can't complicate it any further. Much as I would like to." She hadn't meant to say that last bit out loud, but she couldn't take it back now that it was out.

Patrick gently wrapped his fingers around her wrist, touching a pulse point that suddenly jumped and skittered. There was a deep glow in his eyes, a warning light that meant that he was as serious as she. "Well then, let me give you my perspective on this." His tone was the very definition of patience.

"No woman has captivated me the way you have. I'm almost ashamed to admit how I have had to force myself to get up and go to work, to go on with my day-to-day life as if everything is normal and you having forgotten about me." Patrick fingered her pulse and then raised her hand to kiss the palm.

Then, suddenly, she was free, her hand falling back to the table. Her fingers curled of their own accord, as if to hold on to the warmth of his lips a little longer.

A corner of his lip turned up. "What I don't understand –and maybe you can help me here—is that you seem to want to *complicate* what is really quite a simple thing."

"Patrick--"

"My turn," he told her sharply, inviting no argument. "The way *I* see it, when you have this kind of chemistry with someone, you should see where it goes. It's very natural. Easy even."

Morgana picked up her wine and took a sip that turned into a gulp, and tried to deny that his words struck a chord.

"And I know that I haven't been the easiest person to get a hold of either." Patrick said when she remained silent; a hint of his usual warmth coming into his voice. "I'd like to think that there is more here than a couple of kisses spread way too far apart. So, at the risk of being rejected again, maybe we can take things slow. See where they lead."

Alasdair's words echoed in her ears as Patrick's began to sink in. *Don't turn away.*

"I can't," she said on a sigh, the two hardest words she'd ever said, and got to her feet.

Patrick rose too, gritting his teeth as he levered himself slowly to his feet.

Morgana made a mental note of it as she opened her purse, then remembered that Alasdair had already paid. She snapped it shut and walked from the patio directly into the adjacent city park. Hopefully, a stroll along the small lake in the growing twilight was all she needed to clear her head.

Not likely with him following at a respectful distance.

It had been more than two hundred years since her pulse had quickened in the presence of a man, had a rush of heat burrow into her from a gentle touch. Running for your life every few years was not conducive to a lasting relationship, she reminded herself. It had always been her justification, but now it just felt like a hollow excuse.

If she was determined to finally put down roots here for the first time in her life, why not have the other thing too?

Morgana battled with that thought. Over the centuries, she had never once revealed her secret to the few men she'd allowed into her bed. But none had managed to work their way through the iron-clad defenses she'd constructed around her heart.

With one kiss, the light of a bonfire flickering over her eyelids and his strong arms around her, Patrick had broken through like an arrow to a target. And now, with him only a few feet away, she was finding it impossible to do anything but wish that he would hold her in his arms again. Halfway around the lake, she stopped, rested her hands on the back of a vacant bench, and admired the bright autumn leaves reflected in the still water.

He kept a respectful distance and waited.

A large white duck swam slowly across the water, blurring the reflection with the ripples in its wake. Its mate swam sedately behind, but was slowly catching up. Morgana watched them, absorbed in the beauty of it. Her heart wasn't racing anymore, but neither was it back to normal. So too had her thoughts stopped spinning, but even then, her head and her heart were still at odds.

The warmth of his suit coat settled over her shoulders. Reflexively, she tugged it tight around her, and tried not to be obvious as she breathed in his scent where it clung to the lapels. Then his hands settled on her shoulders, exerting only enough pressure to suggest that she turn around.

The actual motion, she had to do on her own.

His dress shirt clung to his shoulders, top button and tie loosened at the throat. His hair, so stiffly combed when he'd arrived at the restaurant, had been blown wild in the breeze while they'd walked. A lock of fiery hair hung in his eyes giving him a casually rakish look that reminded Morgana of how young he really was. His hands slid up the sides of her throat to frame her face. "Morgana," he murmured, his voice deep and tender. "Please don't turn away. Talk to me."

The similarity to Alasdair's words sent a shiver through her, though he couldn't have heard their whispered exchange. One thumb was absently stroking her cheekbone, his eyes intent on her face.

Morgana closed her eyes against the sweetness of the gesture and the sudden sting of impending tears. She sighed deeply and opened them.

Whatever he saw in her eyes pleased him, for he smiled, and took a step forward to place a gentle kiss on her forehead. It was Morgana who reached up to cover one of his hands so that he would look down at her.

Following her good friend's advice, Morgana gave him a small smile and brought his lips to hers. Her eyes fluttered closed as warmth spread to the tips of her fingers, the soles of her feet. She brought her arms around his neck as he drew her closer until she was unable to tell where one body ended and the other began. It should have bothered her, kissing in such a public place, but the rest of the world could end around them and she'd still be kissing him.

Patrick finally drew back and rested his forehead against hers, their breath mingling. Neither spoke for a long time, it wasn't necessary.

Morgana's heart swelled, only now realizing how empty it had been, and never wanted it to be that way again.

"I've missed you, Morgana," he whispered. "These last few weeks have been an eternity."

She nodded in agreement as he drew her in, resting her head on his shoulder. Her emotions were swirling, but were rapidly settling into a kind of contentment that sent a different kind of shock rippling through her. A moment later, she raised her head and smiled at him.

His answering smile was broad, the dimples stark in each cheek, eyes bright as blue flame.

She eased back and took his hand. "Take a walk with me?"

They wandered in no particular direction, around the lake, up and down secluded paths, stopping occasionally for a quick embrace, a deep kiss in the shadows. Eventually they stepped back out into the city, lit now by the soft amber glow of streetlights, strolling aimlessly down streets full of boutiques, closed at this hour, their windows lit and decorated to invite patrons to return. The cafes were still open at this hour though, their patios bursting with people, kept warm with gas-powered torches.

Pausing to examine a display, Patrick muttered something about there already being Christmas decorations up and it not yet Halloween. Morgana laughed and gave him a playful swat on the arm. They strolled on, stopping at an old-fashioned toy store. Dim lights illuminated a large Ferris wheel made from a brightly colored connector set, still now for the night. Old wooden puzzles were strewn about. Little dolls on unicycles balanced on thin wires along the top of the display.

"I would have loved toys like this when I was little," she said before she could stop herself. As a child, Morgana's toys had been sticks and stones picked up from the ground, a doll fashioned out of wood or straw.

"Really?" Patrick asked as if she'd revealed some deep, personal secret. "Yeah, I love this old-fashioned stuff. Kids these days with their video games... it's a shame, really, that all this stuff is dying out."

"You sound like an old man when you talk that way," Morgana chided him, squeezing his arm.

"Well, I'm only three years older than you. Or is it four?"

"Come now, Patrick, don't you know that you never ask a woman her age?" Her voice was light, but inside, guilt swirled through her at not being completely honest with him. "But in any case, its three." At least for her current back story. If Patrick knew the truth, his eyes would go as wide as the jack-in-the-box in the window.

A quick flash of red in the glass caught her attention. She searched the reflection of the building behind them, resisting the urge to turn around. There, in the shadows of an upper floor fire escape across the street, was a lone figure. Morgana's heart began to pound, her muscles tensing for the fight that could be coming.

Patrick looked over at her.

She only hoped that whoever it was wouldn't attack her while she was still with him. The only weapon she had was a small collapsible knife hidden in her purse. The heels of her boots would do nothing but slow her down.

"You, okay?"

"Fine," she replied. "Come on."

As they continued on, she glanced up over her shoulder. The figure stepped out of the shadows and leaned on the rail. He had a gun dangling casually from one hand, the laser sight, off now, affixed to the barrel. Her eyes traveled up the black leather jacket, but the face was in shadow, the hair covered with a hat or hood. His expression was unreadable at this distance, but if she had to guess, he was feeling smug.

Patrick stumbled as their joined hands forced him to a sudden stop. He tugged gently on her hand, gaze trying to follow hers, but the figure had retreated into the shadows. But he wasn't gone, his eyes were like a weight pressing down on her.

Morgana met Patrick's concerned look and smiled in reassurance as she slid her hand into the crease of his elbow. "The moon came out from behind a cloud for a moment. It was very beautiful."

He nodded and led her away.

"I'm getting a little cold," she admitted, though she still had Patrick's jacket around her shoulders. He must be freezing.

As they turned the corner, Morgana realized the parking lot ahead was the one where she had left her car that afternoon, though they were approaching it from the opposite direction. She released his hand to dig for her keys as they crossed the lot to her little black Audi.

"Drive me back to my office?" Patrick asked. "I left my car there."

Morgana nodded and unlocked the doors with the press of a button. By the second or third turn, it was clear that they were headed nowhere near Davies & McNamara, but he didn't say a word. When she parked in the garage across from her building, there was a split second to decide whether or not she was doing the right thing.

Knowing her address and going inside her apartment were two very different things. Her home was the one place she was safe. If she let him inside, she would be risking everything.

Those thoughts and all others scattered when she took one look at Patrick.

"Are you sure about this?" His voice was deep and oddly husky.

Morgana pushed open her door and put her feet out. When she didn't hear the other door open, she turned back to see Patrick still watching. Still waiting.

She didn't smile, but simply met his gaze. "Come with me."

Eighteen

The night had started out warm with a slight breeze, but had grown cool, almost cold by the time Jacob emerged from the stifling kitchen of *Sophie's*. But the chill was welcome, at first anyway. He glanced around the delivery bay as he shrugged into his jacket. A bus boy leaned against a stack of crates on a smoke break, his face dimly lit by the screen of his cell phone as he scrolled through a news feed. Otherwise, the alleyway was quiet and deserted.

The busboy looked up from his phone at the sound of Jacob's footsteps. He respectfully redirecting a stream of smoke out the corner of his mouth. "Hey, boss."

Jacob nodded in acknowledgement and walked down the steps that led from the loading dock to the service alley. A half block down, and out of sight of the restaurant, he reached for a fire escape ladder and carefully started to climb, avoiding the usual squeaky areas in the eighty-year-old cast iron treads.

The four flights of stairs made for a good warmup for his legs, grown stiff from sitting at his desk doing the books all night. He scaled the ladder that covered the last dozen feet and crossed the roof to the side that faced the front of the restaurant. If he leaned out, he'd see the valet stand, but the marquee for the vintage movie theater below him was too bright to do that without giving away his position.

The low murmur of conversation at street level rose as a movie let out beneath him and the crowd merged with the already considerable foot traffic. Many were smiling, talking, and gesturing excitedly. It must have been a good film. He wracked his brain for what was currently playing. Some action film with the latest musician turned actor, he thought, with surprisingly good reviews. Seeing the reactions below, he made a mental note to call Patrick in the morning and get him out for some fun.

Tonight wasn't a night for hunting, though his gun was in its holster at the small of his back and he'd traded dress shoes for black sneakers. Under his jacket was a white button down and dress pants.

Tonight, he just needed to clear his head and he always did his best thinking from high up.

He turned away from the glowing lights and made his way across the string of buildings, most of which were attached. Those that weren't only had narrow gaps a foot or two feet wide, easily crossed.

The restaurant was booked almost every night. The bar did a roaring trade this time of year, with the hockey season just starting at the arena down the street, and an ever-rotating menu of signature brilliance mixed up by Brennan and his staff for the more discerning crowd in the lounge. The bookwork contributed to some of the mental fatigue, but it also occupied much of his time, grounding him when everything else was uncertain.

Sophie and the baby were doing well as could be expected, but each doctor's appointment brought more and more restrictions, with a little less than two months to go. Not soon enough for him since the less she was allowed to do, the more she fought against the doctor's orders. She was working from home now, and that only increased her restlessness even as it kept her occupied. Jacob smiled, remembering the night before and his wife's look when he brought dinner to her on a tray, and the sigh she had blown out with enough force to lift her bangs from her face.

"You used to love getting breakfast in bed." He'd told her.

She'd scowled. "Yeah, when it was rare, and spontaneous, and romantic." She'd put her hands to the swell of her belly and sighed. "Not when it's every meal, and I'm confined to this bed when I'm perfectly able to cook for myself."

He'd laughed and left her to eat. No use arguing when she was in this kind of mood, and no amount of pleasant conversation would be seen as anything other than platitudes. Jacob laughed again to himself as he shook free of the memory, reaching the end of the row of buildings. He glanced down at the brick pedestrian-only street below. A webbing of lights stretched between the rooftops, looking like so many stars even on the cloudiest nights.

There was a glint of copper below as a couple, both with hair in shades of red caught the light. Jacob recognized his friend's figure almost immediately, and a reflexive shiver went through him at the sight of him down to his dress shirt. He located Patrick's jacket, wrapped tightly around the shoulders of the petite woman beside him that could only be Morgana.

He would have laughed at how the jacket hung almost to her knees, had it not been for the fact that they were holding hands. Last he'd heard, she had kicked him out of her office, and they hadn't talked for almost a month.

Curiosity piqued, he followed them. Patrick had a slight hitch in his stride, though it would be unnoticeable to anyone who didn't know him very well. And Morgana didn't seem to notice as they moved from window to window, studying the displays.

They paused for some time in front of an old-fashioned toy store, heads bent close together, as they pointed at the Ferris wheel and other toys inside. Morgana laughed at something he said, and his arm came around her shoulders, drew her close for a kiss.

Jacob couldn't look away, but his hand twitched with impatience. A moment later, they separated, sharing a smile, gazes locked.

Patrick turned to continue up the street, but Morgana froze when a quick flash of red light reflected in the glass. His friend stumbled to a stop a moment later when she didn't follow.

Jacob's eyes narrowed. He moved a step closer to the edge of the roof, but the flash didn't repeat. After a moment, she responded to Patrick's tug on her hand. Her head turned as she started to move on down the street.

He cursed under his breath as her gaze fixed on the building where he stood and retreated slowly.

How strange that her first choice was to look up...

But her eyes seemed to be fixed below where he was standing. Jacob stepped forward again to peer down. Before he could reach the edge, a familiar figure dressed all in black emerged onto the roof from the fire escape.

The stranger didn't immediately see Jacob standing in the shadow of an air vent only a few feet away. It took only a few quick steps to close the distance and tackle the stranger to the ground. They rolled, sending gravel scattering in all directions.

Jacob batted away the hand that reached for his gun and held it over the man's head, his forearm pressed against his throat to pin him to the ground.

"We need to stop meeting like this."

Jacob glanced around for the stranger's weapon and found it a few feet away. It was out of reach for both of them, so he left it there.

The man tried to sit up and Jacob punched him backdown.

The stranger coughed and turned his head to spit out a mouthful of blood but didn't try to move again. "What the hell, man?"

With the help of the light filtering up from the street, Jacob could make out his features for the first time. He had a sharp nose and deep-set dark eyes along with a dark goatee. "Who are you?"

Instead of introducing himself, the man studied his face. "You're Jacob Martel, aren't you?"

"Depends on who is asking," Jacob replied. "Why were you following my friend?"

"Who?"

"Patrick Davies." He increased the pressure on the stranger's throat. "Why were you following him?"

The stranger tried to rear up and headbutt him, but Jacob was just out of range. He earned a slam back down to the gravel for his trouble. The corner of his mouth turned up at the grunt the man let out. "Want to try that again?"

The stranger glared at him. "Look man, I don't know any Patrick."

"Then why were you following him?"

"I wasn't following *him*."

"Then who?"

"The woman with him."

Jacob hadn't expected that. "Morgana?" he asked and cursed that he couldn't quite keep the surprise from his voice. "What would you want with her?"

The guy bucked his hips to try to roll Jacob off of him.

"Knock it off," he warned cocking one fist back. "Last time. What do you want with Morgana? She's not anyone important, just some auction house manager."

The stranger laughed, surprising him, his lips pulled back in a smile that showed teeth outlined with blood. "And here I thought you were the best Hunter in Western Canada."

Jacob scowled at him, but the stranger must have seen the realization dawning in his eyes.

"Yeah, dumbass, I'm one of you," he said. "Will you let me up now?"

Jacob considered hitting him again just for fun but got to his feet and went to retrieve the other man's gun.

The stranger got up slowly and spat again, then wiped his face with the back of one hand. "Name's Schaffer, by the way. John Schaffer."

The name didn't ring any bells but it sure as hell was the first thing that Jacob was looking up when he got back to the office.

"What do you want with Morgana?"

"I really have to spell it out for you?" Schaffer replied, giving him an incredulous look. "Auction manager, huh? Well, can't blame her for choosing a profession like that."

When Jacob continued to stare blankly at him, that cocky smirk returned. "Alrighty then..." he murmured, then made sure to say his next words slowly, as if talking to a child. "She's not who, or rather what, she says she is."

Jacob was silent for a long moment. "You mean to tell me she's an immortal?"

"Ding ding ding!"

Rage boiled through him. "You do remember that I'm holding your gun, don't you?" He adjusted his grip on the gun but kept his finger off the trigger. "And that you're trespassing in my city?"

Schaffer held up his hands, but didn't apologize. "Not my fault you've had her right in front of you and couldn't figure it out."

"How did *you*?"

"Remember that night that you caught me on the rooftop a couple weeks ago?" Schaffer asked.

Jacob's eyes widened.

Schaffer sketched the same sarcastic salute he'd given that night. "Yeah, that was me." he said. "Anyway, after you so rudely interrupted me, I went back up on the roofs on the other side of the canal and followed her. She got mugged by some street punk, but still managed to scare him off. He dropped his gun when he ran, but not before he shot her in the thigh."

"And she healed?"

The other Hunter nodded. "Confirmed what I already suspected. And man, she stripped that gun faster than I've seen anyone do it and dumped the pieces in the trash before heading home. And with barely a limp."

If Jacob wasn't mistaken, Schaffer was impressed.

"I ran out of roof trying to follow her home, but I saw the direction she went. My guess is she lives only a couple blocks from that gym, given that she was on foot. I was keeping a pretty close eye on her tonight until you showed up." Schaffer glanced down at the street below, but Patrick and Morgana were long gone. "Who's the guy with her?"

"My best friend."

Schaffer had the gall to laugh. "How is it possible that you didn't figure it out?"

"I've only met her a couple of times."

This guy was really not giving him a good reason not to shoot him. *And people say I'm arrogant?*

He certainly wasn't going to admit that one of those visits had been at his own house. At the thought, a different kind of fury burned down his spine, but he forced his voice to remain neutral. "Everything else I know about her comes to me through Patrick. He said she wasn't very forthcoming with information and seemed on edge a lot of the time, especially after our first meeting at my restaurant."

As he said it, it all made sense. Her nervousness around him at the restaurant. At his house.

His house.

A memory of Morgana alone in the upstairs hallway rose up. She'd told him she'd left her phone behind in the library. He stamped a foot in frustration before he could stop himself.

Schaffer chuckled. "I'm guessing that the pieces are starting to fit together."

With a sigh, Jacob took a step toward the other Hunter. He raised the gun and pointed it at Schaffer. Just as the other Hunter started to stiffen and raise his hands, Jacob flipped the gun, grasping the barrel this time and held it out to him.

Schaffer eyed him warily for a moment, then reached out and took the gun back. He flicked the safety on and slid it into the holster on his thigh.

"So, what is your plan?"

The answering smile was more like a smirk. "Still working on it," he replied. "But I'll work together if you're willing."

Jacob still needed to assimilate all of this new information, but he certainly wasn't going to let this guy run around his city unchecked anymore. So, he stuck out his hand.

After a moment, Schaffer took it in a brief, but firm shake.

Jacob reached into the inside pocket of his jacket and pulled out a business card for the restaurant. "You can reach me here. If I'm not there, ask for Brennan. He's my house manager, but he's also my Second."

Schaffer nodded and pocketed the card. "I'll be in touch." He crossed to the fire escape on the other side of the building, and paused, hand poised on the looped railing. "No hard feelings, right?"

"Sure," Jacob muttered. "Just keep me in the loop from now on, okay? You're on my territory. I'm willing to forgive the last however long you've been here, but going forward, full transparency, or there will be issues."

"Works for me," Schaffer replied, and sketched another sarcastic salute. "Nice to meet you, Jacob Martel. Be seeing you around."

He disappeared down the ladder.

Jacob stood still in the middle of the roof grinding his teeth. He wanted to punch something. He wanted to scream. If he hadn't already had an issue with Morgana before for playing with his friend's heart...

A memory clicked in place, and he froze.

"She couldn't have…"

He'd checked the office, and nothing was out of place. Could she possibly have had enough time to get into the computer?

Jacob dashed for the ladder Schaffer had just used and hurried back to ground level. But there was no sign of the other Hunter. He cursed and kicked a can laying at his feet. It careened into a dumpster with a clang and rattled away down the street.

Nineteen

Morgana woke with the sun in her eyes. She closed them tightly against it and rolled over, stretching an arm across the bed to find that the other side was empty. She sat up straight, clutching the sheets to her chest, unsure if it had all been a dream.

A loud crash had her bolting out of bed. Wrapping up in a robe, Morgana retrieved a small throwing dagger from the top drawer of her dresser and eased the door as quietly as she could. She gripped the knife and made her way slowly up the hallway, bare feet silent on the thick carpeted runner. Just outside the kitchen, she caught a familiar shock of red hair and paused to deposit the dagger in the floral arrangement on the hall table just outside the living area. She'd retrieve it later.

Patrick had his back to her, working at the stove. He was bare-chested, wearing only his dress pants with no belt, his feet bare on the cold tile. There was a streak of white across the counter and one of her mixing bowls lay shattered on the floor near the sink, the source of the crash.

She leaned on the door jamb, arms crossed, and watched him with an amused smile playing on her lips. It wasn't every day that there was someone other than her in her kitchen, let alone an attractive man cooking her breakfast.

Patrick continued whatever he was doing at the stove unaware that she was even awake. He turned to the island that stood in the middle of the kitchen for a platter and finally caught sight of her. He yelped in surprise, then pain, as he jumped back directly onto the broken pottery on the floor. The platter dropped to the island where it wobbled noisily for a moment before settling.

Morgana rushed past him while he hopped away and reached the pan of bacon just as it was starting to smoke.

"Watch the floor," he warned, bending to remove a shard of porcelain from his heel.

"I can see that," she chuckled, and passed him a kitchen towel. She turned back to the stove to find a second pan with small rounds of half-cooked batter.

Pancakes. He had been making her pancakes.

She picked up the spatula and flipped them over.

His arms came around her, and he drew her back to nuzzle her neck.

Electricity zinged up and down her spine as his mouth found a particularly sensitive spot behind her ear. "Did you sleep well?"

"What man could sleep with such a beautiful woman in his arms?" he replied. "I didn't mean to wake you."

"You didn't. The crash just got me out of bed." She turned in his arms so that she could put her arms around his neck and resisted the urge to wince. Only moments ago, she'd been prepared to throw a knife at him. "This is very thoughtful."

Patrick grinned and bent to kiss her. It started light and sweet, a soft brush of his lips on hers. He changed angles and deepened the kiss, his tongue sweeping against hers. His hands tightened into fists at the back of her robe, drawing it up her thighs until his hands were gripping her bare hips.

A now-familiar heat was beginning to build deep inside. She yelped in surprise against his lips as his hands tightened and he lifted her onto the island. Her legs locked around his waist, pinning his hips tightly to hers.

His hand eased the robe from her shoulders as he nibbled his way down the side of her neck.

Morgana's head fell back, her hands buried in his hair as his lips made their way to her breasts. Fire swept through her as he drew a nipple into the heat of his mouth while his hands skimmed up her inner thighs, gently pressing her legs even wider apart. She dragged his lips back to hers, needing to taste him again.

The smell of smoke broke them apart. Patrick cursed as he stepped on more broken pottery in his haste to get to the burning pancakes.

Morgana slid off the island onto shaky legs and straightened her robe, dragging in deep gulps of air to slow her racing heart. She grabbed a towel and gathered up the shards, dumping them into the garbage. One piece the size of a pea lodged in her thumb making her suck in her breath.

"What is it?" Patrick asked over his shoulder.

"Nothing," she responded pulling it free. A drop of blood welled up, but by the time she wiped it off on the towel, the wound was healed.

Patrick wasn't so lucky. He favored the injured heel as he came over to dump the ruined breakfast into the trash then dropped the pan in the sink with a clatter. It hissed when he turned on the water.

Morgana finished with the bowl and rose, running one hand through her sleep tussled curls to get them out of her eyes.

"I'm not very good at breakfast," Patrick admitted sheepishly, standing in the middle of the room with his hands in his pockets. Going by the heat that returned to his eyes, he had placed them there to resist the urge to grab her again. "Pancakes are usually about all I can manage. And it seems like I can't even do that today."

"Don't worry about it," Morgana said, touched by the fact that he had even tried, that he had stayed the night and hadn't snuck away after she'd fallen asleep. "But no offense, I don't think my kitchen could take you making another batch. These will have to do." She carried the platter of cooked pancakes to the table, telling him where to find plates and silverware, butter, and syrup.

For Morgana, breakfast was the meal most likely to be skipped. Coffee and croissants from the café across the street from Albrecht were usually the order of the day.

After a few moments, Patrick came up with half a bottle of slightly crystallized syrup out of the back of the fridge and joined her. They shared the cold breakfast teasing and laughing as if they had no care in the world other than to be together. When they were done, and in complete agreement that it was the worst breakfast either had ever had, Morgana took the plates to the sink and began to load the dishwasher while Patrick started a fresh pot of coffee, then tackled the flour covered counter.

Morgana glanced over to see him still leaning heavily to one side. "Foot still bothering you?" It had been so long since she had been bothered by such a simple injury for more than a few minutes. He would be feeling that simple cut on his heel for at least a week. It made her wish that her healing ability extended to healing others.

"It's nothing," Patrick said dismissively as he swept the flour into the garbage he held under the lip of the counter. "Penance for not cleaning up the bowl when it first fell, and then getting *distracted*." He put the bin down and turned, bracing his hands on the counter behind him and watched her, standing casually with his ankles crossed.

Morgana finished loading the dishwasher and closed the door, brushing the curtain of hair back again as she straightened. "A distraction, am I?" The intensity of his gaze had her strolling across the room, placing one hand on either side of his hips. He leaned down and captured her lips.

He pulled back a moment later, one hand now buried in her hair, their bodies pressed close. "So much for taking things slow, huh?" he asked against her lips.

Morgana put her forehead on his chest and laughed.

He put his arms around her waist and just held her.

After a moment she eased back. "I don't know about you, but I have to get to work."

"Work?" Patrick asked as if he had forgotten what that was. Then his head snapped up and whipped around looking for a clock. Not finding one on the walls, he looked back at her. "Wait, what time is it?"

Morgana smiled and pointed at the microwave. "It's almost ten."

"I'm so late!" He cried as he hobbled back to the bedroom.

Morgana followed and leaned on the door frame with a smile playing on her lips as he dug for his shirt, tie, and shoes from the pile of discarded clothing.

"For work?"

"Um… yeah," he said distractedly. "I have to get to work." He brushed past her with a brief kiss, now fully clothed, and headed for the door. He passed the locked door that held the chronicles and stopped. "What's in there?"

"The crown jewels," she answered with a joking smile on her lips that hid the fear suddenly tingling through her.

"No, honestly," he said.

"I have some very old and valuable antiques in my own personal collection." She crossed the room and pushed him toward the door with a chuckle. "And you have to get going so I can go get ready."

He went reluctantly with a parting kiss. Morgana leaned on the door jamb and watched until he got in the elevator, then closed the door and leaned on it, legs suddenly weak. Now alone, the immensity of the last twenty-four hours finally hit her.

"*Mon dieu*," she said to herself.

There hadn't been a doubt in her mind, from the moment she'd put the car in park, that her life would be different. She had allowed Patrick into her apartment, into her bed, where they'd fallen into an exhausted slumber sometime just before dawn. She'd half expected to wake in the morning and find that it had been nothing but a very erotic dream.

Then, burning food had been the only thing that had stopped them from having sex again right there on the kitchen island. Her cheeks heated at the thought. There were no regrets, not really. But she *had* broken a promise to herself that had endured for centuries. Her home was sacred, only Alasdair and Fred had been inside in decades.

And now a Hunter may have been inside.

She closed her eyes. Why was she fighting so hard to poison the feelings she had for him?

No Hunter could be that gentle, that caring and tender with someone that they were sworn to kill. Back in her room, the rumpled sheets, the duvet on the floor, brought to mind exactly what they'd shared in that bed. A thrill went through her at the memory, but she reluctantly forced it away.

And if he isn't a Hunter?

Her usual justification rang a little hollower now. That a mortal's life was so short, only sixty or eighty years, while she remained eternally twenty-five. Patrick cooking her breakfast changed things between them. Away from being something casual, a struck match that would burn out just as quickly. No, Patrick Davies was never going to be just an acquaintance.

That match had touched a place deep inside her where now an infant flame burned steady and true, just waiting to grow and burn away her fear and isolation.

If she dared let it.

Twenty

The folder hit his desk with a resounding slap.

Jacob looked up from his computer as John Schaffer plopped down into the chair across the desk. He was dressed in his usual black, except this time his jacket was unzipped over a plain gray tee. His hat was gone, revealing long, dark brown hair scraped back into a loose knot. Of course, he had to have one of those Viking-style man buns.

"Please, make yourself at home."

A corner of his goateed mouth twitched as Schaffer started raising one leg as if to put it on the desk and thought better of it, ending with his boot crossed over one knee.

Jacob gave him points for style as he turned his head to the door. "You might as well come in Brennan," he said.

His Second strode in from the hall and sat backwards in the other chair, tattooed forearms crossed over the seatback. "I'm sure Schaffer here has something fascinating to show us."

"Can the sarcasm, will you, and look at the file." Schaffer barked.

Jacob caught Brennan's gaze out of the corner of his eye and smirked as he reached for the file. He flipped back the cover and the expression fell away. He yanked the file closer, scattering the stack of photos inside across the desk.

"What's up, Jake?"

The photos came in a wide variety of shapes, sizes, and age though they had two things in common. First, the subject was unaware that the photos were being taken. Some were surveillance camera footage or taken with a long photo lens. And second, they were all of Morgana, except not exactly. In the first few on top, her hair was much shorter. Jacob picked up one where she was dressed in tight jeans and a loose sweater, carrying books, on a college campus somewhere. He squinted at the red brick building behind her to make out the lettering on the sign. Wycliffe College.

He rotated his hand so Brennan could see.

"University of Toronto." Jacob muttered. "Date stamp says ten years ago."

His Second leaned forward and took it from him. "Can't be... she would be a teenager ten years ago." Brennan studied the photo for a moment, his face pale at first, then his cheeks flushed. He stood up from the chair and stepped closer as they fanned out the photos, selecting another at random. Morgana with hair long and straight, in a loose peasant top mingling in a huge crowd with the Lincoln Memorial in the background. "And this, Washington DC Mall... July 1976?"

Martel sat back in his chair with a sigh, and rubbed his face with one hand. When he looked up at Schaffer, the man was watching them with laughter in his eyes, though his face was only smug. "Almost fifty years, and she hasn't aged a day."

Schaffer shrugged.

There were recent photos in the mix as well, through the window in the gym, probably taken the night Jacob had encountered him on the rooftop. Another of her sitting at a table on a restaurant patio while Patrick shook hands with—Martel snatched up the photo. With Alasdair Bromley.

Brennan tossed the photos he held down on the pile and snatched the patio photo out of Jacob's hand. "Two of them?" He cried. "There are *two of them* here in Kingston, right now?"

The boot crossed over his knee hit the ground with a thump as Schaffer bolted more upright in the chair. "Two?"

A satisfied smile broke out on Jacob's face. "Ah, don't know everything do you, Schaffer?" He asked as he gestured with a sarcastic flourish for Brennan to pass the photo over. Schaffer was no gentler snatching the photo himself than Brennan had been. "Meet Alasdair Bromley."

Schaffer studied the photo for a moment, brows drawn down low.

"My contact in Immigration told me that Bromley left again, soon after that photo was taken if the date stamp is right." Jacob looked down again at the pile of photos. Peeking out from underneath the photos were some kind of typed information sheets. From what was visible, they gave biographical data about the identities Schaffer had discovered for the woman who now called herself Morgana Dericault.

"Gone where?"

Jacob shrugged, catching Brennan's cautioning look. "San Diego, was it? San Francisco? One of the San's. I can't remember which."

Schaffer scowled. "Figured you'd be a bit more in a sharing mood considering." He gestured to the desk.

Jacob shrugged and pushed the photos around again. Every time, he saw something new. "Where did you get all this?" Jacob asked.

Schaffer set down the photo he held and steepled his fingers under his chin. "Bit here, a bit there. The stuff from here in Kingston is mine, some from other Hunters. Some of it I even got from the Hunter database, if you know where to look." His words were like a thumb to the nose.

Jacob rolled his eyes toward Brennan and fought the urge to grind his teeth. "Now who's not in a sharing mood?"

Brennan laughed, earning a glare from Schaffer.

Sarcasm aside, Jacob could kick himself for not looking for anyone fitting Morgana's description out of principle. Like any conscientious friend would do when their buddy started dating someone new.

"The database can be difficult to search through," Brennan said with a long-suffering sigh. His tone was defensive, supporting his leader. "It's like a digital box full of newspaper clippings all jumbled together with scattered notes pinned on and no real way to find anything other than to just dig. Somebody needs to recruit a historian or a computer programmer to do something about it."

Jacob snorted. "Or both."

Schaffer shifted forward in his chair. "I'll leave this with you to do with as you will." He said and rose to his feet. He picked up a pen from Jacob's desk and scribbled an email address on top of the nearest piece of paper, which happened to be a food invoice still to be paid. "Why don't you send me what you have on Bromley, and we'll call it even?"

Jacob stayed seated, as did Brennan. Schaffer looked back and forth between the two men. When neither was forthcoming with a handshake or a thank you, he stalked out of the room.

"I better follow him out." Brennan swung his leg around the chair as he stood and stalked to the door. He pointed to the folder spread out in front of Jacob. "We need to start making a plan for that."

Jacob made a noise of agreement as his Second left the room, and looked down at the array of photos, a dozen different identities mocking him. No wonder she had been secretive. No wonder she was skittish around other people, especially him. And now that he knew why...

He woke up his computer and brought up Albrecht's website. He located the staff directory after a bit of searching and scowled. Under the name Morgana Dericault, Assistant Manager, was a short biography, and no photograph, the only staff member without one. He did the same with the website of Bromley's financial firm. There too, for the CEO was a short biography, but no picture. Jacob sat back and clenched a fist, tapping it rhythmically on the arm of the chair as his mind whirled with possibilities.

"Make a plan, indeed."

Twenty-One

Morgana strolled through the door at Albrecht just after noon, her head high and her step light. She'd taken a rare morning off and opted instead to stay in bed with Patrick. They'd spent most of the weekend there, exploring each other, and generally not taking things slow. The pure, boneless relaxation that she'd woken up to each morning in his arms was definitely something she could get used to. But today, the morning was all either could manage. She had meetings, and Patrick had a flight to catch to Toronto for a finance conference.

Alan took one look at her face and dashed across the entryway to loop his arm through hers. He was dressed in an immaculate combination of blue tailored trousers and a fitted suit coat, his brown shoes polished enough to use as a mirror.

His aftershave filled her head, mixing with the usual scents of furniture polish and old paper, as if she needed anything else to make her head spin. The broad grin and waggling eyebrows he turned in her direction were like something out of a black-and-white movie. Comical and overdone. All he needed was a bushy mustache and a cigar.

"Good of you to join us."

Morgana rolled her eyes and put a hand to the heat suddenly burning in her cheek. She strode for her office, heels clicking on the marble floor. "What did I miss?"

"Judging by that glow, I'd say that what you found is a lot more important than what you missed this morning."

Morgana stopped at his desk and swatted away his arm. Her answering smile was coy when she said, "I don't know what you mean."

Alan chuckled and straightened his vest as he circled behind her. He bent over his desk and came back up with a stack of messages and folders. Tucking them into his elbow, he jerked his head in the direction of her closed office door. "Come with me," he said. "And tell me all about what you haven't been up to."

Morgana's breath hitched as a different kind of heat went through her at the memory. The rumpled sheets, their bodies twisted in them. Patrick hovering inches above, his eyes locked with hers as she crested yet another wave of pleasure.

Her thoughts must have shown plainly on her face, for he was laughing under his breath as she reached for the handle and pushed the door open. One of the visitors' chairs was occupied and Morgana smiled, seeing a familiar shock of red hair in the shaft of light from the open window as she had a few months before.

"What the—"

The shock in Alan's voice sent ice water coursing down her spine. She shivered, and when she looked again, the figure in the chair was no longer Patrick, but a tall man in dark clothes, booted feet crossed at the ankle on a corner of her desk.

For a split second, she gripped the doorknob, braced to pull it shut again. But then Jacob Martel glanced up over his shoulder, his chocolate brown eyes meeting hers. He lifted one dark eyebrow and jerked his head in invitation.

What does he *want?* She thought, and wondered whether he was here as a Hunter, or Patrick's best friend. Either way, it wasn't going to be a pleasant conversation. She took the files from Alan's arms and stepped inside.

Alan put a hand out to stop the door and stepped around her. "Who are you? How did you get in here?"

The bustle of the office outside had been replaced by the steady hammering of her heart as it tried to break free of her chest. Morgana took a deep breath and forced her calm mask into place. "He's a friend of Patrick's."

Alan narrowed his eyes. "Friend or not," he said dubiously, "I haven't gotten up from my desk all morning, so I don't know how he got past me. Want me to call security?"

Morgana glanced back at Martel, who smirked and gave Alan a sarcastic, but dismissive salute. She turned to her assistant and gave him her most confident smile. "No, it's fine."

Alan remained in the doorway for several moments as he sized up Martel. With his feet still propped on the corner of the desk, one arm casually draped across the back of the chair, he was the textbook definition of unfazed, despite the piercing look that her assistant was giving him. Martel picked a piece of lint off the front of his jacket and flicked it away. His eyes then turned back to Morgana with a look of pure boredom.

Morgana put her hand on Alan's arm. A murmur had started out in the hall, as others noticed them lingering in the doorway. "It's fine, Alan," she told him, voice steady when inside she was anything but. She put a hand to her forehead and heaved a dramatic sigh. "I forgot that we had an appointment."

She pushed the door closed on him as he continued to sputter and turned to face Martel. The smile she gave him was as pleasant as she could make it as she crossed to the desk and freed her hands. Sweat beaded at her temples and she resisted the urge to blot it with her sleeve.

Martel remained where he was, his posture still relaxed.

A breath of air lifted the fine hairs that had escaped from her bun. The window into the garden courtyard was wide open. Since her office was on the first floor, it was always locked tight, and she thought, alarmed. But the gentle sway of the heavy curtains said otherwise and spoke volumes about Martel's abilities. And his motivation for the surprise visit.

Jake, the best friend, wouldn't have needed to come in through the window.

Adrenaline swept through her body, leaving a fine, tingling vibration in its wake. She hung up her coat without taking her eyes off of him and crossed the room, giving him as wide a berth as possible. When she spoke, it was as Morgana the Assistant Manager, the normal, ordinary, mortal woman dating his best friend. "Hello, Jake," she almost choked on the name. "Is there something I can do for you?"

That smirk returned to his face as he gestured to her desk. A lone brown file folder sat perfectly centered on the blotter. "I was hoping you could look at something for me."

Morgana kept one eye on him as she eased the folder open with the tip of one finger. Inside was a small pile of photographs. She fanned them out on the desk, her fingers trembling slightly. They were photos of her and only a few were recent. Her heart rate ratcheted up as she took in each photograph. Her at university a decade ago, at a peace march in Washinton, DC in the 70s, New Years Eve in Chicago in 1924, her hair cut in a short bob, beaded dress swinging as her partner bent her over his arm in a dance. A half dozen identities stretching back a century were fanned out before her.

She looked up. Martel hadn't moved a muscle, but his eyes were like granite. For a long moment, they looked at each other. Her chest rose and fell, breaths coming faster and faster as if a something inside her was being wound up like a clock, or a jack in the box.

As that spring released, Morgana leapt for the console table. Despite being on the other side of the desk, Martel was a step ahead, and slammed the drawer on her fingers before she could get the hand all the way in. She hissed in pain, certain that a few bones were broken, but swallowed the yelp that would have alerted Alan.

"You know?" she asked, trying to raise a leg to kick him, swing her free hand at him, anything, but he stood too close.

His breath was hot on her ear. "Did you enjoy it?"

"Enjoy what?"

"Your game," he hissed. "Coming into my restaurant, my HOME. Messing with the minds and hearts of my best friend. My WIFE! She's pregnant for fuck's sake!"

Morgana couldn't help trembling. Nausea curled through her from the pain in her hand. "There's no game!" She told him. "I'm not a threat to any of you."

Martel laughed. A cold, cruel sound. He drove his hand into her hair and yanked, exposing her throat. The other hand came up under her chin.

Her teeth clacked together, and she struggled against him, rooting around with one foot trying to spear him with her heel.

Martel stepped in even closer, his muscular chest pressed tight against her back, and yanked again, turned her chin up at a sharp angle. "Stop struggling or I snap your neck." He warned. "It won't kill you, not permanently, but it will knock you out of commission while I finish the job."

Morgana didn't doubt that he would make good on his threat. And though it probably was the stupidest thing to do, she found herself asking, "What will you do, Martel? Drag me out the window? Or will you just leave my body to bleed all over the rug?"

Martel growled in her ear and jerked her chin up another inch.

Black spots started to cloud her vision; her mouth sawing open as she struggled for air. She scrabbled with her free hand, yanked at his iron grip.

His bruising fingers clamped down on the veins in her neck.

"I wasn't playing games," she croaked with the little air she had left. "But can you fault me for being a little cautious?"

Martel didn't speak but he loosened his grip just enough for her to speak, and nothing more. "Yes, I know what you are, too." She whispered. "And then Patrick came into my life. Then I found out that he is your best friend, I had no way of knowing if he was one of you or not."

His grip shifted in her hair, but he didn't release her, merely turned her chin to face him. The expression on his face was pure Hunter, one that enjoyed the pain he was inflicting. The hatred in his brown eyes went soul-deep.

"I didn't know it was your restaurant until we were already seated at the table," she continued, voice cracking. "And yes, I did accept Sophie's invitation to the house, and yes, I'll admit to snooping around when I was there. But I did what I did to make sure that I could stay one step ahead of you, to stay hidden."

"You expect me to believe that?"

"No, Jacob Lembaye Martel, I don't. But I'm not exactly in a position to lie now, am I?"

He stiffened as her use of his full name sunk in, then his hands tightened, her chin yanked back up until only the slightest additional pressure would snap her neck.

She grunted, her breath choking off, the black spots returned. Whatever she had planned to say next was lost as her brain fogged. The muscles in her legs trembled. Only his grip on her neck held her up. In desperation, she gathered what strength she had left and drove her knee up into the console table. It slammed against the wall, and the blue glass bird that perched on one corner tumbled to the floor and shattered.

Her office door flew open, crashing against the wall.

Martel released her and stepped back.

She pulled her hand free from the drawer and retreated to the other side of the desk, clutching her throbbing fingers and dragging in ragged gasps of air.

Alan rushed over and put an arm around her shoulder.

"I'm okay," she told him, eyes fixed on Martel, who now lounged against the table with his hands in his pockets as if Alan had disturbed something more intimate than attempted murder. From a distance, with her disheveled hair and labored breathing, and him having been pressed so close to her, it could have looked like a much different embrace.

Her stomach twisted, both at the thought of his hands being on her in that way, and at the pain coming from her fingers as she surreptitiously straightened each one, pulling and smoothing down the length of each bone to set any fractures before they healed. The act threatened to drive her to her knees, but she bore down on the pain and stayed upright.

Alan stalked over to Martel. "You need to get the hell out of here, right now!"

Martel had at least three inches and thirty pounds of muscle on Alan, but he didn't protest as her assistant started to herd him to the office door. He winked at Morgana as he passed, playing up the aggressive, but jilted would-be lover that Alan clearly thought he was.

As they approached the doorway, a tan uniformed security guard finally appeared and seeing Alan's expression—and her disheveled appearance—took both of Martel's hands and held them behind his back. Again, Martel allowed it.

"I'm going to call the police," Alan said, reaching for the phone on his desk.

"Don't bother," Morgana said from the doorway. She brushed a lock of hair loosened from the pins back out of her eyes. "Let him go."

Alan gaped at her, the handset halfway to his ear.

Morgana squared her shoulders and turned to the security guard. "Please, just escort him out."

The guard didn't hesitate as he led Martel to the door, his hands still held behind his back, and gave him a none too gentle push out into the alleyway. Her last sight of him before the guard closed the door was of his face. All traces of the mild-mannered façade had vanished, gone hard once again, an unmistakable promise in the depths of those brown eyes that the next time they met would end very differently.

Twenty-Two

O
ver the next few weeks, as autumn began to lose its brilliance and faded towards winter, Morgana didn't see much of either of the men in her life. Patrick traveled to Toronto frequently for business, and was often out of touch for several days at a time. But when he was in town, they would meet up a few times a week, exploring the restaurants, cinemas, and museums of Kingston. Nights were spent at Patrick's place exploring each other.

As for Martel, she had seen him only briefly at a baby shower for Sophie held at the restaurant. Morgana had stuck close to Patrick, while Martel had spent the party tending bar with Brennan and sending the occasional meaningful glare her way when his friend wasn't looking.

Every spare moment was spent examining the files that she had taken from Martel's computer. Since the discovery of Martel's Hunter lineage, she hadn't found anything else of interest in the unsecured files, just more financial statements, this time for the restaurant, and more photo albums. She had moved on to the secured files, most of which seemed to contain some kind of medical research.

She'd searched for any kind of summary or report to translate but it must have been in the files she'd been unable to copy. Without it, very little of the data made any sense, but she kept trying. Medicine was not her forte, but the file had come from the cache with higher security, so it had to be important.

After a morning of meetings, Morgana had opened her laptop and settled in for yet another afternoon slowly scanning through the raw data until her eyes started to cross. With a sigh, she tossed down her pen and sat back to rub her eyes. There was a knock on the door and Alan poked his head in.

"Sorry to disturb you," he said with a cautious look on his face. "I have those expense reports you asked for."

Morgana closed her laptop and motioned him inside. "Please, I need to take a break."

Alan smiled as propped a hip on the arm of a visitors' chair and set the reports down on the corner of her desk. He studied the chaos of papers and files, at her laptop perched precariously on a pile of books.

Since Martel's surprise visit, he had turned into a bit of a mother hen, checking her office, peppering her with questions when he brought tea or a snack at any opportunity in hopes of getting details, all while looking at her as if he was still trying to rate her love life on his scale of none to scandalous.

"Don't give me that look," she grumbled but with a smile, fairly certain that he was judging her for the cluttered desk.

HUNTED

Alan held up his hands innocently and laughed, a deep, throaty sound. His eyes fell on the battered blue cover peeking out from under the files he'd just delivered and pulled it out. "What's this?"

She half-considered reaching out a hand for it, but what was the harm? "Oh, just something I picked up recently."

Alan turned the book to read the spine and pursed his lips. "Gulliver's Travels…" He opened it to a random page in the middle and the frown deepened. "In German? I thought they hated Swift in Germany?"

Morgana smiled. "Very good," she said. "That's what intrigued me."

He snapped the book shut and replaced it on the top of the pile with a shrug. "*Jedem das Seine.*"

The perfectly accented and off-hand delivery of the phrase "to each their own" startled a laugh out of her. "I didn't know you spoke German!"

His smile was more than a little smug. He straightened his glasses on his nose and stood. "Have you heard from Patrick yet today?"

Morgana shook her head. "He's supposed to be back from Toronto today."

Alan gave her a sympathetic look at the frustration in her voice and got to his feet. "I'll just leave you to it then."

Morgana sat back with a sigh as the door closed with a soft click. Her eyes fixed on the book where it now lay in a shaft of light from the window. She rubbed at the sore spot in the middle of her chest where the now familiar pang of guilt twisted and took a sip of coffee. The bittersweet hazelnut flavor coated her tongue, a bit of warmth kindling in her belly that radiated back up to color her cheeks. The desk chair creaked as she bent forward and picked up the book. She set the mug

211

aside and held it in both hands for a moment before turning back the cover.

Shortly after the party in Dane, she had transcribed the cramped words onto loose pages and slipped them into the right chronicle. Now the book was just a reminder that she had stolen from Patrick's family.

Her chest throbbed again, and Morgana tossed the book down on the desk as if it was suddenly burning her hands. She propped her chin on one hand, one finger thoughtfully rubbing across her lips.

So far, when she was with him, she'd been able to separate the Ancient from the woman and just be Morgana. By avoiding her place, and its mysterious locked door, she had so far been able to avoid the serious conversations, the serious truths. But once she was alone, the pain of drawing the two disparate halves of herself together again was almost unbearable. As her feelings for him deepened, it was becoming harder and harder to do.

But Patrick had secrets of his own, she reminded herself. There were times, like that first morning, where he had run off without explanation. When he traveled, he was practically unreachable, though they had cell phone service in Toronto as much as in Kingston.

She reached for the phone and dialed his number from memory. This time it rang, but still rolled over to voicemail. Worry and anger battled inside her as Morgana shoved her feet back into her heels and slammed the phone down as she got to her feet. She quickly packed up her computer and scooped up the book. Her coat wrapped around her head when she yanked it down with more force than necessary. She batted it away and bundled it under her arm with a growl.

Alan looked up as she stomped by, but wisely didn't say anything. The look on her face was enough to warn him that his job would be at stake if he did.

From the moment the elevator doors slid open, something was different about him. He was dressed casually in sweatpants and a loose shirt, his feet bare. His face was drawn; deep circles shadowed eyes which had lost some of their gleam. They brightened a little at the sight of her. "Morgana! What are you doing here?"

Much of the fire that had driven her across town froze in her veins. "I'm sorry to just drop in. I did try to call."

Patrick rubbed the back of his neck with a sheepish expression on his face and stepped back, sweeping one arm out in invitation. Morgana pressed a quick kiss to his lips and put her things down on a living room chair. She turned back to find he had followed part of the way, but now stood awkwardly in the middle of the room.

Their gazes met and he just looked at her for a long moment, but then a slight smile appeared on his lips. "Are you hungry?"

Morgana leaned against the counter while he prepared a simple meal of fried chicken over spaghetti. He seemed relaxed enough as he monitored the chicken, but something was setting off a dim warning bell. Her mind drifted back to the encounter with Martel and her hand twitched, though it had long ago healed. There was something about Martel's reaction to her words, his protectiveness for both his wife and his best friend, almost in equal measure, that almost convinced her that Patrick was not a Hunter. Almost.

Yet their strained conversation still gave her pause, and each bite of her food, though delicious, hit her stomach like a lead weight. Patrick had something on his mind, but when she asked him about it, he wordlessly took another bite of his food. More than once, she thought about leaving, that he had only invited her in out of politeness.

As conversation waned, her focus kept drifting to the hallway as the silence dragged on. Not to the bedroom, but the office, and the contents in the safe. She didn't dare ask him about it, but she needed to do something to get some kind of emotion out of him. So, she blotted her mouth with her napkin and rose to her feet and retrieved the battered blue book from her bag.

Her feet felt leaden as she carried it back to the table and uncertainty coiled through her gut as she resumed her seat. She put her napkin back on her lap, but didn't resume eating.

His brow lifted as he looked down at the object next to his plate. He wiped his mouth and set his napkin back in his lap before tilting the book to read the spine. The eyebrow came back down, furrowing in confusion as he studied the title a little closer, to be sure he was reading it correctly without his glasses.

Morgana glanced around the room and didn't immediately see them.

The book looked so much smaller in his hands. "Gulliver's... Travels?" He guessed the second word, then opened the book to a random page near the middle and squinted at the dense type. "In German? Um... thanks?"

She managed a weak chuckle at the utter bafflement on his face and rose half out of her seat to reach across the table and flip back to the inside of the front cover. Her hands were nearly trembling with nervousness, and she clenched them into fists under the table.

He looked at her out of the corner of his eye with a wary smile, then looked down. His eyes sprung wide with shock. "Where did you get this?"

Her heart clenched. "That doesn't matter," she replied, hoping that she put enough casual dismissiveness into her voice. "But I recognized the writing from that story you showed me."

His eyes narrowed slightly in irritation at her tone as he studied the cramped script that filled the inside cover. "But these notes are in German too," he said, almost a groan. "How can this be the same handwriting?" Then a thought seemed to come to him, and he flipped frantically for the title page. "Wait, this can't be right..."

"What?"

He pointed furiously at the printer's mark. "Look here, this book was printed in 1864!" He went back to the written-on pages. Morgana cringed at the rough handling. "But-but this is Jacqueline d'Arnault's handwriting!"

He closed the book with a snap and rose quickly from the table, meal forgotten, nearly toppling his chair over. He beckoned to her, and she followed down the hallway to a small office. He moved quickly, but with a stiffness as if a muscle had tightened in the short amount of time that they had been sitting.

Despite the amount of time she had spent in his apartment, Morgana hadn't ever stepped foot inside his office. The room was set up to work comfortably from home with a large electric standing desk, monitors, and a laptop set between two floor-to-ceiling windows. A plush cream desk chair was tucked in against it. To her left, along the wall that separated this room from the living area was a fireplace, with built-in bookcases on either side. The walls were a cozy dark green, the trim, bookcases, and mantle all a crisp white.

As she entered the room, he already had a lower cabinet door open, from which emanated the beeps of an electric lock being disengaged.

He carried the suede-wrapped tome from the safe to his desk, and flicked on the lamp. He dropped into the desk chair and opened the chronicle to a random page and set the copy of Swift down on top of it.

She wrung her hands as she came up behind him.

His head twisted back and forth between the two books and then turned to her. A finger jabbed the cramped handwriting on the smaller pages. There was a fire in his eyes that threatened to burn her with its intensity, but at least he didn't look quite as tired.

"How can you deny it now?" he asked, but he was excited, not accusing. "Look at the shape of the letters, the loops, the slant. The same person wrote these, but four hundred years apart!"

Morgana leaned over the two books, making a show of glancing back and forth between them. "I can't explain it."

What had she been thinking?

The irrational urge to tell him everything was a physical thing rising up her throat and she clenched her jaw tightly to keep it in. Connecting the two writers was one thing, she told herself, admitting to *being* that writer was something like a bandage she wasn't quite ready to rip off.

"This proves that the stories are true!" he told her almost bouncing up and down like a child who had just been handed his most coveted toy. He squinted again at the handwriting, scowled then rushed out of the room as fast as he could, and returned with his reading glasses in hand.

Settling these on his nose, he dropped into the chair to read. Within moments, he'd propped his elbow on the desk, hand buried in his hair.

Morgana stood behind him, hand on the back of the chair, her fingers inches away from his chestnut waves, as he slowly muddled his way through the scribbled notes. From over his shoulder, she read much more quickly than him about Emilie Jardin's search for a safe place to stay in Munich in 1874.

After a while, he sat back with a sigh, scrubbing his face with both hands, nearly dislodging his glasses. "It also proves that my German is terrible."

Morgana laughed, in spite of her nerves. "It seemed like you were doing well enough."

Reluctantly, he closed the book. "Sophie knows German better than I do," he said, fingers absently stroking the leather. "Maybe I'll have her translate it for me."

"No!" Morgana barely stopped herself from making a grab for the book. One look at the book, she suspected, and Sophie would know where it had come from.

"Why not?"

"Um, it's just that she has so much to do right now," Morgana said hastily. "With the baby coming, you know?"

Patrick studied her for a moment.

Morgana forced her best innocent look on her face.

"Of course," he said finally. "You're right." He opened the book and had another go at the German, reading slowly and with much difficulty. Morgana stepped even closer behind him and started kneading his shoulders. His hair, that glorious combination of everything from deep chestnut to strawberry blonde smelled of some faint but sharp smell. Eucalyptus, or tea tree, maybe.

She shook her head to clear the scent from her head and looked back down at the desk. From this vantage point, her own handwriting stared back accusingly.

"Yet I cannot understand how easily they always seem to find me," Patrick read slowly. "Despite my most cautious—no, wait... it's careful," he amended, "my most careful efforts, by keeping to myself, making no lasting attachments, I am not safe."

Patrick stopped there and glanced over his shoulder at her. "How sad." he said, their faces only inches apart. His eyebrows drew down. "What is it?"

Morgana resisted the urge to wipe away the moisture coating her lashes, and banished the memories swirling through her as best she could. "Nothing," she told him, giving his shoulder a reassuring squeeze. "It *is* a sad story, but not all of it. You get a little closer to the end and she isn't quite as lonely."

"Really?"

Patrick went to turn back but she reached down, took his hand off the book and closed it herself. She brought her hand up to rest on his cheek, drawing his full attention back to her. Their eyes met and held.

Patrick started reaching for his glasses.

"Leave them on," Morgana said, brushing his hand down. He turned it over, linked his fingers with hers. "I kind of like them."

"Oh, really?"

In answer, Morgana bent to capture his lips with hers. It was a brief kiss, but there was nothing simple about it. She pulled back and looked at him. The glasses truly did add an academic allure to his natural charisma.

A slight tug on their joined hands brought her sprawling across his lap. His arms settled around her hips, hers around his neck as they watched each other, waiting perhaps to see who was going to lose this particular game of chicken, though both, in fact would win.

His hair fell over his glasses and into his eyes.

Morgana moved to brush a lock back and cupped his cheek.

Patrick gave her a dreamy smile that had her heart fluttering.

Fearing that the depth of her feelings was showing too much on her face, Morgana kissed him again. Her eyes drifted closed, but she could still feel his gaze on her even as their tongues danced, and he drew her even tighter to him.

It was a long time later when they finally came up for air. Her head came to rest on his chest as she breathed in the scent of him, that musky cologne he favored, the strong, reassuring thump of his heart under her ear.

His head tilted to rest against hers, and the gentle kiss he pressed to her forehead was almost more intimate than the longer one they'd just shared.

Her heart swelled even as her dinner tried again to turn sour with guilt.

Patrick settled her against his chest and turned in the chair, so he faced the books. He ran a loving hand down the page of the larger book. The words were more organized and uniform than those in the margins of Swift. But no matter how faded the ink, the shape of the letters was clearly the same.

"How is this possible?"

Morgana raised a hand and brought his face back to hers. "Let's not worry about that right now."

She removed his glasses and set them down beside the books with a soft click of metal on wood. His eyes darkened as their gazes met, evidence of his arousal pressed against her hip.

They came together again with a crash, lips and hands searching, grasping. He lifted her shirt over her head and trailed a line of fire down her neck, along her collar bone.

Morgana eased off his lap and grasped the collar of his shirt, tried to yank it over his head but his arms got stuck. She laughed and pulled again. The shirt slid free and she tossed it aside.

Patrick was grinning but there was a dark, wicked gleam in his eye as he surged to his feet. He engulfed her in his arms, her back pressed tightly to his chest, and buried his face in her neck, finding that place beneath her ear that made her heart beat so fast, made her core come alive.

Morgana ground her hips back against him. His growled response sent a spear of heat through her as his hands drifted down to release the button of her trousers. He herded her into the hallway, his hand slipping into her waistband, moving with agonizing slowness towards that place that was aching for his touch.

Morgana reached back to wrap an arm around his neck as he trailed a line of kisses along her shoulder. Her breathing turned ragged as he slid a finger through her wetness, to trace slow circles around that tender bundle of nerves. She gasped out his name, as a release started to gather from his touch.

Before it could overcome her, he removed his hand and spun her to face him.

The sound she made at being left on that torturous edge was nothing short of a frustrated whimper. But he immediately captured her lips, desperate, hungry, and slid his hands under her ass and scooped her feet off the floor.

She gasped against his lips as her core came into contact with his hardness through the layers of clothing between them. Her ankles locked around his waist, heels digging in to pull him even closer against her. Her hips rocked against him, chasing that peak that hovered just out of reach. But it wasn't enough.

He shifted her weight to have one arm under her while the other slid up to release the clasp of her bra. The garment slid off her shoulders and was cast aside. He captured one nipple in his mouth, circling the sensitive nub with his tongue, teeth gently nibbling. Electricity zinged down her spine to that part of her that was more than ready for him.

Despite the earlier hitch in his step, Patrick carried her to the bed as if she weighed very little and turned to sit with her on his lap. He slowly leaned back with her stretched at length on top of him.

Morgana lifted their intertwined hands up over his head and pinned them to the bed as she took her turn exploring his body. Her lips trailed down his neck, his chest, drawing out a series of soft moans from him before returning to his mouth.

He tugged his hands free and buried one in her hair, the other moving to her hip, then suddenly she was underneath him in the middle of the bed, their mouths fused together, tongues exploring. He broke free a moment later, but only to shed his remaining clothes.

She lifted her hips, and he made quick work of her pants. Then came back over her, and she opened herself to him. He slid inside in a single, smooth thrust, their bodies fitting tightly together like two pieces of a whole. He groaned and paused for a heartbeat, two as he filled her up. And then he started to move.

Morgana moved with him, quiet gasps escaping her lips as his mouth once again found a nipple. One of his hands braced beside her head as he withdrew almost completely before plunging in deep. Again, and again. Deeper and deeper. Her hands grasped his hips pulling him into her with each trust. Her heart thundered, her breath coming in short pants as her release built once more.

He was close, too. His back and shoulders gone tense under her fingers, his movements started to quicken and then slow, quicken and slow as if he was reining in a frantic pace that would end things much too quickly.

But she didn't want slow, or gentle, and pulled his head down for another passionate kiss as the first tremors began. "Faster," she whispered in his ear.

He pressed his temple to hers, drew one of her knees up higher and let his body take over, increasing the speed, the depth. A breathless moment later, she came apart from the inside out, wave after wave of pleasure coursing through her. Her body convulsed, chest lifting off the bed to collide with his before falling back. Another thrust, two, and he followed, crying out as he found his own release.

He continued to move, but languidly, as the waves of pleasure eased until she relaxed completely beneath him. He withdrew then and rolled onto his back and gathered her against his chest. One leg draped over his and within moments she was asleep.

Twenty-Three

M organa awoke the next morning to a bedroom full of light. She froze mid-stretch when Patrick murmured in her ear and drew her closer against him, their skin nearly fused from head to toe. The bicep under her head flexed briefly, the other remained wrapped around her waist, fingers splayed across her stomach. Her hand came up to cover his but otherwise she remained still in his arms, so she wouldn't disturb him.

Memories of the night before began to filter back, followed by a wave of guilt. After falling asleep, they had awoken in the middle of the night and made love again, this time climbing under the covers before falling asleep once more. Her goal to cheer him up with the book containing Emélie Jardin's notes had succeeded, but it had only served to create more questions, another complication. Then she'd used seduction to distract him from asking the most important questions, the ones that it was growing harder and harder to leave unanswered.

The silence was shattered by the sound of Patrick's cell phone ringing from across the room. Morgana raised her head trying to locate the sound.

Patrick threw back the covers on his side, the movement taking all the warmth with him. He scrambled through the pile of their clothes until he found his dress pants and pulled the phone from the pocket. He looked at the display and his eyes grew large.

"It's Jake," he told her and answered with a cautious greeting. With his sister being on bedrest and her due date growing nearer and nearer, his alarm and apprehension were understandable.

She tugged the covers around her as if Martel had just walked into the room rather than being on the phone. Her heart rose into her throat, as Patrick's body went as taught as a bowstring.

"Is Sophie okay?"

From her place across the room, Martel's voice was just a garbled mumble as if from a cartoon she had once seen. Whatever his friend said made all the tension leave him in a rush.

Patrick covered the mouthpiece and turned to her. "She's not in labor."

Morgana sighed with relief but didn't speak, adrenaline flooded through her just knowing who was on the other end of the call.

Patrick listened to whatever Martel was saying for a moment and then looked down at himself, realizing that he was standing naked in the middle of the room, not that Morgana minded in the slightest.

He got back under the covers. Morgana reclaimed her spot curled against him and draped an arm across his chest with a contented sigh, not caring if Martel heard her. Secretly, she hoped that he had.

Patrick murmured her name a moment later.

A little satisfied smile came to her lips. She traced the muscles of his stomach with her fingers while he talked with his friend, the occasional hitch in his breath proving that he was not immune to her touch. As her hand drifted below the edge of the covers, he released a shuddering sigh, and his free hand came down on top of hers.

"Yeah, yeah, I'm fine," he responded to a question she didn't hear, an amused but cautioning glint in his eye. "Sure, come on over... see you then." He hung up the phone and set it on the nightstand.

Morgana stared up at him through her eyelashes, her hand still poised below his navel, but the urge to move it lower had evaporated with the news that Martel was on his way.

He glanced down and one corner of his mouth lifted. He pulled her closer and dropped a kiss on the top of her head. "Sorry about that."

Her eyes drifted to the window across the room. It was a clear morning, with tattered white clouds in the sky over the rooftops. "It's okay."

His heart beat a strong rhythm under her ear as his hand gently stroked over her hair. Any other time, it would have calmed her, but now, each beat seemed to reverberate through her like a stone ricocheting between her ribs.

Her stiffness didn't go unnoticed. He pressed another kiss to her temple. "What is it?"

"Nothing."

But the morning's glow had been shattered. Gripped with the sudden urge to move, she turned back the covers and reluctantly withdrew from his arms. The coolness of the room hit her bare skin and made her shiver as she crouched to sort through the pile of clothes on the floor. She could feel Patrick's eyes on her as she dug for her shirt, before remembering that it would still be in the office.

"Why do you keep doing that?" he asked from the bed. His voice was quiet, but it had an edge.

The tone brought her head up. "Doing what?"

"Close up. Pretend that nothing is wrong when I can tell that something is bothering you," Patrick answered, "something you're hiding from me."

"I'm not hiding," she said, voice sounding *almost* sincere even to her own ears. "I should be going."

Patrick's eyes narrowed. "You were quite happy to stay before the phone rang." He retrieved his pants from the pile and forcefully shoved his legs in. "Is it me?"

"No!"

He took her hand in his.

She looked down, at the scars from years of sports and a mischievous youth, where hers, so small and delicate by comparison, were unblemished.

"Is it Jake?" Patrick asked suspiciously. "What is it that you don't like about him?"

Want a list?

"It's not you, it's not Jake," she protested, with only a slight hesitation on his first name, and finally broke Patrick's hold. "I have to go."

Morgana left the room and went to the office to retrieve her shirt and tugged it on. She turned back to the door as she put her arms through the sleeves. Patrick's body filled the doorway, arms braced, blocking her way.

When she stepped closer to leave the room, he didn't budge. "Oh, no you don't."

Her muscles tensed, fighting instincts coming to life. "Please," she said, standing in the middle of the room, with no way out. "Let me go."

He shook his head and continued to crowd the doorway. And unless she hit him, which she would never do, or stooped to an undignified dash under his arm, she wasn't going anywhere.

Morgana cursed under her breath in French, then squared her shoulders and met that flinty blue stare. "*D'accord,*" she nodded sharply and straightened to her full height. "If you must know, your friend Jake makes me uneasy, and I do not think that he approves of me. And despite your faith and trust in him, I'm not all that keen on being in this apartment when he arrives to watch him scrutinize me yet again."

None of it was a lie.

Patrick's head tipped to one side as he leaned on the door jamb, though he still blocked her way. "Morgana, I know Jake," Patrick said, clearly taking sides, and it wasn't hers.

She wasn't prepared for how much it would sting and was momentarily breathless.

"He hasn't said anything to me. If he had concerns, he would have said something. Trust me."

"Does he know we're sleeping together?"

Patrick actually looked sheepish. "That's nobody's business but yours and mine."

Inwardly, Morgana sighed in relief, but it was fleeting. The weight of his disbelief was crushing her, and she struggled just to remain upright and breathing. Patrick took her silence in a different direction than she'd intended. She was simply at a loss for words. "But that's the problem, isn't it? You *don't* trust me." His face was set in hard lines. "Why?"

Morgana had no explanation; none that he would believe in his present frame of mind. "I don't know," she confessed, voice only a whisper for she could barely force any air past the lump in her throat. When she took a step towards him, he moved aside and let her pass. She crept into the living area, taking in their half-eaten meals left abandoned on the table, and hesitated, remembering the events that had interrupted the meal in the first place.

Her legs were heavy, as if the floor was trying to suck her down, keep her there until all her walls and secrets crumbled around her. But Morgana pushed away the memories and retrieved the empty satchel and her coat from the chair.

His voice called after her. "I really do care for you Morgana, more than you know." Words that should have calmed and steadied her were each like a dagger of ice to her heart. She stopped in her tracks in the middle of the room, clutching the satchel to her chest, and turned back to see him leaning on the wall by the dining table. His arms were crossed, eyes sharp and blue as glacier ice. "If you go now, don't expect me to see you again until I know that you'll trust me with the truth you've been hiding."

Morgana only nodded her head woodenly, unable to believe that the gentle man she knew could turn this cold and deadly serious. It went a long way to proving her earlier fears that there was a side to Patrick that he didn't let her see. And even though she knew that there were secrets on both sides, the instinct to run sent all thoughts of challenging him back right out of her mind.

"I understand."

She crossed the room and pressed the call button. For half a moment, with the guilt twisting her stomach into knots, she almost turned back. This was foolishness. Patrick deserved to know the truth. The words were so close to the surface. All she had to do was open her mouth and they would come tumbling out.

But what if he didn't believe her?

What if he did and couldn't handle it?

Could her heart withstand it?

The internal battle lasted only a few heart beats. As if on its own, her chin slowly started to turn, and their eyes met. He remained leaning against the wall, one foot crossed over the other, but his expression changed slightly as if sensing the conflict in her. Cracks appeared in the icy mask, hurt leaking through.

Her lips parted but the chime of the arriving elevator sounded, and the words died in her throat.

He took a single step toward her.

It took every ounce of strength she had to walk into the elevator. Once inside, the door slid shut with a clang that reverberated through her body. Her knees wobbled, the paneled wall the only thing between her and the floor.

As the elevator descended, Morgana felt as if a part of her had been left behind on the top floor, her body stretching with each passing floor. But before she could tear in two, the elevator dinged, and the door slid open.

Jacob Martel stood in the doorway reaching for the call button. His eyes popped wide. He took a step back into a fighting stance and his hand snapped to the back of his belt where he must have had a weapon.

"No," Morgana moaned before she could help herself, frozen in place in the middle of the elevator car. For the second time, in almost as many minutes, there was nowhere to go.

Martel's eyes flashed with satisfaction. "Where do you think you're going?"

Morgana tried to hurry past, but he grabbed her arm in a vise-like grip, grinding muscle against bone. He pushed her across the elevator until her back collided with the wall. Stars exploded in her vison when her head followed. The doors started sliding shut.

A whimper tried to force its way up her throat as she staggered, still held tightly in his grip. She swallowed it down and snapped a fist into his cheek. It was his turn to stagger and his grip loosened enough for her to pull free. Morgana crashed into the doors, and forced herself through the slowly widening gap before he could grab her again. She fled across the lobby, oblivious to the curious looks from residents who had witnessed the whole scene.

She burst out the front door and kept moving up the street as she dug for her keys. What was happening to her? Gone was her stability, her unflappable confidence in herself. Even three months ago, Morgana would have been prepared for any encounter with Martel with a quick wit, a sharp tongue, and a cool head if and when she had to fight her way to safety. A wild rabbit punch and a mad dash in pure blind fear was not like her. And it was not an experience she wanted to repeat, especially if she wanted to stay alive.

She didn't stop until she was safely within the confines of her apartment with the door bolted. Despite her racing and unsettled thoughts, or perhaps because of them, Morgana soon collapsed into the caramel-colored chair in her office, picked up her pen and began to write.

For once, she didn't care about handwriting, or style, or any of the other things she usually worried about as her hand dashing frantically across the page as if time had been put on fast-forward. She got up only once to mix a new bowl of ink. The rhythm and flow of turning thoughts into words and transferring them to paper worked to settle her mind, and helped her work through the heartbreak, guilt, and panic of the last few days. She filled page after page, ignoring the tension in her legs from sitting, the cramping in her hands and shoulders, intent on getting everything out.

Finally, she ran out of words.

When she tried to set the pen down, she found that her fingers had frozen around it and she had to carefully peel each one away before she could finally set it aside. As she massaged her palm, she surveyed the damage. It looked horrible, blotchy and a little crooked. But the words were legible, and all the truth was there, and that was what mattered.

Her mind was clear, but her heart empty as she pushed out of the chair and left the room on wooden legs. Emerging into the hall, she found it dark, the only light coming from a lamp on a timer in the living room. It had been ten in the morning when she'd sat down to write.

The sudden rumble of her stomach reminded her that she had also not eaten all day. She hobbled into the living room and stared at the mantle clock in disbelief. Ten hours had passed while writing in her Chronicle.

Morgana turned to the window and stared for a moment at the twinkling city lights. Her own reflection in the window looked back at her accusingly. She could almost hear her reflection demanding in an echo of the last line she had written.

Why couldn't you have just told him the truth?

Twenty-Four

T he elevator door slid open, and Patrick paused in clearing the table to look up. His bruised heart started beating a little quicker. Maybe Morgana had changed her mind and come back? But it was his best friend that strode out, eyes blazing, and face flushed. Jake didn't even glance in his direction as he stalked straight into the kitchen and started digging in the freezer.

Patrick's shoulders slumped as he heaved a sigh and followed him into the kitchen to deposit the dishes in the sink. "What's wrong Jake?"

His friend pushed away a few butcher paper wrapped packages and made a satisfied sound as he stood and pressed a bag of frozen vegetables to his cheek. He drew in an angry, shuddering breath and blew it out.

"She hit me!"

"W-wait, what?"

The brown eye that wasn't covered by white plastic rolled, and his free arm gestured pointedly to the pans still on the stove from dinner.

Patrick's mouth dropped open. "Morgana hit you?"

"I was just standing there, waiting." The contents hissed as he shifted the bag to another part of his cheekbone. "And then the door opened, and there she was, looking pretty upset. I reached for her as she passed by to ask what was wrong and bam! She hit me."

Patrick leaned against the counter and buried his face in his hands for a moment. He scraped them back through his hair and sighed. When he met Jake's eye again, there was a glint of amusement mixed with the irritation.

His friend, damn him, hopped up on the counter and propped his elbows on his knees and tossed the bag back and forth between his hands. He didn't speak, but stared at him intently in that way he knew Patrick hated, the one that usually got him talking within seconds.

He sighed again. "I think it's my fault."

Jake lifted an eyebrow.

"She's keeping something from me, something big." Patrick told him. "I called her on it, and she refused to tell me what it was."

One side of Jake's mouth twitched as he looked down at the counter next to him and spotted the open bottle of wine left out from last night. He held it up to examine the label and the level of liquid in the bottle, then raised it in salute and took a healthy swig. He held it out to Patrick who scoffed.

"Jesus Jake, it's only ten a.m…"

Jake just smirked again and took another swig then wiped his mouth with the back of his hand. He held the bottle out again.

Patrick stared at him for a moment with as much seriousness as he could muster but laughter soon bubbled out of him, and he snatched the bottle away. He took a sip, the rich red wine exploded on his tongue. Warmth kindled in his stomach.

"What do you think it is?"

"Huh?"

"What do you think she's keeping from you?"

Patrick took another swig of wine and set the bottle aside. "I have no idea," he said. "Every time the conversation turns to anything about her past, she closes up or changes the subject. And for some reason, she does the same whenever you come up."

"Me?"

Patrick nodded. "I just wish I knew why." He murmured. "Why doesn't she trust me?"

Jake seemed to think about that for a moment and then grinned. He opened his mouth, probably to say something sarcastic, but the expression quickly turned to a wince, and he clapped the bag of peas back over his cheekbone. He chuckled ruefully almost under his breath. "I don't know man. Maybe I remind her of someone she knew?" He hopped off the counter and reached for the wine. "I can tell you this, she has a good right hook. That boxing practice is paying off."

"Boxing practice?"

"I saw her at the gym not too long ago." Jake said. "She was working with a heavy bag, looked like she had *many* years of practice."

Patrick thought back to the night before, to the feel of his hands roaming over her body, her skin so soft and smooth over lithe muscle like that of a dancer or a gymnast.

He shrugged. "Add that to the list of things I didn't know about her." It came out on a surprised chuckle, but his heart still twisted a little.

"Any idea what you're going to do?"

Patrick turned to the dishes in the sink. As if on cue, the muscles in his leg started to throb. He leaned against the counter and flexed his knee a couple of times to relieve some of the tension. "I have to go to Toronto in the morning and I'll be back at the end of the week." He said and started scrubbing one of the pans in the sink. "It's on her though. There is definitely something between us, Jake, something that I've never felt before. I know she feels it too. But I can't waste my time on someone who won't let me in, who keeps secrets, not again."

Jake was silent for a moment. When he spoke, the sound of his voice, somewhere between curiosity and distaste, brought Patrick's head up. His friend's mouth had a wry, bitter twist as if he'd eaten a lemon. He tossed the bag of peas at him. "Almost sounds like you love her."

Patrick dropped the sponge and got his hand up just before it collided with his face. He tossed it gently in the air once, twice as Jake's words sunk in and kindled a warmth in his chest, though it quickly cooled to shards of ice that pricked at his heart. He took a deep breath and met his friend's eyes. "You know what?" he murmured, "I think I do. And that's why it hurts so much."

Twenty-Five

Alan's cheerful voice greeted Morgana before she had even fully stepped through the door. She removed her sunglasses and blinked to adjust to the dimmer interior of the entrance hallway. It could only mean that Alan had been waiting for her.

And that was never good.

Morgana rubbed the spot over one eyebrow where a headache had been brewing all morning and inched her way across the hall toward him. "You know, you remind me a lot of a friend of mine," she told him.

Alan glanced down at this suit and back up. With his immaculately-styled hair, and the glasses, he was a Cuban version of Alasdair.

"Is that a good thing, or a bad thing?"

"Depends on whether you're going to hand me that stack of messages."

Alan's hand froze in the midst of doing just that. He withdrew his hand and followed at her heels and went to pour her a coffee. As he placed it in her usual spot on the desk, he placed the phone messages by the phone.

Morgana rolled her eyes and settled into her desk chair with a sigh. He straightened the stack of folders on the corner of her desk and looked up, "Are you alright?"

Morgana didn't hear him at first. Her eyes were fixed on the empty visitors' chairs. Her heart twisted, thinking back to the bright, sunny day months ago, the sparks of flame the sun brought out in Patrick's hair. For one desperate moment, she wished she could go back in time and start over.

Alan repeated the question and the words finally registered.

She shook off the memory and looked up to see him eyeing her carefully. She managed a smile, though it was weak. "Yes, Alan," she replied, forcing herself to be present. "I'm fine. Thank you for the coffee."

"Of course," he replied. "Anything else I can get you?"

She eyed the stack of files. "A lighter?"

Alan laughed, came around the desk and placed a hand on her shoulder. "I'll see what I can do." He said and grasped the doorknob. "Oh, before I forget. Lawson said to tell you he's looking for that budget proposal you've been working on."

She stared at the back of the door grinding her teeth.

Albrecht's fiscal year was coming to a close and, for only the second time, Morgana was thrust into the world of financial statements and budget planning for next year. She'd put in extra hours, took work home, but that didn't seem to be enough for Gavin Lawson, Albrecht's owner, even though her deadline wasn't for another two weeks. For not the first time in as many days, she wished that she had someone to help her navigate it all. Alasdair was back in San Francisco and Patrick...

Patrick still wasn't answering her calls.

It had been three days since he had made his ultimatum. Calls to his cell phone went directly to voicemail, and when she'd broken down and called his assistant at Davies & McNamara, a bubbly woman named June had informed her that he was out of town but was due back soon.

As for Martel, she kept wondering where she would see him next; around the next corner, on every rooftop, standing in the middle of her living room when she got home. He hadn't struck yet, but she didn't dare leave the house without carrying at least one weapon. She'd started mixing up her routine, sometimes driving, other times taking a taxi, but always using different routes between work and home to confuse anyone who might follow. She also avoided the gym or anywhere else that put her out in the open or somewhere easily cornered.

Morgana pushed her racing thoughts into a corner of her mind and got to work. The hours passed in a blur, and she only stopped to eat because Alan brought her a plate of bread, cheese, and fruit around midday. Even then, she'd only pulled it closer and nibbled as she worked, occasionally brushing breadcrumbs from her files.

A knock sounded at her door sometime later, and Alan took a half step inside. He had his coat on, a designer silk scarf tucked under the collar. "Staying late again, Morgana?"

Her eyes widened and she glanced down at the clock in the corner of her laptop's screen, and sure enough, it was almost five o'clock. "Oh my, is it really that late?"

"Time flies when you're having fun," he said with a chuckle. "Sorry I couldn't find that lighter."

Morgana surprised herself by laughing, Alan practically beamed at the sound. "I think I'll work just a little bit more," she said. "I feel like I'm making some headway."

Alan nodded. "Anything I can get you before I go?" he asked, and when she shook her head, he added. "Well, then, have a good night!"

"Good night, Alan." He closed the door and left her to her work. The sounds of people saying good night to each other slowly died off, the lights dimming as the motion detectors took over. Morgana logged the last figure and decided to take a break for the night.

The Tiffany lamp cast a pool of light around the desk, the only light in her office. From underneath a scatter of papers, her phone rang. Morgana excavated the phone and glanced at the screen. The number wasn't familiar, but she answered anyway in case it was Patrick finally reaching out. She scrubbed her hand over her face. "Hello?"

"Morgana?" The voice was feminine, and vaguely familiar.

"Yes, who's this?"

"It's Sophie Martel," she replied. "Sorry, I hope I'm not bothering you?"

"Not at all, I was just wrapping up at work." She placed her laptop into her briefcase with the files and ran a hand through her hair to get it out of her face. "How are you feeling?"

"Fine," Sophie answered. "They've got me on full bed rest now, but we're good."

The memory of swollen ankles and a belly so large it was almost impossible to move rose up. Morgana cursed silently at how quickly the image had come to mind and shook like a dog shedding water from its coat and moved the phone to the other ear.

"What can I do for you Sophie?" she asked, trying not to sound like she was trying to hurry the woman off the phone. She wasn't really, but she knew that the longer she talked to Sophie, the more the lid that covered the box labeled Patrick in her mind would start to come loose.

"I've been meaning to reach out, thought maybe we could get together for coffee or dinner." Sophie said and there was a note of expectant hope in her voice. "But now that I'm not allowed to leave the house, I was wondering if you would come here to Dane?"

"I don't know..." Morgana said. *Does she know about the fight we had? That her brother isn't exactly on speaking terms with me at the moment?* Obviously not, she realized, when Sophie continued.

"I know it's a lot to ask, but Patrick's just got back and already said he'll come, but I was hoping that you'd come early, say five o'clock tomorrow night?"

Morgana glanced down at her date book and winced. Tomorrow was Friday, and five would be only mere hours after what she was sure would be a tiring and frenetic auction day.

"Morgana?"

She juggled the phone as it slipped from her shoulder. "Oh Sorry," she replied as she put it back to her ear. "Sure, I-I'll be there."

"Excellent," Sophie's voice was warm, and Morgana found herself smiling. Truth be told, Morgana had a deep affection for Patrick's sister despite the fact that they had only met the once. If she had been in a habit of making human friends, Sophie certainly would have been a likely candidate, despite the Hunter connections.

Though friends didn't steal from each other.

Morgana didn't want to think about that right now.

"Will it just be us, or will Mar- I mean, Jake be home?"

There was a slight rustle as if Sophie was shaking her head. "Oh no, he'll be long gone before you even get here." Sophie told her. "I haven't even had a chance to mention it to him to be honest. He's been in Kingston a lot lately."

Morgana was relieved to hear that they wouldn't have to pretend he wasn't out to kill her while politely passing the mashed potatoes. It was much easier and far less tiring to be open about it, but Sophie was in too delicate a condition to learn that her husband was a cold-hearted sadistic bastard. Even if she hadn't been pregnant, the truth would crush her.

"Well, that's good," Morgana said, trying to convey only a portion of her relief to keep Sophie from becoming suspicious. "I'll be there. Do you want me to bring anything?"

"No," Sophie answered. "Jake's already been to the market for me."

Outside her office, a metallic rattling echoed through the hallway, but the lights didn't come on. Morgana's eyes snapped to the doorway, and her breath froze in her throat. When the hallway remained quiet, Morgana slowly exhaled and reached for a notepad to start listing all of the things that still needed to be done before the first gavel fell while they talked. When she couldn't think of anything else, she read over the dauntingly long list, and estimated how early she would have to arrive to get it all done.

Through the phone, Morgana heard a loud buzzing. "I've got muffins in the oven," Sophie cried. "I have to get going."

"Sophie, baking is not bed rest!"

She laughed at Morgana's reproachful tone. "Now you sound like my husband," she said, a smile in her voice. "See you tomorrow."

Suddenly the lights outside blinked on, and there was a slam followed by a loud "thunk" as something collided with the desk outside.

Morgana swallowed her cry as she leapt to her feet. Papers scattered and her chair collided with the console table behind her rattling the bar tray.

"Tomorrow," Morgana confirmed quickly, and hung up. She gripped the phone in her hand and retrieved the dagger from the console's drawer. Slowly, she inched her way to the door and pressed an ear to the wood. She waited and a few minutes later the lights went dark again. Either whatever, or whoever, had tripped the sensor was gone. Or they were waiting motionlessly somewhere inside.

Morgana put her phone in her pocket and eased the door open a few inches. When the lights stayed off, she eased an eye around the door frame. In the glow from the exit sign over the employee entrance, the door stood wide open, a scatter of curled leaves and shredded paper spread across the threshold onto the rubber mat. The lights finally came on as she took a step out, the dagger gripped tightly in one hand poised to throw.

She didn't dare call out, but her eyes carefully searched the hallway to her right that led to the galleries and the wider stretch of the entranceway straight ahead. All of the office doors were closed tightly and there were no nooks or crannies in which to hide. Morgana checked behind Alan's desk and then slowly made her way toward the open door and examined it for damage. Finding none, she pushed it closed and locked it, deciding that someone must not have pulled the heavy door all the way shut when they left, and a gust of wind had blown it open.

Some gust, she thought with a sigh, she turned back toward her office, still on alert for someone to appear from the hallway. A glint of light on metal drew her eyes to Alan's desk where a military-style utility knife, six inches long was stuck point-first an inch into the wood. She grasped the handle and wiggled it free. Morgana turned it back and forth in the light. At the base of the blade was an engraving, the square cross of the Hunters.

Her blood ran cold as she ran a finger over the mark. The blade had an oily sheen as if it had recently been cleaned, or—

Before her eyes, the skin that had touched the blade turned red, and her fingers began to tingle then burn. Morgana dropped both of the weapons and dashed up the hallway to the restroom and shoved her hand under the tap, water as hot as it would go. She soaped up her hands, which by then had started to blister, and screamed through gritted teeth as she scrubbed as hard as she could under the water. The top layer of skin sloughed off, the soap stinging her raw skin, but she kept scrubbing.

It took several repetitions of scrubbing and rinsing for the pain to fade, replaced by the low electric hum of healing. She sagged to her knees, clutching the sink for support and took a deep breath, and then another. Once her heart slowed to a more normal rhythm, she stood and turned the water off. Grabbing a towel on the way to the door, she peered out, to find the hallway still empty.

The daggers lay innocently on the marble floor where she'd dropped them. The Hunter blade glistened in the light. They called it Glisane. A poison more potent than even an immortal's healing ability could keep up with, it was bad enough on the surface of the skin but excruciating when it got inside from a knife or bullet wound.

Using the towel still clenched in her hand, she retrieved it from the floor, heart beating a furious tempo in her ears, and deposited it in her briefcase. She gathered her belongings faster than she ever had.

"Miss Dericault?"

She froze halfway out her office door and whipped around. A uniformed security guard was striding up the hallway from the galleries. She recognized his dark, shaved head and put a hand to her pounding heart. "Are you alright, ma'am?"

She swallowed and cleared her throat before she could speak. "Yes, Joseph. I'm fine."

"I got an alert that the door back here was open." He said, glancing over to see it now shut.

Morgana nodded. "It was," she said. "Wind must have blown it open or something."

The guard glanced at the door, thought for a moment, and then shrugged. "On your way out?"

"I am." She replied with a nod, "good night, Joseph."

After a few steps, she turned back. "Actually, can I ask you to walk me to my car?"

Joseph smiled. "Of course. It's getting dark so early all of a sudden."

Morgana cracked a smile and nodded. "I'm just across the way in the garage."

He used his keys to lock the door behind them, then crossed the wide alleyway to a set of unlocked double doors that led to the elevator and a stairwell. Joseph pulled his access card out on a cable and scanned it before she could dig hers out. Morgana hitched her briefcase up on her shoulder and led the way to her car.

Joseph waited until she backed out of her space before he waved and walked away. Morgana sighed with relief as she put the car in drive and eased her way around the neat lines of cars to the other side of the garage. There were two other cars in line for the unmanned liftgate when she pulled up and as she waited for her turn at the barrier, a flash of red filled her car. Her head whipped around to the driver's side window.

A figure dressed in black stepped forward from the bottom of a nearby stairwell. His face remained shrouded in darkness, but it was the same masculine figure who'd stood on the fire escape, the same gun. This time, his arm extended out of the shadows, pointing it directly at her.

Her foot slammed down on the pedal just as the gate rose. Horns blared as she shot out into traffic, but Morgana ignored them, tires squealing as the back end of her Audi skidded from the tight turn and she roared away into the night.

Twenty-Six

F ueled with anticipation and half a pot of coffee, Morgana had half of her list checked off before her staff began to arrive at seven. They made short work of the rest, prepping the lots to be sure that everything was tagged, in order, and ready to go. When auction time came and the customers took their seats, Morgana stood at the back and watched proudly as things went as smoothly as ever. All in all, she was surprised that there had been no hiccups.

It was as if the fates knew that the difficult part of the day was yet to come and they were giving her a break, for once. The cleanup and paperwork were straightforward, easy even, so when the afternoon rolled around, she still had time to catch up on some of the work left undone after her mad dash home.

As she drove to Dane, Morgana almost wished that Martel would be there just to put an end to these cat and mouse games. After everything that had happened, first with the encounter in her office, and then last night with the poisoned knife and the parking garage, she had walked in the door, locked everything tight and went to bed with a knife clutched in one hand.

But Martel wouldn't be home, and her shoulders relaxed as she found the house from memory. There was only one car in the driveway, a sleek silver Volvo that must belong to Sophie. Martel drove either a black Land Rover or the beat-up Blazer for Hunting that wouldn't look out of place on the roughest streets in Kingston and likely never left the city limits.

It took a long time for Sophie to answer the doorbell, but she beamed at Morgana as she held the door open for her. Morgana slipped by, just barely fitting between the doorframe and the bulge of Sophie's pregnancy, which had grown substantially in size since the party. She marveled at how the young woman's petite frame was managing.

Or wasn't, she amended, with her on bed rest.

Sophie closed the door and drew Morgana in for a hug. "I'm glad you came."

She led the way into the house, one hand under her belly, the other at the small of her back as she waddled back to the kitchen. "Can you cook?" she asked, settling slowly into one of the padded chairs at the table and then propping her feet up on another. She closed her sapphire eyes, with a contented sigh. Her redhead's skin, normally milky pale like Morgana's, was flushed from the short walk.

The look on her face was eerily similar to one her brother often had, but usually after more... vigorous exercise. A rush of heat went through her at the thought, but it was quickly squelched like a blast of ice water by the memory of the expression on his face, leaning against the wall of his apartment.

Thankfully, Sophie's eyes had been closed while her emotions warred with each other. She cleared her throat to try to loosen the sudden tightness there and replied, "I'm not a *chef de cuisine* or anything, but I can hold my own."

Sophie opened her eyes and smiled. She scraped her long, straight red hair back into one hand to get it off her neck and secured it with a clip. "Good," she replied. "Would you mind if we bring everything to the table and I'll direct you? Doctor's orders, you know?"

Morgana smiled at the sarcasm in her voice. The last thing Sophie wanted to do was sit still and twiddle her thumbs for the next month. "In fact, I insist," she concurred. "What are your orders, chef?"

"Peppers are in the bottom drawer of the fridge, and some chicken on the middle shelf. And there's a bag of onions on the counter. Patrick's partial to Chinese food and there's this recipe that I've been dying to try out."

"*Oui, Chef.*" Morgana replied mock-serious, already halfway to the fridge. She retrieved the ingredients and dumped them onto the huge slab of red oak, which bore its liberal scattering of scratches and dents like badges of honor.

Sophie followed Morgana's gaze and ran a hand lovingly over the wood. "Like it?" she asked. "It was a wedding present from Jake's parents. Been in his family for two hundred years."

Morgana passed her a cutting board and knife. "It's beautiful," she replied. "This kind of craftsmanship lasts forever."

Sophie waved a dismissive hand. "The Martels came over as fur traders in the eighteenth century and branched out from there. Jake's great-grandfather made his money in some kind of shipping."

Morgana contemplated that as they set to work. Given what she suspected about Martel's connections to the Lembaye Hunter family, the money likely came from something more nefarious than shipping. Unless they were shipping out the possessions of dead immortals straight into their own coffers.

Morgana shook those morbid thoughts off and focused on what she was doing. Sophie chatted away as she chopped the peppers and onions quickly and competently from her seat, Morgana a little slower from her standing position beside her. They chatted amiably about everyday things like books read recently, movies seen, and the recent increase in crime in Kingston. Though no one had been killed, police were baffled by the large upswing in reports of gunshots over the last couple of months. Her thigh twitched.

Sophie worried about her husband being in the city late at night.

Morgana bit her lip, thinking of the night before, and the shadow that had pointed a gun at her and reflexively gripped the knife tighter. She kept her voice neutral as she told that shadow's wife that he looked like he could take care of himself.

They scraped everything into a large bowl, and Morgana took the cutting boards to the sink to wash them. Sophie watched, gently rubbing her belly. The baby was active making ripples under Sophie's shirt.

Morgana slid a clean board and knife over. "Thanks. Let's just dice the chicken, then I'll have you get out the pans."

"Okay."

Morgana reached for one package but then dropped it as Sophie started to get to her feet. "I forgot the rice!"

Morgana held up a hand with a smile. "Just tell me where everything is."

Sophie settled back with a long-suffering sigh and pointed out where to get the pot and lid, the measuring cups. Morgana put the water on to boil and went back to the table to start in on the chicken.

Their conversation so far had been full of pleasantries, and for the most part, mindless. But with the slicing of the meat, Sophie didn't waste any time getting to the more substantial conversation. "You and Patrick seem to be getting along very well," she observed. "I remember the story last time you were here was you had just met, and you weren't dating."

"That's true."

"Yet, here you are," Sophie murmured. "How is it going with you two?"

Morgana glanced up. Sophie's tone was simply curious, and there was no hint of anything else on her face. "You don't know?"

Sophie paused mid-cut and shook her head.

"Well, Patrick's not exactly speaking to me at the moment."

"Oh, really?" Sophie's eyes widened, and she set the knife aside. "And you still you came?"

Morgana shrugged. "You asked me to come, so I came."

Sophie considered that for a moment, her gaze turning inward, then focusing again. "So, tell me, Morgana," Sophie asked, spearing her with those sapphire eyes. "What exactly is it about my brother that is frightening you?"

"I'm not frightened," Morgana protested.

"Come now," Sophie said pleasantly, leaning back in her chair. "Forget for now that he's my brother. We're just two friends having a nice chat."

"Okay," Morgana agreed curiously, drawing the word out. She cut up another chicken breast and added it to the bowl. "If you must know, it's not Patrick."

"Then what is it?"

Morgana sighed, set the knife down and wiped her hands on a towel. "There's just so much going on in *my* life right now." The excuse sounded lame even to her own ears. "My career is taking off, and it has me very busy. My personal life is complicated to say the least, without adding him into the mix."

Sophie's eyes narrowed a little. "I'm not going to ask what happened, but I saw the way you looked at each other at the barbecue, even though you had only just met," she replied. "And I have to tell you that I've never seen Patrick look at someone the way he looks at you."

Morgana swallowed and looked away. It really was a beautiful kitchen.

Sophie reached her hand across the table and tapped her knuckles on the wood. It took a couple of moments for Morgana to meet her gaze. "He's been hurt before by women who took advantage of him; married a woman who spent money uncontrollably and lied about it. Then she had an affair with a colleague at her work and well—" Sophie's words choked off and her eyes reddened. She smiled weakly and cleared her throat while she shifted to sit more upright in the chair. "Let's just say, he's very trusting and fiercely loyal, and some have taken advantage of that. I just don't want to see him hurt again."

Had that been the bikini clad brunette on the beach?

Morgana took up the knife again to keep her hands busy even as snakes writhed in her belly. Again, the memory of Patrick leaning against the wall, that mixture of ice and pain in his eyes returned. The ultimatum he'd made. It made more sense now, even if he'd been completely right to call her on it. If only she'd had the courage to stay, to tell him everything.

"I don't want that either," she said, shocked by how small her voice sounded.

"Then what is it?" Sophie asked. "Are you married?"

"No."

"You have another boyfriend?"

"No!" Morgana brought the knife down with more force than necessary, narrowly missing her hand in the process. "Sophie, honestly!"

She held up her hands apologetically. "Sorry, I had to ask."

Morgana could almost hear the gears beginning to turn in the other woman's head as she tried to work it out, though Morgana knew she would never believe the true reason.

"Even Jake says that my brother has love in his eyes now when he talks about you."

The knife skittered off a partially frozen spot and sunk deep into the meaty part of her hand between thumb and forefinger. Morgana pulled the knife free, droplets of blood splattering the cutting board and table. The knife clattered to the table as she clamped a towel to the wound.

"Oh!" Sophie gasped.

Morgana raced to the sink, partly to protect the other woman from the sight of so much blood, but also to delay the inevitable for as long as possible. Her heart pounded as the cold water washed the blood from her skin. Soon, it would become clear to Sophie that not only had the bleeding stopped, but the wound had healed completely. Then there would be a lot more explaining to do.

A gasp came from over her shoulder. Hastily, Morgana shut off the water, dried her hands on a second towel and led Sophie back to her chair where, if she happened to pass out from the shock of what Morgana had to tell her, at least she wouldn't fall and hurt herself.

Sophie sat, blinking like an owl, but her hand darted out and caught her wrist as Morgana took a step away. Morgana settled slowly into the chair beside her. A finger traced the thin red line that stretched halfway across the back of her hand, but even that was visibly fading.

"The cut," Sophie breathed, voice trembling. "It's completely healed! How is that possible?"

Morgana swallowed hard. "It's complicated."

"Is this *the* 'complicated' personal life that you mentioned earlier?"

Morgana just looked at her for a long moment, and nodded. "I'm not quite sure how to explain," she said and truthfully, she didn't. It had been a very long time since she had told her secret to anyone, let alone someone that she didn't know very well, yet still strangely wanted approval from.

"Don't worry about how, just tell me," Sophie urged gently, though her eyes were still very wide. She sat back, hands draped over her belly and waited.

"Okay, here we go." Morgana took a deep breath and began. "I was born in a little village in southern France called Arricau in the year 1287. I am one of *L'Ancienes*, the immortals written about in the chronicle Patrick brought to me."

Sophie gasped, her hand flying to her mouth, eyes gone even wider than Morgana thought possible. "We can be injured, but as you can see, we heal remarkably fast."

The hand pressed to her mouth visibly shook. Whether it was to stifle a scream, or a laugh was unclear. After an eternity, Sophie brought her hand down to her throat, and took a deep breath before she spoke. "Yeah, that could complicate things."

Morgana laughed sadly.

"And you haven't told him," Sophie guessed. "And that's why he's mad at you... because he knows that there is something you're keeping from him."

Morgana nodded.

"Why not?"

"I've asked myself the same question." She rested her elbows on the table and buried her face in her hands, the rest of her words slightly muffled. "I almost did, the last time I saw him. I've had a lot of time to think over the last few days and all that I can come up with is that looking and finding are two very different things. And I didn't know him well enough to take the risk that he couldn't reconcile the two."

Morgana turned her head and rested her cheek on her clasped hands.

Sophie just gazed back, her expression unreadable, one hand rubbing small circles on her belly.

"What would he say if he knew that I've been alive for more than seven hundred years?" She paused before she spoke the more important truth. "And not only that, but that I am the one he was looking for. The one who *wrote* the Chronicle."

Sophie gasped at this last, though why it should startle her more than finding out that the woman across from her was immortal, Morgana didn't know. "I have been Jacqueline d'Arnault, Aline Caro, Emilie Jardin, Aimée Danté, and a thousand other people. Constantly moving from place to place, never having a home, always alone."

"Oh Morgana." Sophie said quietly, then made an apologetic noise for interrupting.

Morgana gave her a watery smile. "I was content with a solitary life. It was easier, safer. And I thought that it was what I wanted, that it was the only way to make the passing years bearable." Morgana told her. "Until I met your brother."

Sophie released a shuddering breath, her eyes brimming with tears.

"I haven't aged a day since I was twenty-five. I starved to death and woke up to find that the passage of time would never touch me again." She released a shuddering breath, and found that now that she had started, the words just seemed to tumble out. "A mortal will age and die and we're the ones who remain forever the same. I have lost those that I cared for more times than I can count. Centuries ago, I decided that I couldn't go through that again and survive. Immortal, or not."

"Centuries—" Sophie murmured to herself, as if calculating that kind of time in her head. "The son you said you lost long ago..."

Morgana nodded. "He died a month before I did."

A lone tear slipped down Sophie's cheek. She didn't speak, but for a moment her arms wrapped just a little bit tighter around the swell of her belly.

"But then your brother came into my office and tore all of those promises and convictions to shreds. I resisted for as long as I could, believe me."

"Sounds like Patrick," Sophie commented, but Morgana was continuing as if she hadn't heard.

"He worked his way into my life and into my heart so quickly and easily that it terrified me." She turned to face her. "I don't get scared Sophie; I can't afford fear when there are men hunting me just for being what I am."

Sophie's eyes went wide again. "But why be afraid of Patrick?"

"My people can identify each other with a kind of a sixth sense, but the Hunters are mortal. They could be anyone. I had no way of knowing if Patrick was one of them."

If her conversation with Martel in her office hadn't been convincing enough, the look on Sophie's face told her how absurd that thought was. Morgana bit her lip and reached across to where Sophie's hand rested on the table. Their fingers met, and Sophie pulled back, both hands wrapping protectively over her belly.

Morgana slumped back in her chair, heart squeezing tight. Was it fear or surprise that made Patrick's sister pull away? Neither were good.

Her next words were almost a whisper. "I fell in love."

Sophie blinked, sending tears falling down her cheeks. She pushed back with her feet to sit up even straighter in her chair and swiped at her cheeks with one hand. "You love him, but you can't bring yourself to tell him the truth?"

The disbelief in her voice hit Morgana like a physical blow and her shoulders curled in. "That's why he hasn't answered the phone, hasn't called me back." She admitted, voice small. "He knew that there was something that I was keeping from him, and he insisted I tell him. When I refused, he told me to leave and not come back until I was ready to be honest and trust him with whatever I was hiding."

Sophie winced.

Morgana caught it out of the corner of her eye and looked up. "But he's hiding something too. Something he doesn't want *me* to know," Morgana replied, wringing the towel in her hands. The tears had been threatening, but irritation burned them away. "He disappears for days on end, and won't tell me where he's gone, and when he comes back, I can tell that something is wrong. Yet he has the audacity to spout ultimatums and insists *I* don't trust *him*."

Sophie had turned away to the window, but her eyes were unfocused.

"What is it?" she asked. "Sophie, what's wrong?"

Something twisted Sophie's features, her breath hitched in then shuddered out before she turned back to Morgana.

Adrenaline tingled through her as she waited for Sophie to speak.

"It's not really my place, but I could tell you something that could shed some light. Especially why my brother has been out of touch the last few days, and all those times before." Her voice wavered slightly as she drew herself up even straighter in the chair and took a deep breath before she continued. "Patrick's dying."

It was as if Sophie had picked up the knife between them and plunged it into her heart.

"What—what's wrong with him?" Somehow her voice still worked, though not very well. Everything else was frozen, rigid, and immobile.

"He has cancer."

Morgana gulped for air, struggling against the terrible weight that sat on her chest. *It can't be true*, nearly every part of her screamed. Though there was one little part of her that had known all along that something was terribly wrong.

Sophie was going on, barely breaking through the roaring in her head. "They found it three years ago when he broke his leg skiing with Jake in Calgary and it refused to heal right. Osteosarcoma, the doctors said. They did aggressive chemo on and off for six months until he could barely get out of bed. We thought we might lose him, but he got better, his leg got strong again. He was in remission, and we thought that he was out of the woods.

"The doctors were hopeful until about six months ago when the cancer markers began to show up in blood tests again. He started chemo, and it was working, but much more slowly, and then it wasn't doing anything at all. Something in his tests prevented them from giving him a higher dose. That was when he started getting experimental treatments in Toronto every few weeks."

"That's why he's been gone..."

Sophie nodded stiffly.

"How long—" She choked on the lump in her throat and swallowed hard. "H-How long does he have?"

"They don't know," Sophie said. "It shouldn't have come back. The doctors were so confident that the relapse took them completely by surprise. Six months ago, they gave him a year, and he's still here. He's been trying everything to stay ahead of the game, but with the chemo not working, the treatments are only delaying the inevitable now."

Morgana couldn't deny the threatening tears any longer, and let them flow freely down her cheeks, to drip onto her shirt. Six months ago, would have been shortly before they'd met. Patrick had come to her with the Chronicle looking for help, not as a curiosity, she knew now, but as a way to save his life. When he had insisted that the Ancients had some kind of magic that kept them alive, he had been looking for something, anything, no matter how farfetched to keep death from his door just a little longer.

"But why didn't he tell me?" She moaned.

"Can you really blame him?" Sophie asked. Her eyes were dry, defeat hollowed them out. "Would it honestly have made a difference?"

Morgana gaped at her. "If I could give my immortality to him Sophie, I would. In a heartbeat. But it's impossible." She replied. "I have spent my life trying to find out why for some mortals, when their life ends, death doesn't come. Even if Patrick had read every single page of every single book, it wouldn't have changed anything. But I could have been there for him, gone with him for his treatments. Not wasted so much time with my own fears."

Sophie lowered her feet to the floor and leaned forward, lacing the fingers of her hands together on the table. "So, he would've had to reveal his most vulnerable truth to you, for *you* be honest with *him*?" She asked incredulously, then scoffed with a sharp shake of her head. "You two make quite a pair."

Morgana rose to her feet and started pacing the kitchen. "You're making it sound like I've been selfish."

Sophie crossed her arms over her belly and leveled those blue eyes on her in an eerily similar expression to the one that Patrick had had on his face when they last spoke. "What else would you call it?"

Morgana braced her arms wide on the kitchen island, her face expressionless. "Survival."

"Well, I'm sorry, Morgana," Sophie said, though her tone was anything but apologetic. "When this is all over, you'll still be here. My only hope is that he makes it long enough to meet his niece or nephew." One angry tear slipped free to burn down Sophie's cheek.

"A *month*?" Morgana murmured, her knees buckled, but the island caught her.

Sophie didn't move, just watched as Morgana struggled to draw in a breath.

"I need to go." She said, once her legs could hold her up, and gathered her coat and purse from the island in front of her.

"I think that would be for the best." Sophie replied. Both knew that she was just running again. One glance at Sophie said that Patrick's sister thought less of her for it.

Morgana left Sophie surrounded by cutting boards, and bowls of ingredients, the table spattered with her blood. She staggered up the hallway toward the front door, her eyes gritty and swollen but dry. The door opened as she reached for the handle and she lurched back, expecting that Sophie's husband had unexpectedly decided to come home. But it was Patrick who came in, his face going impassive and closed upon seeing her, though surely, he had seen her car. His expression turned to shock and concern when he got a good look at her face.

He said her name as he took a step toward her. She shook her head furiously and retreated back, any words she could have said frozen in her throat. Before he could think to stop her, she slipped by him and was out the driveway before he could follow.

Patrick left the door open and stalked into the kitchen to find his sister alone at the table, weeping silently into a dish cloth. Spread around her were the fixings for some kind of chicken dish. But there was blood all over the table. He dashed to his sister and took her hands and held them away from her looking for damage. "Sophie, did you hurt yourself? Is it the baby?"

She shook her head. "No, we're fine. Morgana cut herself."

Before Patrick could ask more, the smell of something burning began to drift across the room. "Damn," he muttered seeing smoke, not steam, and raced to take a saucepan from the flame. It was scorched beyond future use, the water inside having completely boiled away. "How could she leave everything like this?" Patrick asked his sister as he tossed the pan into the sink.

There was more blood here, in the sink, drenching the towel beside it. Where had it all come from? There hadn't been any blood on Morgana as she'd fled the house, or any visible bandages on her hands. He took a deep breath and fought to keep his voice steady. "Is she okay?"

"More or less." she said dismissively. "You need to follow her. I'll clean up here."

Something wasn't right. "Sophie, what's going on?"

She rose to her feet and slowly crossed the room to place a hand on his cheek. "She knows the truth now," she said. "About you."

Patrick reeled back as if she had slapped him. "How could you?" He exclaimed. "You had no right to do that!"

"She needed to know," Sophie told him. "And she has something she needs to tell you. Now get out of here."

Patrick eyed her stomach warily and knew that she shouldn't be on her feet much less cleaning up the kitchen. He reluctantly allowed his sister to herd him to the door. He drove back to Kingston, breaking as many speed laws as he dared, but when he went inside, Fred told him that Morgana had already come home and left again with a small bag over her shoulder.

No, she hadn't told him where she was going.

Patrick left a message with the doorman and went back to the car. He tried her cell phone and, getting no answer but her voicemail, left a hasty message and admitted defeat, at least for tonight.

Twenty-Seven

S omething's not right.

Alasdair parked his car and looked up at his home. The grounds were peaceful and quiet, the gardeners had come and gone leaving pristine lawns and trimmed shrubbery. There were no cars in the drive beyond his. But still Alasdair had a bad feeling.

Cautiously, he climbed out and looked around, waiting for the pop of gunfire or the whistle of an arrow, but only the quiet rustle of the breeze in the trees came to his ears. He tried to relax, telling himself that he was being foolish, that no one was watching, and no Hunters were hiding in the bushes.

But still, he gripped his keys as a make-shift weapon and crept toward the back door, passing windows, their heavy curtains drawn tightly closed. If only he could see inside to have an idea of what he was facing. He reached for the doorknob, heart pounding in his ears, and froze as another sound greeted him. Not quite music, but not quite noise, this sound didn't come through his ears but rang in his mind.

His shoulders dropped away from his ears as he unlocked the door, ready to make the dash to the alarm controls. But of course, she had already turned it off. Alasdair found her asleep in one of the spare bedrooms, a throw blanket draped over her legs for warmth, dressed in yoga pants and a sweatshirt. Deep circles cut under her eyes, her complexion splotched and red.

"What have we here?" Beside the bed was a small duffel bag with something like a pile of fine black threads lying beside it. A wig.

He hated to wake her, but only something terribly important would have brought her to cross an international border to him. While he himself had risked it several times recently with no ill effects, it only took one Immigration agent with Hunter ties to cause a whole mess of problems.

He sat on the edge, brushed a lock of hair from her face. She woke instantly and captured his wrist, the bones grinding together under her fingers. Her eyes focused a split second later and she sighed, fell back, eyes closed again.

"Ally, it's you."

"Of course, it's me," he said gently, but amused. "It's only my bloody house, isn't it?"

She smiled briefly and released him. He fought the urge to rub at the ache in his wrist, but the discomfort soon faded. Slowly, she levered up into a sitting position and yawned, stretching up high to ease cramped muscles. Her sweater rode up to reveal toned muscle and, had it been any other day, he probably would have looked. But it was the deep shadows in her cheeks, the purple smudges under her eyes, that caught his attention.

"How did you get in?"

She gave him a look out of the corner of her eye.

"I forgot," he said with a chuckle. "Keys are for amateurs."

He cupped her cheek and tilted her chin to bring her eyes up. "Not that I'm not delighted to see you darling, because I am, but what in God's name are you doing here?"

Morgana tried to smile at him, turning her face into his hand, then all at once she folded into herself, her body wracked with sobs. He slid into bed next to her and tucked her against his chest. Her arms went around him and held on tight.

"Hey, hey, what's all this?" he asked, running a hand up and down her back. After a few moments, Morgana eased away and sniffed loudly. Alasdair pulled a clean handkerchief from his jacket pocket and passed it to her. She wiped her streaming eyes, blew her nose, then offered it back with a twinkle in her eyes.

"No love, you can keep it," he said with some alacrity, giving her hair a teasing tug.

She tried to smile again but it was brittle. A fat tear slid its way down her cheek.

"You know that this is only the second time I've seen you cry in the past two hundred years? The first was three weeks ago." His concern for the state of her mental health went soul deep. If it was possible for an immortal to have a nervous breakdown, then she might be only a small step away.

"Are you pregnant?"

While they didn't know if it was possible, it had never happened, and he knew that the absurdity of the thought would make her laugh. She only made a face.

"Did someone die, then?" He asked instead.

Morgana's eyes filled and she ducked her head so that her hair hid her face. Then she buried her face in his chest, crying harder than ever.

"Patrick?"

She shook her head but didn't look up, her breath hitched as her lungs struggled to get air. "But he might as well be," she said in a voice so quiet and broken that Alasdair barely heard it.

"What was that, love?"

Finally, she raised her head, her eyes red and bloodshot, still brimming with tears. "Patrick...is...dying." She gasped for air between words.

Alasdair thought that he knew what shock was, but the electricity burning through him was a new definition. "They're all dying darlin', sooner or later, it's a fact of life with them."

His attempt at levity was lost on her. She shook her head furiously. "No," she insisted. "He has cancer. He's only got a few months left. If that."

"Oh, dear Lord," Alasdair gasped. "Oh love, I'm so sorry. Here I am making jokes."

She squeezed his hand and failed in an attempt to comfort *him*. "I don't know what to do, Ally." She moaned and fell back into his arms. "I don't know what to do!"

Alasdair had no words and simply held on to her in silence while she rebuilt her composure brick by brick. Once her breathing was under control, he left her only long enough to fill a glass of water at the kitchen sink and bring it back. The bed dipped as he sat back down and handed it over.

Morgana levered herself up against the headboard and curled her legs underneath her. She looked so tiny and fragile in that position, dwarfed by the bed. Her hands shook so badly that she had to use both to raise the glass to her lips.

"How do you know that he only has a few months to live?" Alasdair asked. "They have treatments now, cures. Surely, you're taking this out of context."

Morgana shook her head sadly, staring into the glass of water as if searching for something in her wavering reflection. "He's not responding to treatments. Sophie's only hope is that he lives to see the baby."

"Sophie?" Alasdair asked, searching his memory. "Ah yes, the sister."

She nodded. Then slowly told him the story, beginning with the invitation for dinner at the Martels' that had finally and completely torn down all the barriers around her heart only to leave it shattered upon the rocks.

"I love him," Morgana said. "I love him more than I ever thought was possible."

"I know darlin'." He'd known all along. Even while she fought it, he'd known that she had fallen even before she had recognized the first step.

She blinked at him, at his open honesty and sighed. "I was finally prepared to spend a lifetime with him. Fifty, sixty years, maybe. This isn't enough!"

He had nothing to say to that and was sure that his sympathy showed plainly on his face. There was an unfamiliar tightening in his throat which he forced down with a hard swallow.

"I gather you haven't discussed any of this with Patrick."

"I couldn't," she told him, voice tight with despair. "He came in as I was leaving, but I couldn't even look at him. I knew, at that point, I would have shattered like glass. Problem is, it's happened anyway."

Hours later, spent and exhausted, Morgana fell asleep.

Alasdair found himself awake, cradling a steaming cup of coffee, staring out at the night. The air was clear here, but most of the stars were blotted out by the lights of the city around his house. He took slow sips and struggled with his own thoughts.

It was as if his own life had suddenly been forced under a harsh light after everything they'd discussed. Through all his casual relationships, he'd thought that the comfort of a woman in his bed for a night, regardless of whether he would ever see her again or even remember her name come morning, was enough. But now, he knew that he'd give up countless centuries for a mere moment with one woman who meant everything.

He took another sip, eyes drifting to the ceiling, his thoughts reaching for Morgana, wishing that there was something he could do to ease her pain. Fate was truly a mysterious thing with one sick sense of humor. But even fate couldn't be so cruel. There had to be a reason that Morgana and Patrick, had been brought together.

If only he knew what that was.

Morgana returned to Kingston the next day, expecting a full Hunter welcoming party to be waiting at the gate. But it didn't come, and she wasn't sure whether to be relieved or insulted as she hailed a taxi and watched the streets pass by. Martel had had two days to prepare in her absence, to ready the killing blow. She knew it was coming, but not what form it would take.

The taxi pulled up in front of her building. For a moment, she simply stared up at the sturdy, red brick edifice, almost identical to its neighbors, but unmistakable to her. It had been her home, that top floor, almost completely hidden from the street by the wrought iron fire escape. Its walls guarded her life and her life's work.

She took a step forward, but then stopped. Had that curtain just moved? She sighed, braced herself for the inevitable, and walked inside.

Fred looked up and beamed at her. "There you are, Miss Dericault!" He excitedly waved his arm. "I've been worried about you. Your man too. He's been by two, three dozen times since you left."

"Really?" The ground tilted under her feet. "Has he been by recently?"

Fred shook his head. "Not since maybe eight this morning."

Morgana glanced at her watch. It was almost one. "Has anyone else come looking for me?"

"No, ma'am."

Her heart began to pound in her ears.

"Are you all right, Miss Dericault?"

She schooled her expression with what little composure she had left. "Fine," she answered mustering a smile from somewhere. "Thank you, Fred."

He nodded and went back to his work, unaware that anything was wrong. Perhaps nothing was, but she had learned long ago that it was better to feel foolish afterwards than to be foolish and unprepared ahead of time. Morgana went toward the elevators, then made a sharp turn for the stairs. The bare concrete steps with a red-painted steel rail were little used but clean. Utilitarian in a building that was all grace and beauty. It also echoed much more than she would have liked. Luckily, she had not worn heels for the flight, but quiet rubber soled shoes. The boom of the door opening made her cringe. That alone would have carried all the way to the penthouse, alerting any sentries Martel had left posted while he took up position in her apartment.

Cursing silently and fluently in several languages, Morgana slid the bag from her shoulder and left it just inside the door. She stepped to the base of the stairs and cautiously looked up through the narrow gap between the spiraling flights, but the top was hidden in shadow as she started up.

By the third floor, her heart was pounding; but by the fifth, the icy calm that had been missing all these months, the kind that made her the hunter, not the hunted, had wrapped around her like a mantle. Just as she approached the next landing, the door closest to her opened. Morgana retreated a step and brought her hands up, ready to deflect a blow swung her way. Her foot slipped, and for a breathless moment, she teetered on the edge of falling before she gripped the railing.

A tumble down the stairs wouldn't kill her of course, but it would hurt a lot, and would leave her vulnerable for several precious minutes while she recovered. But the woman who entered the stairwell wasn't a Hunter, just one of her fellow tenants. The woman hesitated, her hand on the still-open door, a basket of laundry balanced on her hip. Morgana gave her a sheepish smile as she skirted the door and resumed her climb.

The woman shook her head dismissively and continued down the stairs.

Morgana put the woman out of her mind and stopped at the next floor. With only two left, there should be some sound, some sign. But there was no murmur of voices, no heavy breathing typical of Martel's men so she continued on to the top floor. Cautiously, she eased the door open a crack. The echo at the top reverberated through the stairwell as much as it had from the bottom, and she braced herself for whatever might be waiting.

The door to her apartment was easily visible through the crack, but she could see little else. Taking a deep breath, clenching the only weapon she had, a fist, Morgana pulled the door open the rest of the way. She leapt into the foyer to find it empty. Confused now, she crossed to the door to her apartment and put a hand to the handle and turned it slowly. Expecting the door to open under her hand, she instead found it securely locked.

Maybe she had imagined the movement she had seen from the street?

Morgana fitted her keys to their locks and opened the door. "Hello?" she called into the apartment, legs braced for an easy leap back into the hallway, to close the heavy oak door against a hail of bullets or crossbow bolts.

There was no answer. She took a cautious step inside, reaching immediately for the small satchel that hung from a peg just inside the closet. She flicked open the blade as she crossed the entranceway and looked up the hallway. The door to the office was closed, the keypad lights a steady red. She continued toward the living room and stopped dead in her tracks.

The window along the fire escape was broken. In the middle was a hole the size of her hand, or the toe of the boot that had likely made it, a spiderweb of cracks radiated in all directions. The shards of a porcelain vase full of dry flowers lay scattered on the floor among the glass.

"Hello?" she called again.

When there was no answer, she crept across the room and looked out the window. The room was empty, as was the fire escape outside. The hole in the glass wasn't big enough for a person to get through. Whoever had broken it hadn't done it to get inside. Or maybe they had, to reach for a release that wasn't there, and gave up.

She crouched to examine the debris on the floor and found a wad of paper among the shards of glass. With shaking hands, Morgana pinned a corner to the carpet with the knife and, remembering the poison-covered dagger, shook her sleeve down over her hand to smooth the paper flat without touching it with her bare skin. There was a single word written in thick black marker.

Soon.

Twenty-Eight

M organa cleaned up the glass and taped a piece of plastic over the pane to at least keep the cold out and, asked Fred to tell their superintendent to come fix it, on her way by. She didn't pause to give him any details.

Once outside, Morgana dialed Patrick's cell phone. When the voicemail recording started, she ground her teeth and hung up without leaving a message. She dialed his office next.

"Davies & McNamara, June speaking, how may I help you?"

"Hi June, it's Morgana." She replied. "Morgana Dericault from Albrecht. Is Patrick in?"

"You just missed him," her voice already cheerful turned excited. "His sister went into labor, he just left."

"Which hospital?"

"Saint Catherine's."

"Thanks, June." Morgana hung up and walked to the corner to flag down a taxi.

Within moments, a yellow car with a lit sign on the roof responded to her outstretched arm. She gave the driver the destination, which was across town and sat back, one leg bouncing as they wove through the busy city streets. When it pulled up at the emergency room doors, she gave the driver a little extra and got out.

The din of crying children and ringing phones hit her like a physical wall as the door slid open. Morgana pushed against it, ears almost ringing as she wove through the rows of seats and parked wheelchairs to get to the reception desk.

The dark-haired woman with olive skin looked up from a tablet as Morgana stepped up. "Can I help you?"

"Maternity?"

The woman pointed to the hallway behind her. "Take a left at the end, then the elevator to the fourth floor."

Morgana thanked her and followed the directions. The elevator opened into another, quieter waiting room, the walls decorated with pastel rainbows and smiling clouds. She crossed to the nurse's station and gave Sophie's name.

The nurse typed the name and looked back up. "Are you family?"

Morgana hesitated. "Yes," she replied finally.

The nurse nodded and glanced back at her screen. "Looks like she's just come back to her room, and I think I just saw her family heading back there. Room 412."

Morgana thanked her and started walking in the direction the nurse had indicated. At first, she moved with purpose, but the closer she got, the slower her feet moved.

What am I doing here? she wondered, thinking of the last conversations she'd had with Patrick. And with Sophie.

She reached the closed door to Sophie's room, but hesitated with her hand raised. There was a glass pane in the window, with a colorful cling modeled after stained glass stuck to it for privacy. Shadows moved inside, but she couldn't make out who. Just as she worked up the nerve to knock, the door opened and Patrick stepped out.

They collided and clutched at each other as they careened across the hall. Morgana slammed back-first into the wall and narrowly missed hitting her head too. Patrick managed to catch himself with one arm braced on the wall next to her shoulder, but he let out a hiss of pain and hopped on his good leg.

Now that she knew, it was painfully obvious how much he favored the bad leg as he flexed his knee a few times, and didn't quite put full weight on when he put his foot back on the floor.

"Morgana!" His voice echoed in the hallway. "What are you doing here?"

Morgana pushed off the wall, trying to ignore the ache in one shoulder from the impact.

Before she could answer, Sophie parroted her name from inside the room.

Morgana took a step to the right to see Patrick's sister sitting up in bed, looking expressionlessly in her direction. After a moment, she beckoned them to come inside. Patrick looked over at the open doorway and back to her. His expression was cold, closed.

"We need to talk."

He nodded. "Yes, we do. But my sister is calling for you. Whatever we have to say to each other can wait until after."

Morgana held his gaze, swallowed, then straightened the lapels of her jacket, and turned to the open door. Martel sat in a chair on the far side of the bed. He was leaning back, head propped on one hand, but his eyes were fully alert and looking straight at her. She took a deep breath and walked inside.

Sophie was covered in a pile of blankets pulled high on her chest, leaving her arms and shoulders bare, a small bundle in her arms. She looked tired, but happy, though there was a cautious wariness in her eyes as Morgana crossed the room. She eased the baby more securely into one elbow and used the other to push herself up a little straighter. She winced and Martel was half out of his chair before she waved him back.

"How are you?"

Sophie gave her a cautious smile, and turned back the edge of the blanket so Morgana could see a crown of dark brown hair. "Sore, but good." She replied. "I'm just glad he's healthy, being early. Meet Christopher Patrick Martel." She glanced at his namesake when she said the middle name.

"Well, hello Christopher." Morgana reached out a hand and gently ran it over the soft fuzz. The baby stretched, a tightly closed fist waving, and yawned. "Being born is such tiring work," Morgana huffed a laugh through her nose. "Welcome to the world, little one."

Sophie's expression softened. "I'm glad you came."

A little of the stiffness in Morgana's shoulders eased at her words.

Sophie's eyes lifted up over Morgana's shoulder. She didn't need to turn to know that Patrick stood close behind. The icy tension vibrating off him radiated into her back.

"Congratulations to you both," she said, smiling at Sophie, and also at Martel. He was now leaning forward, elbows braced on his knees. His expression was softened for Sophie's benefit, but the Hunter inside was showing in his eyes.

Morgana glanced over her shoulder at Patrick, who raised an eyebrow and made just the slightest jerk of his head toward the door. She turned back to Sophie and smiled again. "I'm going to let you get some rest."

Morgana touched Sophie's arm affectionately, nodded to Martel, and left the room. Patrick said his goodbyes and joined her in the hallway a moment later, coat draped over his arm.

"Take a walk with me?" he asked, his arm sweeping out in the direction of the elevator, and they headed off side-by-side down the corridor. Patrick shrugged into his coat as the car descended back to the first floor. They were outside the Emergency Room doors before either said a word.

"How did you know that I would be here?"

"Your phone was off, so I called your office," Morgana replied. "June told me."

Patrick nodded and for a moment they walked in silence. When he spoke next, his voice was resigned. "So, Sophie said she told you."

Morgana turned and looked up at him. "She did." Despite the stiffness in him, she stepped closer and put a hand on his forearm. "I'm so sorry, Patrick."

He didn't say anything, just looked down at her hand on his arm and then back up at her. There was anger now, and frustration in his eyes. "What the hell happened on Friday night, Morgana? I see you running out of my pregnant sister's house and rush in to find the table covered in blood, a bloody towel by the sink, and my sister crying into a fucking dishcloth saying that you and I need to talk."

He captured both of her hands and examined them closely turning them back and forth under the harsh, but bright lights overhead. "That was two days ago, and there's not a mark on you."

Morgana sighed. "That's why I've been trying to call. I want to tell you everything," she said, looking around. A young woman passed by them headed inside, supporting a crying child with a visibly dislocated elbow. "But not here. Is there somewhere we can go?"

He nodded, then jerked his head, and started walking.

She took a moment to study him. He was the most casually dressed she had ever seen, in dark jeans and a khaki-colored jacket over a cream sweater with the same white sneakers that he'd had on at the party. He moved stiffly, not bending his right knee much, but his face didn't show any discomfort. "Did you drive here?"

She shook her head. "I took a cab."

He stopped and turned back when her voice was further away than expected. "Mine is in the garage a couple of blocks away." He lifted an eyebrow. "Coming?"

She took a couple of running steps to catch up to him. They walked in silence for two blocks, then stopped at the corner under the historic marquee of one of the largest theaters in the city to wait for the cross-walk. The flashing lights advertised that the hottest touring musical was currently playing. The street was crowded even in the dimming light of a late Sunday afternoon, with all the restaurants and theaters crammed into the surrounding blocks.

"The garage is just down this way," Patrick said, pointing left.

"Just a second," Morgana replied. Her eyes had come to rest on a couple nearby who were studying a map that looked like it had seen better days when an actor had been the American President. They were in their fifties at the least, dressed in jeans and windbreakers, weighed down by cameras and backpacks, a suitcase at their feet. They looked thoroughly out of place among the more sophisticated city-dwellers, and completely lost.

The man caught her watching them and held up the map. "Can you help us?"

She gave them a polite smile and approached slowly, giving herself an extra second or two to study them. Their clothes had no tell-tale bagginess or bulges that would suggest concealed weapons. The man had a bit of a paunch, suggesting a desk job, though the muscles on the woman's forearms stood out as she gripped the map. Yoga or Pilates, maybe.

"What can I do for you?"

The wife gestured to the map in her husband's hands and then to the buildings around them. "We're looking for the Mackenzie Arms Hotel." she pushed a few strands of straight black hair behind her ear nervously. "Their website says that they're on Stafford Street, which from what I remember is somewhere around here."

Morgana glanced around and made sure she had her bearings, and then turned back with a knowing smile. "When was the last time you were here?"

"I came here to shop a few times when I was in college, maybe twenty, twenty-five years ago," the woman answered, a slightly sheepish look on her face. "I will admit this area looks very different from what I remember."

"Very different," Morgana agreed. "When they built Saint Catherine's Hospital, they diverted Stafford Street into Pinewood, here," she pointed to the map, drawing the new path with her finger. "The

Mackenzie Arms is still there, but it's a good seven or eight blocks away, and it takes a bit of weaving to get there now. You're best off turning around and going a block back to Mason and picking up the Gold Line train. Go two stations uptown and you'll find the hotel right here," she indicated another spot on the map, "go right at the top of the Stafford side of the exit."

The husband scratched over his right ear and raised the map up closer to his eyes as if he had forgotten or lost his glasses then looked at her dubiously. On the map in his hands, the Gold Line hadn't yet been extended that far north. "The extension opened twelve years ago," Morgana clarified. "Trust me, it's there."

He glanced at his wife for confirmation. "That sounds easy enough."

She nodded and smiled. "Thanks so much."

"No problem," Morgana answered, and turned away with a wave. After a few steps, she stopped and turned back, the husband was still struggling to fold up the crumpled map. "Oh, and you might want to get yourself a new map."

They both laughed. "We will," he said. "Thanks again." He took his wife's elbow gently in one hand, grabbed the handle of the suitcase in the other, and they walked away.

Morgana turned and walked back to Patrick who was waiting a few feet away. His eyes were wide, his mouth slightly open. She found herself smiling nervously. "What?"

"What do you mean, 'what?'?" he asked incredulously, and a chuckle escaped his lips. "That's for me to ask. What the heck was that?"

Morgana shrugged. "Just giving directions."

"I've lived here on and off for half my life and I wouldn't have been able to do that."

"Guess I've lived here longer," Morgana said. He just didn't know how true that was, not yet anyway.

Patrick eyed her suspiciously, but the ice had broken. As they continued on toward the parking garage, the air between them didn't crackle with nearly as much tension. Patrick didn't say much other than to direct her way, but it wasn't out of anger. The parking garage elevator was small and rickety and smelled like urine, but as they emerged on the third level, they both knew that he would never have managed the stairs. But neither did she make anything of it, and he sighed in gratitude. Or it may just have been the relatively fresher air outside the elevator.

Patrick turned left and led the way to where his car was parked. They rounded the corner toward the incline to the next level, and the silver BMW came into view, parked about halfway up. At the same time, there was movement between two cars to her right.

A figure, dressed in black, his face hidden in shadow stood between two vehicles. He raised a hand and a red laser sight trained in the general area of Patrick's kidneys.

Morgana cried out and shoved him out of the line of fire.

He fell to the ground in a heap then whipped his head around. There was loud bang as the gun fired. The bullet hit her in the side, the impact sent her spinning to the ground.

Patrick screamed her name and started crawling toward her.

"No, Patrick," she croaked out. "Stay back!"

But footsteps were already beating a quick retreat, followed by the slamming of a door, and the screech of tires.

Patrick reached her side and pushed her coat back get a look at the wound. A patch of red bloomed on her sweater and was spreading fast.

He cursed, and gathered a fistful of her shirt and pressed it hard against the wound.

Morgana screamed.

With his free hand, Patrick struggled to pull his cell phone from his jacket pocket. When he finally got it out, his hand shook so much he nearly dropped it. "I-I need to call 911."

Morgana's side was aflame, from the wound and from something else. "No," she managed to grunt out. "Don't. No ambulances. No hospitals."

"What are you talking about?" he cried. "You've been shot!"

"No hospitals," she repeated firmly. "Take me home. Please."

Patrick looked at her like she had completely lost her mind.

"Promise me, no hospitals!"

The pain wasn't going away, and the burning was spreading. Morgana cursed repeatedly in French. A Hunter weapon, for sure. Though it made no sense for him to run off and not go after her head. But now wasn't the time to think on that. At any moment, someone could walk or drive by and there would be no way to avoid getting the authorities involved. "Please, Patrick."

After a moment, he nodded though his eyes were wide and terrified. "I promise."

She struggled to get into a sitting position.

"Whoa, what are you doing?"

Without answering him, she took a deep breath, hand clamped down on the wound and tried to get to her feet. Patrick wrapped an arm around her waist and hauled her up against his hip, holding her steady as black spots filled her vision and the world spun around her. But at least she was on her feet.

"Help me to the car."

He put one of her arms around his shoulders and held it tightly by the wrist, then wrapped an arm around her back and placed his hand over hers on top of the wound for added pressure. Together, they stumbled the rest of the way to his car where he helped her stretch out on the back seat. "Keep pressure as best you can."

He closed the door and roared out of the parking space, and sped down to street level in a barely-controlled skid of squealing rubber.

Morgana was jolted back to awareness when Patrick slammed on his brakes in front of her building. She struggled up into a sitting position, but the burning pain and the weight that had settled into her limbs kept her from doing much more on her own. He jumped out of the car and onto the sidewalk, then yanked open the rear door and reached in to wrap an arm around under one armpit and hauled her to her feet. She tried to keep the scream in this time and succeeded with just a grunt of pain.

Another strong arm came around her waist from the other direction and Morgana looked over, just barely able to make out Fred's face through the dark spots in her vision.

"Help me inside."

"Morgana, I really think—"

"Listen to her, son, she knows what's what."

Patrick stared at him wordlessly for a moment.

"I'm bleeding here," she grunted.

Together, the two men helped her inside, her head wobbling like it was on a spring, legs becoming less steady by the moment. In the elevator, Patrick gathered her into his arms when she couldn't stand anymore. By the time they reached the top floor, they bore almost all of her weight between them to her door, which Fred opened with the master key on his belt.

"Shower," Morgana grunted.

Patrick started to protest, but she lifted her head, which weighed as much as a car and leveled him with a pleading look. "We need to wash the wound, and fast."

Once inside the white tiled room, Patrick propped Morgana against the wall and thanked Fred for his help. The bellman looked worried, but he knew her secret and had seen her come out on the right side of worse. Or so he thought.

Patrick shed both of their jackets and Morgana's shirt and tossed them to the floor. He turned the shower on full blast and half-carried her under the spray. The water instantly ran pink at their feet. The skin of the wound, a few inches above her right hip bone, was angry red and blistered. There was no exit wound.

She hissed as the water hit the raw skin and thrust the washcloth hanging from a bar near at hand into his. "Soap this up and then scrub the area around the wound, hard as you can." She told him. Her teeth were starting to chatter despite the hot water. "Keep scrubbing until the color starts to improve. Don't worry if I scream."

"Yeah, sure, don't worry." He swallowed hard but did as she asked.

And Morgana did scream as the friction added to the pain, the pressure of it pushing on the wound, and the bullet still inside. After a few moments, the burning, at least on the surface, was less. Deep down, the bullet was a hot poker stabbing toward her kidney.

"We need to get the bullet out." she told him, sliding down onto the built-in seat, and concentrated on pulling air into her lungs. She pointed toward the vanity across the room. "Top drawer, medical kit."

Patrick went and got it, unzipping the case as he hobbled back. "I don't know about this Morgana."

She managed a weak smile. "It's not very deep, but we need to get it out. It's poisoning me."

His eyes widened even more, if that was possible, but he followed her directions as she talked him through using the scalpel to make the wound bigger, and then the forceps to retrieve the bullet. It took some rooting around, and Morgana's vision grayed out in a familiar, but unwelcome way until, finally, the bullet slid free and clattered to the shower floor.

"Well done," she murmured, her voice barely a whisper, before her vision went completely dark, and all sensation ceased.

Patrick kneeled fully-clothed in the shower, which by now resembled a crime scene. The forceps, still gripped in his hand, started to shake as the enormity of what he had just done hit him. Adrenaline had driven all rational thought from his mind, and good thing, too. If he'd stopped for even a second to think about what had happened since leaving the hospital... well, he didn't know what would happen.

Morgana didn't look good. Her skin was much too pale, though the area around the wound itself had improved after he'd scrubbed the wound. Scrubbed!

Her screams still echoed in his ears. *Why did I listen to her? Why didn't I take her to the hospital?*

"Well done," she whispered. Then her breathing hitched, and she went limp.

The forceps clattered to the bottom of the shower. Her body slumped forward, and he caught her, and laid her down on the rug, calling her name. He shook her and thrust two fingers under her jaw for a pulse but couldn't find one. She wasn't breathing. He cried her name again and again as terror flooded through him.

His brain couldn't comprehend what his eyes were telling him. Sprawled out with her eyes closed, she could have been sleeping, but there was a boneless quality to her limbs that said otherwise.

Patrick scrambled back away from her, his chest heaving. Then he crawled to the pile of coats, covered in so much blood, and dug for his cell phone. Thankfully it hadn't been in his pants pocket, or it would be ruined by now. With trembling hands, he pulled it out and dialed.

His best friend picked up on the second ring. "Hey man, how's it going?"

"I need your help, Jake."

There was the creak of the hospital visitor's chair as his friend got to his feet, then the soft closing of a door as he presumably stepped into the hall. "What's wrong?"

"It's Morgana!" Patrick cried. "I think—I think she's dead."

"Dead?" The sound of running footsteps echoed over the line. "What do you mean dead?"

"We left the hospital and walked to my car and some guy just came out of nowhere and shot her!"

"Where are you?" An elevator dinged. "I'm on my way."

Patrick hesitated for a split second, knowing that Morgana was very sensitive about anyone knowing where she lived. But that didn't matter now. He gave Jake the address and hung up. Crawling back to Morgana's side, he gathered her up in his arms, face buried in her hair, and rocked, his throat choked with sobs.

How could this be happening?

Who would want her dead? Sure, she had her secrets, but never had he thought that any of them would get her hurt, and certainly not killed. But the body in his arms was too limp, and too cold. His mind churned over everything, searching for an explanation, and failed.

Time was already short, but never would he have expected that it would just run out, at least not with him being the one still alive. She had come into his life when he had been at his most desperate. The cancer was back, with him facing a terminal diagnosis before his life had really begun.

Even as he started chemo, then the treatments in Toronto, he'd lost most of his faith in modern medicine and started reaching for straws, no matter how outrageous, ridiculous, or arcane they were. Then came Jacqueline d'Arnault and her book. So much time had been spent getting it translated, learning about the people that couldn't die, trying to figure out how they gained that ability.

And it had all been for nothing.

For what seemed like forever, he just held her, smoothing his hand over and over her wet hair. The tears slowly faded into numbness as he waited for Jake to arrive. He would know what to do. Jake always did.

Just then, her body twitched, then slowly curled around the injury to her abdomen as if still in pain. But the dead didn't feel pain...

Her whole body convulsed once, then she gasped.

Twenty-Nine

Coming back to life hurt like hell.

Death was a dark, timeless abyss. A place where the pain vanished, and her sense of the world disappeared. There was no sound, no light, just an endless drifting without the sensation of either movement or weight, or the passage of time. It was like her body put her consciousness aside until it was healed enough for it to return.

When sensation did return, it started with the extremities. The hardness of the tile, cold and wet. Yet there was also warmth. Arms that surrounded her, cradled her. That warmth grew until it focused into a knot of heat burning in her abdomen. Before her heart started beating, before she had even drawn her first breath, her body began to shiver, to convulse around that pain.

When she did draw in that first breath, the arms around her loosened, and she fell to the floor in a heap. Her body was wracked with a coughing fit that sent jolts of pain through her. When it ended, she moaned and curled into a ball.

There was a tentative touch on her shoulder. "Morgana?"

She forced an eyelid open to see Patrick hovering over her. His face was ashen, his eyes round as marbles. He was soaking wet and there were pink smears of diluted blood all over him. She whispered his name and closed the eye again.

The first few moments were always a struggle, as she adjusted to being out of the void and back in her body. Normal functions like breathing or swallowing took all of her concentration, until her nervous system recovered enough to do them automatically again. Her body convulsed in waves of searing heat and the sting of thousands of needles as nerves, muscles, and tissues reanimated. The intensity of it threatened to sweep her back under.

But somehow, she weathered the storm and the tidal wave ebbed until only a knot of throbbing heat in her abdomen remained. Morgana willed her hand to move inch by laborious inch until it encountered nothing but smooth skin. The wound had healed. So why was the pain still there?

The poison.

Morgana's eyes snapped open, then blinked rapidly at the brightness in the all-white bathroom. She turned her head and looked at Patrick, kept her eyes on him as she levered herself up on one elbow. Though still wide-eyed, he scooted closer to her and helped settle her into a seated position against the side of the tub. Even that effort left her breathing hard. Her body was fighting too many things at once, trying to heal the bullet wound, battle the poison left behind, replenish the blood loss.

She needed food, and water, and rest. Lots of rest.

But Patrick needed answers first. So, she took a deep breath and coughed again, ending on a soft groan, and looked at him.

"Morgana, what the hell is going on?"

She cracked a sheepish smile. "I don't know where to start."

"From the beginning would be nice."

Figuring that demonstrations were always better than words, especially those spoken on a cold bathroom floor, Morgana scrabbled for the top of the tub, and levered up onto a knee, leaning heavily on the porcelain.

"Whoa, whoa, whoa. What are you doing?"

By then, she had one foot under her and almost toppled. He caught her and gently pulled her up. Her legs were rubbery, but he looped an arm around her waist and held her against his side.

Morgana pointed at the hallway. He supported her as she took step by wobbly step, but once they reached the door, she stopped and put a hand on the doorframe to support herself.

"I need you to go get two little boxes," she instructed, fingers sketching out the size, then pointed first toward the spare bedroom. "One is tucked behind the painting over the bed," her finger gestured in the other direction, "the other is up under the bottom shelf on the left side of the bookcase."

He gave her a dubious look, the wheels visibly turning behind those eyes as he struggled to figure out how she had been dead one minute and standing—well, half-standing in a doorway—a few minutes later. But he did as she instructed, returning a few moments later with two small Chinese puzzle boxes in his hands. They were each covered with intricate inlays of different colored wood, about an inch larger than a standard key on all sides.

Morgana took them one at a time from him and slid the panels in the right combination to retrieve the keys, then pushed off the wall and wobbled across the hallway. The intensity of his stare warmed the back of her neck as she turned the keys and then entered the codes on the keypads.

This locked door had been a point of curiosity—if not quite outright contention—between them throughout their relationship, from the first night she had brought him home. Before she opened the door, she looked over at him one last time, partly for her own benefit, partly to make sure he was prepared. He was leaning slightly forward, his lips parted, pupils wide and fixed on the door. With one more deep breath, she turned the handle and pushed it open. He jumped at the hiss of escaping air which carried the scents of aged leather, ink, and paper out into the hallway.

Those familiar smells gave her a boost like a jolt of caffeine on the air. She staggered inside, one hand pressed against her abdomen and settled laboriously into the chair.

It took a moment for Patrick to appear in the doorway. His breath shuddered out of him and he swayed into the doorframe for a moment before taking a few tentative steps inside. His eyes surveyed the endless row upon row of leather-bound tomes each three to four inches thick that filled three walls. An almost daily account of seven hundred years of life took up space after all.

Slowly, he circled the small room, breath coming faster and faster. He brushed his fingers along the spines on one shelf, so similar to the one he had in his safe, and looked at her. At her nod, he picked one at random and turned toward the desk.

Morgana pushed the stand with the current book back and then rolled out of the way.

The heavy book hit the desk with a soft thump. He turned back the cover, but then hesitated. "Should I be wearing gloves?"

Morgana suppressed a laugh and shook her head. But one bubbled out of her anyway when he looked down at the page. If he'd had trouble with the notes in the margins of Swift, he would certainly have problems with that one as it was written in an even older German dialect. Half of it anyway.

The other half was in Russian.

He flipped through it anyway. The words may have been unintelligible, but the handwriting could not be mistaken, even in Cyrillic. He glanced up at her once and then buried his head again.

"Where did you get these?"

Morgana closed her eyes and took a breath, hearing the pure shock and awe in his voice. She didn't speak right away, but pulled the chair back to the desk. Taking the older tome into her lap, she slid the current volume under his hands and flipped back a few pages.

Patrick stepped back in at her invitation to read the entry about the party at the Martels' house in Dane. He braced his arms on the desk and bent over the book, squinting because he didn't have his reading glasses. His immediate reaction was a smile that this one at least was in English, but he only read a few lines before he frowned and his eyes sought hers out. Morgana held his gaze square on and nodded.

"Yes," she said in answer to his unspoken question. "*I* wrote them."

It was a good thing that he was leaning on the desk, because he looked like he was going to fall over. "B-but how?" he asked. "That would make you--"

"Seven hundred and thirty-six last March," she answered, finishing his thought. Patrick put a hand to his stomach as if she had punched him, chest heaving.

"Why didn't you tell me?' He asked. She had expected to hear anger in his voice, but got something more painful. Despair.

"I should have." She hung her head. "But I was afraid."

"Afraid?" he asked as if that was no excuse. "Of what?"

She raised her head again. "Of the look that you have on your face right now. That once you learned the truth, you would leave me, or hate me, because I am not the woman you thought me to be." She was horrified to find that her voice trembled. "But worst of all, I have been hunted all my life, by humans who want nothing more than to see the inside of this room and get at the knowledge contained here. There was no way of knowing if you were one of them."

Patrick stared at her in disbelief, then pushed violently away from the desk took a step toward the door.

Morgana grabbed his arm before he could get far. "Wait, please, hear me out."

He stopped, but he didn't look at her, just stood stiffly, waiting.

"I can sense others of my kind. *Any* mortal could be a Hunter." She told him. "I... I know now that there is no way that you could be one."

"And who exactly *are* you?"

"That would take a very long time to explain." She held up a hand when he started to protest, thinking she was evading the subject again. "But I'm going to tell you. As I said, I have been running for centuries, never managing to stay in any one place for very long. The monastery in the book you have was probably the longest. Other than here in Kingston."

He made a distressed sound. His hand came up and removed hers from his arm, but only to thread their fingers together. The contact grounded her, gave her something to concentrate on other than the pain in her abdomen.

She brushed a lock of wet hair behind her ear and settled into a more comfortable position. "My birth name is Mérande. I was born in Arricau, France in 1287. Five years ago, when I came back to Kingston, I swore to myself that I was going to stop running. That I would stay *here*."

She winced at a sudden flare of pain and took a moment to just breathe. "I chose to become Morgana Dericault for that reason. It's the closest I have ever come to my real name." She met his eyes and gave him a wry smile. "Did you know that I am the only person to have *ever* lived in this apartment?"

Patrick shook his head.

"I commissioned the building, and still own it through a dizzying framework of investment holdings and shell companies. It's my home." A pound of her fist punctuated the last words. She swallowed hard at the sudden tightness in her throat that choked off her words.

She looked down and lifted her hand from the area where the bullet wound had been. It now resembled a six-month-old scar, even though the skin around it was still red and angry.

Patrick dropped stiffly to his knees, and reached out a hand, his fingers cool on her skin. "How is this possible?"

"I usually heal very quickly."

"Usually?" He asked. "You don't consider this to be healed?"

Morgana shook her head and shifted on the chair. She held out her hand and pointed to a thin pink line between thumb and forefinger.

"This is what remains from the cut that left all that blood at your sister's house."

Patrick took her hand in his, traced the line. A shiver went up her arm.

"And I am sorry about that. For leaving the mess behind for Sophie to clean up." When he just blinked at her like a large red owl, Morgana gently withdrew her hand and touched the new scar. "As for this, the Hunters have a nasty habit of coating their weapons in poisons that are stronger than our healing abilities can keep up with. That's why I had you scrub it off, much as it hurt."

Patrick winced as if her screams still rang in his ears.

"Unfortunately," she continued, unable to suppress a grunt of discomfort as she adjusted her position in the chair. "Cleaning the skin and removing the bullet means that the entrance wound has healed, trapping the rest of the poison inside until my body can clear it. And before you ask, I'll be fine, it will just take a couple of days."

"Just don't die on me again."

She chuckled, which ended on a cough that had her curling around the injury. "Not planning on it," she grunted. "Also, don't make me laugh."

"Sorry," he replied. Then he shivered, a full body shake.

Morgana shivered in reflex, and finally took stock of their clothing, noticing for the first time that she was sitting in her writing chair in only trousers and bra.

He was fully clothed, and both of them were still very wet.

She had a sudden irrational urge to cover herself with her hands and brushed it off. After everything they had been through, a little bared flesh was nothing.

She pushed up from the chair to find her legs were steadier, though still very weak.

"Where are you going?"

"To put some dry clothes on," she said, motioning for him to follow. "Go check the closet in the spare bedroom. My friend Alasdair might have left something behind that would fit you."

He nodded gratefully and followed her down the hallway. They parted ways into the two bedrooms and Morgana dropped her clothes into a pile with a wet plop. She wrapped herself in the robe that hung on the back of her door and pulled the lapels tight, glad for any bit of warmth while she dug the thickest, warmest clothes out of the recesses of her closet, coming out with a pair of black lounge pants and a cozy, cream Cashmere sweater. She practically dove into the sweater. The silky softness slid along her skin, and she hugged its warmth to her.

A soft footstep brought her head up. Patrick walked in wearing a pair of straight leg sweatpants and a thermal Henley top. Everything fit just slightly off, the pants too short, the top a bit too tight across Patrick's broad shoulders, but at least they were clean and dry. He was carrying his wet clothes and bent to retrieve hers from the floor as well.

Morgana led the way slowly toward the living room.

Patrick tossed their clothes into the pile in the bathroom to be dealt with later and rubbed clammy hands on his pant legs.

She went to the kitchen and retrieved a couple of bottles of water from the fridge and handed one to him. They went to the sofa and sat close together, but not quite touching. Patrick remained watchful, but quiet, as she told him her story, her words very similar to when she'd told Sophie.

At one point, Patrick's eyes went wide, and he murmured, almost under his breath, as his sister had. "Centuries?"

At some point, she took his hand and held it tightly for courage. The story flooded out of her, but where Sophie had begrudged her secrets, Patrick's response was only one of stunned silence.

"I was almost fifty years old before I first met someone like me, who told me what I was, why I hadn't aged. He taught me how to read and write for the first time, and since then, I've kept a journal of sorts, writing wherever and whenever I could, on whatever was available."

She pointed back down the hall. "The Chronicles in there were started in the early fifteenth century when it was easier to find materials and when it was becoming more and more culturally acceptable to educate women." The derision in her tone brought a hint of a smile to Patrick's lips. "I consolidated most of my original writings into the first couple of books and then just kept going."

"I have a question about that," he said holding up a finger. "Why the hell couldn't you have written the damn things in English?"

Morgana threw back her head and laughed. "Because I didn't *learn* English until I was about four hundred years old."

Despite the fact that she had spent years in Scotland, Ireland, and England, it was true. Most of Ireland had spoken Gaelic anyway, Scotland too. And enough people spoke French. She could probably remember the words now if she tried, though few could understand the ancient dialects she knew.

"I wrote in whatever language was being used around me at the time. You have no idea what running for your life can do for your linguistic skills."

He chuckled, and his chest vibrated with it. "How many languages *do* you speak?"

She thought for a moment. "Twenty-seven, I think. Wait, no, twenty-eight."

He rolled his eyes. "Now you're just showing off."

She smiled and playfully swatted him on the chest. "No, I'm not, I'm just being honest." She said, "although, you would need to be a pretty keen linguist to understand most of it. A temporary deterrent at least for someone who wanted an easy way to get to us."

"Yeah, because I know a ton of people who can read fourteenth century Greek."

"Actually, I spent most of the 1300's in Britain and Scandinavia."

"Oh, excuse me, like Old Norse is that much easier to read," he said tartly, but he was smiling, and it was infectious. Their eyes met and held for a long breathless moment. His smile faded, a familiar heat kindling in his eyes that she hadn't dared hope to see again.

It stirred something deep in her, but she forced it away with a conscious effort. "So, tell me, what do you want to know?"

His eyes cleared and her heart twisted at the loss. "How did they always find you, if they didn't know how to pick you out of the crowd?"

She shivered, and not entirely from the cold.

Patrick reached for the throw blanket draped over the arm of the sofa behind him and wrapped it around her shoulders. His hands lingered, and for a moment she thought he would draw her into his arms, but then he sat back.

Morgana gripped the blanket tightly under her chin. "The downside of never aging I guess, is that we never change," she answered. "For me, it was the red hair. Back then it was even less common and was looked upon as if one had been touched by the devil. I did everything that I could, rubbed soot in it, always wore a hood or a cap. But it didn't matter where I was, they always found me. It really is quite the mystery. Ranks right up there with how I got to be this way in the first place."

"You mean that you *don't* know?"

Morgana shook her head, and took a deep, shuddering breath.

Patrick squeezed her hand, and she held on as if it were a lifetime. What she had to say next was going to be the hardest confession of her life.

"It was the winter of 1312; I'll never forget it. My husband and I had laid in enough provisions to last until spring, we'd hoped at least. But the snow came early and heavily, and we were cut off. For almost two weeks, we couldn't leave our cottage long enough to even gather more firewood. Soon the wood ran out, and then the food froze and since we had no fire to thaw or cook it, we starved. We lost our son Henri first, because I had no milk to nurse him." Her breath hitched around the lump in her throat, but she forced herself to press on, ignoring the quick, wide flare, and then tenderness, in Patrick's eyes at the revelation that she had been married. Borne a child.

She looked down at their joined hands. If she focused on his face, she'd never finish. "I can *still* feel his absence in my heart, so you can probably understand what I was feeling then. It was a month after my son's death that I too succumbed to Death's grasp."

Her eyes drifted closed as she sighed. "But for some reason, he lost his grip, or let me go, and I didn't stay dead." She laughed at that, but there was no humor in it. "It would have been so different if I had. My husband wouldn't have tracked me across Europe and gathered to him men who would become the first Hunters. Because of me, my people are almost extinct."

She buried her face in a hand. "If I had died that cold winter's night, I wouldn't have spent centuries on the run, always alone, never changing. Never daring to let anyone in, because someday they would die, and I would be—"

Patrick glanced up sharply as her words trailed off and took her hand away from her face.

The hands cradling hers were so warm, and so much larger than hers. She looked into his eyes and silently willed him to take her into his arms and take the pain away.

"So that's the real reason?" he asked as it all became clear. "That's foolish, Morgana."

She gave him a sheepish look. "It is the only promise I've made to myself and kept. It has kept me grounded, kept me sane."

"But all this time? Alone?" For a long moment, his eyes lost their focus as he retreated into his own thoughts. When they focused again, there was something in their depths that she hadn't quite seen before. "I wish that I could have been there to walk the centuries with you."

Her throat closed, her reply a deep, breathy whisper. "So do I." But the lift in her heart at his words was swiftly slammed back down by a wave of regret as the reality of that hit her, and how empty her life had been before him. How little time they had left.

"What changed your mind now?"

"You," she answered. "You broke apart every barrier I'd ever put up between myself and the outside world, and then the thickest one that I'd ever built... around my heart. I don't have mortal friends; I don't have mortal loves."

His lips parted, and there was a slight hitch in his breath.

"Alasdair was right. I had denied my heart for too long and it was dying." She pulled one hand loose to rest it on his cheek. "And the truth of it is that I should have told you from that day in my office when you brought one of the scattered pieces of my life back to me, because that's when I think I fell in love with you, and I should have been honest from the start."

"Morgana, I—"

The phone by the front door rang, cutting off anything he was going to say.

Her head snapped over to it, and she and Patrick rose to their feet at the same time. "What the—?" She turned her head back to him. "Who is it?"

He looked at her and there was a hint of sheepishness in his expression.

"Who is here, Patrick?" She demanded though inside, she already knew.

"Jake."

Thirty

T he name hit her like a physical blow. "How could you?"
"You were dead, Morgana!"

She didn't have a reply for that. If she had been in his shoes,
would she have done anything different than call her best friend for
help?

When she remained frozen, he walked past her and went to
answer the phone. "Hello, Fred," he said, his voice far too casual.
"She's fine. Yeah, not much can keep her down apparently." He
laughed, but it was brittle. "Yes, he's a friend of mine. Let him up."

Morgana's heart was fit to beat out of her chest as he hung up
the phone. She turned away and went to close the office door, there
was no way she was letting Martel in there. When she turned back,
Patrick was right behind her.

She jumped back with a yelp.

"Are you going to tell me now what it is about Jake that bothers you?"

Morgana sighed and brushed by him, heading back to the kitchen with him in her wake. "Morgana?" he prompted.

"Please, let's just get through this right now and I'll tell you." She took up position so the kitchen island was between her and the door, with the knife drawer under her right hand. "Look, you are one of only a few people who know where I live. My life depends on that list being very, *very* short."

His shoulders hunched. "He's my best friend, Morgana. I don't keep secrets from him."

"And I don't want to ask you to do that," she said. "I completely understand that I'm putting you in a difficult position. If you want, let me handle everything. That way it won't be you lying to him."

Patrick studied her for a moment as he thought it over. "Semantics," he growled finally and ran a hand through his hair as he stalked past her to the fridge. He pulled out a yogurt and brought it over to her, reaching without looking into the silverware drawer to grab a spoon. "Here, you need to eat something."

A burst of heat broke through the terror writhing through her, an odd sense of satisfaction at how familiar he was with the kitchen, how easily he located what he needed. Morgana accepted the food gratefully and tore the lid off the container. She needed calories; lots of them, and soon. A moment later, she scraped the last of the yogurt from the bottom of the cup and set it down on the island.

As if the cup had struck the elevator bell instead of the counter, a chime rang in the foyer. Bracing herself on the marble top, Morgana drew herself up as tall as she could, though it made the half-healed wound scream. Martel had seen them only an hour or two earlier and she hoped that, other than clearly having taken a shower, she didn't look too badly off. Otherwise, she was sure that he'd take one look and decide to take another shot at her, or worse finish the job, best friend or not.

Then Martel was pounding on the door, calling Patrick's name. At her nod, his friend went to the door and let him in. Martel hesitated only slightly and as he entered, his eyes looked everywhere, finally coming to rest on Morgana, where she stood on the far side of the kitchen alive and mostly well.

"What's going on Pat?" His eyes narrowed in confusion. "I thought you said that she was dead."

Morgana laughed, despite the fact that it hurt, and tried to keep her voice as casual as possible. A difficult feat with the last person in Kingston that she ever wanted to grace her doorstep standing just inside. "Oh, Patrick, is that what you told him?" she chided. "I'm sorry that he brought you all the way over here. Work was really busy today and I forgot to eat. Went to take a shower after we got back, and I passed out. Must have been pretty scary, huh?"

Patrick looked at her with an odd expression on his face, as if mesmerized by her ability to lie so easily. Inwardly, she winced, but only slightly widened her eyes. Patrick finally got the cue though he was clearly uncomfortable. "For sure," he replied slowly. "If you'll excuse me for a moment, I need to use the washroom."

Morgana watched him go, the hitch in his step a little more pronounced after having been on his feet for a while. Concern warred with the relief to have him out of the room, even momentarily. With Patrick gone, Martel was looking at her as if only truly seeing her for the first time.

"So, now that we're alone, want to tell me what really happened?"

"What do you mean?" she asked. "I passed out."

"Oh please," he quipped. "You look like death warmed over, and not two hours ago, you were fine. And for someone like you to look like that, something pretty serious had to have happened."

She took a deep breath and fought the urge to lean on the island. "Patrick and I left the hospital and headed for his car," she told him. "We were almost there, when someone shot me."

"And Patrick saw it?"

She nodded, "though I wouldn't think I'd have to tell you that," she quipped, "it was probably you who pulled the trigger. What did you do, follow us?"

"Excuse me?"

"Dressed all in black, red laser sight, bullets coated in Glisane. Ring any bells?"

His eyes narrowed, and he waved a hand demonstrably at his jeans and gray jacket. "I came here straight from the hospital, where I have been the whole time. My wife *did* just have a baby."

Her heart stuttered. "Then who was it? One of your men?"

Martel's piercing brown gaze, which until then had been burrowing into her, went unfocused as he thought for a moment. Then his head tipped back, and he rolled his eyes.

"Schaffer." The name sounded like a curse.

"Who?" Morgana asked, but she didn't have time to panic about there being more than one Hunter actively, well, hunting her, not with one standing less than five feet away.

"It has to be him," he snarled, then a cruel smile spread across his face. "I should thank him for trying to take you out, but to do it in front of Patrick was just sloppy." The smile dropped from his face. "Does he know?"

"What?"

"Clearly you convinced him to bring you here and then died on him, or he wouldn't have called me in such a panic." Martel replied. "But now he seems his usual self, more or less."

Morgana resisted the urge to look over her shoulder and risk drawing attention to the office door, and simply nodded. "He knows."

"What did you tell him about me?"

Morgana shrugged. "It wasn't my secret to tell, given that he is your best friend, and that you have known each other all your lives." She answered. "Despite what you think about me, I understand the value of such a connection."

"That's oddly moral of you."

"You don't know me, Martel," she snapped. "You think I'm so evil, that I have this grand design to destroy humanity or take over the world or whatever the hell it is that you think we want. Get over yourself!"

He glanced towards the hallway as if her outburst would summon Patrick back into the room. When he didn't appear, Martel turned his gaze back to Morgana.

She clenched her fists and took a deep breath before continuing. "You know, I've never really understood what you Jacob Lembaye Martel have against me, or against my people."

Martel narrowed his eyes. "That is the second time that you have thrown my middle name at me as if it was some kind of revelation."

"It's one of the oldest Hunter lines, is it not? Descended from Roul de Lembaye, of the first band of men to come together to hunt down an immortal?" She scoffed, her mouth pursed at the bitterness coating her mouth. "Though, at the time, they thought they were hunting a witch or a demon who had stolen a child from his father. But my husband, with Roul and his men, created a mob of hate that has continued to pursue me ever since."

Martel staggered back a step. "W-wait, you mean to tell me that *you're* the First Hunted?" The shock, and oddly enough, reverence in his voice at the title startled her.

"I don't think I've ever heard that term. But I guess... yes, in a way the Hunters exist because of me," she replied, bracing herself against the island as a wave of grief flooded over her. All those lives lost. "But that was centuries ago. What I want to know is how you personally got involved. What could I, or any of my people, have done specifically *to you* to make you the way you are?"

He was silent for so long that Morgana began to think he wasn't going to answer. But just as he opened his mouth, a door in the hallway opened and Patrick's slightly shuffling step started up the hallway. He came over to her and put an arm around her shoulder, placing a quick kiss to her temple so he could whisper in her ear. "I took care of the cleanup."

She nodded. With her eyes still trained on Martel, she'd seen the flash in his eyes at Patrick's easy affection. It had surprised her too. They still had a lot to talk about, but with the truth had come acceptance and, hopefully, the beginnings of forgiveness. For one truth at least.

But they had only moved on to the next secret, one that spread tentacles through Patrick's whole life. Unsure, she waited to see what Martel's next move would be. He leaned casually and braced his forearms on the kitchen island.

"Everything okay out here?" Patrick asked, glancing between them.

Morgana could only guess at how much he had heard, if anything. "Yeah, fine." It wasn't exactly a lie.

Martel spread his hands. "Just fine. And delightful as Morgana is for company, I'm still confused about why I'm here. You wouldn't have called unless it was urgent, and I'd say thinking your girlfriend was dead is pretty fucking urgent, Patrick."

Morgana and Patrick exchanged a quick look.

"I'm sorry, man," he said, rubbing the back of his neck. "I panicked. But as you can see, she's not dead."

At least not yet, Morgana thought to herself. She needed to get Martel out of the apartment and to start thinking of next steps now that her home was no longer a secret from the Hunters. As if on cue, she swayed against Patrick, as the adrenaline that had been fueling her since she'd awakened finally started to run out.

Patrick gripped her shoulder a little tighter. "I think I need to get this one to bed," he told his friend. "Give me a second, and I'll walk you out."

Even though she hated leaving Martel alone in the living area, black spots had begun to swim at the edge of her vision and soon standing wouldn't be an option. Patrick tucked her in and went back out to his friend. Despite the lead weights that forced her eyes closed, Morgana tried to listen for any conversation between them, but only heard a quiet murmur as the front door opened, and a short moment later, the dim chime of the elevator. Staying awake after the events of the last few hours was a losing battle, and exhaustion pulled her under before the front door closed again.

Thirty-One

The room was dark when she awoke. With the curtains drawn, and the door mostly closed, the only light was a sliver spilling across the foot of the bed from the hall. She stretched experimentally. The burning in her gut was less, but still simmered like an ember planted above her hip. She pushed the covers aside to get a look at the wound. The scar itself hadn't grown any smaller yet, but the spiderweb of angry red was gone, the skin much closer to a normal color and texture.

The room spun for a moment when she stood, but the walls quickly settled into their proper places. There were slippers waiting and she slid her bare feet into them gratefully.

She eased the door open. The apartment outside was silent, but the smell that drifted down the hall immediately had her stomach growling. The lights on the office door shone green in the dim light, the keys were still in their locks. Morgana hit the reset buttons and continued on up the hallway.

Morgana glanced into the kitchen and found a pot on the stove, flame on as low as it would go. She padded over and lifted the lid and breathed in fragrant steam, redolent of herbs, beef, and a red wine gravy. After giving the thick stew a stir, she turned back to the island and found her cell phone plugged in to charge. She tapped the screen, and found the usual notifications for unread spam emails, but little else. Nothing from Albrecht.

She started to glance down at the time on her phone, but a rustling sound from across the room brought her head up. After recent events, her first instinct was to reach for a weapon, but a quick glance at the locked front door gave her an idea of the source of the sound. Still, she approached the sofa slowly and craned her neck over the top. She smiled, and exhaled in relief as she took a seat on the coffee table gazing down at Patrick's sleeping face.

His long body barely fit on the sofa, the blanket she'd discarded in panic at Martel's arrival draped over his legs, but his eyes were closed, his body fully relaxed. She hated to wake him, not knowing how long he had been sleeping. His clothes were different from this morning, and there was a small duffel next to the couch. At her hip was one of her chronicles, his reading glasses rested on top. She lifted the cover high enough to identify it as the current volume and let it fall, cheeks heating. There was so much she had written about him in there.

Underneath was a familiar cloth wrapped bundle. Morgana slid the chronicle on top aside and removed the cloth from the much older tome and ran a hand down the worn cover.

"I thought it was time to bring it home to its rightful place."

Morgana turned her head to find his eyes were open, though he hadn't otherwise moved. "Hi," she said, unsure what else to say.

Patrick gave her a sleepy smile, the kind that made her heart race, but in a good way. "Hi." He sat up, and scratched his scalp. In the tight space, his knees ended up one on either side of hers, but she didn't feel crowded. "You're awake."

"How long was I out?"

Patrick glanced at his watch. "If you only just woke up, it's been about... oh, eighteen hours."

Morgana's eyes widened. "Oh my."

"Don't worry, I called Alan and took care of Albrecht. Besides, you clearly needed it." he said, then started ticking a list off on his fingers. "You know, after getting shot, poisoned, and then dying and coming back to life."

His tone was dry, almost sarcastic, and it startled a laugh out of her. "And yet you're still here."

"Well, I went to work for a little while today, and went home to get a couple of things, but yeah, I know what you mean. I'm still here."

Her heart warmed, and they sat for a long moment just looking at each other. Then her stomach growled again, and she put her hand to it as an embarrassed blush spread across her cheeks. "You must be hungry."

They stood at the same time and collided. His arms came around her to steady them.

She looked up in time for his lips to capture hers, stealing her breath. Her arms wrapped around his neck and held on tight as the pain and fear of the last few days melted away in his arms. He sat back down on the sofa and drew her down with him to straddle his hips, her breasts crushed to his chest.

The knot of pain in her abdomen flared as she sank against him, but she barely noticed as his hands slid down her back, and he slowly began to rock his hips beneath her. Pressed as close as she was to him, she could feel how much he wanted her through the layers of their clothes and a different heat ignited further down.

He broke the kiss and started moving down her neck. Her gasp when he found a sensitive spot brought his smoldering sapphire gaze back to her face. He was an inch from combusting, and she'd happily burn with him.

She captured his lips in a brief, but blistering kiss and then eased back. He raised an eyebrow at her, but she just smiled and twitched her chin in the direction of the kitchen. He took a deep shuddering breath and set her back slightly on his lap, but far enough to tamp down the flames a bit, and laughed.

"Right, you meant the stew."

Morgana pressed forward and slid once along him, just for the satisfaction of seeing his eyes darken before she climbed to her feet and reached down a hand to help him up. He followed close behind her to the kitchen and buried his face in her neck while she reached for the big soup bowls and filled them to the brim.

"Get the bread," she told him.

Patrick dropped his forehead to her shoulder and chuckled, and finally released her to cut up a loaf of bread.

She set the bowls down and took a seat at the island. The bakery logo on the bread bag caught her eye as she tore off a chunk of bread and popped it in her mouth.

"I remember when that place opened," she said as she chewed. "Giuseppe Sciardi and his family had only recently moved to Kingston.

They were one of the first Italian families to settle in what was predominantly a French-Canadian neighborhood. With the textile mills so close by, they did very well for themselves."

Patrick came around and took the other seat, shaking his head in amazement. "When was that?"

Morgana thought for a moment. "June of 1925, I believe."

Patrick laughed and shook his head as he picked up his spoon and dug in.

"What?" She asked, then blew on her spoon before taking a taste. Her eyes fluttered closed as the beef, richly flavored with red wine and fresh herbs, nearly melted in her mouth.

"I'm just amazed at how much you've seen. How much you've experienced."

Morgana ate another delectable spoonful. "And now that there are no secrets between us, I want to tell you everything."

For a while, the only sounds in the room were the clink of spoons on porcelain and the crunch of bread. Patrick returned to the stove to refill both bowls and to cut more bread. He took his seat and resumed eating. "Let's start with what happened to the window."

Morgana almost choked, pivoting in her seat to find that the pane had been fixed. "Fred came up with the maintenance man this morning before I left."

"Ah," Morgana said as she got up from her seat and retrieved a wide, flat cherrywood box from one of the shelves. Patrick watched as she withdrew the Hunter dagger and set it down between them. He reached for it, but she grabbed his hand away. "Only touch the handle. The blade was coated with the same poison that was on the bullet. I wiped it down but I'm not sure if I got all of it off."

Patrick put his hand safely on the countertop and leaned in closer. "I recognize that symbol from your books," he said. "It's the Hunter's mark?"

Morgana nodded. "And there's this." She placed the note that had been left on her living room floor on top. The black letters sent a shiver through her.

"So, a Hunter threw a dagger through your window?"

"No, the dagger was thrown at my assistant's desk at Albrecht," Morgana corrected. "I think the window was just kicked in from the fire escape, and the note left to let me know that he's getting closer."

Patrick swallowed. "Closer?"

"The last few weeks, I've been seeing a figure dressed in black. Taunting me. First was just the flash of a laser scope in a toy store window." She nodded in confirmation when he gave her a questioning look.

"Next was the dagger. I was working late one night last week and he must have picked the lock on the employee entrance and threw the dagger at Alan's desk. And right after that, as I was leaving the parking garage, he had his gun pointed right at me. Then the window."

"And then yesterday." Patrick said, voice almost trembling with rage. "But why?"

"In a word? Fear."

She returned the items to the box and squarely met his gaze. "He actually had the gun trained on you." She swallowed, as just a fraction of that terror gripped her chest and squeezed tight. "That's why I pushed you out of the way. I couldn't let you get hurt."

"Because you love me?"

Morgana ducked her head, cheeks flaming, and nodded.

Patrick reached out and lifted her chin, raising her eyes back up to his. "I love you, too." He drew her in for a kiss, then retreated to whisper against her lips. "I think that we can save the rest of my questions until morning."

Thirty-Two

Morgana awoke to the sound of her cell phone ringing from the kitchen. Laying on her side with Patrick's breath warm on her neck, she debated letting it go to voicemail. But, given that it rarely rang unless the call was important, she grudgingly removed Patrick's hand from her waist and climbed out of bed.

"Where are you going?" he asked only half-awake.

"Go back to sleep," she said, "I'll be right back."

She hastily wrapped herself in a robe and ran from the room. She scooped it from the island and tapped the green button. "Hello? Hello?"

At first, she thought that she'd missed it, but then a voice spoke, one that made her blood run cold. "Hello, Morgana."

"How did you get this number?"

Jacob Martel laughed then tsked at her. "You left your phone unattended when Patrick put you to bed."

Morgana leaned on the countertop and put her head in one hand. "What do you want Martel?" she asked, her voice low and unemotional.

"Going by your voice, I'd say you're not alone," he said, and she could picture the sneer on his face. "Can we meet?"

Morgana lifted the phone away from her ear and stared at the screen, as if she could stare through it and see Martel's face, gauge his emotions. The screen said, "Unknown Caller."

"A blocked number?" she asked, and added changing her phone number to the growing mental list. "Really?"

"Force of habit."

She snorted a laugh. It was ridiculous considered she knew where he worked and where he lived. As he knew hers. "How can I be sure that this isn't a trap?"

"You can't," Martel told her with a satisfied chuckle. "But I give you my word that I only want to talk."

She pulled the phone from her ear again to check the time, she needed start getting ready for work, but there was still a little time. "Fine, but I pick the place," she told him. "Gransome Park, by the marina, half an hour."

He agreed and hung up.

The phone clattered to the island. Morgana put her face in her hand and took a deep, steadying breath then went back to the bedroom. She lingered in the doorway and studied him, truly studied him, for a moment.

His eyes were closed, and he'd rolled onto his back. One arm was draped above his head while the covers pooled low around his hips. He was thinner, leaner than he had been, like his muscles had drawn in

317

against his bones. His clear complexion was flushed slightly from sleep and light from the window caught sparks of fire in his hair.

Remembering that she was on a clock, she crossed the room and sat next to him.

The sinking of the bed had him cracking his eyes open. "Everything okay?"

She leaned in close. "Yeah," she said with a quick kiss. "But I have to get going."

His arm came up around her back and held her in place. "Are you sure?" He pulled her in for a longer, more thorough kiss.

Morgana allowed him, but when he tried to pull her on top of him, she slid away. "Not that I don't want to stay in bed all day," she said, detaching his arm and standing up. "But I have to go."

His arm flopped back on the bed with a huff, and he rolled his eyes. "Spoilsport."

Morgana laughed, surprised how easily it came out of her now, especially with him. She patted his leg and headed for the closet.

Patrick watched her dress, his eyes hooded and smoldering. Forget a striptease, the act of putting clothes *on* in front of him sent waves of heat through her, to pool deep in her core. If she went anywhere near the bed, she'd never leave, and Martel was waiting for her.

Ice water doused the heat at that thought. She broke free of Patrick's gaze and turned to dig in the closet for shoes. "You should probably get going yourself, right?" she asked. "It *is* a weekday."

There was a rustle and a groan as Patrick turned back the covers and sat with his feet on the floor. His hands rasped over the stubble on his cheeks. Coming out of the closet, shoes in hand, Morgana got a glimpse of a lot of exposed skin before she forced herself to turn away. If she stopped to get a better look, she'd never leave the room.

As tempting as it was to leave Martel waiting, Morgana left Patrick to dress and went to gather her work bag, phone, and purse. Halfway out the door, she paused and opened the front hall closet and pushed through the curtain of coats to reach the safe at the back. She retrieved the small handgun, slid the clip in place, and chambered the first bullet. After checking that the safety was on, she added it to her purse. Much as she hated carrying a gun, she knew how to use one, and at this point, with nearly all the chips on the table, she didn't trust Martel not to spring something on her.

Morgana descended to the lobby and spent only a moment with Fred, assuring him that she was okay. It wasn't a lie. The burning pain in her side was finally down to a level she could ignore. By the end of the day, it would be gone. Before walking away, she crooked a finger at him, and when Fred leaned forward, she hopped up and kissed his cheek. "Thank you."

Flustered but pleased, he waved her off.

Once outside, she tipped her face up to the bright sunshine and drank in deep gulps of clean, fresh air for the first time in days. The honk of a passing car jolted her back to reality, and she reluctantly made her way to the parking garage. With the Hunters closer than ever, she gave her car a thorough once over before getting in. Even then, she squeezed her eyes shut while turning the key. Her breath left her in a rush when the engine roared to life and nothing else happened.

Gransome Park was on the waterfront, a long, narrow strip of green sandwiched between the bay and Oceanside Boulevard. It had a popular bike path that weaved on and off of a chain of small barrier islands housing playgrounds and a public beach closed now for the season. The marina was in a similar state, with only a handful of boats still moored up. Martel's Blazer was in the front of the parking lot when she pulled in and parked nearby. The man himself sat on a bench facing the water about a hundred feet away, his back to her.

Morgana got out of the car and shouldered her purse, the unfamiliar weight of the gun inside bounced off her hip. She kept one hand within easy reach of the weapon as she crossed the open field, eyes and ears alert to any company that Martel may have brought with him.

With his legs casually crossed, and an arm draped over the back of the bench, Martel was the definition of relaxed. Sunglasses shaded his eyes from the light reflecting off the water and his hair, freed from its usual ponytail, lifted in the gentle breeze. He turned his head as she approached from the far side of the bench.

"Well, hello there," he said as if she was a long-lost friend. "Please take a seat."

Morgana didn't move. "You said you wanted to talk?"

"You're looking well, Morgana, so much better than you were yesterday."

She scoffed at him and took a step back toward the parking lot.

His hand darted out and caught her arm in a firm grip, just tight enough to keep her from going any further. "Come on, have a seat."

Morgana shrugged free and sat, putting her purse in her lap. "Okay, I'm sitting." Morgana spread her hands in invitation. "Now what?"

"Now, I think it is time that we had a real conversation. Since we know each other's secrets, I mean. Just you and me, Hunter and Ancient."

Morgana nodded and looked around the area again. There were a couple of families on a nearby playground, a few joggers and cyclists on the path. "So, what's the plan then, Martel? Get me talking so your people can sneak up on me from behind?"

A corner of his mouth twitched at her use of his last name, like it was a curse word, but just shook his head. "Not at all. We are far too out in the open for that."

"Then how about this? Why don't you answer my question?"

Martel narrowed his eyes at her. "And what question was that?"

"What prompted you to join the Hunters?"

Martel leaned back and ran a hand through his hair. "Ah yes... well, if you remember from the party at my house," he paused to glare at her, "I didn't exactly grow up in a very good neighborhood. My dad was in and out of jail and ran with some pretty rough people and the apple didn't exactly fall very far from the tree so to speak."

"Went into the family business then?"

"More or less," he replied with a shrug. "I found out one day in my teens what the group I ran with was really about when we were chasing down a man who we were told had been dealing on our territory. We pinned him down in an alley, and a gunfight erupted. One of my closest friends --besides Patrick, I mean-- was shot, right next to me." He closed his eyes briefly, and when they opened the chocolate of his eyes was almost black with rage. "I shot back, hit the bastard straight in the chest, and I bet you can guess the rest."

Morgana nodded. "I probably can," she replied. "I'm so very sorry about your friend, but not all of us are like the one who hurt him. We're human too, some good, some bad, we're not all the same."

321

He snarled. "You're not human, you're abominations! Creatures that threaten mankind."

"Mankind is a threat to itself," she retorted. "Most of us only want to be left alone to live out our lives in peace. Instead, we are forced to hide in the shadows, to run from those that should have nothing to fear. Yet fear us you do, and that is why you hunt us."

"I fear nothing."

"Oh really? Then take a shot at me, right here, right now." When he hesitated, she threw her head back and laughed. "But you can't do that, can you? By your own admission, we're too out in the open here."

Martel glared at her, his face flushing red.

"So, here's what you need to know about me. I am not a threat to you or your family. I care about them more than you could know, or believe, given your prejudices against my people. Your wife has been incredibly kind and welcoming. And Patrick? Well, Patrick has helped me to open up my heart and learn to love again."

"Love?"

Morgana nodded. "Love."

Martel considered that for a moment. "Despite the fact that you had been lying to him about who, and what you are?"

"He knew I was keeping secrets, so he gave me an ultimatum to come clean," she replied. "That's why I went to the hospital. To tell him everything. We were walking through the parking garage when, suddenly, there was a laser scope pointed at Patrick's back."

Martel's eyes widened at that.

"Yes, at *him*, not me. I pushed him out of the way and took the bullet myself." She put a hand to where the wound had been. "I was planning on breaking the news to him gently, but Patrick got the crash course instead."

Martel looked away from her, out at the water, as he worked out some kind of puzzle in his mind. The revelation that the other Hunter had targeted his best friend, and that she had sacrificed herself for him, had turned the conversation in a different direction. "It's not every day you see someone die right in front of you."

"Even temporarily," she amended. "Though Patrick didn't know that yet. And, for the record, your friend is using an incredibly potent form of Glisane. I don't think the bullet wound alone would have killed me."

Martel ground his teeth.

"And now you're closer than ever," she continued, heat flushing her face. "This Schaffer, I believe you called him? He's been circling for weeks."

"I know," Martel answered. "I've been following him as much as he's been following you. He's not much of a team player. The laser sight, the knife, those were all him."

"Right before I went to the hospital, I came home to a broken window in my apartment, and a note among the glass shards. It had one word on it. 'Soon'."

Martel whistled in amazement.

Morgana narrowed her eyes at him.

Before either of them could say more, his phone began to ring, the ringtone indicating that it was a video call. He retrieved his phone and checked the caller ID. "Speak of the devil..." He answered the call. "Hello, Schaffer."

Martel held the phone so she could see just make out the face on the screen but could not be seen. How thoughtful of him. Schaffer was dressed in black, with dark hair, but his face was fully visible for the first time. Mentally, she compared the man on the screen with the one who had been following her, the one who had shot her, and it was all too easy to connect the two.

"Martel," the other said by way of greeting.

"What do you want?"

"Remember that immortal that you were tracking recently? The associate of the woman?" Morgana's eyes shot to Martel. He didn't acknowledge the accusation on her face though his jaw did clench briefly.

"Of course," Martel said with a tone of voice that encouraged Schaffer to keep speaking.

The other hunter must have pushed a button on the phone, for the camera suddenly flipped in the opposite direction. The area wasn't as well lit, and Morgana strained to make out any details beyond the distinct gray shades of concrete and steel. A warehouse or basement maybe?

Schaffer took a few steps forward, the video jerking with the movement. A hand appeared in view and grabbed a dark piece of cloth and pulled it away. Schaffer took a handful of dark blond hair and raised Alasdair's bloodied face to the camera.

Thirty-Three

M organa's hands flew to her mouth, smothering the anguished cry that rose up her throat.

Martel's eyes widened slightly, but he didn't speak.

Schaffer smirked. "Now, I know we've had our differences, but I wanted to know if you wanted in on this one? Then, I'll help you with the woman."

"Where are you?"

"A warehouse in the Mission District, San Francisco." Schaffer released Alasdair's hair and brandished a blade, similar to the one that he had left embedded in Alan's desk.

Morgana watched in horror as he held it under Alasdair's chin and pressed the flat of the blade to his skin. She buried her face in her hands, chest heaving, and fought the sudden urge to vomit as her friend started to scream.

"Call me when you land at SFO and I'll talk you in."

Schaffer ended the call, cutting off the screams.

"What the hell is going on?"

Both jumped to their feet to find Patrick standing a few yards away, his face pale with shock.

Morgana went to him and buried her face in his chest. Every muscle in his body was rigid, but his arms came around her, one hand buried in her hair, while she trembled against him. "Jake?"

"Patrick, I can explain."

"You're one of them?" Patrick asked accusingly. "A Hunter?"

The tremor that went through him under her cheek told her Martel had nodded. "And the man on the video?"

"His name is John Schaffer."

"And his prisoner?"

Morgana raised her head and looked up at Patrick. "My friend Alasdair."

Patrick ground his teeth and skewered his friend with a glare. "Will he kill him?"

Martel nodded. "Eventually," he said. "Once he's had his fun."

"And you were going to help?"

Martel started to speak, and Patrick raised a hand and cut him off. "I don't even know who you are." He looked down at Morgana, at the desolation on her face.

"He's the closest friend that I have," Morgana moaned. "I can't lose him. I need to get him back."

Patrick nodded, still looking at his friend. "I don't care what history the two of you have." His tone invited no argument. "That man is already expecting you, so you'll go, and get Alasdair back."

"I'm going too."

Patrick stared down at her. "Morgana, no."

"He's my oldest friend, Patrick," she informed him. "And I bet he wasn't even on the Hunters' radar until he came here, because of me."

"That's not exactly—"

Patrick glared at his friend. "You're arguing right now?"

Martel closed his mouth. Clearly, this assertiveness was not something he was used to seeing in Patrick. It was nice to have that icy stare trained on someone else. Especially if it was Martel.

"I'm going," she said again.

Patrick stared down at her for a long moment and, when she continued to look right back, he finally shook his head and muttered something about stubbornness under his breath. She fought a smile.

"Okay, fine." Patrick turned Morgana, so she stood against one hip. "I'm in no shape to travel, and I'm no fighter. Jake, you'll take Morgana with you and get Alasdair away from that psychopath. When you get back, you and I are going to talk."

Martel swallowed hard and exchanged a look with Morgana, icy stare to raised eyebrow. Finally, he nodded. "I'll need a couple of hours to book the flight, make sure Sophie is set, and I'll come pick you up."

He looked between them one more time and then walked off.

They turned and watched him get in the Blazer and drive away. Once he was gone, Patrick stumbled a few steps and barked up against the back of the bench, gripping the worn wood for support. He took a couple of deep breaths to steady himself, then looked at her with a slight reddening of his cheeks.

Her breath blew out in a rush that ended in a laugh. "What was that?" She asked, looping an arm around his back.

"I haven't seen that truck in ten years."

"Not the truck," she said, swatting him gently on the hip. "Where did that whole performance come from?"

He shook off her arm. "I'm not all that happy with you either for not telling me about him."

She blinked and gripped her hands together in her lap, though she should have expected the admonishment to come. "It wasn't my story to tell," she said. "I told him the same thing."

Patrick's head tilted to one side as he considered that, and then looked at her with a pleading expression. "Please tell me that that's it. No more secrets. I don't know how much more I can take."

"No more secrets." Morgana reached over and threaded her fingers with his. She gave the hand a tug, pulling him down for a kiss. She'd meant it to be brief, but once their lips touched, and his lips parted under hers, it was several minutes before they parted.

Patrick gave her a wry, dreamy smile. "What was that for?"

"For standing up for me to your friend. I've never really had anyone do that," she told him. "And I know it's been hard, finding out about everything the way you have."

"I hope you're not expecting something corny like 'the things we do for love,' right?"

She laughed. "No, but I know the sentiment is there."

Patrick squeezed her hand and smiled, then jerked his head in the direction of the parking lot. "Come on," he said.

Morgana wrapped her free hand around his arm and walked close. For the first time, he accepted the support without tensing or making a face, but he was limping badly and breathing hard by the time they got back to the vehicles.

She helped him inside, her heart pounding. "Are you okay?"

He nodded, though there was sweat on his temples and forehead. "I've been a little more tired lately." He started the car and put the window down, then pulled the door closed.

Morgana leaned down with her forearms crossed on the door frame. He put his hand on her arms. "Go, I'll follow you home."

Home. The word went through her like a shock of static. For the first time, the Hunters knew exactly where she lived. And she had no idea how far that information had been shared. Even if they were successful in rescuing Alasdair, Morgana was beginning to think that her time here was limited.

"What is it?"

Her eyes focused on him. "Nothing," she said and leaned in for a kiss. "I'll see you at home."

Thirty-Four

As soon as they returned to her apartment, Morgana dug out a small duffel from the recesses of her closet and started gathering what she needed. It had been a very long time since she'd needed to go on the offensive against the Hunters, and the items she wanted were buried in the bottom of drawers, or tucked in the back of the closet.

Patrick sat on the end of her bed as clothing landed around him. He reached up just in time to catch a dark jacket as it flew at his face and grunted at the unexpected weight.

She turned at the sound to see him studying a sleeve. "I know, it's surprisingly heavy." She said, smiling. "It's not bulletproof, but there's enough reinforcement to stop a knife."

Patrick's eyes widened as he pinched his fingers, testing the thickness of the sleeve. He folded the jacket and set it aside, then started folding the clothes scattered around him. "Are you sure you need to do this?"

Morgana took a folded shirt from him and packed it away. Then another, and another, until the whole bag was packed. As they worked, she studied him. The dark circles under his eyes that hadn't been there this morning, a tightness to muscles in his neck and shoulders. Her heart clenched at the thought of leaving him, even for something as important as this.

"Alasdair has been my closest friend for more than two hundred and fifty years," she replied finally. "He is not a warrior, he's a businessman. You saw him on the video! He's not going to be able to get himself out of this."

"Morgana."

Socks, she needed socks. "He cared enough about me to risk crossing over an international border, not once, but *twice* in the last few months. The Hunters have him because of me."

Patrick wrapped his hand around her wrist when she started to turn back to the closet again, a swirling torrent of anger heated her blood. Anger at the Hunters. At herself. She wanted to punch something, she wanted to run, in part to hide how angry she really was. "Morgana, stop."

She turned back and let him pull her closer, until she was standing between his knees. "You seem to blame yourself for a lot," Patrick observed, putting his arms around her hips. "For things that are not your fault. You can't help being what you are, or that there are those who are frightened by that. But it's not your fault, Morgana. Do you hear me? It's *not* your fault."

All Morgana could do was nod, her throat suddenly thick with emotion. Her hands came up to frame his face, one hand smoothing back the hair that always fell in his eyes. "I love you."

He tightened his arms and leaned back until he was lying flat, with her stretched out on top of him, her knees split around his hips. "I love you, too." He replied and lifted his head to capture her lips with his.

The anger melted away as each stroke of his hands down her back left a different heat in its wake and she allowed it to sweep her away, losing herself for just a few moments in his arms, his lips. Her breath came in pants as she sat up on his lap. She unbuttoned her dress shirt and tossed it aside, followed soon after by her bra. Patrick's hands slid up her sides and over the backs of her shoulders and into her hair scattering pins around them. Her curls cascaded down like a curtain.

Her hands dove under his shirt to stroke the muscles of his stomach and chest. He groaned as her lips followed her hands as they traced the ridges of muscles, rucking his shirt up higher and higher. She bypassed his mouth and used the shirt to pin his arms overhead.

He took advantage of her position and captured a nipple with his mouth, grazing his tongue and teeth over the sensitive peak. Each nibble and swirl of his tongue sent shocks of heat directly to her core until she was quivering over him. He filled his hand with the other breast, his thumb slowly sweeping across her skin. Then he was kissing a trail across and gave it the same attention with his mouth. Then, suddenly, she was underneath him as he settled between her thighs, raining kisses along her collar bones.

Morgana gripped the comforter with both hands as he worked his way down her stomach, removing her remaining clothes as he went. He then stood and shed his clothes before returning to her, and began kissing his way up her calf, the inside of her knee and thigh. He skipped the most sensitive part of her, the part that craved his touch the most, to trail kisses down the other leg.

She cried out when his fingers parted her and his mouth found that sensitive bundle of nerves and latched on, licking and nibbling. She buried one hand in his hair, and her back arched as he slipped a finger, and then two inside. It was a matter of moments before she came apart, his name escaping from her lips. He gave a satisfied chuckle, and slowly kissed his way back up until he was stretched out beside her, nuzzling her neck as she recovered.

As her breathing calmed, she lifted his chin and captured his mouth again. The kiss was languid, unhurried. Morgana leaned into him until he was again on his back with her stretched at length on top of him. He ran one hand down her back to grip her hip, the other buried in her hair. Then she reached between them, wrapping her hand around his hardness.

They both moaned as she lowered herself onto him, just a little at first, only to lift up, and lower even further, torturing them both until she had taken all of him. Then she paused, and their gazes locked. His eyes were dark, hooded, his hands came to rest on her hips. When he tried to move beneath her, she pressed down, pinning him.

"Stay still," she ordered, though the movement had her biting her lip.

He bucked once more with a mischievous glint in his eye that made her hiss in a breath before he subsided beneath her, waiting.

When she did move, it was with a slow, gentle rocking of her hips, rising and falling an inch, two. Morgana savored the feel of him so deep inside her with each unhurried stroke, stoking a fire so hot it threatened to fuse them together. Neither in any hurry to reach completion for both knew that this time together could be their last.

When it was over, she would be leaving.

She leaned forward to capture his lips, sharing their breath, tongues dancing. He took the opportunity and wrapped one arm around her back, holding her to him while he pressed up from below, driving even deeper. He took a firm grip on her hips, and lifted her almost to the tip then pulled her back down. Both groaned, their faces close together.

They soon found a rhythm, moving together. Her breathing was coming in short pants by the time she planted her hands on his chest and sat up.

His hands roamed her body, stroking her back, massaging her breasts as tension began to build deep in her belly as she continued to force the torturously slow pace. The flash in his eyes was the only warning, before his hands gripped her hips tighter and he quickened the pace again, physically raising and lowering her with each thrust from underneath, their hips collided only to part and meet again and again.

Morgana reared back and cried out as she crested that delicious peak and crashed over the other side, her body shaking above him as she came apart. He pressed up into her once, twice more, then gave in to the rhythmic clenching of her muscles around him and pinned her hips tightly to his as he lost himself inside of her.

She went boneless on his chest as aftershocks rippled through her. For a moment, they lay together still joined, their foreheads pressed together, breath mingling. Then she slid away. He tucked her against his side, holding her tightly to his chest.

Patrick gently ran his hand up and down along her hip and gave her a drowsy, satisfied smile. "Go ahead, sleep," he said in response to her struggling to keep her eyes open. "Jake said it would be a few hours, we have time."

Morgana turned her head and placed a kiss on his shoulder before snuggling in and closing her eyes, drifting off within moments.

They awoke sometime later. Patrick remained stretched out under the covers, and watched as she slid out of bed and moved naked around the room, gathering up a change of clothes from the pile that had been kicked to the floor. The sight of her compact and toned body, the fact that she was completely at ease and yet perfectly aware that he was watching her, had part of him stirring to life again.

She gave him a smile as she disappeared through the door, and a moment later there was the hiss of the shower turning on. He rolled onto his back and stretched muscles pleasantly sore from recent exertion. The ache in his right leg, which radiated from knee to hip, was much less pleasant. Sleep tried to pull him back under, but he resisted, they had so little time before she had to leave.

His brain still spun with everything he'd learned the last few days. That she was a seven-hundred-year-old immortal. That his best friend was someone who hunted and killed those like her. His heart squeezed tight.

It was no secret that Jake had had a rough life, becoming involved with a gang at a young age, getting into fights, carrying a gun, disappearing for days on end. Though by some miracle, he'd always avoided getting into any major legal trouble. And after opening the restaurant, Patrick assumed that he had left all of that behind when he followed Sophie out west.

Or so he'd had thought.

Sophie. His heart clenched again. What did she know? And how would Patrick break the news to her if Jake didn't come home? And even if he did, how were they going to move on now that he knew?

He looked up as Morgana walked back in, her hair wrapped in a towel, dressed all in black. She smiled, seeing him still lying in bed, one arm thrown up over his head, though she couldn't know the turmoil in his mind. She gathered up the duffel bag that had been kicked to the floor and set to refolding. She disappeared into the closet and returned with a pair of black boots. She walked around the side of the bed and sat next to him to put on her socks. He ignored the ache as he sat up and placed a kiss on the point of her shoulder. She glanced over at him with a sweet smile, then looked away, reaching for a boot.

She let out a startled yelp, then laughed as he wrapped both hands around her waist and hauled her onto his lap. The weight of her on his leg was uncomfortable, but worth it. The boot tumbled back to the floor. He sent the towel after it and filled his hands with wet curls, dragging her to him for a kiss.

She released him with a sigh a moment later. "I'll never leave if you keep kissing me like that."

"Well, that's the idea."

She slid off his lap and gathered up the boots, pulling them on her feet and lacing them up at the dressing table so he couldn't tempt her back in. He gave her a theatrical pout, which made her laugh. When he turned back the covers and reached for his pants, he saw that the skin of his thigh was red, and warm to the touch. He swallowed a groan of a different kind as he stood and fastened the button then bent to retrieve his shirt from the floor.

Morgana started heading up the hallway, duffel in hand.

He followed, appreciating how the clothing hugged her curves. The muscles in her back and arms, normally hidden beneath the loose-fitting sweaters or boxy suit jackets she usually favored, were clearly on display.

"Are you hungry?" he asked, going to the fridge for a bottle of water. She shook her head. "I'm too keyed up to eat."

"Even immortals need to eat," he admonished and went back in for meat and cheese. While he assembled sandwiches, she roamed about the living area, gathering a surprising number of weapons from various hiding places, some of which were unnoticeable until she opened them. She set them out on the other side of the island, an array of small throwing daggers, and a handgun she retrieved from her purse of all places.

She gave him a sheepish grin. "I didn't know what your friend had planned when he called this morning."

The casual way in which she offered that explanation surprised him, though given her history, maybe it shouldn't have. He sliced the sandwiches and pushed one over to her. She took one look and went back to the bookcase, returning with the Hunter dagger, the one possibly with poison still on the blade and added it to the pile.

Patrick gestured to the meal and gave her a look that invited no argument. She sighed and took a bite of turkey and cheese.

"Good?"

She stood on the rungs of the chair and reached across to steal his water bottle. "Very." she replied after a long pull of water. "Thank you."

"While I have to admit that I'm impressed at your arsenal, what are you going to do with the weapons?" he asked. "I wouldn't think that airport security would let you take them on the plane."

"Modern technology can be such an inconvenience." She sighed dramatically, and then laughed. "I can take some of this if I check the bag, though you're right about the gun." She picked it up and popped the clip out with a casual flick of her thumb, ejected the round from the chamber, and slid it back into the clip.

He must have been staring because she lifted an eyebrow at his expression.

"I am not a fan of guns," he said as heat curled in his belly. "But that was hot. So smooth, like you've done that a million times."

She winked as she rose from the chair and opened the closet door. "Maybe I have."

Her tone was coy, as the coat hangers screeched in protest at being shoved aside. Then there were the beeps of a keypad and the grating of metal on metal as a safe door opened and the gun placed inside.

"How many more hiding places do you have?" he asked when she returned to her sandwich.

"A few more," she admitted.

He looked at her in amazement.

"Most of them were in the original design or added as the technology evolved. The office was always reinforced, and fire-proof, but I added climate controls and security over the years. The closet safe was a tumbler lock initially, later upgraded with key codes and biometrics."

"But you said you've only been here five years." Patrick said. "What am I missing?"

"This time." She took another bite of sandwich. "I've been back this time for five years, remember."

"Oh, right."

"In all my years, after everywhere I've been, this is the one place that has felt the most like home," she said, and the earnestness in her eyes, as if she was trying to make it a reality by sheer force of will, made him want to do whatever he could to make it true.

"I am sorry, Morgana, for my part in revealing this place to your enemies." Patrick grimaced at the thought that her enemy was his best friend.

"You had no way of knowing," she said, carrying her plate to the sink. "At this point, I don't know what will happen. I just need to take things one step at a time, and first is getting to Alasdair before anything else happens to him."

"But he's immortal like you, right?"

She nodded, glancing at him over her shoulder as she turned the water on. "We *can* be killed for good," she said, "if we are decapitated."

Patrick swallowed, his hand going reflexively to his own throat. "Oh."

She turned back to the sink and loaded the few items already in the sink into the dishwasher.

He reached around her to add his plate then gathered her into his arms and just held her for a long moment, face buried in her hair which by now was mostly dry and filled his head with the scent of honeysuckle.

All too soon, the phone by the front door rang, though neither of them could have ever really been ready for this moment to arrive. Morgana went to the phone and told Fred that she would be right down. She went one more time into the front closet, coming back with a knife holster and a long piece of cloth that turned out to have pockets for the throwing knives. She added the weapons to her duffel.

She shrugged into the armored black coat and Patrick walked over to straighten the lapels. She threw her arms around his neck and raised up on tiptoes to kiss him.

He parted her lips with his and tasted every part of her mouth, searing the feel and taste of her into his memory. When she finally pulled away, her eyes were brimming with tears, and one slipped free to slide down her cheek.

Patrick wiped it away with a thumb. "I'll say goodbye here."

She nodded and stepped back with a sniff, picked up the bag and slid the strap up over her shoulder. "Stay as long as you want," she said. "I love you."

He captured her hand as she started past him and placed a kiss on her palm. "Say that again."

She smiled, and it sparkled in her green eyes, and repeated the words.

He kissed her one last time, and finally released her hand. "Come back to me."

Morgana met his eyes one more time. If only he could freeze time, hold her with him forever. But too soon, her hand slid from his and she walked to the door and out to summon the elevator. He moved to the doorway and watched as she got in and turned back, giving him a soft, sad smile and a wave as the door slid closed.

He continued to stand there for a few moments, almost hoping that she would change her mind on the way down and send the car right back up. But several moments passed, and she didn't come back. He sighed and went back inside the empty apartment.

Thirty-Five

The drive to the airport in Martel's old truck was one of the longest of Morgana's life. He'd barely acknowledged her when she walked across the lobby, only walked outside, and waited behind the wheel. His only reaction was a lifted eyebrow when she shoved her bag through the window and the weapons inside clacked together. He stared straight ahead as he drove, radio and heat both off, either broken or off deliberately to make the trip as miserable as possible.

Within five minutes, she'd rolled down the window, and left it open, even on the highway. She filled her lungs with fresh air, tinged with the salt tang of the ocean, visible only as an inky blackness in the distance to their right. She wasn't in any kind of mood to talk either, even if there was something to talk about. Her mind kept drifting back to Patrick, silhouetted in the light from her apartment. He had tried to put a brave face on, but she had seen past the façade to the fear hiding in his eyes, fear that this could be the last time they saw each other.

As they passed a sign announcing they were leaving the Kingston City limits, Morgana forced herself to stop, and concentrated on putting all thoughts of Patrick into a corner of her mind so she could focus on what lay ahead.

The airport soon came into view off to the left, the terminal rising in the distance at the other side of the taxiways like a mother goose spreading her wings protectively around the planes lined up at the gates. The main runway ran perpendicular to the highway, ending at a fence a short distance from the pavement. A row of short poles, each bearing an array of blinking amber and white bulbs, extended across the highway from the end of the main runway.

A large passenger jet took off, the roar of its engines shaking the truck as it passed close by overhead. Morgana laughed nervously as Martel negotiated the exit. They waited at the light, but when it changed, he went straight instead of following the signage that pointed right toward the passenger terminals.

Morgana sat up stiffly in her seat and braced one hand on the dashboard so she could turn her torso toward him, eyes narrowing. "Where are we going?"

He didn't respond, didn't even turn his head, and she flopped back in her seat, arms crossed. Their destination became all too apparent moments later when a smaller airport terminal came into view with several private airplanes parked along the taxiway. Martel pulled up to a security barrier and swiped a badge through the reader attached to the guard booth. When the lift gate rose, Martel wove through the lot, parking the Blazer in a numbered space near the entrance to the low, cinder block building. It reminded Morgana more of a rural bus stop than an airport terminal, but the planes lined up nearby were mostly new, and expensive.

She got out of the truck and retrieved her bag from the back and followed a few steps behind Martel. Inside, the small space held a ticket counter and security scanning equipment near the door on the far side, along with a coffee bar, a few vending machines, and a scattering of overstuffed leather armchairs arranged in small conversation groups. The room smelled of coffee and jet exhaust that the ventilation system couldn't quite keep up with. The building was empty except for a lone woman in a maroon suit standing at the ticket counter. She smiled warmly at them as they approached.

"Good afternoon Mr. Martel, Ms. Dericault," she said cheerfully. "Can I see your passports please?"

Martel's eyebrow twitched at the blue Canadian passport she placed on the counter but didn't say anything. The woman in maroon gave each document a cursory glance and slipped a boarding pass into each one then handed them back. "Have a safe flight."

I hope so, Morgana thought as she followed Martel as he skirted around the baggage scanner and walked through another set of sliding doors straight onto the tarmac. She glanced at the scanner, which looked like it was only there for decoration, and hurried to catch up.

A short distance away, a clean, white plane idled. There were no markings beyond the number on the tailfin above a pair of jet engines that spun slowly and emitted a quiet whine. Light shone out through the half-dozen windows along the fuselage, and spilled out the open hatchway. The lowered door doubled as a staircase and led into a space that more resembled a living room than the interior of a commercial airplane. Decorated in warm shades of cream and tan accented with polished wood inlay, the space smelled of leather mixed with the faint tang of jet exhaust that drifted in through the open door.

The pilot emerged from the cockpit and held out his hand to Martel who shook it warmly. "Hey, good to see you again, Jake," he said with a voice as warm and rich as the caramel color of his skin. He turned to Morgana. "You must be Miss Dericault."

"Call me Morgana," she replied, taking note of the calluses on his palm as she shook his hand. Flying planes wasn't the only way he spent his time.

"My name is Adrian, and I'll be flying you down to San Francisco today. Flight time should be a little over three hours," he told them. "My co-pilot Jane is up there finishing our pre-flight. Make yourselves comfortable. There are snacks and drinks in the bar area at the back."

With that, he returned to the cockpit. The blonde in the other chair, who appeared to be just on the younger side of thirty, glanced back at them with a smile and returned to the checklist on the clipboard in her hand.

Martel stowed his bag in a compartment underneath the bar area. He stepped aside to pour a cup of coffee, but left the door open for her as he sat in one of the plush-looking leather seats that wouldn't be out of place at a night club except that it had a seat belt attached.

Morgana added her bag and shut the door. She surveyed the options arrayed in small baskets and carafes, but her stomach was too tied up in knots for anything beyond a bottle of water. She sank deep into the sofa that stretched across four of the plane's windows, aware of Martel's eyes on her as she unzipped her jacket and crossed her legs at the knee.

A few minutes later, Jane exited the cockpit and brought the door up with a few quick pulls of the cable that doubled as a handrail, the muscles in her forearms flexing with each practiced movement.

"Buckle up, we'll be taking off momentarily," she requested, her voice kind but professional as she secured the door, and retreated to the cockpit and closed that door as well.

Martel set his coffee on the arm of the chair long enough to gather the straps on either side of the seat and click the buckle. He wrapped a hand around his coffee while scrolling through something on his phone.

After some searching, Morgana located the seatbelt retracted between the cushions and buckled in as the plane started moving. She stared directly ahead out the windows on the other side though there was little to see outside besides an open field. The plane slowly rolled forward for a few moments and then stopped.

"We're next in line, folks," Adrian said over the intercom. A moment later he made a wide right turn and wasted no time accelerating and getting the plane up into the air, leaving Morgana's stomach on the ground.

Morgana couldn't take the silence anymore. "The flight crew, are they Hunters?"

Martel scoffed but didn't look up from his phone. "No," he said. "I use this charter service when I can't fly commercial."

"When you need to keep it off the radar, you mean?"

He finally looked at her. "Or when I need to transport weapons," he said, his tone implying that he was questioning her intelligence.

Morgana bristled. "Look, it was an honest question." She snapped. "I don't know what I expected when you said you would be booking flights, but it wasn't this. Kind of ironic, don't you think?"

"What's that supposed to mean?"

"Just that a restaurant owner wouldn't be able to fly private, which means you're using the family money to do this. Hunter family money, to help out someone like me."

His eyes narrowed. "Are you seriously begrudging me for it?" He asked and pointed at the cockpit door. "Say the word and I'll tell Adrian to take us right back."

Morgana sighed. "That's not what I meant," she replied. "I just mean that it's a little ironic. And not something that I would ever expect someone like you to do."

"Someone like me..." His voice trailed off, but his eyes were hard as he stared at her.

Morgana gazed right back for a moment and then cursed under her breath in French. "Regardless, flying private does work in our favor since you saved me from having to explain my bag to airport security."

That got her a ghost of a smile. "What did you bring?"

Morgana unbuckled and went to retrieve her bag and set it on the floor at her feet. She retrieved the two bundles and set them on the table with a clatter. She untied the strings around the bundle of throwing knives and unrolled it to reveal the neat row of short handles each topped with a round finger loop.

Martel nodded in approval and reached over to lift a corner of the black cloth, revealing the dagger. His eyes widened and he pushed the rest of the cloth away, leaning in close to study the engraved Hunter's mark. "Where did you get this?"

"Embedded in the wood of my assistant's desk."

"Come again?"

His confusion spoke volumes. "I take it this belongs to Schaffer, then?" Morgana asked. At Martel's nod, she told him about the late night in her office, the break in, and the calling card thrown from the doorway.

Martel looked impressed, which only made Morgana glare at him. He let out a low whistle. "Like a cat and mouse."

Morgana rolled her eyes. "As the mouse in that particular analogy, I can't say that I feel the same."

He barked a laugh, then caught her glare and, surprisingly, looked sheepish, but he didn't apologize. He put a finger through a loop and slid one of the daggers free. He examined the blade appraisingly. "How much experience do you have with these?"

Before he could even look up, Morgana had slid another dagger free and leapt from her seat. She grabbed one arm and twisted it behind his back, slamming his chest and cheek into the table. Morgana put her lips close to his ear, the tip of the blade pressed just below it. "Enough."

He grunted from the impact and trained his eye on the blade but didn't resist.

She pressed the blade closer, enough to dent but not pierce the skin. An odd thrill went through her at having him at her mercy. It would only take a bit more pressure to puncture the artery beneath. The temptation was there, but she needed him to rescue Alasdair.

Martel must have realized it too, for his muscles went slack in her grip and his eyes closed. He opened his hand and the knife clattered to the table.

She released him and replaced the two weapons in their slots with short deliberate movements, then sat on the sofa and crossed her legs again.

Martel sat back, rubbing his wrist, his face expressionless.

For the first time in his presence, she felt fully at ease, confident in her own experience and skill with a weapon. "I know that helping me rescue another of my kind from one of your own people is the last thing that you want to be doing." She draped one arm across the back of the sofa. "But can we at least be civil with each other?"

He lifted an eyebrow but eventually nodded. He glanced down at her open bag beside the table and frowned. "No guns?"

She shook her head. "You didn't tell me that you were booking private."

"You can have one of mine," he replied. One corner of his mouth lifted up. "You *do* know how to shoot, right?"

Morgana gave him a look.

He smirked and held up his hands, as close to an apology as she was going to get.

"So, what *is* the plan?"

"We have three hours to figure that out." Martel admitted. "When Schaffer first came to town, I reached out through my contacts. No one really knows all that much about him. He doesn't have any formal affiliations, so no one knows if he's a lone wolf or if there's anyone that he runs with. But he does have at least three confirmed kills."

Morgana closed her eyes with a sigh, thinking of the lives lost. "And he'll have a fourth if we don't get to Alasdair in time."

"He won't do anything before we get there."

"It looked like he'd done plenty already."

"Nothing permanent, anyway," Martel amended.

Morgana snapped in French, "as if that makes it all right?"

Martel shrugged. If he didn't understand her outright, he got the gist from her tone.

"Like I said before, Alasdair has never been a warrior." She took a steadying breath. "He was an aristocrat, and now a businessman. He fights with a pen, not a sword or a gun."

Martel reached into his pocket and pulled out his phone. He scrolled for a moment and then nodded, finding what he was looking for. "Alasdair Bromley, CEO of Amity Financial in San Francisco for the last ten years."

"How did you know that?"

"Six months ago, my contacts with Immigration informed me of a man just arrived in Kingston whose passport had flagged one of our databases using facial recognition software," he told her. "He was here for a week or two and then came back a couple of months later. I'd tracked him down to The Mason, but that's when I met Schaffer and my focus shifted."

"To me."

Martel nodded. He lounged in the chair, arms spread wide like a king on a throne. "He had information on you, and I had information on your friend. We compared notes."

Morgana blinked, unsure if he was fully conscious of his flippant tone or not. "This isn't a game, Martel. These are people's lives. And when he failed at killing your friend, it looks like he decided to go after mine."

"Or maybe, given your relationship with my best friend, he figured that I would consider it an even swap. He'd take care of Alasdair and leave you for me."

Morgana sighed, not at all pleased with the thought of being something to be traded. "So, it sounds like you don't know much at all useful about him."

One side of his lip curled up, though she didn't know if he was sneering at her skeptical tone, or because she'd spoken the truth. He raised a hand with only the pointer finger extended. "One, since he's unaffiliated, it's likely he's not going to have anyone else with him, or at least not many." He lifted a second finger. "Two, he asked me to come, which tells me that he enjoys showing off." A third finger lifted. "And then there's the call. He wanted to show me that he had done what I hadn't."

"Arrogant then, for sure. Think that might make him over-confident?"

"Possibly," he considered. "He doesn't have any reason to believe that I wouldn't be coming alone. But I also think that he's thorough. He chose a warehouse for a reason."

"Out of the way of prying eyes." Morgana agreed. "A place with open spaces, yet also places to hide, either for people working with him or other means of defense."

Martel nodded in agreement and, if she wasn't mistaken, approval. "Not knowing where we're going limits our options."

"I'm sure that was deliberate," Morgana said. "What do you remember from the video call? Anything that could be useful?"

Martel shook his head. "I couldn't really see much of the background at all, it was too dark. The Mission District is the oldest part of the city, mostly residential, so if he's in a warehouse there, I'm guessing it's probably more the size of a small machine shop, maybe an auto repair garage or something like that rather than what you'd find down by the docks on the east side of town. I could really only make out that the building was steel and concrete, and I didn't get the impression that the ceiling was very high."

"That's something at least," she replied. "All I could see was Alasdair and it looked like Schaffer had already done so much to—" Her voice failed, and she reached for the bottle of water.

She didn't expect any sympathy from Martel, and he didn't offer any. Instead, he gave her space by sitting back in the chair, propping one elbow on the arm of the chair and his head on his fist as his eyes lost some of their focus. Leaving him to his thoughts, Morgana rose and went to use the lavatory. When she returned, he hadn't moved, and she settled in on the sofa to wait.

Thirty-Six

B y the time the plane landed and taxied to the private terminal, they were no closer to having a solid plan, not until they knew more about the building where Schaffer was holding Alasdair. The door to the flight deck opened and Adrian emerged. "We just have to wait here for Homeland to send someone over, and then we can get you on your way."

Martel nodded and went to collect his bag from the back of the plane. Morgana had transferred the throwing knives to the belt that would be hidden under her jacket but had stowed it with the dagger back in her bag for now. No use clueing in the pilots, and especially the immigration officers, on the fact that they had weapons regardless of what friends Martel may have.

About ten minutes later, a knock sounded on the exterior of the plane and Adrian went and opened the door. A man in a blue jumpsuit with a gold badge on his shirt came up the stairs. There was a second officer standing at the bottom of the stairs, his blue ball cap just visible through the hatch. The officer took their passports and asked all the usual questions, but something in the looks that he exchanged with Martel said that it was just for show. He removed an ink pad and a stamp from the cargo pocket on his thigh and bent over the low table to stamp their passports.

"Welcome to the United States." He said as he handed the passports back and turned to check the credentials for the cabin crew before ducking his head and descending from the plane.

Martel stepped close and murmured, "now, he *is* a Hunter."

Morgana shivered, partly at how close he was standing, but also at the reminder that the Hunters had a network where they could pass over international borders without much by way of inspection or security. And hadn't he mentioned something about facial recognition and databases?

Martel picked up his duffel bag and motioned for Morgana to do the same. The flight crew descended from the plane, each carrying a small suitcase, and Martel followed. Morgana hesitated for a moment at the top of the stairs when Martel shook hands with the immigration officer who had remained on the tarmac. As she stepped down, the officer pressed something into Martel's hand.

Martel struck up a conversation with the officers as the cabin crew disappeared into the terminal. Reminded that she was alone, in a relatively isolated area with a group of Hunters, Morgana stood to one side and gripped the strap of her bag a little tighter, her other hand poised to reach for a throwing knife, though it would do little good against the handguns holstered on the immigration officers' belts. When none of the men acknowledged or even looked over at her, she left them on the tarmac and also headed inside. A few moments later, Martel walked in alone.

"Let's go."

"Go where?"

Martel held up his hand and jiggled a set of keys. "I have the address. I called Schaffer when I was outside."

Morgana hesitated as he walked away from her toward the exit. When she didn't follow, he stopped and turned back. "What is it?"

"Did you tell the officers who I am?"

Martel shook his head, which Morgana did not expect. "Despite what your death could do to my reputation, we didn't come this far for it to happen here," he told her, and gestured for her to follow him outside. To their right was a long, narrow parking lot with roughly a dozen cars scattered through it.

Martel clicked a button on the key and a small green Jeep flashed its lights. They walked over and loaded their bags inside. As they got in, he spoke, and his tone was uncharacteristically soft. "You have my word that you have nothing to fear from me, at least as long as Patrick is alive."

Morgana stared at him, struck both by his vow and the prospect that their truce might not last all that long. And for just a moment, his eyes were as soft as his voice. Then the wall came back down as the Jeep roared to life. It idled for a moment as he pulled up the navigation app on his phone and entered the address Schaffer had given him.

"First time in San Francisco?"

He shook his head, "no, but that doesn't mean that I have the whole city memorized." His tone was back to the gruff one she was used to.

"Give me the address, I'll see what I can find out about the building."

Martel told her and backed out of the parking spot. The sun was setting over the water, as they turned on to the access road that ran between the main runways and the bay. A seaplane bobbed at anchor, silhouetted with red and gold.

Morgana searched for the address on her phone and studied a satellite image. "Looks like a one-story cement building with a rubber roof, limited windows only along the front." She told him, using her fingers to zoom in and turn the image. "One set of glass double doors at the front, and what looks like a loading bay near the back with a steel roll-up door with a normal entry door beside it. There's a maintenance hatch on the roof, but no visible access to it from the ground."

She hit a button to request a general internet search and scrolled through the results until she found the city records. "Over the last ten years, the place has been a weightlifting gym, a studio for an artist who made metal architectural sculptures, and most recently an automotive glass fabrication shop. It's been vacant for two years, owner is listed as ANH Holdings, Inc. Does any of that mean anything to you?"

"No," Martel answered with a shake of his head. "But vacant usually means unmonitored. Schaffer probably just scoped the area for a while before he took your friend and took advantage. Makes me think there won't be any cameras, unless he's put some in himself."

"So, what are you thinking?"

Martel merged onto the northbound highway and thought for a few minutes. "Schaffer is expecting me, not you," he said as he changed lanes. "I'll drop you off a block or so away, and pull up out front, go in the main doors. Are you any good at picking locks?"

Morgana nodded with a sly smile, and he smirked. "Good, then you can go to work on the locks on the side door and hope that it isn't otherwise bolted on the inside. If it is, I'll see what I can do, but no promises."

The drive took another fifteen minutes before Martel exited the highway and merged onto a wide boulevard. A few blocks up, he turned into a dimly lit parking area on the side of a building. He reached into the back seat and tugged at the zipper on his duffel, extracting two small cases. He passed one to her and set the other in his lap.

Morgana opened the case to find a deconstructed pistol, the pieces fit into slots cut into a protective layer of foam. She didn't quite roll her eyes as she picked up the parts and assembled the gun with ease, ending with sliding the clip in and chambering the first round.

He let out a low whistle. "Touché." There was the slightest smile on his lips as he passed her a holster, and a small pouch which contained lock picking tools.

"Just because I don't like to use guns, doesn't mean I don't know *how* to use them." Morgana said as she checked the safety, and slid the gun in the holster. She reached in the back for her own bag and dropped it at her feet. "Your people saw to that."

Martel didn't respond as she strapped on the belt of throwing knives and slipped the holster into the space between two looped handles. She put Schaffer's dagger in one of the pockets, still wrapped in the black cloth, the handle in easy reach. She patted the pocket. "I'll be glad to give this back to him, if I get the opportunity."

"The building is the next block up," Martel said consulting his phone. He looked up and pointed ahead of them. "That cell phone billboard is on the roof."

Morgana nodded, and reached into her bag one more time, coming out with a black knit hat. She twisted her hair up and pulled it on, making sure that her distinctive shade of dark red was not visible. She took a deep breath and reached for the door latch.

"Wait!"

She paused and looked over her shoulder.

"Good luck."

"You, too." Morgana said and got out of the truck.

Martel pulled back out onto the road. A moment later, the flare of brake lights blazed through the night as he rounded the corner, disappearing in front of the building.

She adjusted her jacket and started up the street then stopped halfway down the next block where the last building ended and the vacant lot on the corner began. There were piles of trash and the odd pile of rusting car parts, but no real cover between where she stood, and the recessed white steel door facing the empty lot. It was almost full dark now, but there was enough light to show that there were no visible security cameras, and if Martel's theory was correct, even if there were, Schaffer likely didn't have access to them.

Still, Morgana put the car parts and trash between herself and the building until she had to make a dash across an open area about ten feet away. There, she crouched in the shadows of the doorway, retrieved the lockpicking tools that Martel had given her, and got to work.

Thirty-Seven

J acob left the brightly lit boulevard and parked the Jeep in near total darkness. He climbed out of the vehicle and studied what he could see of the front of the building. If someone were to walk or drive by, they would think the building was completely abandoned. Narrow windows flanked the large double glass door in the center, all dark. But wait, was that a light in the left window?

He clipped the holster to his belt and pulled his jacket down over it, then swung the door closed and locked the vehicle. After checking to make sure his phone was set to silent, he looked up and down the street and reached for the door. He hesitated for a moment when a chime sounded somewhere in the back of the building, but Schaffer already knew that he was coming.

The dim light from outside revealed a short breezeway that opened into a small reception area where he could just make out the outlines of a desk and a couple of chairs. Then the exterior door closed behind him, and the space was plunged into total darkness. Jacob drew a small pen-light from his pocket and shone it around. To the right was a doorway into a space that could have been a coat room but was now packed with stacks of half-crushed boxes. Ahead to the left was a single steel door that led deeper into the building.

Jacob stepped up to the door and grasped the handle with the hand holding the flashlight, the other hand already curled halfway behind his back. He eased the door open slowly and took a few steps into the much larger space. The flashlight glinted off racks of stored glass and illuminated humped shapes of machinery draped with tarps. The building must have been abandoned in a hurry, with this much inventory just laying around.

He passed between a pair of bookcases into an open space that served as the loading dock, making out the two doors. From across the room, he could see that the smaller access door had only a handle and deadbolt but no additional reinforcement. If Morgana was as good as she claimed, she should make short work of those locks. He just hoped that there wasn't any buzzer or alert when the door was opened.

If so, there went the element of surprise.

A soft, wet thumping sound, followed by a quiet grunt came from somewhere ahead, and then another. Jacob turned his head to the left towards a doorway where a faint light shone. Jacob put his hand on the gun at the small of his back, but didn't draw it as he moved around a tall pile of pallets that obscured the loading dock from the area where Schaffer was holding Alasdair prisoner.

The sounds stopped as Jacob grew closer. He didn't bother turning off the flashlight as he rounded the last corner; the other Hunter already knew that he was there. Alasdair sat bound to a tall steel chair beneath a single bare bulb dangling from the low ceiling. Schaffer stood just behind him, one hand resting on the back of the chair. Morgana's friend was wearing dress pants and what had once been a white dress shirt. It was stained now with blood, as was his face, which sported cuts and bruises in various stages of healing. His arms were strapped to the chair, with gaping wounds seeping blood, dripping off his fingers to the floor. He was curled forward and would have slumped to the floor had he not been bound.

For the wounds to stay open and bleed like that, the blade had to have dug deep and been covered in Glisane. The bruises on his face would keep healing, though the pace of that had to be slowed by the number of injuries his body was trying to heal all at once. Alasdair's breathing was labored, each exhale ending on a soft groan.

Schaffer clearly liked to play with his prey.

"There you are, Martel!" White teeth flashed in the light. "Glad you could join me."

He greeted Schaffer tersely and clicked off the flashlight. "From the looks of it, you didn't need any help from me."

Schaffer laughed. "I knew you were after this one, so I figured that you'd want a piece of the action." He said. "But I couldn't help myself in getting a head start."

Jacob stepped up and studied the man in the chair. He was conscious, but barely, his head hanging loose on his neck. Shivers wracked his body from the pain, and the poison burning through his system. Underneath the blood and the bruising, the man looked incredibly young, no older than early twenties, though that meant nothing.

Morgana had said that her friend had been an aristocrat, and he certainly looked the part. The clothes, while simple, were tailored and looked expensive. Tied as he was to the chair, even if he did have fighting skills, they wouldn't do him any good.

"What are you planning to do with him?"

Schaffer looked down at his captive. "These creatures really are remarkable." He circled around Alasdair and came to a stop next to Jacob. "Their healing ability takes care of superficial wounds in minutes; more severe injuries take longer. I intend to figure out how much this one can take before he succumbs to death. And when he comes back, I'll do it again. I'm in no hurry."

"Clearly."

"A little squeamish there, Martel?"

Jacob turned to face him, leveling an icy stare, and shrugged out of his jacket. He retrieved a utility knife, much like Schaffer held, from his belt. "Where do you want to start?"

Morgana turned the last tumbler in the deadbolt, and it finally slid open. Some time had passed since Martel had gone inside, at least ten minutes, but she hadn't actually timed it. She stowed the lock picking tools in her pocket and she drew the gun from its holster. Gripping the door handle, she took a deep, steadying breath before slowly pushing it down.

It turned easily, with only the barest of creaks, but even that sounded loud to her ears. She hesitated a moment before pushing it open, preparing herself for the door to be rigged with some kind of alarm, or worse, an explosive. But when only silence met her through a crack, she risked pushing it open just far enough for her to slip through, before easing it closed again.

The only lighting the loading dock had of its own was the red emergency light over the door. The air was redolent with machine oil, wood, and the moldering piles of cardboard stacked against the wall next to her, and faintly, the iron tang of blood. Directly ahead were tall piles of pallets about eight feet high forming a sort of wall. Light filtered through the gaps, as did the low conversation of two male voices, and the moans of someone in pain.

Alasdair.

Morgana gritted her teeth as a wave of anger went through her. Before advancing further into the room, she pulled two throwing knives from her belt and tucked the blades into pockets sewn into the cuff of each sleeve, added another pair to slots on her upper arms. She gripped the gun between both hands and moved slowly and silently across the floor. She pressed her back to the pallets and took a deep breath, then poked her head out.

Bloodied and bruised, Alasdair was securely bound to a chair with rope around his arms and legs. His feet dangled just above the ground, and his head fallen forward as if his neck couldn't support it anymore. The two Hunters were slowly circling him. Morgana stifled a gasp when her eyes locked onto the knife in Martel's hand, its blade coated in blood.

As she watched, he reached out and ran the dagger down Alasdair's arm between two loops of rope. Her friend's scream echoed through the room, and it took all of her willpower to stay in her hiding place. Martel circled Alasdair as if planning his next move, then bent and made another slow cut to his calf, finding space between turns of the rope to slice through his pant leg and into the flesh beneath. This time Alasdair only grunted, trying and failing to lift his head.

Anger flared again, this time directed at Martel, and herself. How could she have been so gullible? To think that Martel had come to help her get her friend free, yet here he was, helping to inflict the torture right alongside the other Hunter. Unwilling to let him get a third strike in on her watch, Morgana stepped out from the shadow and raised the gun, flicking off the safety.

The click froze both men in place, then they both slowly looked over at her. Martel's expression was blank. Nothing showed through his eyes, neither guile nor guilt. Alasdair managed to turn his head enough to see her out of the corner of his eye. One corner of his mouth twitched, about all the recognition that he had the strength for, but it sent a wave of relief through her at the sight.

Schaffer threw back his head and laughed. "Well, well," he crowed. "Just what do we have here?"

Morgana took a step forward. "I'm here for him." She jerked her head in Alasdair's direction.

"Oh really? One immortal against the two of us?"

Quick as the blink of an eye, Morgana pointed the gun at the ground an inch from Schaffer's foot and fired. The bullet sent chips of cement flying, and both Hunters danced back. She raised the gun back to aim at Schaffer's heart. At the same time, he drew his own weapon and pointed it at her. Martel, still poker-faced, passed behind him and took a step toward Alasdair, and then another, brandishing the knife. Morgana shifted her aim to him, and he froze.

"Back up."

Martel complied, hands raised.

"Now what?" Schaffer asked, and shifted his aim to Alasdair. "I could shoot your friend, though that would ruin my experiment until he's had a chance to heal up again. Since you've taken one of these yourself, you know how it feels."

Morgana's fingers tightened on the gun and fought the urge to pull the trigger, Even if she shot him, Schaffer could still shoot, and Alasdair had already been through so much. So, they remained frozen for a time. Schaffer's aim didn't waver, and she certainly wasn't going to be the one to end the stand-off, though her arms wouldn't be able to hold the position forever.

Martel was the wild card, but he just watched her. She met that blank stare again, and as she did, his eyes flicked up over her head and widened slightly.

Before Morgana could turn, a body collided into her from behind. She staggered forward as a burly dark-skinned arm looped around her chest, the other slammed into her right arm with enough force drive it down to her side. The gun was easily stripped from her numb fingers and clattered to the ground only to be kicked out of reach as she struggled.

His hand came up and held her chin, lifting her up at an uncomfortable angle. It wasn't lost on her that Martel had used the same tactic back in her office. But unlike Martel, this man had at least six inches and a hundred pounds on her.

Schaffer chuckled, and lowered his weapon, considering the threat neutralized. "You couldn't possibly have been stupid enough to think that I was here alone."

The vise-like grip across her chest was cutting off her air and her neck was twisted at an unnatural angle. Struggling only earned her a tighter grip on her chin, lifting until her feet only grazed the ground.

A kernel of panic expanded in her chest as black spots started to dance in her vision, the muscles in her limbs going numb and weak. Her hand trembled as she cocked her wrist and palmed the throwing dagger and drove the three-inch blade into her captor's thigh with as much force as she could muster.

His arms loosened as he yelled and scrabbled for the blade. Morgana slipped free and fell to her knees at his feet. It put her at the perfect height to swing up an arm between his legs, colliding with the most sensitive part of him. He groaned and collapsed to the ground next to her with a thud.

She tried to scramble away on her hands and knees, but her arms threatened to give out with each wracking cough as she struggled to pull air into her lungs through a bruised throat. She reached a work bench and slowly dragged her feet under her and started lurching toward Alasdair and the gun near his feet.

Hands grabbed at her again, but this time it was Schaffer. A fresh wave of adrenaline pulsed through her veins as she pulled a blade free from her sleeve and swung it at him in a wide arc.

Schaffer danced back, giving her the space to grab another dagger. She snapped her wrist out and flung it at him, but he dodged and charged. She blocked and countered a flurry of punches and grabs as he tried to pin her arms or throw her to the ground. Her hat came off in the scuffle and her hair swung free to get in her eyes. More than once Schaffer wrapped it around his hand as an anchor to land blow after blow before she could pull away. More than once, one of her daggers sliced the skin of his forearm, the back of his leg but it didn't slow him down.

In their struggles, Alasdair's chair was knocked over and he hit the ground on his back with a crash. She couldn't spare any concentration for him, or for where Martel had gotten to, as she drove a punch into Schaffer's eye, connecting with both bone and soft flesh.

He grunted and responded with a punch of his own to her abdomen that drove all the air out of her lungs. As her knees started to give way, Schaffer landed a punch to her cheek. Pain exploded in her face as she spun to the ground. Rough hands flipped her onto her back but before he could land another blow, Martel grabbed a handful of the back of his jacket and yanked.

Morgana rolled to her knees, her right arm pressed tightly to her throbbing ribs, and gulped for air as the two men struggled. They were evenly matched and traded blow after blow. Schaffer stepped in and threw Martel to the ground, but he rolled away and back to his feet as if he had practiced the move for years, bouncing lightly on his toes, hands at the ready like a boxer or martial artist. The two men watched each other, looking for an opening, and then came together with a crash, grappling together like two hockey players, slowly turning, landing a punch to the side, a knee, a swinging elbow.

BANG!

Thirty-Eight

M organa froze, waiting for the stinging pain. When none came, she looked over at Martel and Schaffer, still locked in each other's arms. She could see Martel's face over the other's shoulder, and his eyes were wide. Then Schaffer's legs gave out and Martel let him drop. He flopped to the ground, eyes staring sightlessly at the ceiling.

Martel put his hands up and Morgana turned her head to see Alasdair, lying on his side, gun pointed squarely at Martel's chest, a faint curl of smoke slowly dissipating over his head. The laugh bubbling up her throat became a yelp as a hand clamped around her ankle and yanked her backwards. She was rolled onto her back, the dark-skinned Hunter pinning her with a knee on either side of her hips. He planted a hand on the middle of her chest, pinning her to the ground, the other held a machete up high, ready to swing it down at her neck.

A second gunshot rang out and a red spot bloomed across his chest. The machete clattered to the floor, and he slowly collapsed to the side. Morgana kicked at the deadweight to free her leg and crawled a distance away on her knees. Her head swung frantically around the room looking for the next attack.

Martel stood with smoke curling around his head, his weapon pointed in her direction.

Before she could react, another shot rang out and both she and Martel dropped to the floor.

Morgana turned her head to see Alasdair's quivering arms adjust his aim downward readying for another shot at Martel.

"Stop!" She cried.

The gun rang out again, the bullet sending chips of cement flying a foot from Martel's face.

"*Pour l'amour de dieu, Ally!*" She cried, scrambling towards her friend. "Stop shooting!"

Alasdair looked her way, his bloodshot and bruised eyes wide and unfocused.

Morgana reached his side and gently pried the gun from his hand. Movement across the room brought her head around to see Martel cautiously levering himself up on his forearms. He met her stare and raised his hands, his finger held away from the trigger.

She nodded her head in a signal to him that the coast was clear.

Martel got to his feet and holstered his weapon. "You, okay?" he asked as he dusted the dirt from his shirt.

Morgana nodded and looked down at her friend, who now lay still on the ground, his eyes closed. She reached under his bloodied chin and searched for a pulse. It was there but weak. "Ally, can you hear me?"

He groaned and his eyes cracked open. "Barely."

She laughed with relief and gathered him into her arms, cradling his upper body in her lap. Slowly, his hand came up and wrapped around her forearm.

Martel was moving around the room, checking the two bodies, confiscating weapons.

Morgana focused on her friend and smoothed his bloodied, sweaty hair back from his forehead. Now that the danger had passed, her heart finally began to slow, the aches in her body fading as her body repaired the damage to her neck and trachea. Her breathing evened out, though the air was hardly fresh, cloying as it was with gun smoke and blood.

Martel finally came over and crouched by her side. "How is he?"

"Alive," Alasdair murmured. "Can't say I'm all that well. Thanks to you lot."

Martel had the good sense to look sheepish. He produced a small black bottle and pulled the cap off. Taking one of Alasdair's hands, he started spraying directly onto each laceration. Alasdair winced with each spray.

She gripped his wrist. "What are you doing?"

"It's an antidote to the Glisane. I found it in Schaffer's pocket." Martel shrugged out of her grasp and switched to the other arm. "I don't use the stuff personally, but any Hunter that does needs to have some of this on them in case of accidental exposure."

Morgana flexed her hand, remembering how quickly her skin had blistered from just the slightest contact to the coating on a blade, not to mention how it continued to eat her from the inside after being shot.

For a mortal, who did not have her healing ability, the stuff would be as deadly as a venomous snake bite if not neutralized almost immediately.

"Just what the hell did you think you were doing joining in?" Morgana exclaimed. The only thing keeping her from climbing over her friend to punch him was the fact that the spray seemed to be helping. The fine tremors wracking Alasdair's body were starting to ease. "I saw you using your knife on him."

"I had to make it look real," Martel replied brushing off her accusing tone with a shrug, Morgana glared at him for the nonchalant tone in his voice. He held up his hands defensively for a moment then went back to spraying. "I used my own weapon, which was clean and tried to keep the cuts as superficial as I could without arousing suspicion, and each time I made a cut, I also cut the ropes."

"Most of them snapped when I fell over," Alasdair confirmed. "I was able to crawl to the gun while everyone else was distracted."

"Nice shot, by the way," Martel said, capping the bottle and shoving it into a pocket of his jacket. "The first one, anyway."

Alasdair scoffed. "Too bad the rest missed."

Now, Morgana did laugh and once she started, she found it difficult to stop. It was part relief, part amazement that, in his condition, Alasdair could still be his normal sardonic self. When she finally stopped, Martel was looking at her as if she had lost her mind, but Alasdair was smiling.

She looked down at her friend. "I'm still amazed that you hit anything at all."

Alasdair chuckled, and it turned into a cough that ended on a groan. "You and I both."

"We need to get him out of here."

Together, they pulled Alasdair to his feet then caught him as he immediately started sinking to the floor. Martel pulled one of Alasdair's arms around his neck and propped him against a hip. "I'll call some people, take care of all this."

Morgana scooped up the fallen pistol and holstered it, then ducked under Alasdair's other arm and together they got him outside to the Jeep and into the passenger seat.

Martel followed her around to the driver's side and reached in for his duffel, then passed her the keys. "You and Alasdair take the Jeep. I'll meet you at the airport in the morning," he said, "Be there at nine."

"Are you sure you want me to leave you here?"

He nodded. "Schaffer told me earlier that he had taken Alasdair as he came out of work," he said. "I don't want to know where he lives. There are already enough questions that I don't have answers to."

Morgana nodded and got into the driver's seat, put the keys in the ignition. "See you in the morning then," she said. "Just don't leave without me."

His smile wasn't very reassuring as he closed the door for her and walked away.

Morgana glanced over at Alasdair and found that his eyes were closed, but his chest was rising and falling in a deep, even rhythm. Leaving him to sleep, Morgana backtracked to the highway and merged into the northbound traffic. Alasdair's house was across town near the Palace of Fine Arts, but she knew the route well.

When they arrived, Morgana opened the gates with the keypad and pulled under the archway by the side door.

Alasdair stirred, cracking his eyes open slowly.

"Home again!" Morgana said cheerfully. "Think you can help me get you inside?"

Alasdair moved his legs back and forth. "I think so," he replied as he released the seatbelt. "Whatever was in that spray has worked wonders."

Relief flooded through her as she came around to open the door for him. As he emerged from the Jeep, the light illuminated bruises on his face that had already faded to a yellowish purple. Under the dried blood, most of the cuts had closed up. By morning, they would all be gone. She eased him out of the vehicle, and he found that his legs did support him, at least well enough that Morgana could get him into the house on her own.

The stairs were a challenge, but they managed, though both were breathing heavily when they made it to the master bathroom. Morgana left him leaning against the marble countertop and turned on the shower. "Cheers, love," Alasdair said. "I think I can manage from here."

Morgana smiled and closed the door behind her. She went back down to the vehicle and retrieved her own bag then carried it to the bathroom attached to the guest room she always used. Starting the shower, Morgana shrugged out of her jacket and let it fall to the floor. The weapon belt followed.

She paused to study her reflection, arms braced on the countertop. Dirt and blood smeared her cheeks and crusted around her nostrils where one blow had given her a bloody nose. Her hair was a riot of dirty tangles.

Morgana turned from the mirror and bent to remove her boots only to find the laces knotted and caked with dirt. The room filled with steam as she struggled with a particularly stubborn knot. She was half a breath away from reaching for one of the daggers when the knot slid free. The boot clattered to the floor, and she shed the rest of her clothes and stepped under the powerful spray.

The water at her feet ran black and red as she scrubbed her skin and hair, the air filling with eucalyptus and lavender. She remained under the spray long after she was clean and just let the water pummel the tension from her muscles, as she breathed in the perfumed steam that rose around her.

Nearly a half-hour later, with the water starting to cool, she reluctantly turned off the shower and stepped out, wrapping her body in a plush cream bath towel. She dug in her bag for fresh clothes, pulling free the loose sweater that she had added almost as an afterthought. Morgana dressed and wrapped her wet hair in a towel, then bent to examine her dirty clothes. Most of it was not worth saving so she left it all on the floor and gathered her bag, jacket, and weapons belt in her arms.

She sat on the side of the bed and stripped the remaining throwing knives from her gear, replacing them in the suede roll. There were empty slots now where the one she'd thrown and the one she'd left in the dark-skinned Hunter's leg should have been. Maybe Martel had collected them.

The opportunity to "give" the Hunter blade back to Schaffer had never presented itself, so it went back in her bag as a souvenir. Morgana reached into the other pocket for her cell phone, frowning in dismay to find the screen was shattered. She pressed the power button, and nothing happened.

Morgana cursed and tossed the dead-weight down on the bed. She pulled the towel from her hair and used it to rub some of the excess water from the heavy curls as she walked back to the bathroom. Next to the sink she found a bottle of her favorite conditioner left behind on her last whirlwind visit and she worked some through her hair as she padded barefoot down the stairs to the first floor.

The kitchen lights were on, the air redolent with chicken broth and herbs. Morgana continued to run her fingers through her hair as she stepped inside the brightly lit space that wouldn't have looked out of place in a Tuscan villa to find Alasdair at the massive stove stirring something in a pot.

His light brown hair was still wet, thick locks falling into his eyes making him look like the rakish teenager he had once been. He was dressed in lounge pants and a waffle knit long-sleeved top. His feet were bare, but the terracotta tiles were warmed by the heating system built in underneath.

Morgana glanced at the clock on the wall, shocked to discover that it was nearly midnight. He looked up as she approached, then turned his attention back to a thick stew of chicken and vegetables. Beside the stove was a bowl of herbed dough waiting to be added to the top.

"You were kidnapped, beaten, nearly killed and now you're making chicken and dumplings?" Morgana asked him with a laugh. "Shouldn't *I* be cooking for *you*?"

"Call it a thank you then," Alasdair said. He brushed some herbs off his hands over the stew and put a lid on the pot. He turned to Morgana and took her hands. "And I mean it, Morgana. Thank you. I owe you my life."

Morgana wrapped her arms around him, and he buried his face in her shoulder. They stayed like that for a long time, relief coursing through her that they were both safe and whole. "You don't owe me anything. You're my oldest friend, there is nothing I wouldn't do for you."

Alasdair stepped back and picked up a spoon to stir the soup. "Including working with a Hunter it seems."

Morgana sighed. "That's complicated."

Alasdair laughed and started carefully placing scoops of dumpling batter onto the top of the soup. Once finished, he replaced the lid and took the bowl to the sink to wash. "That will take about fifteen minutes to cook." He shut the water off and dried his hands on a towel. "Come sit and tell me about it."

Morgana went to the fridge and pulled out two bottles of flavored water, passing him one as they settled onto the padded benches at the breakfast nook. She tucked one foot underneath her and twisted the top off.

Alasdair listened with rapt attention as she recounted the events of the last few days. He roared with laughter hearing how Patrick had ordered Martel around. "I knew I liked him!"

Morgana smiled. "I wish you could meet him," she replied, sadness sweeping over her. "Really meet him I mean."

Alasdair took one of her hands in his and gave it a reassuring squeeze. "Me too," he replied. He couldn't come back to Kingston with him on the Hunters' radar. His days in San Francisco were also likely numbered. He had a little time, since the Hunters didn't have his home address, but not very much.

A few moments later, Alasdair rose to check whether the dumplings were cooked. Morgana got up and set the table while Alasdair filled their bowls. Her mouth watered at the steam rising up as he placed one down before her and she dug in, barely hesitating long enough for a breath or two to cool the broth. The dumplings were tender, the stew perfectly seasoned with thyme, sage, and garlic. They quickly emptied their bowls, and both went back for seconds. Alasdair, in particular, needed the calories to help with healing his wounds.

Finishing the last bite, Alasdair dropped his spoon with a clatter and yawned hugely.

"I'll clean up," Morgana said. "Go get some sleep. I'll say goodbye before I leave in the morning."

He didn't argue, and just gave her a tight hug, and a quick kiss on the mouth, then headed off. As Morgana filled the soup pot to soak, she found herself yawning. She finished loading the dishwasher and turned out the lights as she made her way back upstairs, her limbs growing heavier and heavier with every step.

Once inside the bedroom, she only had enough energy to clear off the bed, put her hair in a braid, and set an alarm on the bedside clock before sliding under the down comforter to let sleep take her.

Thirty-Nine

T he alarm clock jolted Morgana awake in the morning. She rolled onto her back and stretched under the layers of luxurious bedding, marveling at how a delicious meal and a full night's sleep could work so much magic. All the aches from the night before had vanished even if the memories had not. It would be some time, she knew, before she'd stop seeing Alastair's beaten and bloody face every time she thought of him. Maybe if she just stayed under the blankets, their warmth and weight like a comforting embrace.

But there was another embrace that she wanted, needed, to feel around her again. Reluctantly, she sat up, threw the covers back, and perched on the edge of the bed, scrubbing her face with her hands. She unbraided her hair and made herself as presentable as possible with a brush and water. She carefully folded the heavy coat inside out to enclose as much of the dirt and grime as possible and stuffed it inside her duffel bag, she added the useless brick of a cell phone on top and zipped it closed. The clothes from the bathroom she just bundled in her arms to dispose of on the way out.

Alasdair was in the breakfast nook sipping a cup of coffee when she came downstairs and watched as she deposited the armload of soiled clothes in the trash. "Good morning," he said, his normal cheerful self. On the table next to him was a plate of fresh crusty bread, cheese, fruit, and jam, her favorite breakfast.

"How are you feeling?" She slid into the seat across from him and loaded her plate with apple slices and sharp cheddar cheese.

"Surprisingly well, all things considered," he replied, studying her over the rim of his cup. "Coffee?"

"Please."

Alasdair filled her cup from the French press carafe at his elbow and gestured to the creamer and sugar bowl even though he knew she preferred to take her coffee black.

She thanked him and tucked into her breakfast. When she was finished, she sat back and sipped the last of her coffee. "Well, I hate to rescue and run," she said with a wink, to which Alasdair laughed. "But Martel said to be back to the airport by nine."

He glanced up at the clock and coughed. "You better get a wriggle on, then."

She laughed, as she always did, at the saying. "My phone was broken yesterday in the fight," she told him. "I'll call when I get home."

He rose with her and gathered her into another hug.

Morgana's vision blurred as she eased back, a lone tear slid down her cheek.

He reached up to thumb it away, then cupped her cheek. "I'll see you soon."

Knowing that it could be some time before she saw him again, she nodded and brushed away another tear that had escaped down her cheek. Morgana shouldered her bag and headed for the door, snatching up the keys she'd left on the hall table on the way by.

Alasdair followed her to the doorway and waited while she put her bag in the back, and then turned and blew him a kiss before climbing inside and driving away. From the rearview mirror, she could see him continue to watch her, one arm raised in farewell until the gate opened. Then she turned onto the street, and he disappeared from sight.

The drive back to the airport was slow, the highway snarled with rush hour traffic. By the time Morgana pulled into the parking lot, it was nearly nine and the drive had taken twice as long as it should have. She swung into a parking spot with a screech of tires and threw the gearshift into park, barely remembering her bag as she locked the doors and ran for the terminal.

Inside Martel was pacing back and forth, causing the door out to the tarmac to repeatedly open and close, earning him glares from nearly everyone in the small terminal. "There you are!" He stalked over and grabbed her arm and dragged her to the ticket desk. "I've been trying to call you all night!"

"My phone broke." Morgana shrugged her arm free, and gave him an annoyed look. The woman behind the desk took her passport when she handed it over, eyeing Martel as if he was a bomb that was about to go off. "What's wrong?"

The woman handed her passport back with a look that said, "better you than me."

A corner of Morgana's mouth twitched, and she turned to find Martel tapping his foot in the doorway, an exhaust scented breeze blowing in around him.

He held out a hand. "Keys."

Morgana handed them over and followed him to their plane, which was idling a short distance away. The same two immigration officials were already waiting for them at the bottom of the stairs. Martel passed the keys back to one, who tucked them into a breast pocket and plucked her passport from her hand for them to inspect, if only for appearance's sake. The officer flipped the passports closed and passed them to Martel.

"Have a safe flight, Jake," he said curtly, and turned away without another word.

Morgana glanced at Martel and raised an eyebrow, as the immigration officers returned to their truck and drove off, yellow lights flashing on the top.

Martel shrugged. "Let's go."

She followed him up the stairs and into the plane, vacillating between annoyance and anger. Once aboard, she stalked up to him and spun him around to face her. "Will you please tell me what the hell is going on?"

To her surprise, his gruff façade cracked, and he seemed to deflate before her eyes. "It's Patrick."

Her knees gave out and had the arm of the chair not caught her, she would have been on the floor. Martel looked apologetic as he eased her onto the seat and pressed a bottle of water into her hands. Co-pilot Jane appeared from the flight deck and secured the door, then left them with instructions for them to buckle their seatbelts.

Martel sat down on the sofa and clicked his belt on, while Morgana struggled in a daze to remember how to secure her own. With a sigh, Martel unbuckled and shifted forward so he could do it for her, pulling on the strap with a touch too much force and then returned to his seat.

She ignored the tight belt since there wasn't any air getting into her lungs to begin with. "What about him?" Her heart was pounding in her ears so loud that she barely heard the engine noise increase as the plane started to move.

"He's in the hospital," Martel said. "He was keeping an eye on Sophie. She said he was only in the bathroom for a few moments and then she heard a crash, so she tripped the call alarm. The nurses came running and found him unconscious on the floor, a gash on his forehead where he'd hit the sink on the way down."

Morgana's hand flew to her mouth, not quite muffling the small scream. "Oh, *mon Dieu*," she whispered. "I thought you were going to say that he was already dead."

Martel shook his head.

She took a moment to really get a good look at him. His face was drawn with dark circles under his eyes as if he hadn't slept at all the night before.

"No, not yet," he replied, "but it isn't looking good."

The plane suddenly accelerated, pressing Morgana back in her seat, further crushing her heart. "I didn't know he was that sick."

"None of us did," Martel's voice broke, and he swallowed hard before he could continue. "I think Patrick kept it to himself. The doctors said that the course of treatment he was on had stopped working weeks ago."

The words drove out what air she had in her lungs, sure as if Martel had punched her in the gut. She buried her face in her hands. "I wasted so much time!"

A hand settled tentatively on her shoulder and this time she didn't shake him off. "Don't blame yourself, Morgana."

It was the first time that he had used her name on the trip and that alone brought her head up. His bloodshot eyes were full of sympathy, as if he only now realized how much Patrick meant to her. For now, and for as long as their truce lasted, they were just two people facing the prospect of losing someone they both loved in the very near future.

Morgana wiped her eyes and sat back. His hand slipped away. She tried to speak, choked, and cleared her throat. "You should get some sleep," she told him. "There's nothing that either of us can do for the next three hours, and not to be indelicate, but you look like shit."

The fact that Martel only smirked said a lot about his condition. He unfastened his seatbelt and stretched out on the sofa. "Better hope we don't hit any turbulence." He said and closed his eyes. Within moments, his breath had smoothed out into the rhythm of sleep.

For a moment, she envied his ability to fall asleep so easily. Unlike him, her skin was practically vibrating with nervous energy. Despite having just told Martel that there was nothing *to* do, she found herself wandering the cabin, peering into cabinets and drawers, but found only snacks and emergency equipment. Emerging from the lavatory, she spotted another door at the rear of the plane which opened into a small office space. There was a desk, barely large enough to hold the keyboard attached to it, with a computer monitor mounted to the wall. It was all wired into a small docking station, though no computer was connected to it. On a corner of the desk was a printer, barely larger than the paper it held.

Morgana smiled, and withdrew a stack of blank paper from the tray. Pens and a clipboard were in the middle drawer. She took her finds back to the main cabin and buckled back in. After fitting the stack of paper to the clipboard, she uncapped one of the pens and studied its tip, then drew a series of test lines and curves in a corner. Satisfied, Morgana started to draw, sketching first Martel's sleeping face, then Schaffer's face as she would in her Chronicle. She wore out one pen, and then a second as her hand drew line, and contour, and shading. When the cabin crew signaled a half hour warning, waking Martel from his nap, Morgana was drawing Patrick's face.

He sat up and scratched a hand through his hair. Seeing the scattered paper on the table, he braced his elbows on his knees and leafed through the completed drawings. "Wow," he remarked, running his fingers over the one of him stretched out on the sofa. "These are very good."

"Thanks," she said. "Though do I have to say that it's more than a little ironic for you to say so."

"Ironic?"

"You're complimenting my drawing skills when it is the main reason that the Hunters have been chasing me. Because my chronicles are full of drawings of people like me."

Martel made a grudging sound of assent in his throat and pulled out one of Alasdair tied to a chair. She'd drawn him sitting in a pool of light, his head falling forward from exhaustion and pain. "Was your friend alright?"

Morgana nodded, her hand still moving, shading the area under Patrick's jaw. "He seemed right back to normal this morning." She set the clipboard down in her lap, and gave him her full attention. "I saw how that Immigration agent acted towards you this morning. Did you have any trouble after we left?"

Martel assumed his customary legs-crossed, head-propped-on-hand position. "I called in a couple of Hunters that I knew, including those two who work for Homeland Security. They came and took the bodies. And I don't think they were all that happy about it. My not answering their questions probably had something to do with it."

Morgana chuckled.

"They confirmed that Schaffer was a lone wolf," Martel continued, "and the other guy... his name was Atufo... Marcus Atufo, I think. According to the local leader, he had been part of a group out of Los Angeles until about a year ago when he hooked up with Schaffer."

Morgana thought back to that night, more than six months ago when she'd gone up to the rooftop of Albrecht for a breath of fresh air and had ended up running across the rooftops of half of downtown, pursued by two Hunters. "It was them."

"What was them?" Martel asked, his eyebrows drawn down low over his eyes.

"Sorry, I didn't realize that I said that aloud." She replied and went on to tell him about the rooftop chase, the first time she'd had issues with the Hunters since returning to Kingston and how she had been sure at the time that the one firing at her had been the man sitting across from her. "Schaffer had much the same build as you, but I had never seen someone the size of Atufo moving in your circles. Now, it makes sense."

He shook his head with a rueful chuckle. "Wish I could take the credit for that one."

Morgana rolled her eyes at what she hoped was a joke and returned to her drawing. The plane started to descend into Kingston and soon enough they were on the ground and taxiing to the private terminal. She gathered the drawings up and put them in her bag.

Martel paced the small space inside the aircraft as they waited for Canadian immigration officials to arrive, then he and Morgana ran to his battered blue truck and wasted no time getting back on the road. He wove through the light traffic with a recklessness that made her glad to be immortal, in case he caused an accident, but they arrived at the hospital safely and in record time. He parked in the garage attached to the hospital. As they walked toward the entrance, Martel pulled out his cell phone and dialed.

"Hi Soph." he said. "Yeah, we're here. How is he?" He listened for a few moments. "What room is he in? 3261? You're there with him? Okay, see you in a minute."

He hung up the phone just as they reached the glass door and yanked it open. He ushered Morgana in ahead of him, and hurried across the catwalk that stretched over the open atrium lobby.

Sophie was perched in the visitors chair dressed in a robe tied over a hospital gown. She looked up as they entered and, seeing her husband, rose wearily out of the chair and threw herself into his arms. He gathered her close, tucking her head under his chin, one hand buried in her hair. She turned her head and looked at Morgana, her eyes red and bloodshot.

Morgana gave her what she hoped was a comforting smile. After a moment, Sophie extended her hand. Morgana gripped it warmly. Sophie mouthed a hello, and she mouthed back.

"He's sleeping," she said, turning her head to look up at Martel. "He's done a lot of that since..."

Morgana slid her hand out of Sophie's grip and walked over to the bed. Patrick was buried under a pile of blankets tucked up to his chest with his arms on top. An intravenous drip ran to the back of one hand, a white monitor was clipped to a finger. There was an oxygen tube in his nose and a huge bruise on his forehead, partially covered with gauze. Beside him, the monitors beeped a steady rhythm.

"He bumped his head when he fell," Sophie explained, resisting her husband's attempts to get her to sit.

Morgana carefully brushed his hair back from his face and placed a kiss on the unblemished side of his forehead. Patrick stirred, drawing in a deep breath and cracked his eyes open. His blue eyes were unfocused at first, then he slowly blinked, and they fixed on her.

"Morgana." His voice was sleepy, and terrifyingly weak.

"I'm here," she said, gripping one of his hands, and eased a hip down on the bed next to him. Martel and Sophie stepped up behind her. Patrick's eyes drifted up.

"Hey, buddy."

"Hey, yourself," Martel answered. He tucked Sophie against his side and put a hand on Patrick's shoulder.

"How's Alasdair?" Patrick asked, his eyes returning to hers. His hand squeezing hers, though it wasn't by much. "Is he safe?"

Morgana smiled at him. "He's safe."

Patrick breathed a sigh and closed his eyes for a moment. "Good," he said. Then he looked up over her shoulder, at his best friend. "Can I talk with Jake alone, please?"

Morgana and Martel exchanged a glance. "Of course," she answered, and leaned in to press a gentle kiss to his mouth. "Sophie and I will go get something to eat."

Martel pressed a kiss on the top of his wife's head, and she adjusted her robe and headed for the door with Morgana in her wake. Martel followed them to close the door behind them.

The two women looked at each other for a moment, then Morgana opened her arms. Sophie hesitated for only a moment before she stepped in close. "Oh, Morgana," she sighed. "I'm so sorry about... about everything."

Morgana could only smile and hold her a little closer. "There's nothing to apologize for." She replied. "I would have done the same had I been in your place."

Sophie stepped back. "I still haven't processed everything you told me, and I'm not sure that I will truly understand or accept everything, but I really am glad that you're here."

"Me too."

"Come on, there's a cafeteria on the other side of the floor where we can talk."

"Should you be walking this much?"

Sophie just gave her a look that hit her like a punch in the chest, but at the same time made her want to laugh. It was so much like the one that Patrick made when he was annoyed.

"Never mind," she said with a chuckle.

To her surprise, Sophie slid her hand into Morgana's elbow and together they set off down the hall, the soft scuff of Sophie's slippered feet setting the pace. The smell of food grew stronger as Sophie expertly navigated the twists and turns until they emerged into a cafeteria-style serving line. Morgana selected a salad and a bottle of water. Sophie got a chicken sandwich and a coffee and gave Patrick's room number to the cashier. They found a table off to one side and sat down to eat.

"How's Christopher?"

Sophie smiled. "He's great. The nurses are keeping an eye on him in the nursery." She adjusted the neckline of her shirt. "Speaking of... I'll need to stop up there and feed him before I go back to the room. It has been a while, and my boobs are killing me."

Morgana laughed and stabbed up a mouthful of salad. "Jake told me that he fell?"

Sophie's sandwich dropped onto the plate as if she had lost her appetite. "Patrick was keeping me company upstairs while Jake went to help you with your friend." She tapped the heel of her hand softly on the table as she considered her next words. "I'm not going to pretend that I know what the emergency was, but it had to have been important."

Morgana opened her mouth to say something but found the words weren't there and snapped it closed again. She nodded.

Sophie sighed and wrapped her hands around her coffee cup. "Anyway, he went into the washroom and then I heard a crash." Her face went bone white. "It was so scary, Morgana!"

"What are the doctors saying?"

Sophie lifted the cup to her mouth with trembling hands. "They said that he passed out because his blood pressure was low. The cancer has spread beyond the bones and his organs are starting to shut down."

"It's too soon." Morgana's voice was barely a whisper.

"For someone who has lived as long as you have, this time must seem like a blink of an eye." Sophie covered one of Morgana's hands with her own. "The thirty-two years that I've had with him as a brother aren't enough."

They ate in silence for a few moments, neither able to think of what to say next. Sophie's phone chimed from her pocket. She pulled it out and studied the screen. "It's Jake. Patrick wants to see you."

They pushed back from the table and tossed their half-eaten meals into the trash and headed back across the floor. Morgana left Sophie at the elevator and continued on alone. When she entered, Martel was sitting in the visitor chair, but rose and left the room without a word.

Patrick was sitting up in bed now and looked much more alert. But still, his skin had a slight yellowing of jaundice, and there were deep shadows under his eyes. "Hey, you."

"Hi." Morgana bent to kiss him on the lips. Weak as he was, he found the energy to reach up to cup her neck and hold her for a slow, deep kiss. When she eased back, he shifted over on the bed and made room for her, the beeping from the monitors spiked faster from the exertion. Morgana's heart twisted with how much effort it took.

"I don't think I'll fit."

"Nonsense." He patted the bed next to him. "I'm willing to chance it, if you are."

Morgana slid out of her jacket and climbed up onto the bed, snuggling close to his side, her head pillowed on his chest. His arms came around her and she tried to tune out the beeping of machinery, to pretend that it was any other day. For a minute, or an hour, or however long they lay there in that bed, she'd pretend that time couldn't touch them.

"Why didn't you tell me?" she asked finally. Her throat thickened, but she kept the tears at bay through sheer force of will.

Patrick placed a kiss on the top of her head. "Would it have really changed anything?"

Morgana considered that for a moment, but he was right. Whether she had forty to fifty years or four to five months, no amount of time would have been enough. She shook her head, words failing her.

"I'm sorry, Morgana," he said. "I am sorry that I came into your life when I did only to leave it again."

"No, don't apologize." She snuggled closer to him as if she could hold him to her forever. If she could pass her immortality to him through their skin, she would, but it didn't work that way. She closed her eyes and tried with her whole being anyway.

"You taught me the difference between just living and truly being alive. You showed me what it is to love again after centuries of being alone. I can never thank you enough for that."

"I love you, Mérande," he murmured in her ear. His use of her birth name made her lift her chin to look up at him with a smile, their faces only inches apart. A lone tear escaped to drip on his chest. "*Je t'aime.*"

"*Je t'aime.*"

Patrick lifted his head to capture her lips briefly, then lowered it back to the pillow with a sigh. His arms tightened around her, and she tipped her chin up to see that his eyes were closed. She snuggled back in, and just listened to his heartbeat under her cheek; feeling the rise and fall of his chest. The steady beep of machinery evened out as he fell asleep.

After a few moments, the beeping began to slow. At first, she thought the change was just his body relaxing into deep sleep, but she couldn't hear the beat in his chest as easily as she had before. Morgana turned her head to the monitors and watched as the numbers that represented his heart rate and breathing fell. A moment later, alarms started blaring from the machines. Morgana leapt to her feet as Sophie and Martel came flying into the room, closely followed by two nurses, who shooed Morgana away from the bed.

Martel held his wife while she called out questions to the nurses. They didn't respond as they administered medications to try to stabilize him. Morgana stood helplessly beside them, her heart hammering in her throat, as adrenaline and anguish coursed through her.

The numbers continued to drop. "Why aren't you using a defibrillator?" she demanded of the nurses.

"He has a DNR," Martel murmured over his wife's head. Sophie was now staring wide-eyed at the bed, clutching her husband's arms.

The alarms continued to blare as the beeping went to a solid tone. The nurses ran out of options that they had authorization for and stopped fussing over him. One held her fingers over the pulse on his wrist and stared at the monitors. After an endless moment, she nodded and the other nurse turned the monitor off, glancing up at the clock. "Time of death, thirteen forty-six."

Forty

S ophie let out a cry of anguish and crumpled. Martel tightened his arms around her and buried his face in her hair, holding her while she fell to pieces. Morgana walked on wooden legs over to the bed, as one nurse slipped the monitor from Patrick's finger and removed the IV from his hand. The other reached over his head to turn off the oxygen and gently slid the tubing from his face. When they finished, the one closest to her, a plump blonde in maroon scrubs put a hand on Morgana's arm and gave her a sympathetic look. "We'll give you a few minutes to say goodbye."

Morgana nodded and sat on the edge of the chair next to the bed. The figure on the bed became blurry as her eyes filled with tears. She took his still-warm hand and held it under her chin between both of hers.

Martel led Sophie over to the other side of the bed and she took her brother's other hand. She didn't know how long they all stayed like that, but it had to be at least five or ten minutes before Martel gently detached Sophie's hand.

"It's time."

She looked up at her husband and then down at her brother and nodded. She sniffed and wiped her eyes, and braced one hand on the bed so she could bend down to press her lips to Patrick's forehead, her eyes squeezed tightly shut. Tears fell from her eyes onto his hair. She was trembling so badly that she needed Martel's support to straighten back up and stay on her feet.

Martel took Patrick's hand and leaned over to smooth his friend's hair back. His forearm came to rest on the pillow as he lowered his head until their foreheads touched. He closed his eyes for a moment, his lips moving as he murmured a silent prayer. Finished, he also kissed Patrick's forehead before withdrawing.

His eyes met Morgana's as he stood. She watched as a lone tear slid unheeded down his cheek. The anguish on his face mirroring her own.

He tucked Sophie against his side and turned her to the door. "Let's get you back to bed."

Their steps were slow, reluctant. Both knew that once they left the room, it was over.

A ringing started in Morgana's ears, faint at first, but growing fast. Like the ringing of bells, the roar of the ocean, but at the same time neither. The sensation coursed through her, spreading like lightning through her body, growing until her whole body vibrated with energy. She sucked in her breath with a hiss and put a shaking hand to her forehead as her temples started to throb hard enough that it took a moment for her brain to process where the sensations were coming from.

"Wait!" she cried and waved her arm to beckon them back.

Martel turned them both back to face the bed, his arms seemingly the only thing keeping Sophie on her feet. Their faces bore the same dazed expression, down to the wrinkles in their foreheads. For them, nothing had changed.

"What is it?" Sophie's voice was raw, barely more than a whisper.

Morgana's head snapped to Patrick's face. The sickly yellow-gray pallor his skin had taken on when the nurses shut off the monitor was disappearing before her eyes, as was the bruising on his forehead. She rose to her feet and gently removed the gauze. Underneath was smooth skin, the color improving by the second. She put a hand above his head, leaned toward him. "Patrick?"

"Morgana, what is going on?"

She glanced up at Martel, a knowing smile starting to spread on her face. She eased a hip onto the bed and reached over him to take both of his hands. They weren't limp and lifeless anymore. His fingers twitched in her grasp.

A moment later, Patrick drew in a deep breath, and opened his eyes.

Forty-One

T ears streamed down Morgana's face. For a moment, Patrick stared sightlessly ahead. Then he bolted upright, clutching his throat. Sophie shrieked and covered her mouth with her hand. Morgana gently pushed him back down, her hands circling his wrists and lowering them to his sides. His eyes were wide and panicked. His mouth opened and closed his mouth like a fish out of water, gulping for air.

"What's wrong with him?" Sophie shrieked, forgetting that only moments ago, her brother had been dead.

Morgana locked eyes with him and took exaggerated deep breaths, encouraging him with a nod of her chin to breathe with her. "Just breathe."

She glanced over her shoulder. "It takes a little while for everything to come back." she explained as she turned back to Patrick. "That's it. Keep breathing."

After a few moments, some of the tension left his muscles, his breathing eased, and became more natural. He tried to speak, but only a croak came out. After another breath, he cleared his throat weakly, and tried again. "W-what happened?"

She reached up and swept the hair from his eyes, her fingers brushing over the area that had been marred by a deep purple bruise not that long ago. "You died."

He looked at her, a deep wrinkle in his brow. Then one hand rose shakily to his forehead. Feeling no tenderness or pain, he lifted his hand and stared at it, then put it back to his forehead. Slowly, he began to move his arms, his legs, as if taking inventory of the aches and pains that were no longer there. He looked at Morgana again, realization dawning in his eyes.

All she could do was sniff and wipe her streaming eyes. And grin like an idiot.

"Patrick?" Sophie had detached herself from her husband's arms and was inching her way over to the bed. She stumbled into it and gripped the side rail for balance, and fumbled along the rail until she reached his side. Her trembling hand grasped his, then moved to his shoulder, his face, as if making sure it was really him.

He looked over and smiled. "Hey, Soph."

"What is going on?" she asked, looking wide-eyed between her brother and Morgana.

"He's immortal."

It was Martel who had spoken. Morgana looked up, half expecting to see disgust or anger on his face, but it wasn't there. "He's immortal," he repeated with a little less fascination the second time. "And we need to get him out of here before the nurses come back."

Morgana got to her feet and looked back at Patrick. "How are you feeling?"

He pushed himself up a little higher in the bed. "Better than I have in a long time."

Martel had already gone to the small wardrobe in one corner and was pulling out Patrick's clothes. He tossed them onto the foot of the bed and bent to retrieve his shoes. Then he was standing beside his wife, dropping the bed rail and throwing the covers off of his friend's legs.

"Come on, get dressed."

Patrick looked back and forth between his best friend and Morgana, then pulled the pile of clothes closer.

Morgana reached behind him and released the ties on the hospital gown so he could shrug out of it and pull on the long-sleeved t-shirt. There were a few spots dried of blood on the shoulder from the headwound, but they didn't have an alternative.

He swung his legs off the bed and shook out the jeans, hesitating for a moment, looking at his sister.

Martel's lips twitched and he wrapped an arm around his wife's shoulders. "I need to get this one back to her room." he said. "If you go to the right, there is a staircase, and you won't have to go anywhere near the nurses' station. Take this." He tossed a knit beanie down on the bed. "To cover that hair. Just in case."

Sophie pulled away and ran back to her brother, who wrapped her up in a tight hug, two bright heads bent together.

"I'm okay, Soph," he reassured her. "I swear."

After a moment, she stepped back. "Love you."

"Love you, too."

Martel held out a hand to her and Sophie took it. Before walking out, he dug a set of keys out of his pocket and tossed them to Patrick. "You guys can take the truck."

He wrapped his arms around his wife again and led her from the room. As they turned the corner, he whispered in her ear, "act sad."

The excited, hopeful look on her face disappeared, replaced with a droopy expression that wasn't exactly convincing.

Morgana chuckled under her breath as Patrick pulled his legs into the jeans and slid off the bed onto his feet for the first time to pull them the rest of the way on. He plucked the gown off of the floor and dropped it on the bed, reached for socks and shoes. Fully dressed, he turned to Morgana, with the biggest smile she had ever seen on his face. "It has been years since I could stand without pain."

She picked up the hat from the bed and pulled it over his head, deliberately tugging it down over his eyes.

He laughed. The sound was music to Morgana's ears as she straightened the hat. He reached up and captured her hands. Their eyes met and held. He drew her arms around his neck. Then his hands were sliding along her ribs, drawing her close. He bent and captured her lips, his mouth opening, his tongue seeking hers.

Morgana's lips parted, and his tongue swept in, swept everything away. She buried her hands in his hair and poured all of the relief, and wonder, and celebration into this kiss. This first kiss of a new life.

A moment later, she reluctantly pulled back. Her breathing was ragged, her body already heated. "We need to go. Now."

He nodded, and released all but her hand, lacing his fingers with hers as they headed for the door.

Morgana leaned out into the hallway and looked both ways. It was practically deserted, only an orderly with a cleaning cart a few doors down. She jerked her head, signaling an all clear and turned right down the hallway. They walked for about twenty feet, with Patrick keeping his chin lowered in case of cameras. Morgana pushed the bar and the door opened into a clean, linoleum tiled stairwell. They descended to the first floor, emerging into a hallway near the emergency room and continued through the waiting room and out through the sliding doors.

Once outside, Patrick pulled off the hat and took a deep breath of salty fresh air. He let out an exhilarated laugh and jumped up and down like a child. He bounced back and forth from one foot to the other, and then swept Morgana up in his arms, spinning her around and around in a circle. She was laughing too, her hands on his chest for balance when he set her back on her feet. "Where was I?" he asked, a glint in his eyes.

She cocked her head to one side and raised an eyebrow, knowing exactly what he was thinking.

"Oh, right."

He bent his head and kissed her again, reigniting the heat that swirled through her and settled deep in her belly. Their tongues danced as her hands slid up and burrowed deep in the russet waves, holding his head to hers. Her body pressed tightly against his as if she could fuse them together.

The rattle of the emergency room door sliding open broke them apart. While they were outside, they weren't exactly in the clear yet. She took his hand and led him to the parking garage where she and Martel had left the truck.

Patrick opened the driver's side door, but Morgana reached around him and plucked the keys from his hand. "I'll drive," she said, and slipped around him into the seat. "You did only just come back to life, after all."

Patrick chuckled as he circled around to the other side. He climbed in and shut the door. He turned to her, his eyes bright. "Let's go home."

Epilogue

Sometime later, Morgana awoke in her bed, tucked against Patrick's hip, her head on his bicep. The sun was setting, sending an explosion of orange and red streaming across the room. Patrick was studying his hand as he moved it in and out of a sunbeam, turning this way and that, curling his fingers tight and straightening them again. She lifted her chin. There was a crinkle between his eyes, and she reached up to smooth it away.

He started at her touch, then smiled, and captured her hand, studying it instead. His fingers traced each oval nailbed, examining the faint lines of old scars.

"What's on your mind?"

He tucked their hands against his chest and turned his head to look at her. "I guess I keep waiting to feel differently."

"Apart from no longer dying of cancer?"

His chest vibrated under her hand as he laughed. "Apart from that, yes."

"Well, in my experience, you don't really change all that much when you become immortal. You just gain the ability to heal from most wounds and come back from the dead from all but one fatal injury."

Patrick shuddered. "Not an experience I want to repeat any time soon."

She made a sympathetic sound in her throat and stretched her body at length against him.

He raised an eyebrow, the arm under her slid from her shoulder down to her hip and drew one of her legs over his. "Did you know?"

Morgana shook her head, understanding what he meant. "No. I didn't know." She slid her hand from his and reached up to brush a lock of hair out of his eyes. "You were gone for maybe five minutes when I felt it. Then, I knew you were coming back."

"Oh right, 'it'." He captured her hand again and pressed a kiss to her palm. "Do you ever get used to that?"

"Not really. I get a migraine every time, even now."

He grimaced and kissed her temple.

She slid her hand from his and draped her arm across his stomach. "Physically, you'll stop aging. You'll remain as you are now for the rest of your life, which will hopefully be a good long time."

Her hand started moving down his side and across his hip.

A shiver went through him. When he spoke, his voice was deeper, rougher. "Remain forever in the prime of my life, huh?"

"Uh-huh." Her hand slid under the sheet.

"So, tell me. Where do we go from here?"

She sighed, and her hand stilled just above its target. "The hospital is going to wonder what happened to you, and there will be questions. Questions we can't answer." She traced the muscles below his navel, his hip bones, which stuck out far more than they should have. But now that the cancer was gone, he would regain the lost weight easily enough. "We're going to have to disappear for a while."

"We?"

"Of course."

He lifted his head to capture her lips in a brief, but thorough kiss. "You told me once that you had come back to Kingston for good, and here we are talking about leaving again."

"It's all right," she told him with a sigh. "I always said that this place, this apartment, felt like home. But I've actually found a better one."

"Oh?"

Morgana levered up onto one elbow, so she could look down at him properly. She tapped her hand over his heart. "Right here, in your arms, *that's* home. Whether we are here in Kingston or somewhere thousands of miles away, as long as I have you, I'm home."

His hand floated up to cup her face, drawing her down for a kiss that was as binding as any contract.

"And some day, maybe someday soon, we'll be able to return."

He nodded and reached over to pull her on top of him, her legs splitting around his hips, and clasped his hands at the small of her back. "For sure," he agreed. "We do have forever, after all."

Acknowledgements

Hunted has been a labor of love nearly twenty years in the making. But this was the kind of love that was neglected, given only the slightest bit of attention for much too long, only to be cast aside before the hard work really began. But that spark never truly went out, and one day, with a little fuel, and a challenge from a good friend to give it a go, it has finally become what it was always meant to be.

To the small but mighty army of people who have come along with me on this journey: You helped me kindle the ideas, to read this book in its earliest, roughest form, and most importantly, you were there with generous amounts of encouragement to put in the real work to complete it, and to send it out into the world.

To Carol Jayez: You have been my sounding board, my collaborator, and all around E.B. for as long as I can remember. You were with me long before I put the literal pen to paper on my first stories and you were there to help me first start developing the little spark of an idea that became this book over AOL Instant Messenger. Yes, it was that long ago, and yes I still have the conversation.

To Mary Frame and Rachel Hawk: Without you, I never would have gotten out of the corner I'd painted (written?) myself into and finally get this manuscript out of the "would be nice to finish" pile and put an ending on this story. Your encouragement, insight, and willingness to share your publishing experiences has been invaluable and I'm forever grateful for your friendship.

To Amanda Norris: You took an interest in this story from the second you heard about it and gave me the best compliment ever when you said that you had to force yourself to put the book down or you'd be a zombie at work the next day. And then when you finished, you asked for more. To that I say, who knows?

To Shanny Keady: Thank you for being my found family when both of our own live so far away. What started as coworkers living on opposite ends of two commuter rail lines into Boston has become a friendship that I couldn't live without. And although you live in the ass-end of nowhere, I never mind the drive if I get to spend time with my chosen sis and her family.

To Kyley Krueger: Thank you for giving me the real New Adult perspective on this book and for your diligent editing and suggestions. I'm glad your mom came into my life because you got to come with her.

To my mother Sharon Kerr, my really great aunt Sandy Kerwin, and the rest of my family: Thank you for your support of my writing and for taking the time to help me any way you could. Your eagle eyed editing was invaluable getting the manuscript ready to publish. I know there may have been times when my stories were not your cup of tea, but you always listened and that is all that matters. I'd like to say that I'm sorry for making you reach for that box of tissues at the end, but hearing that the story had that kind of emotional effect is also one of the greatest compliments that an author could receive.

And to you, Dear Reader: If you have made it this far, I hope that you enjoyed Morgana and Patrick's story as much as I enjoyed telling it. Thank you for taking a chance and buying this book. Here's to the future, and to the books yet to be written. I can only hope you'll stick with me on this journey, wherever it leads.

About the Author

Molly Kerr grew up with a pen in her hand. It started with sneaking to the back of Miss Campbell's second grade classroom for extra sheets of lined newsprint paper to practice her lettering while telling the story of a kingdom inhabited by butterflies. For many years, writing became purely academic or as part of her full-time job without any room for writing for fun. Now, many years later, *Hunted* is her debut novel. A native of Tonawanda, New York, she currently lives in Lowell, Massachusetts with her beloved Black Lab, Remy.

Use the QR Code or visit
mollykerrauthor.com
to join my newsletter!

Printed in the USA
CPSIA information can be obtained
at www.ICGtesting.com
LVHW091243230424
778174LV00006B/599